FAREWELL TO THE SEA

ALSO BY
REINALDO ARENAS

Hallucinations
El Central

FAREWELL TO THE SEA

A NOVEL OF CUBA

REINALDO ARENAS

TRANSLATED BY
ANDREW HURLEY

VIKING

VIKING
Viking Penguin Inc., 40 West 23rd Street,
New York, New York 10010, U.S.A.
Penguin Books Ltd, Harmondsworth,
Middlesex, England
Penguin Books Australia Ltd, Ringwood,
Victoria, Australia
Penguin Books Canada Limited, 2801 John Street,
Markham, Ontario, Canada L3R 1B4
Penguin Books (N.Z.) Ltd, 182–190 Wairau Road,
Auckland 10, New Zealand

English language translation
copyright © Andrew Hurley and Reinaldo Arenas, 1986
Copyright © Reinaldo Arenas, 1982
All rights reserved

First published in 1986 by Viking Penguin Inc.
Published simultaneously in Canada

Originally published in Spanish as *Otra Vez El Mar* by Editorial
Argos Vergara, S.A., 1982

LIBRARY OF CONGRESS CATALOGING IN PUBLICATION DATA
Arenas, Reinaldo, 1943–
Farewell to the sea.
Translation of: Otra vez el mar.
I. Title.
PQ7390.A72O8   1985   863   85-40106
ISBN 0-670-52960-5

Printed in the United States of America by
R. R. Donnelley & Sons Company, Harrisonburg, Virginia
Set in Trump Medieval
Designed by Joe Marc Freedman

For Margarita and Jorge Camacho
For Olga Neschein
                    thanks to whom this novel
    didn't have to be written a fourth time.

CONTENTS

PART ONE

Memory is a present which
never stops going past.
Octavio Paz

The ocean. . . . Blue. . . . Not at first. At first it's sort of sallow. Ashen, you might say. . . . Although it's not ashen either. White, perhaps. But not white meaning transparent. White. And then—though, still, almost at first—it turns gray. Gray for a while. And then dark. Covered with even darker furrows, cracks in the water. . . . Perhaps they're waves. No— just mirages of water, and sun. If they were waves they would reach the shore. That is, the *sand*. But there are no waves. Just water. That almost clumsily hits the land. . . . But it doesn't *hit* it. If it did, you'd hear some sound. There is silence. Just water, touching earth. Not *hitting* it. It comes—white, not transparent—touches it, clumsily, and retreats. Not *earth*; it's *sand*. When the water rises, without waves, perhaps the sand breathes a sound. Satisfied. From here I don't hear a thing. The water rises, but you can't see it go down. The sand absorbs it. Underneath it goes back to the ocean. . . . And farther out, it's no longer gray, but dun-colored. Very dark. Almost black. Until finally, it really is black. But by then it's very high. It joins the sky. You can't make out where the two, as separate things, begin or end. So really, to be precise, it's never blue. . . . Hector drives slowly. There's no wind. The wet smell of the sand reaches the car. Sometimes there are a few leaves borne on the water. Not many. The leaves stay on the sand, as though they were pasted there. The water vanishes. Lighting a cigarette without any trouble, with the window open, I actually have to blow out the match. Today, end of September, with no wind. He acts like he doesn't see me. He drives slowly. His mouth is closed. I might have offered him a cigarette. But he would have said no. Thank you, he would have told me, I don't smoke this early. Finally he looks at me. He'll say, Do you feel all right? I'll say, Perfectly. Then he won't speak anymore. Neither will I. Or perhaps I will. Perhaps at last I'll say his name. I'll smoke another cigarette. I'll toss the cigarette butt out. The butt falls on the sand. The water, without waves, soaks it; it feebly tugs at it; it dissolves it, sort of accidentally. Now he opens his mouth. "Do you feel all right?" "Perfectly." . . . The car goes on. I don't know what will have become of the remains of the cigarette butt by now. Perhaps it made it to the ocean. You still see the pine trees. Motionless. No—*very still*. The pines in a row, right along the edge of the ocean. Their shadow is fixed on the water. You can see another stand of pines there too. With a background of sky. When a stone is thrown in the water, it all blends. The pine grove, the sky, clouds. The whole scene is nothing but a shine of colors on the water. If you ducked under the water you wouldn't see anything at all. Opening your eyes wide— sand. Making gentle, barren little hills. And sunlight, like shards of glass. Under water, with my eyes open, very near the shore, the sun in splinters on the bottom, I might, I think, see other things too. The big yagrumo tree in the yard at home. In the country. Turning loose its leaves, white and green at the same time. On windy afternoons the leaves fall before me; I watch them, I gaze at them as I sit on a stool. Sitting there, leaning against the kitchen door, in the yard. The leaves fall. White on one side, green on the other. For a second there's a glimpse of ocean. Pines on both sides of the highway. Their low branches completely shut out the view. Pine nuts, dry, in the middle of the road, pop almost noiselessly as the car passes. Crabs scurry from their holes—their eyes like antennas, as though jumping out of their heads. Some of them, terrified, try to flee, running madly back and forth. So the car goes along squashing them. The bursting of the crabs when they're squashed is different from the pine nuts'. It's a brittle noise, like dry soil makes when it crumbles. The sun, now higher than the pines, blanches the road covered with seeds, leaves, and fleeing crabs. Stop, I'd like to tell Hector. Put on the brakes, give them time to get away. But how silly. That's senseless. We couldn't go on. He'd laugh. . . . We go on. Again I see the ocean. This time between the trunks of the pine trees. Like a very still river, barely flowing. White, behind the trees. Then the popping of the crabs and the pine nuts becomes almost inaudible. Hector has speeded up. I look at him, although I'm not going to say anything. Although, actually, I didn't want, for now, even to look at him. Tomorrow. And the day after. And always. . . . But for now I'd rather not look at him. I look at him. He looks like a boy. Although he no longer is, really. But sometimes he surprises me. Especially when he smiles. Then he's almost a child. Other times he's startled me—suddenly I don't know how, he's turned into an old man. That's how he is—a boy, a child, and an old man too. But every time I see him pose as older or younger than he really is, I feel sorry for him. Anyway, I know very well that he is not an old man—although now he's not a child anymore either. His lips are set, perhaps because he's driving faster. Now he's an adolescent. We pass the pine grove. We go into the stand of almond trees. Almonds are the only trees here that methodically give up their leaves, every year, observing seasons that don't exist here, at this latitude. Poor trees, they haven't lost their memory. They go through that unnecessary ceremony, stripping themselves and then covering themselves up again. Uselessly. The leaves—yellow, sometimes completely red—fall slowly, unhurriedly. . . . As though they understood the uselessness of the tradition. Poor trees, undressing. Having to take this sun without a single leaf of protection. Just a ritual, a habit. . . . Now it's not the bursting of the crabs but the crackling of dry leaves. They sound like scorched pages, perhaps, that you step on as you walk. Some of the leaves are swept against the windows of the car, roll toward the windshield. Constantly there are moments when they almost don't let you see the road. Hector winces. I look at him again. Now he's an old man, horrible of course. . . . Hector. But I don't say a word. Don't call him, don't speak to him. Just think it. . . . It may be that he can hear me better that way. For a time—a long time— I thought all words were futile, that talking could better be done by not opening your mouth. Now I doubt that, although I could be mistaken. Although of course I still think that words are worthless. Perhaps for saying yes or no they serve a purpose. But when they're needed for other things, they fail you. What's more, you can affirm or deny without having to open your mouth. Sometimes I can think what he thinks, although it terrifies me.

You never know where that will take you. Or you know, and that's much worse. That's why perhaps from time to time you have to speak—meanwhile you generally aren't thinking about anything. . . . And if we made the effort, if suddenly you started thinking out loud? Shouting. . . . Well. We go on. We've almost left the almond trees behind now. Little by little the baby's crying comes through to me. Perhaps he's been crying a good while and neither of us has heard him. He's behind, in the back seat. I've never been able to hold a baby for very long. I think it's going to come apart in my arms. And too, back there lying down, alone, he must be more comfortable. Lying on his back, he cries and lifts his arms and legs. I pass my hand, but without touching him, across his face. He stops crying. He closes his eyes. He seems to have gone back to sleep. What a crime, I tell myself sometimes, looking at him, he'll never forgive us—like I don't forgive my mother—although perhaps he'll never reproach us, either. And if he did, if he reproached me, I wonder what answer I would have for him at that moment. . . . He opens his eyes. He smiles and stretches his arms out to me. I turn my back and go on looking down the road. He begins to cry again. But I don't hear him anymore. Hector, absorbed in his own thoughts, drives. We go on. We leave behind the rows of cabins, some high on the line of the horizon. Soon we'll take the avenue where the oleander flowers burst. For a while we won't see the ocean. Once more I almost start to speak, to use, manipulate words. How stupid, when I had thought I had done with them for good. Could I really use them to show someone that there, in the road, to one side, a dinosaur is now strolling slowly down that dazzling path? Nevertheless, there he is, lifting his imposing head to the sky, watching us pass by in the glare, which is already unbearable. . . . Deafening screams. And beyond, out toward that point, where the beach turns to rocks and open sea begins, another group of animals, to all appearances dancing. How useless words are. All you'd have to say is "Look at them" for them to disappear instantly. I don't say a word. I close my eyes. There they are, lifting their enormous wings, gesturing, off along the beach. But above all, the calm. Over all the ruckus, the calm. I open my eyes. The dinosaur moves aside with that legendary gait that seems so melancholy to me, and lets us pass. Then he howls with laughter. Or perhaps he's shouting at us. I don't know. But above everything, the calm. That is, the semblance of calm. Since, doubtless, we'll have to go on. Have to arrive. Havana. We will arrive. Or worse, we'll always be arriving. . . . After three or four hours, perhaps more, perhaps less, depending on our speed, the traffic, the weather, the baby, we'll get there. Here's our street already. Say hello to the neighbors. Go on, say something. Smile. Terrific vacation. That's the word: "Terrific." God. And now, once you've said hello, even asked about their health, you go into the house. You put the baby to bed. Open the windows. Hang up the bathing suits to dry. Fix dinner. We eat. Tomorrow you go back to work. The vacation is over. Hector fell asleep a long time ago. I undress him. I sit for a minute on the bed. I lie down next to him. I cover my face with the sheet. Suddenly the cicadas begin to whistle. Hector sometimes says they screech. But perhaps we're both mistaken—they neither whistle nor screech. They simply make noise, out of habit; perhaps because that is their password—but they don't know that it's been used so much that it isn't any good anymore. . . . But That isn't right, he tells me. They screech like that because summer's over now and they are about to die. . . . Now they are all making that noise at once. You can hear nothing but that monotone clamor—that cry, it may be. Soon it will cease, all at once. Then a single cicada will start to whistle, slowly, by himself for a while, until another, and another, come in to accompany him. For a few seconds the racket will be unbearable. Not the sound of the engine or the baby crying or the crackling of the leaves—you can hear none of that. It's all drowned out, erased, reduced to silence by that other noise, by this kind of maddening concert—the sound of millions of cicadas, unseen, throughout the stand of pines. I know very well that even if I put my hands over my ears—as I do—I'll go on hearing them. They're on the leaves of every tree, on the rocks and grass by the roadway. I think they must have taken up residence on the roof of the car and they're whistling from up there, upstairs. The noise has suddenly grown even louder. It's unbearable. The only way to stand it is to listen to it. Now, once nothing but that clamor exists—What can hold us back, who can resist, who can not see, not see, not understand, not have a foreboding . . . White, white. . . . Hector—and the boy, who really is beautiful, lying on the sand, perhaps asleep. Pretending to be asleep. Hector—and the boy, floating on his back, very near the

---

7

shore. Applause. He has finished speaking. Someone hands him the belt with his pistols. They sing the "Internationale," everyone clasping hands, swaying. The mosquito keeps on inside the mosquito net. It buzzes above my head. Someone told me the mosquito you hear is not the one that bites. I hope that's true. Anyway I can't sleep. I go out onto the cabin porch. . . . Such silence. Only the sound of a sheet of zinc, come loose from some roof, that slowly stirs—for there is no wind. Along one side of the pines comes the boy. He walks slowly; his white clothing seems to float in the darkness. He pauses, looks back. It's early morning, I think. It will soon be dawn, I say to myself, and I go on waiting. And in these moments we have turned onto the avenue where the oleanders blaze. Oleanders of such a strong red that it isn't red anymore—pink, yellow, white oleanders. There are no leaves, no stalks, just flowers. On both sides of the avenue, and down the center. Flower after flower after flower. The oleander flower has no scent, or such a faint one that it is hardly perceptible. I have raised one to my nose—I can't smell a thing. Young lady, says my mother, don't smell that flower, it'll give you cancer. . . . My God, getting cancer from smelling a flower. And then the explanations follow: The-oleander-has-little-tiny-ants-that-live-among-its-petals-if-you-smell-it-those-bugs-go-up-your-nose-&-they're-what-give-you-cancer. Mama, I've smelled an oleander. I'm going to get cancer for sure. My God! You did it on purpose, to spite me! . . . There's also a poem about oleanders. It's in *My Second Reader*. "High and alone lives the sad oleander," it goes. Then of course it goes on, but I don't remember. The poem tries to explain that since the oleander is a poisonous plant, nothing can grow in its shade, not even the tiniest blade of grass, and that's why, according to the poem, it's alone. But really, I say to myself, what fault of the poor oleander's is that? But the truth is that it is alone. That is, except for other oleanders. If I sit under an oleander bush, if I lie down, if I fall asleep. . . . Don't digress, don't digress. No matter how much you try, and you're already trying, you're not going to escape. *High and alone, high and alone*. . . . I look at Hector again and light another cigarette. The baby is sleeping. We're making good time. Soon we'll leave the avenue of the oleanders and come out onto the highway. I look at my hands. My index and middle fingers yellow from cigarettes. A smell of gasoline begins to grow, almost pleasant, in the midst of the heat and the shimmering brightness. I open my eyes. I look at the buttons of the radio, at the closed glove compartment, all plated with aluminum; the cigarette lighter (which doesn't work) glints in the light. On top of an armrest, near the window, there's a screwdriver, a little rusty. For a while I stare at the screwdriver. Finally I begin to cry. Silently, with my mouth closed. The tears fall onto my arms. I cry a little harder now. For a second I almost started to raise a hand to my face. But I controlled myself. *This* time it looks like I'm going to escape. I look out the window. Through the tears I see a landscape utterly distorted, as though everything were under water. Above the ocean, which now rises behind the pines, I make out a bird that rises and then dives. Perhaps a hungry gull. But from here it's just a bird that descends and rises. There's nothing sure you can say about anything.

Except the day's great calm. The morning's. It's so early that no one has gone to the beach yet. Ocean and pine trees. And nothing else. I always wanted to spend some time at the beach. Now that we've come, everything is so bright, everything is so close, everything is so real that it doesn't seem true. Moreover not a soul, not a movement to be seen. Is anybody here? Hector calls, banging his fist on the counter. Coming, coming, at last says a voice. A disheveled woman appears carrying a mop. The baby in Hector's arms wants to get at the contract for the cabin. Hector finally hands the contract to the woman and she gives us the key. The baby looks steadily at the woman as she puts the paper in a desk drawer. We go in a short Indian file toward the cabin. He goes first, with the baby and the suitcase; I, behind, with the rest of the bags. The baby looks at me as though to say There you come; no problems. I stick my tongue out at him. Here it is, says Hector now, discovering the indistinct number encrusted on the cabin wall. We go in. I lay the baby on the couch. Besides the couch in the living room—which doubles as a dining room—there are two armchairs, a table with a lamp and four chairs, a refrigerator, and a cupboard that also serves as a partition between the refrigerator and the bedroom. It looks like everything works, says Hector surprised. He turns on the kitchen tap. A stream of cold water spurts out, gushing eagerly. The water splashes all over Hector's shirt; laughing, he opens and closes the refrigerator door. It works too, he says. He turns on the living room lights, they light; the bathroom's, they light. I go to turn on the porch light, but I realize the bulb is missing. Doesn't matter, says Hector, tonight we'll steal one from one of the other cabins. Now to get these clothes off, he says. Through the blinds I see the ocean. The baby raises his arms. I pick him up and carry him to the bedroom. There are two narrow beds pushed together to make one big one. There is a bunk bed too. I lay the baby on the lower bunk. I go to the bathroom; for a second I look at myself in the mirror above the washbasin, but I don't get close to it. When I open the door Hector, already in shorts, is folding his pants and putting them over a chair. What time is it? I ask. *I* don't know, he says. If the baby's asleep we can go to the beach right now. Or do you want to eat? I'm not hungry, I say, while I look for my bathing suit. I didn't think we forgot anything. . . . We brought the most important thing, he says, taking two bottles of rum out of a bag. And suddenly I hear a voice as though very distantly, beyond the ocean, or over the ocean. "We brought the most important thing." And it's Hector in the middle of a waste of sand that seems more like ash, with pieces of stone emerging from it; but perhaps they aren't stone. They seem to assume menacing positions, as though waiting confidently for him to bump into them so they can cut him to shreds. "We brought the most important thing." And the voice, cracking, is lost in a dull boom of echoes. He stumbles, his neck strikes against one of those sharp not-stones. His head rolls through the dust and comes toward my feet, slowly. "We brought it," the unbleeding head says to me, and the words can be heard running, fading away through the stony place. I go over to the bottles that are miraculously unbroken. I pick one up. I open it. I stand and begin to sprinkle the whole bottle of rum over the severed head. The falling liquid washes its eyes, its still-shining hair, its cheeks, its muddy eyebrows. Don't tell me you've forgotten your bathing suit, he says to me. Here it is, I say, taking it out of the bag. I go to the bathroom and begin to undress. Now I hear music from the portable radio he's turned on. I hear him singing to the beat of the music, perhaps to make me think he's happy. Now with my bathing suit on, I go to the bedroom where the baby, in spite of the music, is still asleep. I go back to the living room. Have a drink, Hector says to me. He's sprawled in an armchair, and indicates the two glasses already filled. Whenever you want, he says, we can go. I go to the kitchen with the glasses and let the liquor run down the drain. It would be better to take an ice chest to buy soft drinks. This is too strong by itself, I tell Hector. Let's go, he says. I'm coming, I'm coming. But first I go to the bedroom again. The baby is still asleep. I look at him a second. And go out onto the porch. It's now, for the first time, that I hear the noise. Perhaps I had heard it before, in passing, or in my imagination, but I don't remember ever having heard it like this—utterly, absolutely unbearable. It comes from among the pines and is like a whistle that's not a whistle, like a dull cheep, high monotone and desperate. It's the cicadas, Hector says; now that summer's over they start screeching like that and don't stop till they burst. They're spring insects. . . . I take my hands from my ears. The noise grows softer and softer until it becomes barely audible. We go down the steps from the cabin porch to the tile path and walk along it toward the ocean. The noise, unexpectedly, with not a cicada straggling, ceases. They all burst at once, I say, looking toward Hector. Don't you believe it, they're still screeching, just very very softly, he answers. He walks in front now, in his shorts and tennis shoes. I like him walking ahead of me, in his tennis shoes and shorts. I like to watch him walk, I think. You seem to have been here before, I say to him. No. Not much, he says quickly; he seems almost flustered. I only asked because you seem to know the place. . . . And not for a long time, he adds. But what difference does it make whether you've been here before or not? I think. Yes. I think I came once before, in the summertime, when the other beaches were full of people. . . . But where does all this explaining come from? I wonder. Now we've come to a narrow walk that goes along under the almond trees. Oleanders start here and run right down to the sand. The ocean, so high and bright, looks like a white wall rising to the sky. If I said that to Hector, he'd laugh. "You're making literature too," he'd say, "or copying it, which amounts to the same thing." And that's true, since I read something in some book about the height of the ocean in these places, but I don't remember where. But when we come to the end of the path that carries us in a straight line down to the ocean, I see that the waters dissolve just at the level of our feet. Hector, leaving everything on the sand, takes off running along the beach. It's wonderful today, he says. It's always wonderful, he says. Now down the beach, he plunges into the water. But listen, listen, maybe you'd better stop, maybe it would be better if you slowed down, if we just got home, after all, since, perhaps, everything is futile. My God—although I shouldn't think about God—perhaps, really, everything is futile—and after the noise, the twisted metal, the blood, and all the other disasters, that other hell really does exist, and he's waiting for us up there. He, unspeaking, walking slowly, assured, abstracted, unassailable, mocking, across the clouds. He and that radiant darkness of his, which emanates from who knows where (perhaps simply from his youth), lying on a cloud, on his back, in shorts, basking in the sun. His legs slightly arched, so apparently innocently. All glowing, mocking, bending us to his will, destroying us, saying, *Here I am, here I am again.* . . . Uh-huh, I say—thinking Drive carefully, don't drive too fast, for I'm sure he'll be there, waiting for us—It's wonderful, it's wonderful. And Hector, nodding, dives again, reappears higher up, in the dark blue band. Wonderful, he repeats now. And plunges in again. . . . But who's that talking, who's that shouting, who's that interrupting me with these prophecies, so alarming—which for that very reason shouldn't surprise me, since they will undoubtedly be fulfilled? . . . He springs up again, disappears, and emerges at once, drenched and sparkling. His knees break the waves, his legs now overcome the water, his feet (and he hadn't taken his shoes off!) stride the sand. Water trickles down his body, bending the fleece which looks like grass matted by a rainstorm. I lie down beside him, a little higher than he, and close my eyes. Suddenly a wave, since now there's some surf, almost fiercely breaks over my legs; I see the last bubbles dissolving on my thighs. I feel my bathing suit soaked. Soon I'll swim out to that far point in the ocean where the waters turn dark. My feet toward the horizon, my head toward the sand. The incoming water breaks against my legs, making little waves, fanning out my hair. He starts to float too. I hear him breathing. If you get tired you can rest on me, he says. We can stay like this all day. Except finally he goes a little way off, perhaps carried by the surf. I turn over. I breathe deeply. And it's the ocean. The smell of the ocean. . . . I wonder what becomes of people hundreds of miles from the ocean. . . . I go out onto the balcony every once in a while, leave my washing, let the baby cry in his crib, open the curtains, look at the ocean. There it is, there it is, I say; the rest hardly matters. The pale ocean rolls among the buildings which rise against a backdrop of blue almost white that then, later, now, darkens, glitters, until it fades away. I pick up the baby; holding him I go on washing, hang out the clothes, go to the kitchen, make lunch. But I know very well that *it is there.* And, in a second, I'll stick my head out on the balcony again and see it, swelling, rising, pulling away. . . . That's why a town in the interior is so terrible, a town in the country, or the country itself with no ocean, just a ravine that dries up when it stops raining. My mother takes me to the ravine on those days when there is plenty of water, when everything is covered with cassia blossoms and there are nighthawks fluttering and alighting everywhere, in every tree, even around the tall antennas for the crystal radios. My mother bathes in her slip; I am naked. She does not go into the ravine, but stays on a rock over which the water runs and falls in a single stream into the pool where a few leaves revolve. It's a whirlpool, she says; if you go in, it'll swallow you right up. Mama finishes bathing and puts on her clothes. Then she pees. She almost always pees standing up. Her pee falls on the dry leaves, and a lizard that was underneath runs out, soaked. . . . Almost out to the great blue band, I go under, I let the current carry me to the bottom, I open my eyes—I see my shadow under the sea, making the same motions as my body (but more serene, more remote), the sun breaking into splinters, tiny rocks, shells as white as though they were really . . . I stretch my hands out even farther. I bump my nose on the sand. I rise without breaking the surface. The luminous flickering of the seabed. Now they are leaves. Leaves passing under my body. A huge whirlwind of white, green, silvery, small, enormous leaves that crackle, that make no sound, that sway, that flicker, that go on marching past. The great yagrumo tree at home has grown so that its leaves fill the yard. A few branches have grown out over the roof so they shade it; iridescent green and purple blackbirds perch up there. Every afternoon, like now, I'm sitting on the stool, leaning against the corner beside the door to the yard. In the shade of the yagrumo. I listen to the leaves come loose, flutter, fall at my feet. Sometimes, when the wind is strong, they fall by the hundreds. I look at the air, white from so many leaves. If I stand up, if I leave the stool and begin to walk, I'll hear the rustling of the dry leaves that crumble to dust when you step on them. And still when all the bags are packed, and my mother has stirred up the ashes so not a single brand still glows (since it would bring bad luck), has closed the windows and is wandering from the horse with its baskets full of crockery to the cart the furniture goes in, I am here, still, now, standing (because the stool goes into the wagon too), gazing at the leaves. And it seems to me (*and I feel*) that for this alone one could stay here forever. But finally they ask where I am. My mother and the neighbors that have come to say goodbye to us are calling for me. Before I answer and come away, I look up again. Many leaves come loose and one, large and dried-out, like a dead bird, dives straight down and falls between my feet. What are the voices saying? What are the voices asking? What do the voices advise me to do now? *Throw yourself onto the highway. Open the car door and jump. Disappear once and for all.* . . . LA DOMINICA CUBA'S BEST CROQUETTE. Because now we've left the avenue of the oleanders that lead to the ocean and you're on the highway with not a tree, lined with shining slogans and faded signs. . . . Cane-trailers, buses, trucks, military vehicles pass us snorting. CROQUETTES AND MEAT FRIED PIES. The voices don't say a word, nor does the weather, nor do I. Just the smell and sound of the engine and the swish of other cars. The air filtering in through the wing vent stirs my hair. I turn. I look toward Hector. I begin to get used to seeing him again. His face, mouth, eyes. It all belongs to me. Now more than ever. So much so that if I wanted to I could touch him right now, put my arms around him, speak to him. So, happiness comes to me. Comes, like always, for no particular reason, while I'm looking down the highway, at the puddles—not *puddles*, mirages the sun makes on the shimmering pavement. Happiness comes to me for a moment. Then instantly, just like always, it's gone. And I'm left saying to myself, Idiot, idiot, idiot. . . . The baby has gone back to sleep. Perhaps it's the heat or the noise of the engine. What does that happiness mean? Where do you get that urge to laugh? the voices say to me now. You're alone, like always, but you haven't even the right to be proud of your solitude, since obviously there is somebody with you. And you feel it, that solitude, churning in your belly, beginning to rise in waves, then going down—and it spreads now through the stiff, numb landscape over which not cars, but rather witnesses to your helplessness, travel now. . . . I see the dinosaur again, lying in the middle of the road, calmly lifting his head, gazing impassively as we approach. Only when we're practically up to him does he stand on the end of his tail, give a hop, slip into the thin clouds, and appear farther on, descending above the nonexistent puddles. . . . A small red vehicle comes up over the horizon. It approaches; it passes clattering next to us, falls behind. There will still be air for a while yet; we can breathe. Later the brightness will be a blinding glare. The earth will burn, as it does every day. "The trees will turn to a smoke of fury," I think, imitating you, not looking at you. But for now I'm under water. I can still feel myself in the water; come out floating. Swim. Lie, like this, next to you on the sand. Let time go by, and forget. . . . But listen, listen: What do you have to forget? What are you complaining about? I come out of the water; we take the ice chest and go toward the café. We come back with the chest full of soft drinks. . . . The pavement now at noon almost burns. . . . We go into the cabin and I begin putting the clothes away in the closet. Hector's shirts, socks, underwear, books. He comes up to me now holding the baby. He hasn't taken all his milk, he says to me. He never does, I think. You brought too many books for a week, I tell him. I've already read some of them, he answers, but I'm going to go back and look over them again here. You should have brought something for yourself, he adds; that *Life of Helen of Troy* you're always reading, he ends mockingly. I already finished it, I tell him. The worst thing is, he goes on, that those books are not only full of lies, they're stupid too. It's amusing, I answer. . . . Well, I'll find you some novels to amuse you without wasting your time. But please, don't correct me, I think, don't try to "enlighten" me, and above all, stop using that tone of voice, that smug, weary, pitying tone of voice, as though before you "pronounce" your advice you already know how little attention I'll pay it. . . . Read great poetry, you say now, is what we must do, and forget that we only have a week of life. You leave the baby in an armchair, take the book, and go out onto the porch. You might as well be at home. Because he does the same thing at home; he comes in, already carrying a book. Often he doesn't even take a bath, he just sits there, with the book practically glued to his eyes, covering his whole face. You should see an eye doctor, I tell you. Yes, he says, but he hasn't really heard me. I leave him alone. I cook dinner. Dinner's ready, I tell him. But you keep reading. Until finally I come up and brush against your shoulder. Dinner . . . You don't let me finish. I'm coming, you say; I'm coming, you suddenly say, too loud. But I know you'll stay there a while longer yet. I put the baby to bed and go out onto the porch too. Hector is reading and talking to himself. If he started writing again, I think, he might feel better. But he isn't going to start, mark my words, and deep down you're glad that that's the way it is. That at least allows you to console him. Because you want to be his consolation, his refuge. You want him to come and beg your protection. Help me, help me, his eyes say. You go up to him with an enormous rope, walking laboriously, pretending the rope is even heavier than it is; you come to where he's sinking; you take a few steps. . . . With great effort, at the last second, you throw him the rope. . . . A seagull, motionless, floats in the sky, above the ocean. It isn't gliding; it hovers, suspended, still, as though held by an invisible cord. Bring me something to drink, says Hector, still with his back to me. I come back with the drink. He's totally wrapped up in himself. I put everything on the little table between the two chairs, on the porch. Thank you, he says now, while I watch the seagull as it rises, dives above the ocean, skims the water, stirring an explosion of spray, and rises instantly, fixed once more in the sky. It would be nice if we could stay here, far away, he says. I go in and come back with more to drink, I bring the ice chest, glasses of ice. We drink. At the beginning, he is reading in the back bedroom, still in town, in my mother's house. Every day, as soon as he comes in from work, he goes into that bedroom (which he can't close up because the bedroom doesn't have a door) and begins to read. He came fleeing his grandparents' house, his other aunts' house, since there, believe it or not, it was worse. Here my mother, just to pester him (not for nothing is she known as Obnoxious), goes in and out of the bedroom talking loudly, screeching, saying any stupid thing that comes to her mind, and asking questions. Sometimes he does nothing but make some gesture and go on reading. Up here, in the bedroom Mama and I sleep in (my cousin Eulogia inhabits the other one), I'm getting dressed to go to the park. How I detest these walks in the park, this town where everybody knows everybody else, my cousin Eulogia and the retinue of boys who follow her all around the park like a pack of rutting dogs. And her giving herself airs, fluttering her petticoats, talking to me about some silly thing it's not worth my bother to listen to, since what interests her is showing off, standing out, letting them see the way she moves, laughs, speaks to the others. . . . Son, my mother tells him, go take a bath. He doesn't answer, he just closes himself up in that bedroom with no doors. When we come in from the park (my cousin still babbling nonsense), the light is still on and when I go to the bathroom, I look in and see him, see Hector. He is lying on his back in bed, dressed, with his shoes still on, motionless, not reading, in another world. Now I imagine you're among the mourners in a corner, sitting among the wreaths and blankets of flowers. In the other bedroom there are the sounds of Mama's crying along with the other aunts, and the shrieks of Eulogia, who screeches louder than anyone, so she'll be noticed. But it's you I see; it's from you that, without hearing you cry, I hear the sobbing come. But you don't say a word, don't do a thing, and perhaps that's why you're the center of all the talk. When they come to take out the coffin, when the few wreaths are carried away, there is the sound of a sob in the bedroom, a brief sob that no one hears. That is when I come close and touch your shoulder and (later) take your hands. . . . Going by, on the way back from the bathroom, I look at you again. You're still lying on your back, now, apparently, contemplating the opening for the door. And since you've seen me, or I think you've seen me, I say good evening. Good evening. . . . Now you're in the bathroom (my cousin Eulogia, in the living room, chatters with her friends; my mother is clattering around in the kitchen); I hear the water from the shower falling over your body. Slowly I approach the bathroom door, closer, hold my breath. I do this, every day. Not seeing you, I hear the water rolling over your body. Young lady, says my mother from the kitchen, come help me. I go, and get to work. By early morning I am still awake. But as the dawn light grows I begin to fall asleep. When I open my eyes Mama is standing by the bed. I'll have you know, she says, that your cousin has run off with one of her boyfriends. She took all her clothes with her. Who cares, I say, still half asleep. . . . Well, *you* ought to care. It disgraces us all. But you're just like Hector, who cares as much about God as he does about a horse—you're always walking around with your head in the clouds. And I laugh, happy that she's compared me to him. And that excites even more rage in my mother. . . . Hector, I say (the gull has disappeared, probably has dropped or risen out of sight), let's go to bed. Pour another drink, he answers, and lights a cigarette. The sun has been stealing across the porch, and now we have to drag back the chairs and the table with the drinks. Don't you feel like going swimming again? he asks. Maybe later, I answer. Now I'm a little sleepy. Go lie down, he says. I'll be right there. Off to one side of the pine grove the whistle of the cicadas begins ascending. While we have another drink the whistle swells to a din and even a seagull (perhaps the same one as a while ago) flies off as though frightened. What a racket, I say; now I *am* going to bed. When I go into the bedroom I see, through the blinds, the ocean. And suddenly, as I fall into bed, millions and millions of agile, white, thin, delicate, fugitive insects in procession, gliding along. . . . Until he bumps the door open, comes in, and lies down on the bed beside me. For a second I feel him moving; instantly he is still. The cool air coming in through the blinds flows over our faces. Little by little I open my eyes, not much, so they still look closed. The first things I see are his tennis shoes, then his legs, his knees, his shorts, until I come to his chest, his neck; I watch his face awhile. His eyes are closed, but I know he isn't asleep. I inch toward the edge of his bed pushed next to mine. I close my eyes; for a while I stay that way, not saying anything, breathing. Listening to him breathe. I move closer, put a foot between his legs. I stay like that another little while. I slide my body next to his and let my hand touch his stomach for a moment. I raise my head and see his nose, his closed lips. I place my head in his hands. The cicadas' whine begins again. I get up and sit on the edge of the bed. (The ocean is still there motionless behind the pines.) I begin to take off his shoes. I run my fingers over the bottom of his feet. At once I lie down beside him. For a moment it seemed to me he had half opened his eyes. I slide my body closer and let my bare feet stroke his. Slowly I touch his neck, go up to his lips; I run my fingers along his nose. I let my hand, now spread open, slide down his chest, around his waist, under his shorts. And form an arch over his sleeping sex. My throbbing, slightly perspiring hand gently begins to caress it. Hector, I say, not too loud, since I know that I don't need to call, don't need to speak, that he hears me. Hector, I say, and as I open my eyes

I almost brush his, still closed. Hector, I say, and my eyelids little by little begin closing, as though in a drowse that will not be sleep. Hector, I say, and down there I feel him begin to throb slowly, timidly, slowly filling my cupped hand. The immense procession has reached the ocean. There, it takes flight. Hector, I say again, and feel the throbbing die; it stops. My hand covers the slightly warm, once more sleeping flesh. Hector, I say, do you want us to get under the sheet? Be still, he answers. I place my head in his hands again. And through it all, the torpor of the afternoon makes us drowsier and drowsier. Until I wake up in my mother's bed, in the country. Outside you can hear the tumult, not loud, of the night. Crickets, an owl now and then. Inside, my mother praying. First *Our Father*, then *Hail Mary*, then the *Credo*. . . . When she begins to pray, I pray along with her. I accompany her almost always to the first amen. But by the time we come to "Holy Mary Mother of God" I'm falling asleep, and since I don't know what the word "intercede" means, that's where I fall asleep. When I wake up I'm covered completely, with the sheet stirring from the air coming in the window or through the blinds. I don't quite know where I am: at first I think Havana; then, in the country. When I open my eyes everything looks somehow blurry. Only now, when I hear the ocean, do I realize I'm at the beach and Hector is asleep beside me. Then another distant noise begins to reach me, till I realize it's the baby crying. He's red and his face is soaking wet. I pick him up, dandle him, coo to him. Hush, I tell him, you'll wake your father. I walk about the room, rocking him slowly in my arms. But he doesn't hush. I go into the living room. I try to get him to take some food, but he spits it out. I sit on the porch. Hush, I say to him softly, but he goes on screaming. I walk back and forth on the porch. Look at the ocean, I tell him. Look at the ocean, I croon to him. I raise him as high as my head and show him the ocean, now almost golden, since by now it's afternoon. Want me to take you for a walk on the beach? He goes on screaming. . . . But listen, I tell myself, look at the pine grove, look at the sky, look at the water, and stop feeling so bad. All babies cry; they spend their lives crying, over any little thing. . . . Near the coast there are some seagulls. They rise, fade off to one side of the sky. In a straight line, keeping the same intervals, they appear again over the pine grove. People are leaving the beach. Someone throws up a ball that shines as it is lit for a moment by the sun. As it comes down it grows darker. This is the only moment you can breathe, look at things without their blinding you. But the baby goes on crying. His screams now seem aimed at bothering me, doing it now of all times. Hush, I tell him, raising my voice. If Hector woke up right now I'd give him the baby and run away. Wake up, come get this screaming monster. . . . But I don't want to call him. And meanwhile I'm losing the only moment of the day that's worth hanging on to. I feel it eluding me, as though it were slipping away from me through the screeches. . . . And in these moments the sun drops onto the ocean. The sea, touched by the sun, is covered with an orange braid. . . . But why won't he shut up? You must be sick, you must have something. Or you're crying just to bother me, to upset me! I tell him. And he screams louder and louder, trying to drive me crazy. I'm sure he does it on purpose. Good lord, I don't know how to take care of children. I don't like babies, I detest them. They're wet, smelly, screaming, cruel. . . . I hate them. I don't know what to do with this one. Somebody take him. . . . I lay him on a porch chair; I leave him alone, choked with crying. I go to the other side of the porch and stand there, still, leaning against the railing. I stand there like that a moment, looking at the ocean. But the screaming won't let me. I listen to his screaming. I pick him up again. I love you, I tell him, I love you so much, I tell him. I walk back and forth all over the porch holding him. Hush, I tell him quietly. Hush! . . . I lift him, I shake him, I skip softly with him. But he goes on like before. I sit down in the armchair. Be still, be still, I tell him over and over very slowly, and I begin to rock him. Hush, I tell him, and begin crying with him. Shhh. . . . And the two of us go on crying together, while we rock. Hector appears now. Take the baby, I tell him. He takes the baby and in a minute he stops crying. But it is already night.

I've never seen a night so black, says Hector. Now we do have to find that light bulb. Carrying the baby piggyback he is walking around the pitch-dark porch. Immediately he takes the baby to the bedroom and comes back. Let's go, he says. . . . But why did he have to come before the baby would stop crying? He does it to spite me. And now he doesn't even ask me why he was crying.

He does that on purpose too, I'm sure of it. Although perhaps he has intentionally not said anything, so I won't feel bad. . . . We walk through the glowing oleanders. In the darkness there is a sense of the flowers' perfume, although it doesn't quite reach the point of being perfume. Cautiously we slip behind the plants until we come to a cabin that seems not to be occupied. Here, he says, and he's already climbing on a chairback. I sit on the chair and watch him, from below, as he maneuvers, now touching the porch roof. I see his legs trying to balance, his shorts, his waist, his arms stretched toward the bulb. Suddenly his body lights up. Someone inside—since the cabin is occupied, after all— has turned on the light. Hector jumps, and we both take off through the oleanders. Once almost to the pine grove we stop, panting and laughing. Maybe we'd better go to the restaurant to get something to eat, he says. We order beer and spaghetti, which is the only dish they have today. We leave. We come to the clearing in the pine grove. I begin picking oleanders. I break off leaves, whole branches full of flowers, buds. Hector comes up to me as I am going on intently and begins to put flowers in my hair. He puts his arms around me and lifts me up. Now he flings handfuls of sand into the air. Sand falls on us like a rain shower, over our heads and shoulders. It falls on the pines and the olean- ders too, pittering on the leaves. Look how it looks, when every- thing is covered with sand, he says. And we both watch as we (I do it too now) go on taking handfuls of sand and throwing them into the air. Now we come to a place where the pine trees make a real forest. From here, if you listen a little, you can hear the racket the cicadas make, that now, perhaps because it's night- time, is not a racket anymore, but rather a distant murmur. We come out onto the open beach. At night the ocean is not so dark as it looks when you aren't close to it. Although there is no moon, the whole surface of the ocean shines as though a glow spread across it, a sort of radiant fog that comes right up to the shore. Farther out (almost out to the horizon, I suppose), you can see flickering lights. They burn brighter at times, go out, wink on again. . . . I go down to the very edge of the ocean. My feet sink into the sand. On the seabed there are lights too. They're like little fireflies lighting up the submerged sand. From time to time the waves drag these luminous rocks to the shore, where they stop shining. I pick one up. They're phosphorescent stones, Hector says. They shine in the daytime too, but the daylight is so bright that you don't notice. He walks off along the beach. He squats down and splashes in the water; he washes his face. He moves back a little way from the waterline and stands with his hands stretched out, looking at the ocean. For a second I hear him whistling. Suddenly he strips off his shirt, runs, and dives into the surf. I feel the sand moving, vibrating under my feet. I stand looking at it, until I realize it's crabs. Hundreds and hundreds of crabs begin emerging from their holes and running all over the beach. Some of them crash into my feet. Hector comes out of the water. Look, I say to him, pointing toward the stampede. It's nothing, he says, this afternoon there were lots more than this. Let's go, I'm shivering. Don't worry, he tells me, opening the cabin door, tomorrow we'll get the light bulb. Inside now, I run my fingers through my hair; they snag on oleanders still clinging there. Carefully I untangle the flowers and place them in an empty bottle. I go over to the sleeping baby and pick him up. He cries feebly, not really awake. When I turn on the light, he wrinkles up his whole face. I fix milk for him and he drinks it unprotestingly. Almost immediately he falls asleep again. I lay him down, cover him, pass my fingers down across his face; but I don't kiss him. I straighten our beds—Hector's, mine. I put up the baby's mosquito net. I go into the living room. He is still lying there with his head propped on one of the arms of the couch. He is reading. I light a cigarette and go out onto the porch. Little by little, out of the darkness, another, thicker darkness begins to take shape. It's the trees, which are silhouetted blacker, although barely silhouettes at all, against the blackness. I lay my head against the back of the chair and smoke. A mosquito whines and tries to light on my nose, but I wave him away; more come. I hear them buzzing all around me. I smoke another cigarette. Perhaps the smoke will drive them away. The cicadas begin their whistling, which drowns out the buzzing of the mosquitoes. I go into the cabin. It's awful how many mosquitoes there are out there, I say. He goes on reading. Ah, I think he says now. But I don't know whether it's because of what he's reading, what the book makes him feel, or what I say. Perhaps what he meant by that "Ah" was "Leave me alone, get out of here." I go to the kitchen and fix two drinks. Thank you, he says. He takes a drink and goes on reading. I sit down in a chair with the glass resting on my stomach. Sitting there, I try to concentrate on something, anything. I go to the table and try to find something on the radio. *Making a palm-leaf hat,* says the voice of the woman speaking, *is not easy. We're at the "Martyrs of Girón" unit where the workers go all out to surpass their production quotas for palm-leaf hats, trying to keep up with the needs of our men and women who work in the fields. Let's listen to Isabel Monal, one of the most productive workers here. She has far outstripped her daily goal, weaving more than two hundred fifty hats in eighteen hours of volunteer labor. The technique for weaving a hat from the thick fibers of the husk of the palm branches, explains Comrade Monal, is as follows: Take two long thin strips cut from the husk and tie them together at one end. First step: Fold the strip on the right over the left. Second step: Pass the left strip under the right one, crossing them alternately one over the other to make the first braid, which we call the "initial braid." This plaited piece—* I turn off the radio. Perhaps I should pour myself another drink, but do I really want one? He hasn't finished his yet. He hasn't so much as tasted it again. He's been talking to himself for a while. Perhaps he's only moving his lips as he reads. *Behold loathing,* he seems to have said. *Behold the place in flames,* I'm sure he said just now. But listen, listen, why such rage? Why such a feeling of resentment, impotence, loneliness, if I'm here? Don't I count? Can't I help you at all? There is nothing, nothing you can do, the voices say. Look at the ocean, think of the ocean; think of the ocean and be comforted. Be comforted knowing that it is there, that it marches along beside you, behind the trees. A little farther on, when you cross the bridge and top the first hill and lose the imaginary odor of the oleanders, you will see it once more. I will smell that smell of salt and washed land, and I will be able to breathe. Now, control yourself, pay no attention to the sun. Close your eyes. Close your eyes. . . . There is the dinosaur up there, once more right in the middle of the road, waiting for us. The car draws closer and closer; it looks like we're going to smash to pieces against the beast. I open my eyes—walking slowly and deliberately the dinosaur moves to one side of the road. When we pass beside him he takes out (I don't know where from) an enormous lipstick and paints his lips. What in the world, I think. And the dinosaur roars with laughter. His teeth like great whetted axes glint behind the red rind his mouth has become. The car speeds on and the howl of laughter falls behind, echoing wider and wider. . . . A trailer-truck approaches, making a hellish racket. It's an enormous vehicle apparently loaded with merchandise, although it's completely covered by a tarpaulin. But listen—think, reason, meditate. It may not be merchandise, it may be weapons. Secret weapons. Machine guns, cannons, bombs that can flatten a city with one blast. Because we are at war. Constantly, ceaselessly, we are now at war, said one of the highest officials. We are at war, do you hear, we live in dread that they will strike us dead with firebolts, we live under the threat of lightning, we live in a never-ending struggle that extends beyond the battlefield, that sometimes, *always*, surpasses the battle itself in horror. . . . Who cares about my tragedy, when this minute we could all perish in a clap of doom? It's really terrible, says Hector, and I listen to him (now on the way to work, waiting for the light to change), terrible always living under threats, warnings, that this miserable day could be your last. Even within horror there must be some stability, you need to be able to stop at some point, say Here I stand, I will start out from here, given these conditions I will try to survive. But we don't even have that, he says (and now the car begins to move forward; soon I'll get out and go in to work), not even that. Open warfare is preferable. I'd rather all the bombs were dropped at once. That way, at least there would be an end, the chaos wouldn't just go on and on. Perhaps one might even start over again. . . . Another trailer-truck goes by, fast; then another, and another, all loaded down, with the enormous tarpaulins covering the "merchandise." It's a real caravan of trailers threatening to run us over, run us off the road, taking up the whole highway and raising a hot wind that blows into the car. . . . But listen, listen, pay attention, think—if it were lemons or oranges, any kind of fruit, they'd have to be covered because the sun spoils them, rots them, ruins them. . . . Yes, perhaps it's lemons. . . . And now we are crossing the bridge and now we are topping the first hill. The car's engine sounds tired, as though it were making an effort not to give up. Hector accelerates and we finally reach the top. The sound of the engine returns to normal. We go on. The fresh air of morning comes in; the heat, for a moment, seems to be lessening. I look at the baby, who is still asleep, and now, more calmly, light another cigarette. . . . On one side of the highway, you can see the ocean; on the other a few yellowish solitary pine trees dried out by the wind and sun. On one side of the highway you can see the ocean; on the other a few almost motionless cows grazing uninterestedly. On one side of the highway you can see the ocean; on the other a house of unplastered cinder blocks, unshaded by trees, with four windows and a tower, or something that looks like a tower—I can't imagine what it's for. I see the house from afar as we pass. It looks pathetic there in the middle of the flat field, having to take the force of the wind and the sun. The car goes on but the house stays a few seconds in my memory. . . . On one side of the highway you can see the ocean; on the other a billboard with immense letters: YOU ARE ENTERING THE MONUMENTAL COFFEE BELT OF HAVANA. On one side of the highway the ocean; on the other a gigantic fence: EIGHTY THOUSAND HAVANA WOMEN TO THE CANE-CUTTING! On one side of the highway the ocean; on the other a sign: WE HAVE REACHED 100,000 COFFEE SEEDLINGS PLANTED! A sign with an athletic arm, its hand gripping a rifle. TO THE ATTACK—WITH FIDEL BEFORE US! A military post with two armed guards at the entrance. A great banner: YOUNG PEOPLE TO CAMAGÜEY FOR THREE YEARS! Two rumpled women under a bus shelter. A gas station. A gigantic placard: AT YOUR COMMAND, COMMANDER-IN-CHIEF! A sign: THE SCHOOL IN THE FIELDS IS THE BEST EDUCATION! A mural: WAR TO THE DEATH WITH LONG-HAIRS AND WORMS! A scaffold with NO QUARTER GIVEN IN THIS WAR painted on it. A stockade which has been used for another sign: GREAT PROVINCIAL NURSERY. PATRIA O MUERTE! A faded red canvas banner arching across the highway, with a smiling man planting a coffee tree drawn on it: TO DRINK IT, YOU'VE GOT TO PLANT IT! Another huge billboard with smiling men and women lifting their blades: ALL WE'VE GOT FOR TEN MILLION TONS OF SUGAR! Another sign: LEAVE NOT A SINGLE CANE STALK STANDING! Another: PUT YOUR SHOULDER TO THE FIELD! Another: AGRICULTURE IS FOR A CUBAN WHAT MOUNTAINS ARE TO GUERRIL-LAS! Another great mural with a gigantic figure: AT YOUR COMMAND! Another illustrated platform: TO PINAR DEL RIO FOR WOOD-GATHERING—THE TOBACCO MUST BE DRIED! Palm trees with their trunks papered with a sort of breastplate of photos—JUST GIVE THE WORD! Photo after photo after photo.

Another great sign emerging: TO THE FINAL CHARGE! Another: IF YOU STICK OUT YOUR NECK WE'LL CUT OFF YOUR HEAD! Another: HARK TO THE CALL OF THE FATHERLAND. Another: LEAVE NOT A GRAIN ON THE GROUND. . . . But listen, listen, look, listen to me: On one side of the highway you can still see the ocean. The ocean, so smooth. The ocean flowing timeless, the ocean sliding along under a flock of seagulls gliding gently. The ocean, clear at the shore (almost transparent), green farther out, then blue, then indigo farther still. Glittering black, out there, where you can't tell how huge it is. The ocean. The ocean. Listen to me, pay attention: white, green, blue, echoing, deep, black, still, transparent, ceaseless, fixed, immense. The ocean. . . . The ocean can hardly be heard from here. As I close the blinds of the cabin and am putting up the other mosquito net I can't hear it if I don't concentrate. I think: The day is over. We're coming to that great calm in which the peaceful water flows noiselessly, not hitting the shore, not rising. The quiet, transparent water, flowing slowly, constantly. And if I leaned out over that flowing water, flowing nowhere in particular, itself a prisoner, if little by little I leaned over, gently, just a little fall forward, then a slow rocking. . . . Floating, perhaps, for a while, then sinking slowly. Feeling the water flowing around my sides, *take me*, little by little rising muffled and embracing, *take me*, ceremoniously circling me, *take me*, flowing up around my neck. . . . But the battle is not over, do you hear? It hasn't even begun, you mark my words. When I have the mosquito net up I listen to the beating of the tide. And I know it will never be over. For a second I look toward the still-sleeping baby. I go to the living room, where Hector is still deep in his reading. A mosquito buzzes between his nose and the book. I go out onto the porch, and under the silhouettes formed by the almond trees I pick out the gleam of our car parked there. I go in. For a moment I stand in the living room. Immediately I go into the bathroom. I turn on the light and look at myself in the mirror without looking at myself. I really don't feel like it. Or perhaps I *do* feel like it. But I can't permit. I can't permit . . . I can't. . . . My mother is calling me. My mother calls me and says, You spend hours in front of that mirror, looking at yourself like some silly twit; you must think you're so pretty. . . . Someone comes in all of a sudden and adds that if a person spends so much time looking into the mirror, he finally sees himself dead. "You wind up seeing just a skull, your own skeleton." I test that assertion. But I can't permit. But . . . I turn off the light and begin undressing. Little by little. I don't want to cry. I calmly unfasten the bathing-suit straps, unzip it down the back. Not wanting to cry. Now just letting the bathing suit roll down between my legs and lifting my foot leaves me completely naked. Then, without turning on the light, I sit on the toilet and begin to pee. I'm peeing with the lights out; and I cry slowly, softly, so that I don't even hear it myself. Now in the bedroom I take a pair of panties out of the drawer, crawl under the mosquito net, and lie down. Light is coming in, but not harshly. And, of course, I could close my eyes. But for a while I keep them open. Little by little the cicadas' noise swells. And swells. Suddenly, it falls. Now you can't hear it. In a second I'll wash my face and put out the light. Since I'm not sleepy I'll stay awake. After a little he'll come in. I'll hear him go into the bathroom, turn on the light. I'll hear him undress and see him naked. Immediately he'll turn out the lights and slip under the mosquito net, trying not to make any noise. You can hear him breathing. You can hear the light rustle as his body stretches out. He covers himself with the sheet. We are next to each other. Are you asleep? He doesn't answer. I bring my body closer to his. Like always, with my head in his hands, on the pillow. . . . The great fog rolls in. . . . And the leaves. More and more leaves, now changing into green parrots, the parrots fluttering down and alighting to form an empty beach. . . . And there she is. Sometimes I only see her a few seconds. Other times, she stays awhile. And we talk. Or really, she talks. I contemplate her. She has that regal, desolate bearing that I will never have, even if I suffer worse things than she. Her clothes by now are shabby and she herself, even she, has noticeably aged. Nonetheless she is beautiful still. There, on the seashore. On a beach that I will never visit, with no trees, no grass. Just sand. Bright sand that turns to rocks farther on. You'd think she had been swept up here by the tide. She looks like she's from another world. But I recognize, identify her at once, by her sad (*tragic*) countenance; I look on her as someone I know and, indeed, admire. Because you have at least been able to *be*—I mean, you exhausted all the possibilities. My defeat is my triumph, you can say. . . . But *I* . . . I am the detested of the gods, you say to me, while I creep forward on all fours. Near her, on the sand, I squat and watch her now in strange attitudes, posing like a model, placing a hand over her mouth. Then she is still and seems to look at me. I hop little by little, still on all fours, closer to her. I can see her muddy feet, her coarse tunic, her hair blowing across her eyes. Somewhere, when I was always on the lookout for information about her, I read, *"The life of the young suitors was very happy, when one day a very beautiful young stranger arrived in Lacedaemon. . . ."* But I know that isn't true, there can be no happiness when everything is ordered and foreseen. I am the whore of Argos, she declares now, so proudly that she might be giving one of her noblest titles. For a while there is silence. Then suddenly we hear music. It comes from nowhere, but it seems to be everywhere. It is a sound of trumpets, choirs, lamentations, songs. I look toward the horizon where the sand becomes a rocky waste. A great army is approaching. She too descries it and begins to wave her arms. The army comes on, like a platoon of war. The soldiers all march directly toward us; their short tunics reach only to their thighs. They are mostly young men, and their looks are made even more breathtaking by their shields and helmets. I step back a little way. I watch her straighten her hair, paint her lips, and try out various smiles. At last she raises her tunic, leaving one thigh bare. Now they are passing before me, looking ahead, toward her, those first warriors. Here are Ascanius, Ialmenus, Ajax Telemonius, Antimachus, Peisander, Agamemnon, Menelaus, Bienor, the deiform Odysseus. All the soldiers come on, both Danaans and Trojans, squeezed into one confused formation. Achilles is the first to reach her. Hurling a shriek, he begins to remove his crested helmet. Then Nestor, who strips off his tunic and golden sandals with a haughty look. The line of men comes on. Now beside her stand Doryclus, of Jovian descent, Pandocus, Lysander, Pyrasus and Pylartes, panting and brandishing their manhoods. Magnanimous Odysseus strokes his thighs and glares all about him. At last the rest of the squadron has arrived. Brave Trojans, extraordinary Achæans are now massed about her. Grief-burdened Menelaus, captain of the army, covered with sweat, goes up to her and attempts to seize her by the arm. But she pulls away, laughing, and begins to dance, brushing against Agamemnon, king of men, with her thighs. He throws down his scepter, strips off his armor, and stands entranced, gazing at her. She goes on dancing, although the music has ceased and now the panting of the soldiers is the only sound heard. A sharp odor of sweat bathes the beach. Deïphobus, completely nude, approaches and goes to trap her in his arms. She caresses his sex with gentle fingers and goes on whirling in her dance. A group of Trojan warriors begins to circle about her, as the sons of Theseus and Peirithoüs, strong as tigers, clasp their members and beckon to her of the white arms, who touches the boys' inflamed virilities with the tips of her toes and runs off pursued by the troops. Down the beach she stops, flings open her dress, and laughs once more. The aroused army encircles her once more. The Achæans, in their cuirasses of bronze, place themselves before her; the Trojans, with gleaming shields, form up behind. Proud Antilochus steps out of the ranks and grasping his member in both hands begins marching toward her, who waits impassively. When the danger is at hand, she touches the staggering size of the young man with her elegant fingers, gives a sophisticated yelp, and flees. In a din of splintering shields, helmets, headpieces, and breastplates, the soldiers circle her yet again. Kind Priam, father of five sons, tries desperately with his erect old sex to open a path for himself through the young men, who pay him no heed. King Priam spews invective and goes on stroking his masculinity. Theseus and Peirithoüs immediately follow suit. Divine Agenor calls up his young herald and orders him to kiss his member. Even Thersites, the ugliest of all the warriors there were in Troy, takes his enormous phallus out and begins to fist it so furiously that blood dyes the sand. . . . She dances once more. Some kiss her footprints in the sand; others, already spent, writhe on the ground and are crushed by those who leap forward in a fever of lust like splendid stallions. . . . Meanwhile, Menelaus, possessed by the Furies, tries to seize her, but Hector, tamer of men, with his turgid phallus deals him such a blow on his back that the son of Atreus lets out a cry of consternation and falls to his knees. Timid Patroclus looks toward Achilles, who shows signs of arousal under the tunic he is wearing still. The young man begins to cry softly as he of the fleet foot supports him. . . . At last the Achæan soldiers, like dogs of prey, rush headlong toward her of the rapacious eyes, just as the Trojans, inflamed, attempt to possess her as well. But she, mistress of magical potions, leaps, and the two battalions clash together: now the battle begins. . . . Splendid Diomedes of potent phallus strikes about with it, dealing death to the young son of Eurydamas, the cunning charioteer. Then, with well-directed thrusts he lays Thymbræus, Thoön, and Deïopites in the dust. Meanwhile Odysseus, equal in prudence to Jove, strokes his member up to dreadful proportions, pierces the breast of Democoön, bastard son of King Priam, and then runs Alastor through, of glorious young age. Deicoön kills Polypoetes; Ajax son of Oïleus kills Doryclus; Euryalus, Dresus; Antilochus strikes Ablerus dead. . . . Dust, carnage, blood—the battle goes on, growing every moment more confused and terrible. The Trojans flourish their sweaty members; the inflamed Achæans brandish theirs, no less bronzed and glistening. Patroclus is almost pierced through by young Peiroüs, son of Imbrasus, who is instantly slaughtered by a blow from Achilles who drops his formidable phallus on the young warrior's head. Meanwhile Agenor with a single thrust spits five Lycian captains on his proud rod. Agamemnon son of Atreus plunges his phallus into young Antiphus's breast and into Sarpedon, of doughty glare. Alcibiades sinks his flaming member into the forehead of Ascanius, leader of the Phrygians, who in his turn destroys Æsepus and Pedasus. Imposing Orsilochus, of divine thighs, methodically riddles twelve Trojan youths with his rosy sword, cutting out their livers and lights; then wielding his member with great fierceness he assails old Priam, who seeking to escape runs with a start of surprise into Achilles, who also sticks him with his golden device. Kind Priam, at the moment when death is at hand, overleaps the Greek demigod's tense phallus and, kicking off from its shining surface, leaps, as from a springboard, over to his warrior friends who receive him and stand in a living fence about him. . . . Hector, enraged by the mishap suffered by his father, runs though six Danaan captains, of lovely cheeks. The two Ajaxes with their supple engines attack again, toppling Pylon, Ormenus, Menon, and Orestes. Peisander, taking advantage of a moment when Achilles is careless, attempts with his tapering sharp prick to prick the hero's heel, but Achilles, abandoning his prey, seizes him by the thighs and pulls him onto his own member, of frightful dimensions. . . . The din of the battle is so great that neither voices nor bodies may be made out. Only a uniform wail is to be heard, an inflamed panting; only a gigantic roiling mass is to be seen, in which all the parts are writhing as well—only the rigid bronze phalluses, like unwearying thorns, stand out clear. They leap, waver, crash, pierce, splash, rebound, sink and emerge, fall defeated, and then, with measured throbs, rise again. . . . Thus continues the battle, and there are now so many dead that on the beach there is nothing to be seen but shattered skulls, viscera, severed heads and manhoods. I look toward her of the white arms and I see her, off to one side, gazing in fascination. . . . When it seems that not a man will remain alive, the distant sound of a trumpet is heard, so remote that perhaps it has been sounding for a while already and it is only now that I hear it. . . . On the horizon appears a ship with full-blown sails. It draws closer. From time to time the sight of it is blocked by the mutilated bodies rolling along like a windrow of seaweed blown by the shore winds. The music is here now. The ship too is very near. It reaches the shore. A young man descends. He gives some order to the ship, which keeps pace as he advances toward us. He is wearing a splendid short tunic which shows off his naked legs and arms; his hair falls over his forehead and shoulders. Helen runs toward him, but he goes on walking straight ahead, indifferent, toward the site of the chaotic battle. Undeterred, she runs all around him, tries to stop him, cries out as she gestures lewdly. But he proceeds; his feet shod in rich sandals bestride the sand. She, the coveted of the gods, embraces only his footprints; she stands up, runs her hands over all her body, then strips off her short vestment and naked blocks his way. But the favorite of Aphrodite goes on with firm tread. Desperate, she throws herself to her knees and attempts to caress the folds of his shining tunic. The tamer of steeds thrusts her aside and goes on toward the battle. First to see him is Achilles, who stops, leaving his victim half pierced. Agamemnon too pulls his member from his opponent's breast and stands observing the youth whom the goddesses dispute over. The two Ajaxes interrupt their struggle to stare inflamed at the trainer of horses. Old Priam stops fighting, entranced before the vision of his son, and his opponent, wily Odysseus, fails to take advantage of the moment to kill the King. Both stand still, contemplating the young man calumniated as a kidnapper. King Menelaus, King Idomeneus, Hector, proud Antilochus, all the Greek soldiers, beautiful as gods, and the Trojans of bronze cuirasses and spendid legs stand still, looking only at the divine male who now passes next to them. Adolescent Patroclus, his breast covered with froth, is the first to follow.

Then Iphidamas, brave and of towering height, Arcesilaus, chief of the Bœotians, Ajax Telamonius, Hector Priamida, Lycophron, of glorious age, immediately join them. The entire Greek army, the most shining Achæans and Trojans, now are coming along behind the one who has lived for love. Helen stands desperate before the throng. Naked, she suddenly begins a dance of unbearable lasciviousness. But no one heeds her. When she persists, clasping indiscriminately at the soldiers' feet and begging to be possessed, the soldiers thrust her roughly aside, calling her "evil woman," "destroying scourge," "shame of Great Hellas," "witch," "shameless whore," and a thousand other insults, until at last they send her off with blows and kicks. . . . The youth whom the goddesses dispute over now marches close to the shoreline. The two armies, that now make one, follow behind him. The tamer of steeds reaches the ocean. The sweaty, inflamed armies too stop, a little way off. He turns toward them and with a firm graceful motion feels the folds of his tunic. Then he walks on. Achilles draws closer to Patroclus; Emoclitus and Theseus surround proud Antilochus, who affectionately strokes the member of Diomedes son of Tydeus. Menelaus, dear to Ares, introduces himself into a valiant group of excited young Trojans. In that way the throng proceeds. Old Priam, almost fainting, runs with great strides, leaning at times on the rigid phallus of his son Hector, tamer of men, who looks vacantly at him and goes on, still aroused. Now the pet of goddesses emits a whistle. His ship pulls ashore. He leaps aboard. Slowly he draws away. Once more, the distant sound of a trumpet is heard. The brave warriors, clasping each other tightly and still more tightly, cast themselves into the sea. Thus they go, deeper and deeper into the water, while bold, prolonged caresses slow their progress, sometimes bringing on a multiple hecatomb of spasms. The submersion and emergence of arms, legs, heads, and phalluses which bob and sink behind the divine one resemble a strange ship where the crewmen, fettered to one another, make up the keel, the stern, the deck, the entire boat—and this boat can no longer be called back; breaching, it sinks over the horizon. . . . The trumpet no longer sounds, the distant speck has disappeared. She is sitting on a rock sobbing. I sit at her side, on the sand. She seems not to have noticed me and goes on crying. Finally she looks at me as though she recognizes me. Am I the whore of Argos? she asks me, and gestures at the now deserted sea. Suddenly she breaks into laughter. Then in a moment she becomes an egg, as tiny as a dove's. I pick it up, gingerly, carefully; I hold it a moment in my closed fist. Now I stand and throw it into the ocean. There comes a terrible roar. I look up. A squadron of yellow planes advances along the sky, like a swarm of wasps clouding over the whole ocean and shore. On the ground and into the sea the bombs fall like a deluge of colors. They fall next to me, raising the sand become dust, and on the waves, which lash, wild and aflame. Everything is burning. They've killed him, I think, now he must be dead, the boat could not have withstood this barrage. I run toward the ocean, but there is nothing I can do. Columns of fire blossom all across the horizon. I am going blind, and I begin to scream. I hear, suddenly, someone calling me. But I go on screaming, until once more I descend—where, I do not know, since now I cannot see. Everything is dark, and I feel cold. My voice descends. I no longer scream, but I am sobbing very softly, so no one can hear me, so no one will go on calling me. As I cry I find the planes have left. There is only a great silence now. A silence as unbearable as the most deafening roar—a great silence and a formless gloom. I walk, I try to walk, and I touch nothing; there is only emptiness, silence, and the vast darkness. I squeeze my eyes even more tightly shut, and in the blackness I see less-black shadows; something moves, variations of darknesses. I release my eyelids—little by little the blackness lightens; the shadows begin to sort themselves out. Now there is contrast, light—I have

FIRST DAY

sobbed, I have been sobbing. My eyes sting. But now, here is daylight. The day grows brighter little by little through the half-shut blinds. Although I still haven't completely opened my eyes, I feel it striking, opening a way, reaching the mosquito net now, passing through it. . . . The light, though it is barely daybreak, is already becoming intolerable; it makes you get out of bed even when, like now, you don't really need to. I begin to identify things: the sheets, the mosquito net, the ceiling, the blinds through which the great splendor shines. Hector has already gotten up. For a moment I sit on the bed, just sitting, thinking of nothing, while I begin to pick out the sounds of daytime. Voices, shouts, people talking, the engine of a car that has apparently just stopped in front of our cabin. Then, mixed into the sound of the beating of the ocean, which is not too strong yet, I hear the whistle of the cicadas. I get up. I go to the bunk where the baby is sleeping. A fly is walking over his lips. They always figure out a way to slip inside the mosquito net. I shoo it away gently, so as not to wake the baby, and cover him over again. I go into the bathroom. Hector, I call, thinking we should probably go to the beach right now. He doesn't answer. No doubt he's already deep into some book. Hector, I say, and go into the living room. He has his back to me, looking out through the blinds. I slowly walk toward him. A car has parked next to our cabin. A woman who looks to be getting along in years is standing by the car and pointing toward the cabin next to ours. A man gets out of the car, but I can't see what he looks like because his back is to me. He opens the trunk and turns to carry in the bags. He is not really a man; he is a young man, a boy. I suddenly feel a dread I cannot explain. Hector is still in a sort of vacant day-dream; he has still not found me behind him. Both of us, very close to each other, stand there and watch. For a moment, when the boy with the suitcases goes up the steps to his cabin, he seems to look our way (although from outside, I think, he couldn't possibly see us) and smile. . . . The baby's crying is too insistent not to be heard. I go into the bedroom, pick him up, and begin to rock him. There are people in the cabin next door now, says Hector, coming into the room. I hope it isn't a big family, I say, thinking of the noise they might make. Apparently not, he answers. Do they have a car? I ask, just to say something. Apparently, he answers. A Ford, in pretty good shape. I hope it stays that way, I say. . . . I feed the baby. I put him to bed again and stand looking at him until, suddenly, I turn my back. I put on my bathing suit and go out onto the porch. There is Hector waiting for me. When we go down the steps I see the boy at the door of his cabin. He's taken off the clothes he traveled in and is now sporting a brand-new pair of gleaming-white shorts. In these seconds the woman, wrapped in a housedress which also looks new, stops at the door and smiles and waves at us, as though saying, Since I'm in the cabin next door we have to be, perforce, good friends. . . . I feel obliged to return her greeting. She then waves again, even more effusively, with an air of triumph. She's the boy's mother, I think; she can't be anything else. I take Hector's hand and we go on toward the beach. The ocean is yellow and reddish, like rivers when there's been a lot of rain and they're all stirred up. Hector stands up to his knees in the incoming waves. He keeps standing like that, with the water up to his knees, and I think, I've never seen anyone so alone. But What can I do to comfort him? What will I say to him if I go up to him? What, for that matter, is there to comfort him for? Holy Mary, what are we going to do, what am I going to do, what am I doing? . . . It's true that I don't bring you flowers anymore, or pray to you, but I still believe, or want to believe. Someone told me I'm young; someone told me when I fix myself up I don't look so bad. But he doesn't say a thing like that to me, and so it's as if no one had told me. . . . I put on my only nice, dressy dress—I just finished ironing it. I turn on the radio, not too loud, and stay in the dining room listening to Pedro Infante sing and looking at Hector standing there, in the middle of the yard. And What can I do, how can I make him aware that I want to help him? . . . I'm writing a letter full of all kinds of foolish things. I'm reading the letter. I'm tearing up the letter. I'm listening to the radio—now Miguel Aceres Mejía is the one singing—and looking at you there in the yard while evening falls. I hear my mother rattling around in the kitchen; she's making (*creating*) dinner. Soon I'll turn on the dining room light, turn off the radio, and help set the table. The three of us will sit on our stools. And an unbearable feeling will come with the smell of the food and fill us with fury. My mother, acting like she doesn't have a conniving bone in her body, *pretending*, will ask Hector again whether there are still no jobs at the factory and when they plan to reopen and whether it wouldn't be a good idea to go look for a job someplace else. Finally she says that a friend of hers, an "acquaintance," told her they needed waiters in who knows what restaurant, and tomorrow bright and early he ought to go and start work. Okay, uh-huh, he says, as he eats. The next day he goes. They'll try him out for a week. At the end of a week they tell him they don't need him. And now I hear my mother shouting in the dining room again. He's a dimwit, she says; the owner of the restaurant told her "acquaintance" that he was too distracted, that he needed a boy who was awake, not a slack-jawed fool people walked out on without paying, was always breaking glasses and spilling milkshakes and being generally clumsy—it's like he was living on the moon. . . . And these days, she says even louder, you can't live on the moon. Living right here, even with your feet on the ground, is hard enough now. And she goes on talking, now calling him a moron, a lazy good-for-nothing. . . . I turn up the radio. Pedro Infante's voice fills the whole house and I start to sing along with Pedro Infante so Hector won't hear the ruckus my mother is making. But it's no use. He probably heard it all, and he's still standing there in the yard, while the afternoon lengthens, not saying a word, because he never says a word. Why doesn't he ever say anything? . . . Holy Virgin, tell me, how can I help him if he runs away from me, if he acts like he doesn't even want to see my face? Sometimes I think he doesn't need anyone. But perhaps that isn't true. Perhaps he needs everyone but no one understands him. If only one day he'd come in and beat my mother and smash the radio and set the whole house on fire. If only he'd do *something*. But he doesn't do a thing. . . . After dinner he goes to his room and starts reading or lies on his back in bed, while Mama takes the flysprayer (just like my grandfather did) and fills the house with that awful smell. And I sit on the porch watching the people go by and saying hello, because everyone in this town knows everyone else. I lie in bed too, unsleeping, thinking, trying to think what he's thinking, but I can't. . . . Dear Mary, don't let my mother find out, but I'm in love with my cousin Hector, and there's nothing I can do to make myself fall out of love with him or make him fall in love with me. And I cry, for him and for myself, but especially for him, because he's a man and it must be terrible to be a man these days, because really a woman doesn't have so much to lose; if she's insulted she can just break down and cry or ask for help. But what can he do when they insult him? And he's not like the rest. They know how to defend themselves; they have those angry words always cocked and ready, those threatening looks they're always stabbing you with. You have to watch out for that kind, they never let an opportunity slip to fondle us or say something crude. . . . We are at the annual gala at the Vista Alegre Club. Everyone is dancing. The young men who didn't bring a date find one immediately, or steal their friends', and go off into the darkest corners. And they do it all in such a natural way (like when they drink beer right out of the bottle) that the world seems made for them, and they understand that and behave according to those rules, *their* rules. They *fit in*, I think. They're *in their element*, I think. But he is standing in one corner of the room with his hands in his pockets, gazing blankly into space, as though he were in another world. But I know (and that is the worst part) that he is not in another world but in this one, in the midst of the hullabaloo and laughter, and that he's making a real effort to put up with it all. That, at least, I know. When the song is over I excuse myself to my partner (who smiles as though to say It's all the same to me, I'll find somebody else) and go over to where he's standing. Let's dance, I say to him. And I take him by the hand. I lead him to the center of the room. While the organ plays I put a hand on his shoulder and draw him little by little toward me. My other hand clasps his sweating hand; I put my head on his shoulder and let my hair touch his lips. He marks off the steps stiffly, as though he's afraid he'll step on my feet, and he doesn't say a word. We go back home. I open the door and like always Mama is waiting up for us. Is this any hour to be coming home? I don't answer her. I go to my room; I undress and lie in bed. I hear her spraying the house and then turning off the lights. Like that, in darkness, it's easier to think. Everything is hidden, blotted out, and although there's no consolation there's nothing noisy or bright or quick, either, calling our attention, diverting our thoughts. So, sleeping in the bedroom that had been my cousin's, listening to my mother snore in the other bedroom, I can put everything in order and when I feel a bit quieter I can think about him. . . . I think that he is there, next door, and that by merely going into the hall I would be in his room. Our Father, I say. Our Father. Our Father. And as I pray I think He is there, just two walls away. Our Father. And he's probably awake, with the lights on. . . . When at last I say Amen, I am still thinking about him, still seeing him, there, alone. And about just getting out of bed and just, on tiptoe, touching the walls, going down the hall. Our Father, Our Father, if I just went out into the hall and then into his room. Holy Mary, sweet Mary. . . . Sleep comes over me, but not suddenly—little by little, rather, without my realizing. The noise of my mother in the kitchen wakes me. Her voice vying with the crash of the pots she is furiously throwing on the fire. Now there's *really* no way out for us, she says, coming into my room, forcing me to listen to her. *Way out, way out,* I say to myself aloud, almost laughing, thinking Has there ever been a way out for us? Things are going from bad to worse, she goes on, not paying me any heed; the rebels are everywhere, in everything, everything is blockaded, not a single potato gets through, now we'll *really* starve to death. So much the better, I say; if they're everywhere that means this can't last much longer, then. She laughs and says, Do you really think it'll topple, just like that? The government has the weapons. What can a rebel mob do without weapons? Eat cows and ruin everything! That's what they're doing, screwing the country up worse every day. . . . Suddenly, hearing her talk like that fills me with fear, not because of what she's saying but because of the way she says it. But listen, I think, this may have happened to me before. Anyway, I never pay any mind to what my mother says, only to the way she says it. And what's more there is always some war or other going on here, an attack, some kind of revolution, some monkey business. . . . At last I reach the conclusion that no war will have any bearing on whether he looks at me or not, listens to me or not, guesses how much I think about him. And so I tell myself, *It's all the same to me, it's all the same to me.* But whether I want to or not, I have to hear all about it all, have to virtually be part of it all. They are out there, somewhere; they take such and such a town, they now control such and such a province; it topples. . . . At last I begin to feel a kind of hope, not fully hope because it doesn't make me happy, but at least it shakes me. And it's due precisely to the fact that, as my mother says, things are getting worse every day. Closed stores, people going off to the mountains; every second I hear someone say the canefields are burning, the country is in ruins. . . . *Ruins! Ruins!* I close myself up in the bathroom and begin to say the word out loud, laughing at the same time. What on earth do I care whether the country is "in ruins"; what does that mean to me? And I laugh out loud. Although I can see that it's all true. Mama rages more every day. Finally we can only eat once a day, and not much at that. *Ruins! Ruins!* And I laugh and think Something, somehow, has to happen. But he is the only thing I worry about. He speaks less than ever now, although every day my mother is more awful to him and now even says to his face that he has to go find a job, he's the man of the house. And she says the word "man" so it sounds like an insult. But he, what can he do, what can he say, where's he going to go? . . . In bed again. The house totally dark. The reek of insecticide drowning everything. There is the sound of shots, a great roar, the racket of police-car sirens, cries. And he is there, just two walls away from my room, as alone as anyone will ever be, for he has never lost anything because he has never had anyone. What is he waiting for, what plans does he have for later, tomorrow, right now? . . . Shots, closer now—it sounds like the world is coming to an end. And then I wonder whether we've ever been in the world. And I wonder what he thinks of the world. I sit on the edge of the bed; I sit very still listening to the uproar. Now I hear my mother's snoring. I stand up and walk into the hall. I come to the doorway of Hector's room. The light is on. He is sitting on the edge of the bed with his hands over his face. I stand just a moment at the doorway and immediately go back to my room. And lie down. Our Father who art in heaven, if only he'd come to my room, if I weren't the one who had to go to him. If only it weren't you who had gone. If only he had come, slowly, barefoot, and pushed open the door. Listen, because I don't latch the door anymore. You don't have to say a word, you don't have to speak—just come in. But you won't come. I will grow old in this house stinking of mosquito spray, watching the door that he's not ever going to push open. Finally, the first light of day, and I am exhausted. . . . I get up and dress. Before my mother starts yelling at me I'm already polishing furniture, surprised that he still hasn't gotten up. I finish scrubbing the floor with water and a broom, polishing the tiles; I think Any second now, since he's still in bed, Mama will start fussing and yelling at him to get up, even if it's just to bother him. And now that I've finished scrubbing down the porch too I begin to feel another worry: Why don't you get up? Perhaps he's sick, really sick perhaps. . . . I walk down the hall carrying the pail; the tiles are gleaming, gleaming so that it makes me even sadder. . . . I come to the doorway of his room. He isn't there. The bed is empty. The sheet, smoothed out, covers only a pillow. Books on the night table. Everything neat, but he isn't there. Where can he have gone so early? I think; when could he have gone out that I didn't notice it? I go into the room once more. I open the chest, even look under the bed. Then, when I am about to leave, I find a piece of paper on the sheet, next to the pillow. *Dear aunt, I am going with the rebels, because I'm not doing*

anything here. Don't let yourselves worry over me. That's what
the piece of paper says. I read it again. Mama, I say, and I don't
know whether I'm happy or sad; happy, I think. . . . Mama, come
here. She comes in. I show her the note. He's crazy, she says,
throwing the piece of paper down on the bed, I think this war is
stupid; that miserable moron, he's as good as dead. Shut up! I
tell her, and I think That's the first time I ever shouted at her.
They're not going to kill him. How do *you* know? she answers.
What do you two know about war? Everybody here has gone
absolutely crazy. She goes into the hall, walks all over the house
saying now we'll really be "disgraced," they'll come and search
the house. That's all we needed, she says, furious and sarcastic
at once, a "rebel" in the family. Now they'll really come down
on us. I follow her around, shushing her, telling her everybody
in the neighborhood will find out. But she goes on yelling, complaining, thinking only about us, about herself. And when she
furiously repeats, convinced, certain, that we can give him up
for dead, that he'll have no idea how to defend himself, he's never
known how to do anything, much less use a weapon, or fight, I
feel such hatred for her, my God, that I walk off and leave her
talking to herself, and I go into the living room. . . . You did it, I
think. I'm glad you did it, I think. And I read the note once more.
Then, reading it, I am suddenly sad once more, because he doesn't
even mention me in it. *Dear aunt,* it says. Poor thing, knowing
she detests him. No doubt he does it out of a kind of remorse,
his way of being considerate; after all, it's her house. However,
at the end he addresses me. Yes, at the end it says *Don't let
yourselves worry over me.* He doesn't speak just to my mother,
he addresses another person in the house. And who can that other
person be but me? I and Mama are the only people who live here.
And it says *Don't let yourselves worry.* I think that at least when
he wrote the word *worry* he was thinking of me too. In fact, if
he put *Don't worry yourselves over me* he did it thinking *only*
of me, because he knows perfectly well that Mama won't worry
herself over him. Then, I tell myself, that word isn't addressed
to my mother at all, it's to me. In fact I might say that he wrote
the whole note to me. But since he's so shy he didn't dare address
it to me. Perhaps he thought Mama might get it before me and
find out. But come now: Find out about what? Realize what? Yes,
I tell myself again, realize that there is some secret between him

and you. Because there is, because it's impossible for him not to have realized it. There *is*. And so he tries to throw my mother off the track by addressing the note to her. And if he tries to throw her off the track, it's because he knows there's something between him and me, even if nothing has happened. And if he tries, as it looks, as it seems, to keep Mama from finding out, it's because he wants to keep it a secret. And if he wants to keep it a secret it's because he's interested in me and he doesn't want it all to end like *that*, all of a sudden. . . . *Don't let yourselves worry over me*, he writes, as though he had written *Don't worry about me*. Then, I tell myself, if he wrote that there's no doubt that it's because he frets over me, because he thinks only of me, because he's in love with me and wants to keep it a secret and doesn't want me to suffer. So this note is a love letter. . . . But when all is said and done, I think now, what is all this plotting, what is all this subtle reasoning? It may be that this is all in my head—daydreams—and he means exactly what he says. So it's no more than a brief informatory impersonal note, addressed not just to us but to all his relatives, the ones in the other house too. . . . Yes, it may be that he isn't interested in us at all. And now I think about what my mother said and see that, in a certain way, she may be right. He is so clumsy about everything—about everything that everyone else does so naturally. What will he do in that life, which must be just as unbearable and even more dangerous than this one? Yes, you must think about it all, even if you don't want to. You have to think that he may be killed, that he may already be dead and you'll never see him again. You must think about it all. . . . *If he'd been with* us *he'd never have done this crazy thing!* I hear someone at the front door shriek. It is Adolfina, my aunt (accompanied by her little monsters Tico and Anisia), who has found out about it all and blames my mother for everything that has happened. She shoves her aside and comes up to me, cuffing me too and grabbing the note. And now she runs into the street shouting, so everybody knows, so he can never even come home again if things don't go well out there. And Tico and Anisia right behind, yelling even louder and laughing like crazy. . . . Holy Virgin, help me, because I don't want them to see me cry. And I don't cry. And I devote myself to waiting for you. For I know perfectly well that you will come back. I know it. You must. If not, what sense would any of this make? There has to be some consolation, some pity, sometime, if disgrace is really going to be disgrace; because if there isn't, then disgrace makes no sense. Therefore, you are going to come back. And so I wait. . . . The rebels cut the power lines. We are sitting in the living room, my mother and I, by the light of a candle that she has made herself out of a piece of soap. Mama is in the rocking chair, rocking; when every once in a while she speaks, it's to complain about something. What a New Year's Eve, she says. I've never seen such a sad New Year's Eve in my whole life. She goes to the front door and opens it. She stands a moment in the doorway; she suddenly slams it again. We may as well go to bed, she says. I undress in the dark and lie down. The gunfire can be heard more clearly now. The sound of a plane too, crossing over the town. Then the bombardment. Sometimes the smell of wet dirt comes in the window. I don't know where it comes from, since it hasn't rained for months. So, lying there, I try to figure out where that smell comes from, until dawn begins to break. . . . In this town, the only sound early in the morning is the crowing of roosters. First one, far off; then another, this time closer, answers him. And so the roof-raising chorus little by little takes shape. And at last, daylight. But at this moment a different sound is heard. Like shouting, the roar of thousands of voices that seem to sing, shout Vivas, cheer. In nothing but the slip which I have thrown on, I go into the living room. Hundreds of people are coming out onto their porches, gathering at corners. From over that way a kind of parade appears, the demonstrators carrying a flag, the rebels' flag—which can cost the person who has one his life. The murderer is gone! someone shouts. It all comes clear to me. I run to Mama's room. She was already awake; she gets out of bed and opens the front door. Be careful, she shouts at a group of men on the porch, you're going to mess up my flower beds! I run cheering into the street too. I run to the center of a commotion centered on several rebels. But he is not one of them. I run in and out of all the groups. I run all through the town. I don't go back home till afternoon. Mama is nervously watching the yard; she goes and looks fearfully out the front door, closes it, and goes back to the kitchen. What a commotion, she says, we'll see what happens. . . . Your cousin, she finally says, it's strange he hasn't come back. He'll come, I say, everyone can't come back the same day. That's true, she says. Lord only knows where he is. For a moment I don't say anything. Don't say he might be dead, I tell her now, raising my voice, perhaps unnecessarily. God forgive you for thinking such things, she says now. You're the one thinking it, I say. You're rude, she answers. And I keep still. But I know very well that that was what she was thinking. She's always thinking the worst. Maybe by now she's so used to unhappiness that a little hope terrifies her or confuses her; she wouldn't know what to do with it. But it may be that I'm mistaken; it may be that it's cruel of me to think that of her. Holy Virgin, I am so stunned by all this that I don't even know what I'm saying. Oh, and forgive me, for I didn't even remember to thank you. . . . The next day. . . . There are more rebels coming down than yesterday. I ask many of them about him. But they know nothing. There are so many, they say, that the whole army won't be here for a week at least. I go back. My mother, calmer, is making dinner. Today there's less food than ever, she says; with this mess of people I couldn't get anything. I don't answer. I go to the dining room and turn on the radio. Some woman is reciting a patriotic poem. I don't know whether this poem is good or bad, no doubt it's dreadful, but I listen and am filled with happiness. So night comes. The two of us are sitting once more in the living room. What they have to do, says my mother, is get the food out and straighten things up once and for all. They'll get everything straightened out soon, I say, and go on rocking, pumping with the tips of my toes, faster and faster. You're crazy, Mama says, behave yourself. I go on rocking until, now later in the evening, she stands up. He isn't coming today, she says. That's what you think, I think. I'm going to stay up a while longer, I say. I hear her spraying all the bedrooms. . . . I undress slowly, listening for every sound. Someone is coming down the street, getting closer; he passes by the front of the house and goes on. There is nothing to be heard now; just, in the darkness, the racket of the Victrolas in Loma Colorada barrio, and the organ lording it over all the other noises. The bars in La Frontera have opened again. That's where, so my mother tells me, the whorehouses are. Sometimes you can hear loud yelling (it's a fight) mixed with the screams and laughter of the women. The music from a Victrola can be heard more clearly now that the organ has stopped. It's some vulgar song, in fashion for two or three months and then no one will remember it. Sometimes, silly fool that I am, I've cried listening to those songs; sometimes, silly fool that I am, I have caught myself singing those songs. . . . I think I heard a tap on the window. Maybe he has come back. Or it might be a cricket, or some other kind of insect. I think—I'm sure now—the tapping really is repeated. I listen, I am stiff in bed. Holy Virgin, the taps are soft, as though not to make too much noise, as though not to call attention to themselves, as though barely to be heard. Only I hear them, no one else. Who could tap like that? Who could be tapping that way, so softly, as though not to be heard? I jump into my clothes and run to the living room. I open the door. And he is there, on the porch, in his faded uniform, a rickety rifle, and a beard that's not a beard, laughing. Laughing, but not loud. . . . Mama, I say then. Hector's here. And my voice echoes through an enormous cave out of which millions of bats begin to swarm, knocking against the walls, streaming like a whirlwind toward the outside. The whirl of their fluttering grows indescribable. It flattens me, picks me up, carries me to the very center of the mountain. Hector emerges, radiant, out from among the immense trees, his arms open wide as though inviting me to marvel at them. . . . He runs to one that seems to split open and shoot into green flares. This is *the manjack tree of lofty crown*, he says. Immediately he jumps to another, thick with flowers. This is *the lancewood tree, which puts out most delicate blooms*, he announces. . . . Taking my hand, pulling me by one arm, he deposits me in the cool shelter of another enormous tree. This is *the broomwood tree of softest shade*, he says. Immediately he gives me a tug and transports me through the air to a sweet-smelling tree whose trunk he begins to caress, saying, This is *the naked-boy tree, with skin like silk*. . . . We leap and come to rest in the top of another immense tree—*the juniper tree, of spreading leaves*, he says. . . . And this (he points as he transports me to another treetop), *with hard, long-lasting trunk and leathery spikes, is the ironwood tree*. And these, he tells me (the two of us floating over the highest treetops), are *the satin-leaf, the monkey-goblet, the yagrumo tree which stanches wounds, the ceiba*. . . . He goes on like that, lifting me up, carrying me with him through the air, showing me, introducing me to all the trees, giving me their names, as they whirl, turn loose their leaves, which fall on us as though in greeting. . . . He comes down through the long lianas and melts into the confusion of greens; leaping, whirling, capering, he fades into the crowd of branches; and then he is beside me, expansive, sober, pointing out another plant, another impressive spread of leaves. *The short straight palm, the thick-trunked oxhorn tree, the pregnant calabash and avocado, the waving reed grass.* . . . As I listen to this murmur, I sprawl on the leaves. Hector approaches me, panting, standing still now, next to me, looking at me. His firm naked feet on the ground, his rising legs, his hair whipping across his forehead, and sweat flowing in rivulets all down his skin—He is a tree, I think. He is a tree too. And I laugh. I laugh like he does and I am entranced, looking at him. . . . *Son!* says Mama with a long shriek, and runs to the door where he is standing, still undecided whether to come in, waiting for me to tell him at last to come in. Son! my mother repeats once more, hugging him. And I am embarrassed to hear her say that word; it sounds so ridiculous coming from her. She hugs him again, she kisses him. She starts to cry. At last she leads him to the dining room, talking constantly. Oh, how worried she was, how happy she is now. Me, behind. Looking at him. Looking at his uniform, his skin tanned dark brown. While Mama begins to prepare him something to eat I sit down next to him on a stool. The two of us are silent. And I am glad he doesn't tell me anything. We remain like that while my mother serves the improvised lunch (or breakfast), always talking, asking questions, chattering nonsense. He answers everything, practically without saying a word. Yes, he says. No, he says. Now you'll be able to get a good job, which is something we all could really do with, says my mother when we're finishing the meal. And I realize that all her unctuousness, every word, had a purpose, a precise, utilitarian end, that it was more than simple hypocrisy. How can she be so self-seeking? I think; how can she be so selfish? But suddenly I'm sorry I thought such a thing. She's not young anymore; after all, she has the right to think of her own security. But she goes on talking to him, giving him advice, hounding him. He mustn't let this chance go by; hurry and get a good position. And he says uh-huh, uh-huh. . . . I get up and go into the living room. But the neighbors come in, embrace him too, ask him a million questions. He has to show them his rifle, give them lessons in assembling and disassembling it. He does everything slowly, hoarsely, clumsily. Be careful with that gun, "son," says my mother. And once more her words sound to me utterly false,

fake. I watch Hector now manipulating some lever on the gun—
I don't know what it's called. The shells fall on the floor and
scatter all over the living room. He bends over to pick them up.
Then I see his hands and realize they're sweaty. And I think, I'm
thinking, that he's the same, the same, Holy Virgin, the same
man that left. He hasn't changed. And suddenly I begin to feel a
sadness such as I've almost never known and then, without
knowing why, I am happy . . . I stand up in the middle of the
living room and speak. You must be tired, you should rest. And
I look at the neighbors . . . Yes, he says, but I think I'll take a
bath first. I'll start it for you right now, says my mother. And
she rushes out. He says goodbye to the neighbors and goes into
the bathroom. Holy Virgin, before he goes in he looks at me and
smiles—although not much—and it was a smile of complicity,
as though he were saying I don't give a damn about any of this
but what can I do? . . . Sitting in the dining room I hear the water
gush from the shower and stream over his body; I hear his soapy
hands rubbing his body. I'm listening until I hear my mother's
voice; perhaps (certainly) she's been talking to me for a good
while. He shouldn't have taken a bath right after eating, she says,
it isn't good for you. And I'm about to answer For all he's eaten,
since you barely let him eat a bite with your chattering. But I
don't say a word. And at this moment, I think, the water is rolling
down his body, sliding down his legs, covering his feet with
soapsuds. . . . We'll see, says my mother, whether things go back
to normal when all this uproar is over. What in the world is
"normal"? I ask. But at that moment he is already coming out
of the bathroom. Do you have anything to do now? he asks me.
Not a thing, I say. We could go for a walk if you'd like to, he
says. I don't even remind him that he must be tired. I put on my
best dress, my best shoes, put on powder and lipstick. When I
come out of my bedroom he's standing at the front door, his hair
combed and his uniform on, waiting for me. Where are you going?
says my mother. For a walk, I answer, already taking his arm.
But Hector, she says—ignoring me—aren't you even going to
wait for your coffee? No, I answer for him, we'll get some somewhere. . . . A constant parade is passing through the streets now.
They have put up loudspeakers at the corner, which pour out one
patriotic anthem after another. Everyone looks at us and smiles—
looks at him, so young in his uniform. . . . Some people say hello

although they don't even know him. We finally come to the highway through the mob of cars, bicycles, and milling people. Although we don't talk it's as though we were chatting about everything. Or perhaps better. Pushing, knocking against people and saying Excuse me we come to the center of town. In one corner of Calixto García Park a large crowd has gathered. Everyone is angry—some women are jumping up and down and shaking their fists, others are throwing rocks. Hector and I walk over to the disturbance. Several rebels are holding their rifles on the crowd, protecting a sweaty man it wants to lynch. Some people manage to dodge around the guard and give him a kick. Shoot him, he's a murderer! yells an old woman. To the wall! To the wall! everyone is shouting now. Finally the rebels, protecting him with their weapons, take him away. Now they cross the park. The procession grows larger and larger as it moves along. We join in too, as I keep holding tight to Hector's arm. Both of us in silence. The unruly crowd follows the rebels to the walled jail, where as I now learn they have already executed several war criminals. . . . We go in with everyone else. We cross the courtyard and at the far end see the high wall that fences in the compound and now acts as the firing squad's backdrop. Everyone clusters around. Some people have climbed up into the trees, others cling to the bars of the windows. Although soon it will be dark it is still terribly hot. I look at Hector and see that he is perspiring too. I try to speak to him, to catch his attention, to tell him that if he wants to we can leave. But he's not looking at me now. He looks straight ahead, to where the soldiers are now lining up just a few yards from the man. Suddenly, there is silence, a silence in which not even our breathing can be heard. Out of this silence comes the unwavering voice of the criminal who (himself) directs the firing squad: *Ready!* he orders with an angry, firm voice, still the boss. The new soldiers obey, raising their rifles. I watch them. They are so young. They wear their uniforms so well. New uniforms, apparently not the ones they wore in the battles. . . . The rifles held to their shoulders: *Aim!* The silence is now unbearable. The mob seems to have vanished, no one seems to surround us, and we seem to be alone, Hector and I, somewhere there's no sound, or space, or anything. *FIRE!* The word is heard, shouted as though very far away. The bullets shatter the man's head. Blood splashes across the wall. The body, perhaps from the force of the fusillade, stiffens upright, stands on tiptoes; its arms shake, its breast, riddled with bullets too, is covered with blood, soaking the shirt; at last it teeters slowly forward and falls. . . . *Viva la Revolución!* cries a voice from the crowd. And suddenly everyone (including us) begins to shout: *Viva la Revolución! Viva la Revolución!* People wave hats, handkerchiefs, little flags. Once more the shouting, this time worse than ever. . . . Mingling with the mob, we come out into the street. I have to cling tightly to Hector so I don't get lost in all the pushing and jostling. Let's go home, he says now. The shouting moves farther off. We cross the highway, go through the deserted field near home. And now I realize he hasn't turned loose my hand—who knows since when? . . . It is the middle of the night when we come in. My mother looks troubled, frightened, unsure, but at bottom threatening. It's late, she says, Come eat something. But Hector disobeys her for the first time. He lowers his head and goes to his room without looking at her. We're too tired, I tell Mama. We saw them shoot a man. Oh, God, she says, crossing herself. I go to the dining room. As I cross the hallway I see Hector, who has sprawled across the bed without taking off his uniform or his boots. You two have to eat something, my mother says now. I've even made you a dessert. I don't answer. I go into my room and sit awhile on the bed without turning on the light. I feel almost dizzy, and at the same time I'm sorry for Mama and would even like to eat something, just to make her happy, but if I did I think I would be sick. I lie down in the dark. Little by little the man appears. He walks steadily. Ready, he says. Aim, he says. His bloody body teeters and falls beside my bed. I pull the sheet up over my head. Once more the man topples beside me. His skull smashes against the chest, his blood spatters the bed. Holy Virgin, Holy Virgin. . . . But the words to the prayer will not come, don't flow, will not appear; I don't remember a single prayer. I only see that bloody body which topples once more. I cried out. Did I really cry out? I may have cried out. . . . But no, if I had, my mother would already be here. I'm so terrified I can't even shout. I'm also certain that I didn't cry out then, either. The surprise was so great that I couldn't have. Thank goodness. If I had cried out people might have thought I was a counterrevolutionary. But I'm sure I didn't shout. Not then or now. And Hector must be thinking about the same thing too. Holy Virgin, he's alone in his room, seeing the same thing I am, not crying out. I listen carefully. I only hear Mama snoring. Little by little a strange uneasiness comes over me, different from any fear I ever had before. My mother's snoring is stronger. I stand up. I open the door. I go out into the darkness of the hallway. I walk slowly, touching the walls with my fingertips, tiptoeing, Holy Virgin, so no one will hear me. . . . I come to his room. The light is on. He is sitting on the bed. Still dressed in his uniform. Hector, I say. He turns and looks at me, not surprised, not elated. He simply looks at me. I go in and put my arms around him. I feel his sweating hands on my back. Still embracing him I only say, Hector, Hector. And we cry. But very softly, so no one will hear us. Then we are still. Just holding each other, just together. All night. . . . Until the shout, just as the light begins to break. Or perhaps before. Perhaps my mother had found us a while ago and was shrieking, and neither of us had noticed anything. It may be. Anyway, now we hear her shouts and sense her blows. For she's hitting us, but not exactly with her hands. . . . You whore! You whore! The daylight grows shrill too and sees me there, almost naked beside him, in bed. She goes on hitting us, shouting at us. You son of a bitch, she says now to him, you animal. Is this the way you pay me back for all the meals I've given you? Then she is rigid in the middle of the room, under the light bulb. Let's go, says Hector, get dressed and let's go. I run out of the room. I put on the dress I had had on in the afternoon, and hadn't even hung up, and the same shoes. I go into the living room. Hector is waiting for me. You miserable whore! I hear my mother behind me. You miserable whore! He opens the door. The two of us go into the street. . . . Holy Virgin, how could I have convinced her that nothing happened, that, honestly, we didn't do a thing? . . . We almost run once more across the highway and come to the bus station. He asks for two tickets to Havana. Still numb, in shock, we get on the bus. It is all like a dream. He puts his head back next to me and is asleep. I only hear the bus's engine; I feel the weight of his body against mine. Until I too lean back against the seat and go to sleep. Now, when I've just waked up, I hear another sound, strange and distant. Beside me, he begins to wake up too. Then he runs a hand over my shoulder and with the other opens the curtain at the window. Look, he says, and I lean over to the glass. I see a great, shining, blue expanse. A huge open plain that begins at the side of the highway and rises away into the distance, growing bigger and bigger, widening, flowing, swelling until it melts into the sky. Holy Virgin, eighteen years of living on an island and I've never seen the ocean! . . . The ocean, I say, as though to convince myself that it really is there, here, right beside me, washing over my feet. Hector swims up to me. Look, he says, such strange rocks. He opens his fist. They are colored rocks, glistening, blue, clear. They're lovely, I say, although I'm sure that isn't the word I should use. Yes, they're strange, I say, trying to erase the other word. But he no longer is paying me any mind. Along the beach our neighbor from the next cabin comes walking. He is coming along slowly. His white shorts, his tennis shoes, all glow white against his body. He is coming straight toward us. When he is almost up to us he turns and goes into the water. But first, I'm sure he looked this way. . . . Yes, says Hector, they're strange, although they may not be stones, they may be pieces of glass polished by the surf. He stretches on his back on the sand and closes his eyes. The boy, near shore, seems wrapped in the shimmering of midday. He wades farther out. The ocean swirls around his knees, his thighs, comes over his shorts right up to his waist. He raises his arms, tenses, leaps, and dives, disappearing. Hector is resting with his eyes closed. . . . But Listen, listen, say the pines, the solitude is within, gnawing. The solitude and the fury are within, waiting. . . . But look here, listen—here I am, beside him, I answer. . . . And Who are you? What do you know? the voices say now, shouting above the noise of the cicadas. . . . He seems to be constantly waiting for the blow. How can you even imagine the terror he has hidden there inside that body in repose? . . . And then the laughter. They're mocking. They think I'm beaten and they laugh. But come now, what nonsense. It's the people on the beach. A woman playing with two children, a nearby radio—people having fun. And the whistle of the cicadas. I am sweating. I'll swim awhile. But listen—the voices return once my feet are in the water—what about desire? You too know what desires are. Enough, I say aloud, looking toward the grove of pines. I came here yesterday and I want to rest, forget about work, swim for a while. That's all. Not even think about the baby—my God, he must have waked up by now, he must be crying. Float. That's what I need to do. You torment yourself over so many insignificant things (*nonexistent things*) that when the real ones come there's no space left for them. Moreover, do you hear me—and I turn again toward the pine grove—above all, there is us: he and I. Enough! Into the water! . . . He and I. Even if only to say to each other, Look, I'm beaten, look, I'm being beaten before your very eyes. . . . If only for that. Into the water. . . . If only to be constantly worried about each other, fearing for each other, hating each other, watching each other. Although I know very well that that isn't true. . . . Into the water! Once and for all, into the water! . . . The uproar ceases. I open my eyes. I stretch out my arms. I float through silence and open space. Blank, everything completely blank and quiet. Until, forced to breathe, I come out on the surface and float. I swim, pulling away from the shore. I come to the great band of blue which, I see now, ends in another even bluer band farther on. I look back toward the beach. The people—although I hear no sound—seem calmer. They are playing, resting, swimming, running. . . . I feel sorry for them. Perhaps, *surely*, I think, this is their only day of rest, and they are trying to gulp it down, wildly, doing everything at once, thinking *Who knows when, who knows how long we'll live?* . . . Yes, now I understand why I feel such pity thinking of them—I'm thinking of myself. Of Hector too, who, by the way, I don't see on the beach. At last I discover him there on his stomach on the sand with his head resting on his arms. I also see the boy, who comes out of the water and says something to him; he lies close by, face down. I forget about making it out to the second great band of blue; I swim straight for the shore. Hector opens his eyes. It's late, I say. We should be getting back. Uh-huh, he says, I was asleep. He gathers up the little stones and stands up. We go through the pine grove where the cicadas' whistling is maddening now, monotonous and, for me, strangely mocking. . . . Hector opens the cabin door. I go into the bedroom. You're still asleep, I say, looking at the baby. He wakes up now, crying slowly, almost whimpering. Shh, I tell him, very softly, and go into the living room with him. There is Hector sprawled on the sofa, his feet on the floor, reading—running away. *That is the most important thing, fleeing, putting yourself on hold while noon goes by* (he thinks that way, I am sure of it) *and everything outside succumbs, everything is stripped of the little mystery that justifies it, and perishes in the shattering light and heat. Not looking*

(these are his very words) *while everything grows deserted, be-*
comes a smooth, white-hot surface where the only thing left is
desire. . . . Those looks, those shameless hands, the way he strolls
along. . . . But enough, enough. It would be terrible to go on guessing, poking into his thoughts. Moreover it might be, in the final
analysis, that I'm mistaken. . . . He's just reading. The rest is
fantasy, the ravings of my *own* desperation. The baby has gone
to sleep again. I'll wake him up, petting him slowly, shh,
shh. . . . What time is it? I ask. What time is it getting to be now?
But he goes on immersed in the pages of that book he isn't reading.
I wonder what time it is, I say aloud. . . . And those spiders, sweaty-
looking, gleaming, as though they had just emerged from a bath
in oil, walking across the ceiling, these spiders that bristle up,
glide and twist all around each other, and skitter back and forth
to the rhythm of the tide: wrapping around each other, inter-
twining, rubbing each other, mounting each other and so, locked
in a mortal embrace—since possession for them ends in death—
being carried by the waves down to the waterline, where the
delirium, the final ecstasy, the madness, is consummated. . . . I
don't know, he says. The watch is on the shelf in the closet. It
must be about two, maybe not that late—and plunges again into
his pages. He doesn't know, he never knows anything. He's always lost in a fog, hazy ("What I talk to you about isn't the
important thing, that's not what's worrying me," I know he thinks),
and I, on the far shore, waving my arms, Don't you see me? Don't
you see me? . . . But it's no use, and now he's gone, high high
away, behind the clouds. I let my arms fall to my sides, and look
at my feet. I turn on the radio. *By applying the methods and*
guidelines of our Commander-in-Chief we will reach ten million
tons of sugar by next year, 1970! . . . In 1960, 1970, 1980! . . . So,
in fact, time does exist. At least for them. Tomorrow, day after
tomorrow, in a month, in a century. My God, in a century! . . . At
last they give the time: *Two forty-five, daylight savings time, in*
Cuba. God, does time exist? The baby still hasn't had his milk.
I heat it for him. I carry him out onto the porch. I sit in a chair
and feed him. I laugh (I *smile*), looking at him: He must have
been starving. He finishes and dozes off once more. I look toward
the pine grove, which seems to wink now in the shimmering
light of midday. The boy is coming along the road; he walks
unhurriedly, barefoot (carrying his shoes in one hand), across the

asphalt. Slowly. In the distance the white shorts glow even brighter against his tanned skin. At times he seems to look up, but
others (almost always) he looks at the ground, just ahead of his
feet. He crosses the avenue of almond trees, passes our car, takes
the path leading to the cabins. Now he exactly crosses my line
of sight, still slowly, not looking at me. But he knows I am here;
he knows I am watching him. Perhaps that is why he lowers his
head even more. That face, always ready to blush. . . . *I couldn't
care less about you* is what his absolute abstractedness means.
I couldn't care less about anything, say his bare feet now, going
up the steps of the cabin. His mother, naturally, goes out to meet
him. Even if I didn't want to, I'd hear a few words from here.
"But child, this is no hour. . . . You must be hungry. I was worried. . . ." Poor kid, I say to myself. Poor kid. But why poor? What
can he and his typical mother possibly matter to me? . . . There
before my eyes are the pines, the pine grove, the highway, the
almonds, the oleanders, and the ocean. Motionless, all of it. All
of it swallowed up in the shimmering haze. Only the ocean, rising
behind the tree trunks, flows slowly, strives to keep flowing. You
can do it, you can do it. . . . But midday prevails, and now, suddenly, the ocean too seems paralyzed. Out of that silent scintil-
lation emerges the whistling of the cicadas. It moves in, marching
toward a stridency it has never reached before. The uproar less-
ens; it becomes a light whisper; it softens into silence. . . . A
gleaming-white egret flies from the motionless pine grove. She
comes down next to the cabin. With her long pink legs she maneuvers over the grass, supple and elegant, a ballerina. I like that
egret. She has that independent, indescribable, free sort of look,
like she's just passing through and therefore nothing can bother
her very much but everything can interest her for a while—even
inspire her pity and praise. . . . She walks erect, stretches her incredibly slim neck; suddenly she takes flight as though frightened. She disappears behind the pines. If she wishes she may
never come back. . . . The sun rises higher. It perches imperturb-
ably in the sky. My cigarette is soaked with the sweat from my
hands. The butt disintegrates and falls like dead weight out the
wing vent. What desolation, I sometimes say. What desolation,
I've never said, since no one has ever listened to me. Anywhere
you look, this landscape is not even sad, just dry and harsh. What
desolation, now, far from the ocean (which has disappeared be-

hind the hills), far from trees and even from road signs (since the highway is a straight line, with not the least curve or bobble). What desolation. . . . Once more the dinosaur rises out of the pavement. He waits motionless for us to catch up to him. Only when we are about to crash into him does he jump heavily out of the way, and he settles down farther on, waiting for us. We go on, we keep going on. Now when we are once more upon him, he moves aside to let us pass. I look now at his head and see that it's become a skull. His body is still the same, but his head, his face, his nose or snout or trunk—whatever you call it—is a blindingly white skull which seems to be crumbling in the brightness. A burst of laughter peals out. The same laughter. We keep going on. . . . I look back and see him (a shining skull), blending in with the whiteness of the day. . . . My God! (although I can't even, shouldn't, say *My God*). Why does everything have to be so obvious? I turn toward Hector; he seems to be driving impassively, unconscious of anything. Stop, let's do something, look at me. But nothing happens. You go on driving, seemingly peacefully. But listen—even if you don't want to listen to me, even if I don't speak, even if we are like this, like now, unspeaking, I know you're listening to me, I know you're listening to me. . . .—The first day, after the burial, the boy's body swells, his eyes burst out of their sockets, a yellow liquid flows from his ears and slides down the back of his neck; his tapering hands are purple and his face, not yet disfigured, takes on that static rigidity of dead skin. Listen—the second day his mouth opens and his tongue, which has swollen out of all proportion, emerges between his teeth. Listen—the third day he is covered with big blackish spots; strange noises come from his belly. His whole body begins to swell and crack and burst. . . . Listen, because you have to listen to me, because you're listening to me, because we both hear the same thing. . . . On the seventh day if you get close, if you lean over and put your ear to the ground, you will hear that constant bustle, *faster, come on—faster*, that unceasing sawing. But listen, listen, what about the eighth day? And the ninth? And on the tenth day? . . . But above all, the calm. Even if you can't see the ocean, even if you think you're never going to stop, that you'll never halt, the calm. I control myself. I light another cigarette. I look toward Hector, there, in profile, at the helm, driving carefully, never taking his eyes from the road; his mouth tightens. Now he's a baby. . . . The cicadas' roar increases. First slowly, then all at once. Now it's two egrets that rise from the pine grove. They climb. Now they are flying over the ocean. Their wings are outspread and motionless. Perhaps they're resting till midday is over. Perhaps they have a nest in some pine tree and have gone out in search of food. I am so engrossed in the flight of the egrets that I haven't even noticed that someone is speaking to me. Now I hear the voice, blending in with the racket of the cicadas. How old is he? it has asked me. How could I not have seen her before? It's the boy's mother. Leaning on her cabin railing, she smiles at me. Oh, just eight months, I tell her. He certainly sleeps well, she says, and settles now even heavier on the railing. Obviously she wants to follow up the conversation. And what can I do to avoid it? . . . Yes, I say, luckily he spends the whole day sleeping. What about at night? she asks—no, there's nothing I can do to avoid it. . . . Well, at night he fusses a lot, I answer. Although it isn't true. Actually, he only wakes up once in a while. . . . That's how my son was when he was a little thing. That's all I needed, for her to start talking to me about her son. He slept all day and at night he didn't let me close my eyes; but I hated to wake him up during the day. You know what I found out did the trick? Quinine water! It's wonderful! She says these words with real enthusiasm. You don't say, I answer. Quinine water, that's all he needed; I suppose he still ought to have a dose of it now and then. What about your son? I ask, although I know what the answer will be. Is he your only child? Yes, my only son! You can imagine, at first it was so hard, being alone with a son. Yes, I say, but he's almost a man now. He must be sixteen years old. Seventeen! she says proudly. He'll be eighteen soon. How nice, I say. She—just as I feared—leaves her porch and comes over to mine. How cute, she says, looking at the baby; it would be good for him to get a little sun. Don't think for a minute it would be bad for him, she says, now switching to the familiar pronoun with me. Morning sun, of course. I took mine out every morning, until about ten o'clock. It's the best medicine for babies. Uh-huh, I say. And before she asks me, I give him to her to hold. Delighted, she rocks him, she coos to him, she tickles the end of his nose—you-sweet-thing-this, and honeybun-that and cootchy-coo-the-other, she tickles him. She's not so old, I think, although she looks like she no longer has any illusions about getting married again—and who knows for how long past. She lives only for her son. How cute, she says, he looks like he's getting his teeth. Yes, I say, although actually I hadn't noticed, but if I say so she might be shocked. . . . And he is your only one? she asks while she walks up and down the porch, rocking the baby. Yes, for now, I say and smile. Of course, of course, she says, now confidential, as though we were the closest of friends; the way things are now, I'd advise you not to be in any hurry. Anyway, you still have time. . . . Yes, yes, I answer—but Who's hurrying? Who has the least intention? Good lord, how can people be so simple? . . . And she looks so happy, with her flowered housedress reaching to her ankles. How can she look so happy? I say to myself; she's not young anymore, her husband must be dead, she must have suffered sometime. And so, while I watch her taking little steps with the baby across the porch and back, laughing in the glow of the afternoon, I begin to feel (for her as well) a certain embarrassment. . . . She settles down in a chair now, in front of me, and sits looking at the pine grove. What a lovely place, she says. I've been intending for years to come here and bring my son; but if it wasn't one thing it was another, until we finally just made up our minds. He needs a rest. He just came back from the farm camp after he passed all his exams. He applies himself to whatever he does, but work in the fields is so hard. What about you two, how long are you going to be here? Oh, I say, just a week. We got here yesterday. Come on, why don't you stay fifteen days, like us? . . . Work, I say. Of course, she says, I spend all day at home and I don't even realize that people have to go off to work. I live in my own little world, I know, of course. Luckily we have a pension; if not, my goodness, with everything so expensive, and keeping a car, too—but I didn't want to sell it. I keep it for him, even though I haven't let him learn to drive yet, he's so young. . . . But Wouldn't you like a drink? I say suddenly, almost enthusiastically. No, she says, thanks very much, but I've got to run. Look at the time—and she points to the sun—and I haven't even started dinner! My son will be starving. And eat! It's one of the things that I worry about most, not being able to feed him well. Rationing hardly bothers *me,* but youngsters—and she grows confidential again—youngsters need nourishment; and even more at his age. Lots of meat, lots of protein. But good lord, these days . . . I always find something, but it's overpriced. It's a racket!

Of course it is. . . . But I'm not going to let him starve to death on me. And she stands up, laughing. I take the baby, whose bright eyes sparkle at her. He's fallen in love with you, I tell her. If you want, I could take him awhile so you two could rest. Not at all, I say, you have a lot to do. I'm going to cook something too. Can you believe that we haven't eaten a bite since breakfast?— Oh, it's a thrill for me, she says, interrupting me, to hold a baby, and especially when they're this age, and they don't fidget and cry. My husband used to say that babies shouldn't ever have more than two birthdays. . . . Poor thing, he never saw his son at two— and she has taken on the confiding tone once more—but really, they're wonderful no matter how old they are. . . . Tomorrow if you want I'll leave him with you for a while, I tell her. Why, certainly, dear, any time you like. See you later. . . . She goes down the steps in little hops. Now on her porch she puts out her hand, euphorically, as though she were waving from a ship. . . . Madame, says a voice behind me, lunch, though late, is served. It's Hector, standing in the cabin door. I fixed up something, he says, but if you want we can go to the restaurant later. We eat. The baby grabs a fork and I have to take it away from him before he throws it somewhere. You should have called me, I tell Hector. I called you, but it seemed like you were asleep. Ah, it's this noon heat, it almost wears me out, and then the lady next door came over. We were talking and she made me lose track of time. Uh-huh, he says. Yes, I say—and take the fork away from the baby again—she's a widow, her life revolves around her son; she does nothing but talk about him. Hector goes on eating. I raise one of the glasses to my lips and begin to cough. This is rum! I say. They both are, he answers, and we still have almost a bottle left. And there must be someplace around here to find liquor. We finish eating. He plays with the baby. *Madame*, he said to me. *Sir*, he says to the baby. He's happy. He talks that way when he's happy. Other times he calls me by my name, or not even by my name. Yes, he's happy, he looks happy. But Why this happiness? But really, Why would one be sad? I brush my teeth, wash my face; I comb my hair, I put on perfume. Now dressed, I spray some perfume in the living room and bedroom too. I go out onto the porch. He, in the living room, goes on playing with the baby. I pour myself another drink; I take my cigarettes and matches and sit down. Here are the swaying pines, the almond trees letting go their leaves, which flutter through the air. Because now there's a breeze. I breathe. I can breathe. You will have the evening. You will have the evening. Even the whistling of the cicadas seems a comfort now. I drink, I light a cigarette. There is the light over there, touching the highest branches. Suddenly, there is a strong gust of the cool of the ocean. I lean back in the chair. I raise my legs and prop them on the railing. I smoke. The ocean breeze washes over my face. A veritable blaze of colors plays across the water. Little by little, silence; or perhaps not silence but shadows, among which sounds seem to withdraw and even the most vulgar noises are transformed. It's like *tolerance,* I think. It's like *pity,* I think. . . . The egrets return again, beating their wings slowly over the ocean. They glide above the pine trees. Suddenly they dive into the dense part of a tree. Listen, it's more than pity, much more; it's happiness, the only happiness you can aspire to. And it's enough. Just like *that,* sitting there, while the colors begin dispersing, not thinking, just looking, feeling, listening. . . . The great calm of the day that is waning at last, but has not yet come fully to night. One moment. Just one moment. Yes, but wonderful. The sky forms incredible cities, violet mountains; the ocean flows behind the tree trunks where cicadas sing (for now they sing). I smoke a cigarette. I drink again. I look at myself, I contemplate myself, there in a practically new dress. I am young, I am young. Although I hardly believe it myself, I am still young. I can look in the mirror—not a single wrinkle. I'm not thirty yet. I am young. My body is thin, my hair isn't bad, my face is attractive. . . . And I have on a new dress! Perhaps that is what makes me so happy. Always, ever since I was a girl, when I wear a new dress I feel very happy. Why? For what? For whom? No matter. Even if I stay at home, even if I don't go anywhere, even if no one sees me, I feel happy and I walk through the living room, listening to the rustle of new cloth, smelling that smell that only new things have. How happy, my God, how happy. I'm young and I have on a new dress. And, more even than any of that, here is the evening—the sky's glow falling on the ocean, the smell of trees and earth growing cooler. What more? What more? . . . I have eyes to see with, hands to touch with, a nose to smell with. And the evening, and the colors, and the smell of things transformed.

What more? What more? Here is happiness. My feet on the railing next to the sea. Thank you, thank you. Thank you.

Whenever you want we can take a walk, says Hector from the cabin door, with the baby in his arms. We turn off the lights and leave. Still bathed in the blaze of the evening, we walk along toward the restaurant. But when we enter, the noise of people, silverware, plates, the harsh light from the bulbs, all bring us suddenly back to the same old reality. *It's already night,* I say to myself. And we sit down. We order only croquettes and beer. For a while we drink without speaking. I pour him a little beer from my bottle. He pays no attention. A little way off, but in front of us, the mother and the boy are sitting. For a while—I am certain—he has been watching us, although now, when he's seen, he lowers his gaze. The mother sees us too and raises her hand, waving with enthusiasm. I smile at her. Pleased, she looks at the baby, at Hector. Everything's fine, she seems to be saying to us, and confers her approval on us. They finish eating. She stands up, followed by her son, and comes toward us. How's the food? You can't ask for anything more, I answer. Give me the baby, she tells me. Don't bother, I tell her gratefully, we're going to bed right away. Well, don't have too much to drink, she teases, familiarly, as she walks away. She is smiling, not without giving her son a glance, as he follows her out. Hector finishes his beer. He seems to be somewhere else, at an inconceivable distance where the cigarette smoke makes a fog, a thick wall he fades into as he runs toward the well, followed by the other cousins. From the dining room, consumed with envy, I contemplate them. . . . Finally he comes out of it, takes out his wallet, and pays the check. We are once again in full daylight. The beast rears again over the nonexistent puddles. Beyond, hitting the deserted land, the ocean. The open sea, taut, like a skin of glass that I would bounce off if I fell. We go on, without looking at each other, without speaking. Now here is the horrible smell, pervading everything. I know you smell it too. . . . The wind comes up, the ocean comes to life once again. It reaches the shore covered with foam, throwing up the boy's dead body. I lower my gaze and look into my glass of beer, still half full. I feel that all the powerlessness in the world is concentrated in those bubbles rising and bursting at the surface. I pick up the glass; I drink down the beer in one gulp. Take the baby, I tell Hector. And we leave the restaurant. Now, listening to the ocean, we walk along the oleander path. He lifts the baby and seats him on his shoulders. Watch out, I might say; but enough of useless words. I simply run my hand along over the flowers and listen to the sound of an engine. We come to the darkened porch. I remind you that we still haven't gotten that light bulb. It's true, you say, we'll look for one to-morrow. The sound of the engine comes again across the ocean. That's the Coast Guard, you say; if someone tried to leave they'd machine-gun 'em. . . . We remain silent, listening to the rattle of the boat's engine grow fainter. . . . Slowly I make the bed, spread the white sheets. Yes, perhaps we suffer more than others—I fluff up the pillows. In your life you've seen nothing but misery, hu-miliations, special favors, privilege, you've been through hunger, real hunger, and you've known the true meaning of the word *horrible,* and you've so utterly rejected *that,* and you see some possibility of change, of hope, and you clutch at it desperately, and then it turns out—I put up the mosquito net—that you now see the same humiliations, the same privilege, the same pov-erty. . . . I go barefoot into the living room. He is standing with the baby in his arms in the light of the lamp, paled by it, lent a complexion by it that is almost not real. . . . *Springing forth,* I thought I heard him say. But perhaps (*certainly*) it was in my imagination. Someone starts whistling outside. It's an unvarying whistle that repeats the same tuneless tune and yet it doesn't remind me of any song I know. Just a whistle, or better yet, a whistling. I open the refrigerator. I pour myself a glass of water. Want some? I ask you. You don't answer. I sit down on the couch and stretch my legs. I keep hearing the whistling, that isn't very loud, not quite loud enough to bother you, or for that matter to entertain you, that follows no particular rhythm, that simply says *Here I am.* You take the baby into the bedroom. I am alone in the living room. I look for a second at the bottle with the withered flowers I gathered last night. I open the refrigerator again, see the pitcher of water, without asking myself why I'm doing this. I close the refrigerator again. I throw the bottle with the flowers into the wastebasket. When I go out onto the porch a swarm of mosquitoes lashes my face. There is the boy, in the overhead light of his porch, whistling, looking, but certainly without seeing it, toward the pine grove. He is still wearing the white shorts and a shirt that looks yellowish under the light bulb. He whistles motionless, leaning on the chair, not paying any mind to anything, not even to his own whistling. Yes, but he knows someone is listening to him. . . . The mother is there too, absorbed in her knitting. I'll leave before she discovers me; as for him, I know perfectly well he has seen me already, although he has not taken his eyes off the pine grove or stopped whistling. But when I slip away and open the door, she instinctively looks up and sees me. Hot, isn't it? And suddenly I'm embarrassed, as though I had been discovered doing something forbidden or foolish. . . . Yes, I say, really hot, I think I'm going to go to bed. And I try to say good night. But she stands up and walks to the edge of the porch. I, she says, use these still nights for knitting. I'm making him— and she points to her son—a pair of white socks. Oh, I say, how nice. And I think that I'm behaving even more stupidly than usual; I might have asked about the knitting, the different stitches, the quality of the yarn. Yes, perhaps it would have been better to have asked about all that, not that *oh, how nice,* how moronic. . . . But why do I have to get tangled in all these complications? I came here to rest, not to worry. I came to rest, not to talk; to rest, not to think. And have you gotten very far? I say, and I'm surprised myself to hear me. Not far at all, really, she says—happy that I've showed interest in her labor—and jubilantly raises her knitting to show me. I started just today—I smile at her and look at a halo of mosquitoes that hovers over her head—but by the time we leave I'll have this pair of socks finished, she adds in a tone of triumph. Yes, I say, I think you'll have time. Imagine, she says, there isn't a single pair in the stores. I got this yarn in exchange for a dozen cans of condensed milk. No kidding, I say, thinking Good lord, twelve cans of condensed milk. . . . But really, what do *I* care about all this? That's her business, let her do whatever she thinks is right. Well, I say, and swat a mosquito on my arm, I think I'll go to bed. It's early, she says, come over, I'm going to make some coffee—it's good, I bought it on the black market. No! I say, so loud that even she, who apparently is never surprised by anything, looks at me slightly disconcertedly. No, I say, now more softly, trying to efface the impression of that first *no*, I have to take care of the baby. And I'm really tired, and Hector's already asleep. I think I've said these last words, as well, a little too loudly, so loudly in fact that for a second I stop hearing the whistling that goes on, indifferent to our small talk. . . . Well, there's tomorrow, she says. At last I can go inside. I go to the chair, pick up the stones that Hector found this morning; now in the glow of the lamp, out of the sunlight, they're simply gray rocks. Before turning off the living room light I throw them under the chair. I go into the bedroom. The baby is covered, sleeping. Hector is already under the mosquito net. I undress, turn off the light he left on for me. I put my head between his hands. And I wait, I wait, I wait. Little by little the great fog comes in. And the leaves. More and more leaves, becoming green parrots. The parrots fuse into a deserted beach. . . . And there she is. Sometimes, although I wait a long time (like today), I only see her a few seconds. Other times, she stays awhile and we talk. Or really, she talks and I listen to her but confine myself, like now, to contemplating her. She is dragging a little cart full of rotten fruit, rags, pieces of wood, and other trash—and atop all that, a huge pumpkin, so big I don't know how she can even haul it along. Her hair is rumpled, and the only garment she wears is a short dirty burlap skirt over her pustule-covered legs. Hector follows her with a kind of spike or pointed stick and spits the huge pumpkin on it. I kneel at his feet and begin to eat the fruit. Helen swings her hips, paying me no heed, as she picks through the trash, looking for who knows what. I am eating, gobbling down the pumpkin, until I feel full, feel I can't swallow another mouthful. Then, still eating, I raise my eyes and see Hector, my husband, ordering me with an imperious look to go on. My face smeared orange, my eyes bathed in tears, on my knees, unable to take any more, I go on eating the fruit, which he now clutches with a look not even of contempt but of hatred, of uncontrollable hate. . . . When I realize that it is utterly impossible to go on I try to stand up, to speak, to make a gesture with my hands and push away the huge pumpkin, but his gaze, furious and steady, his firm body planted before me, prevail, and I go on gobbling. I gesture desperately, I make strangled moans; on the point of death, I look around. Helen, while she hums some popular song or other, I'd say a cha-cha-cha, pulls her pustule-covered arms out of the trash and triumphantly shows me a tattered *Bohemia* magazine with a drawing of a dinosaur on one of its pages. I remember that magazine, it was the one in the trunk in my grandmother's house, with my aunt's empty perfume bottles, rags, and other stuff. . . . But how did it ever wind up here? I look up again. Through my tears I see Hector laughing (clutching the stick with the huge gourd), raging and implacable. I feel so full I cannot breathe. "To Prado and Neptune, da dum da dum, there went a little girl, da da da dum," sings Helen, dancing (yes, a cha-cha-cha). I fall at Hector's feet. He gives me a tremendous kick. I am so stuffed that I roll off down to the ocean. I feel myself sink, downward, to the seabed. I reach the bottom. For a second I ascend, on my back, and see through a lens, the lens of the water which pulls me down again, the sky, low and gray, melting

SECOND DAY

into the ocean, which now covers me completely. The sky is the first thing I see as I open my eyes. Perhaps it is so early that everything else is dark and so only the sky stands out. I think the cold, the wind, has awakened me. I don't have the sheet over me. At any rate, dawn is breaking. I can see the ocean without pulling back the mosquito net—pale, almost white, like a reflection of the sky. But little by little it will grow brighter, reflecting the blinding light. "Intractable brightness." It was Hector who wrote that. Those pages are around somewhere, yellowed, hidden, stored away for I don't know how long, and now perhaps forever. And that is the worst thing, I think while I comb my hair, while I do my face, while I cook breakfast. The worst thing because, after all, the only thing that can save a man suffering under a curse is assuming it, accepting it. But perhaps, *certainly*, he's the one who said that too. . . . I see his body half uncovered now; I slide into bed and lie down again. Hector, I say, Hector; not too loud. And I lie face up beside him. But You've got to get up, do you hear, you've got to get dressed, at least put on your bathing suit and get into the sunshine, you've got to serve breakfast; you've got to go into the pine grove and listen to the racket the cicadas make. . . . He goes on sleeping. I could wake him up, but what for? Moreover, it may be he's not asleep; he's pretending, so I'll leave him alone. . . . Not a sound comes from the other cabin. They're asleep too. And What if no one is there? What if it's just my imagination and the cabin is unoccupied? I had a dream last night too. Like always, I hardly remember a thing of what I dreamed.

Usually I think they're ridiculous, silly things, things it embarrasses me to remember and I will never tell anyone. Moreover, I don't want to remember my dreams; they can be interpreted so many ways, and all of them can be wrong, or right. . . . But the cabin *is* occupied; now I hear the mother's voice as she talks, of course, to the son. I think she's even asking him what he would like for breakfast. Before she opens the door, before I have to say hello, I pick up a towel and a bottle of milk and go out to the beach with the baby. The sand is still cool. For the time being I don't have to go into the pine grove for some protection. I close my eyes. I only hear the ocean. The baby beside me. Let yourself be carried, let yourself be led, have no expectations. Might it not be that when once a desire is satisfied—*momentarily* satisfied—thousands of more pressing demands arise? And those demands met, others—to madness? Until you come to true madness. We still have four days to lie on the sand, to listen to the ocean, to close our eyes and not wonder what I'll cook today, not feel myself duty-bound to read the paper, to offer my opinions, and, above all, to put on a face for other people. But listen, that doesn't solve anything, don't kid yourself, don't try to delude yourself, because you . . . When I raise my head to reply to the voices, I discover we're surrounded by bathers. Women wrapped in loud ugly clothes, children yelling, young people constantly jumping up, big-bellied old men. . . . Everyone turned toward the light. Everyone in an incoherent turmoil, splashing, whirling, shrieking. You'd think it was already high noon. . . . And even when you turn to God, which I doubt you'll do, you will not be saved, the voices say (seizing the opportunity, since I can't answer them); what's more, God isn't going to come and fold you in his arms, he isn't going to come and comfort you, he's not going to come— do you hear!—and take you to bed. . . . God, God, where can I go, where can I hide, so I don't have to see those feet, those bodies, those faces, don't have to hear those voices, don't have to show myself too in this blaze of light? . . . When I raise my head I discover Hector coming through the trees; he's wearing a bathing suit I haven't seen before. God, Hector, *God Hector*. He takes my hand. *This is the house,* he says. We enter, and there is not that great choir I heard singing once from a church—not a real church, one of those film extravaganzas, there, in the Infante Theater, that was a movie house. There is not that choir you'd

expect, that chanting that heralds great events. . . . But there are
chairs, a dining table and four chairs, two bedrooms, a big stove
with four burners, a living room, and there is a porch which opens
right onto the Malecón. *This is the house,* he says. And now,
indeed, you can hear the choir. *Our house,* I think, while I feel
the furniture, touch the doors, admire the walls, squeeze the keys
in my hand. And think How much we've had to suffer, to whee-
dle, to grovel, to act a part, to plead (pretending that we aren't
pleading, that we're just asking), so as to be able, at last, to say,
This is the house. Now we just have to make the monthly pay-
ments. . . . Hector comes, lies on his back beside the baby, and
closes his eyes. I hear you yawn. But when did this feeling start,
this relationship based on hypocrisy? Because at the beginning,
unquestionably, things were different. At the beginning we went
to meetings, listened to lectures, thinking: It's terrific, terrific,
everything is terrific. And the happiness of the moment, the
justice of the moment, the events of the moment, the *passion,*
were so great that I didn't even remember, discover, pay any heed
to the fact that although we were married, although we slept next
to each other, I still was not your wife. Nothing of that sort, at
the beginning, mattered to me. We had so much to do; it was
natural for us to get home exhausted. Those were the days when
we didn't need any promises in order to believe, any words in
order to hope. . . . Your unmoving body in repose. The sand falling
on your body. The sun shining on your body. The sand blowing,
your shut lips, the breeze that ruffles your hair from time to
time. . . . But days pass and words that before gave me heart now
were menacing; hope is, now, as it was before, a useless thing
you grab onto so you can go on waiting. Freedom, which we barely
begin to know, completely disappears, and with it, everything—
enthusiasm, rebelliousness, justice, security, food, and hope. . . .
Your body lightly arching now, shifting on the sand, perhaps
adjusting itself to the sun's rays a little better. I watch you very
closely. I see you come into the bedroom at night—you know
very well I'm not asleep—and I see you sit down and start un-
dressing. You hang up the uniform you hate by now on the clothes
rack (until tomorrow, until tomorrow). I allow these silences. I
stand those silences; I think those silences are terrifying. Until
one day you speak: *The only thing that matters anymore is working and obeying like an animal, lowering our mentality to that*

of a beast, and if you can't manage that, so much the worse for you. . . . And now I think After all, silence was better, ignorance. . . . Your body in the sand, the baby sleeping beside you, *for me, for me,* and once more the racket of the cicadas, the shouting of the swimmers, and, beyond, the boy stretched out just far enough away so I can make him out perfectly. . . . Now everyone scurries, everyone tries to find a position, occupy a post; everyone wants to save himself—as always, at the expense of others. But there are no more posts, so more have to be invented, more "restructurings" have to be effected. But posts can be lost too. You have to make yourself important, show that you are utterly trustworthy; you have to take back what you said in the morning three times a day, and denounce as quickly as possible (before they beat you to it) the person that committed the reckless act of only forswearing twice (he might be the one assigned to spy on you). . . . But even if you do that, security, possibility are still very difficult. And the persecution is under way. . . . The boy stretches lazily; he has his hands behind his neck, his toes wriggling in the sand. *Sauve qui peut! Every man for himself!* That is the secret watchword and we all, all at the same time, are trying to practice it, drowning the next guy, being drowned ourselves. . . . But listen, we have nothing to fear. You're an honest man, head of your household, loving husband, respectful, obedient, and observant of all the rules. Loyal to the system, discreet, without a "past," with no previous life that might be subject to checking. Having sold your soul for it, here is the house—walls, chairs, bedrooms. Let the young hero enter, the new man. . . . Your body is covered with sand, the baby wakes up. I pick him up, straighten the towel, and lay him down again. Now that the— shall we say—fundamental problems are solved—house, food, car, salary—we can devote our full efforts to making life intolerable. We could wipe each other out once and for all with an honest look, but following tradition we poison each other slowly, methodically. We have a drink. You turn on the record player and we dance. Tonight, I feel sure, we'll make love for the first time. I think almost smugly (looking at the furniture), that we might invite my mother to stay with us a few days; she's probably forgiven us by now. . . . The boy pulls his hands from under his neck now and lets them lie on top of his shorts. Everyone that passes, men and women both, stare at him. . . . My God, when did all this really begin? Surely at the very moment we began to feel regrets. Still cross-examining myself I walk through the hullabaloo, behind Hector in his uniform, clinging to his back. We try to push our way through, until we find a good spot, before the reviewing stand. What a clever idea, I hear you say softly, scheduling a mass meeting for one o'clock in the afternoon; they've got it all planned to melt us. They want to see us sweat, see us wilt, pop like popcorn before "His Majesty's" reviewing stand—and now your voice is angrier still, too loud—who will look grim and benevolent upon us, with that thug's face, saying, *Yes, that's it, applaud, applaud, for you are in my hands, and whenever I wish I can open your file, every one of you, and destroy you. . . .* Sure, for whatever you've done, no matter how heroic, so much the worse for you—they'll use it against you. Hector, hush, they can hear us, I say. There, you see, I'm right! you say more irately, almost choking, pointing at my terrified face. And we move forward a bit, under the scorching sun, until we come right to the parade ground where the parade is to pass. Students go by, marching and carrying enormous posters of support and thanksgiving; workers grouped by guilds go by. They've been picked to march, he tells me, and we've been picked to watch them march. I don't answer him, I only make a gesture of powerlessness. . . . And now the army goes by, sounding its fanfares, parading its arms, creating a great din with threatening-looking devices which seem to be on the attack. Who refuses to march? Who is not here, present, cheering? Everyone now tries to push forward, to see, to get right up to the curb. We run sweating too up to the front of the mob, where the others wait for us, the people from work, whom we must parade our loyalty before, enthusiastically repeat those slogans repeated, hammered, screamed out now by the loudspeakers. But when, when did all this start? I ask myself again, not loosening my grip on Hector's shoulders. The worst thing is that there's no specific point of departure, no date, no event to mark the beginning of the disaster, much less its limits; there is no definitive catastrophe; everything seems to be crumbling, rotting—not suddenly, no, but constantly—and only chaos, poverty, fear, incessant harassment remain. Today they abolished such and such a program, yesterday they suppressed such and such a magazine, today they rationed such and such a product, yesterday they arrested such and such a person, today the firing squad executed so many people. Yesterday, today, on and on and on, until the terrible becomes merely monotonous, and one doesn't wonder why, doesn't demand an explanation or a reparation of the injustice—you just want a place to crawl into, breathe, and watch it all from: watch the utter destruction, see the end of everything, see your own destruction, but without losing your mind, without going insane, without actually dying from the brutality of compulsory labor, the implacable laws, the goals beyond all human strength which must be met and surpassed. . . . And now the loudspeakers describe, at great eulogistic length, the "great procession passing at this very moment before the presidential reviewing stand." Oh, God! Oh, God! Who can I invoke? Who might be able to save us? I bump my nose into Hector's back; he has abruptly stopped, as has everyone else. The notes of the national anthem have begun, so I can't even rub my bruised nose. . . . Hector, I say, and on turning over find that he has disappeared. He's gone off without saying a word to me. I look at the sand and see only the print of his body. Almost frightened, I lift my gaze—the boy has left the beach too. Both of them have vanished. And the notes of the national anthem flow from the reviewing stand, from the loudspeakers. Flow over the uncovered heads, over the static sweaty bodies, over a million motionless figures. I breathe deep, squeeze my lips together tight and breathe, lift my head and breathe, still sitting in the sand. There is the great dais, the white statue of José Martí bending over the crowd, the tower with its cannons, the ministerial edifices plastered with signs of colossal arms and fists grasping rifles. Here, the two of us in the paralyzed multitude. My God. . . . But I get hold of myself, I keep standing up by leaning against Hector. I can still stand up. I do everything in my power not to cry. Because you will not cry, you stupid girl, do you hear; you can't cry at these moments, what would they think? . . . And the notes of the anthem flow on. I raise my head, I stand up still shocked, I look toward the ocean. I can't permit other people to realize, I can't permit them to think, to suspect. . . . Look at the ocean, look at the scene—but not with eyes that scrutinize; make them simply contemplative. You're just a woman looking at a landscape, a woman "thrilled by the view." . . . It must be very late. I'm hungry. The baby must be starving too. I stand, brush off the sand, pick up the baby, and begin to walk in the direction of the cabin. A few men look at me, even whistle at me. They enjoy this; they only think about having their fun. Lucky I can still entertain somebody. . . . Little by little I am losing my provincial accent (that singsong talking, as they say here); little by little I stop bobbing up and down as I walk—which there, in my hometown, no one would notice, since everybody walks that way. My hair is becoming straighter, softer; my face is changed too; my voice is growing less expressive, quieter; the way I use my hands, more controlled; my skin lighter; even my vocabulary is improving. Yes, little by little I'm becoming less and less the *guajira*, the clumsy country girl; I'm beginning to fit in, pass unnoticed, blend in with the people in Havana. Now if somebody gets a little fresh with me (like now), I don't blush, I go on walking, indifferent, almost pleased. . . . But that feeling, that sensation, that question *what for, what for* is still the same one that would come to me in the afternoons there in my hometown as I listened to some Mexican ballad, or any song, in fact, as I sat on the stool. . . . The asphalt shimmers, once more the whistling of the cicadas grows; I reach the cabin almost running, so as not to burn my feet. Hector isn't there, I think; he hasn't gotten here yet. But suddenly, joy—the shower is on, I hear it. He's taking a shower, he's taking a shower, I say to myself aloud, and I turn on the radio. I start making lunch. I finish it. I set it out. I feed the baby and put him to bed. I open the refrigerator and take out the bottle of wine. . . . But listen, listen, it shouldn't be too fancy a meal, he might think you're pleased (as you are) because he came straight back to the cabin. But listen, listen— it may be, moreover, that he didn't come straight back at all, it may be he was taking a walk and happened to come in as you did; after all (I go out onto the porch), he left the beach hours ago. It's already noon, which is to say, afternoon. But why doesn't he come out of the bathroom? The food is getting cold. He's had the shower on for over an hour. . . . Oh, oh, ow, says a voice behind me. Ow, I'm melting. And I see the boy's mother, smiling, hopping over the asphalt. She hops along like that until she gets to my cabin. You should put on some shoes, I say, looking at the bright glow of the day. Yes, she says, I should have slipped my house shoes on, but I didn't think the concrete would be so hot. . . . Now, in the sunlight, I can see her clearly, perhaps too clearly. Poor woman, she's so old. At least her body is that of an old woman. Look at those thighs, covered with potholes, almost; and that bathing suit that makes her look so awful. Look at that belly, those baggy arms, those breasts hanging to her waist. How awful! I say aloud. She looks at me. It's true, she says, the heat is awful. And suddenly I pretend to be furious with the weather to hide the fact that I was stupefied by that deformed body. But You too, say the voices (and now they seem to be nesting in my very ears), you too will get that way. No! I shout. And she looks at me, now a little disconcerted (perhaps she was talking and I interrupted her). No, I say, no one can bear this midday heat, no one can go any farther outdoors than the porch. That's exactly what I say, she says, but he's so bullheaded—of course, she's referring to her son; who else could this ruined figure of a woman be referring to that way?—so bullheaded, she says again, he left early and still hasn't come back. He loves the ocean, she says. And, suddenly, it's like a hymn of thanksgiving, flowing now from the pine trees. *He loves the ocean, he loves the ocean*, goes the anthem. Yes, she says, I went looking for him, but imagine, there are so many people. He's probably at one of the refreshment stands. They say you have to stand in line for two hours sometimes to get a soft drink. Uh-huh, I say, and look at her freckled hands. I see she hasn't left her knitting behind. Poor woman, she doesn't even leave her labor to go to the beach. But Why don't you sit down? I say. No, she says, still smiling, I have to go cook his lunch for him. When that boy comes in he'll be ready to eat a horse. And she hops away, laughing and waving goodbye with the knitting. I go in. The food is cold. The shower is still running. Hector, I call from the bedroom door and look at the baby, who's still asleep. Hector. I go closer, hear the sound of the water apparently falling straight onto the floor. I go to the living room, I look once more at the table I set, the glasses filled with wine. I am still for a second, just listening to the brightness of the day, that racket, but, suddenly, the noise of the shower reaches me again, now louder. I almost run to the bedroom. I go in and open the bathroom door. Hector, naked and dripping, is standing before the mirror, stroking his rigid sex, masturbating. The water falls straight onto the bathroom tiles. He hasn't seen me. I step back slowly and close the door. I go to the living room and stand once more before the laid table. My God, I say out loud, I forgot to make a salad! I start cutting up tomatoes. I put everything on the table when I am done. He comes out with his hair still wet and a towel wrapped around his waist. "Sir," I say aloud, "your dinner awaits you." Thank you, he says, in the same tone, I'm starving. . . . We finish eating. I take the baby and sit on the porch. The baby, with his eyes very wide open, observes me. The shadow the roof throws has crept back across the entire floor; soon it will be at my feet. Then I will be face to face with the dazzling light, but at least the sun won't hit me directly. Still, for a moment, before I try to forget this brightness, I hear Hector in the kitchen washing dishes. The baby keeps watching me with his enormous eyes, waiting for me to say something to him. But "I'm not going to make funny faces for you." Other times I've done it and I think he's been a little surprised by it, even taunting me a little for doing it, as though he were looking at me and saying Who asked you to do that, who said you had to poke out your tongue and say all those silly things to me? . . . I don't know, but perhaps that is what he thinks. I decide not to look at him, to go on just staring into the light, listening to the sound of the engine going down the shimmering highway, passing through the nonexistent puddles now; I make out now, there, finally, the dinosaur that vanishes as soon as we get close to him. Poor beast, he doesn't cause me even the least surprise now, let alone fright. There he is, pirouetting, standing on one of his worm-eaten legs. There he is, trying to frighten me. Poor beast, even he has become ineffectual. When we drive past at full speed, I can hear his bones creak. Poor animal, I hear him sort of bawl, sort of bellow beside the ocean. Poor animal, I'm so undaunted when I look at him. I look at him and light a cigarette; I look at him and blow out a cloud of smoke; I look at him and almost offer him a cigarette. Poor animal. Now I watch him make a million incoherent motions. He leaps crazily from one side of the road to the other, pleading for my attention. Poor animal—I hear him roar and I smoke a cigarette; I hear him calling me madly, and I smoke a cigarette. I see him expiring in a fit of mad laughter, and I smoke. I watch him banging his head against the pavement, I watch him jump, rear on his hind legs, paw the ground, open his mouth and stick out his tongue of flame. I watch him go on like that, transforming himself into a pillar of flame, standing on one leg, and I go on smoking. Finally, he dissolves away. When again we shoot like a meteor past his spot, he is nothing but a little column of smoke that instantly disperses over the almost flat surface of the sea. . . . A few seagulls, in spite of the heat, are still flying over the water; they pass through the little column of smoke now almost invisible and go on climbing, pick up speed, and dive straight down into the waves. What are those seagulls after? What do those horrible birds want? Food, do you hear, just food, the voices yell at me, mockingly, from the pines. . . . Awful birds, I think. Yes, because they really are awful. I've watched them from up close. Just a few seconds ago one of them flew past my head, almost crashing (perhaps dazzled) into a porch chair, and I found it was frightening—its head was monstrously out of proportion, its feathers were ashen and dirty; its taloned legs were poised to strike, its beak curved and gray, its eyes round and hard, cruel and alert, looking for any sort of filth to devour. . . . But now it's far away, climbing against the sky. There it is, remote, hovering over the ocean: A white fowl, a shining bird. I look down. I look at the baby looking at me, questioning me. But listen, perhaps his look is no more than the look of a child ready to be amazed by anything he sees. Everything, for that head still unstocked with memories, must be a great event, an experience, a real discovery. How many surprises must this house, my lips, my eyes, the light bulb turned on and off, the ocean, hold. . . . Listen, listen, how can you be so sure that everything is so simple? What if he really is questioning you? What if he really is looking at you stricken with amazement? What if he really is saying *But why, why, why have you brought me to this place I never asked to be?* . . . That may be true too. It might be, after all, that only at his age does the great sensibility remain totally pure, only at his age when we are not yet used to it all, when we are not yet mutilated, stupefied, or tired out—only at his age, perhaps, might it be possible to be astonished, really terrified, to look at things with that scrutinizing gaze. Later the senses are worn down, until the perception of pain is dulled and we do not even keep the memory of before, of that time when we looked at everything with astonishment—when we were not yet old and we could feel (without the promise of a future, without a past which sets up categories within unhappiness) fully terrified. . . . Now only sometimes does there come to us a kind of "feeling," a dull ache, a kind of indefinable memory of a time. . . . But Which one? What time was that? And we find no answer, for memory has of course atrophied; it is now a man's memory. One sees oneself alone, sort of longing for something, something lost that we aren't sure we ever had. One stops and sort of remembers, tries to remember, to fix a place, a river, a bench under the trees, a fragrance, a few gentle, bright, kindly faces, a piece of printed cloth, a passageway, a garden in the rain, a party we all floated through, and make them clear. . . . But we can riffle through our whole life and not run across that river, or that bench, or the garden, or the party, or even that great dog-rose bush that sometimes (*right now*) seems to be spreading over us. . . . Or yes, we do stumble across things, but they are wrong, they are wrong somehow. . . . And yet something tells me that they did exist, that we were close, that we once possessed those things. But I look at the sun, the day vaporizing into haze, glare, and sizzle; I look at the sky with its implacable clarity (not a cloud, not a seagull now), and now I cannot conceive, cannot imagine that such things existed. Slowly, as though from a distant land, a sound is coming. . . . Here it is now, clearly, the baby's crying, and I feel my legs wet. . . . It is my son crying, it is my son who has wet his diapers. My legs feel sticky, I hear the crying. . . . Listen, listen, I say to myself, the same thing happens to all women; all women, surely, have gone through, go through, this. And they don't go mad. Why do you then? Why you then? And I smell the horrible smell of excrement. Hector! I call. But he doesn't come. So I have to deal with it myself. I go to the bathroom. I wash the baby, change his diaper; I put him to bed. Even my hands have taken on that loathsome smell. I scrub them again with soap, I pour perfume all over them. And I feel (though it can't be) that I still have that disgusting smell. I go out onto the porch again. There is Hector now, his back to the cabin, leaning on the railing, looking toward the ocean. I hear him speak. I slowly approach. Hector, I think. He goes on speaking, looking out into the shimmering landscape. . . . *And I will die in this strident land*, I hear him say, *where people communicate with phallus blows and shameless looks.* He goes on speaking, he keeps speaking, but his voice vanishes in the echoes of the day. I hear only murmurs. That angry, resentful, sad murmur. . . . And what would happen if suddenly I went up to him, if I put my hand on his shoulder, no longer as his wife—*Give up, give up*—and began to talk to him? If only I could talk to him, if only find a word, a way to tell him. . . . The heat is terrible, I say behind him, as I sit down on the porch (a word, a cry, a blow, a question). Yes it is, he says, and turns, tosses the book he was carrying onto the chair, and looks at me; maybe it'll rain. And he turns and puts his arms on the porch rail. It's the end of summer, I say out loud. That's when it's hottest, I add. (But the word doesn't come, the cry doesn't come, the conversation won't get off the ground, doesn't start. What conversation? What conversation? shout the voices.) The end of summer, I think, as though there were ever anything but summer here. You said it yourself—twelve months of hell. . . . I wish it would rain, I say. Me too, you say, but not storm—the car is parked down too close to the water. . . . What words, what words, my God, might be able for the first time to make us recognize ourselves and each other, see each other face to face? You speak: We're into hurricane season now, so once it starts to rain it'll never end. . . . There are no words, there are no words, there definitely are no words. And you go on: Other years by this time we've already had three or four. . . . And your voice sounds a little strained, sarcastic, completely mechanical and sure of itself. *Because, listen,* you say, although you don't say it, *not even nature offers us any comfort, it conspires against us too. Poor country, poor country.* And you take on again—although you haven't spoken—that paternalistic, patronizing, contemptuous, superior tone. But listen to me, listen to me, you too, although you consider yourself special, will perish, you will be destroyed, you will be burned to a crisp. . . . But it isn't going to rain, I finally say, it's already past noon and there isn't a sign. . . . *Chains of hurricanes, chains of hurricanes,* you say with your silence (and once more, you dissolve into the shimmering day), *deluge and withering drought,* I hear you say without saying it. And now it's the cicadas that take up our conversation. Just them, speaking, announcing, forcing us to listen to their litany, our own voices, yours and mine, in the evening. For now it is evening. You sit in the shade of the porch with your book and begin to read, your eyes glued to the pages. I'm going swimming, I say aloud and go off in the direction of the ocean. The pavement is still hot; the breeze that blows across my face is hot too. I walk barefooted across the pavement, I breathe that air, I look at the landscape: the corollas of the oleanders reddish, open, moist, saturated, and half drooping; the twined roots of the almond trees, the tight buds the leaves make from which emerge the equally smooth, tight nuts; the pines reproducing, throwing off seeds; the birds fluttering on their branches, preening their feathers, chasing each other through the sky, diving at each other. The uproar of the cicadas rouses it all to an even higher pitch. The earth cracked and split creaks in the glare of the day, in the heat. I look at that landscape, I look at the flowers, I look at the asphalt. My hands are soaking wet. I have sweated through my bathing suit too. I begin to run along the sand; I come to the ocean. . . . The ocean taut as skin licks my feet, comes up to my calves, breaks against my thighs, rises and swirls around my hips, then touches my breasts and shoulders—it comes up to my neck and goes on rising, covering me. Now, extend my arms and stretch out my legs. Float. Out of the uproar, clasped to the ocean. The silence and the thickening waters, the waters that grow thicker and gloomier as I descend vertically. I am standing, almost touching the seabed, swaying as the waves move to and fro. No fire, no light, no cries, no orders, no voices. . . . But I need air; I blow out bubbles, push off and kick toward the surface. Now I am in the midst of the din, in the dazzle of this day that seems never to end. I begin to walk all along the water. High in the pines the cicadas continue their litany. I stroke a hard, thick leaf, almost metallic, on a plant with a thorny stalk; ants trail along its edges; other insects are trying to chew it too. But they won't be able to devour it, I think, not even the most powerful pricks will be able to pierce it. It has learned how to resist, it has lasted, and now it's on top of the situation, of the weather, of the fauna and the landscape. I pluck the leaf off, I fan my face with it and continue my walk. Here the ocean makes little bogs among the roots. I pick up a stone and throw it across a mud puddle. Thousands of blue flies rise from the water and fly off buzzing among the trees. I hurry on too. I push my way deeper into the sea-grape plants. I hear, suddenly, someone shrieking behind me. I stop and look all around. The shrieks have turned to laughter. I bend over slowly and peek between the trunks. A man and a woman, both half naked, are locked together on the fallen leaves as a cloud of mosquitoes hovers motionless above them. They have discovered me looking at them. Sorry, I say, and almost run through the quagmire. My feet are sucked, slowed, by the mud. Behind me I hear the woman break into a peal of laughter. From afar now, I turn and look. They have both stood up. The woman, now completely naked, signals for me to come back and join them. I run on and once more hear the pealing laughter. Stones bruise my feet. I take a trail which carries me to a little fort from colonial times. It's a building with a high ceiling supported on four stone walls that rise now above creeping vegetation, cans, and empty bottles. There is a plaque at the entrance: THE CITY OF GUANA-BACOA PAYS TRIBUTE TO PEPE ANTONIO (1740–1762) FOR HIS HE-ROIC RESISTANCE IN THE DEFENSE OF THIS CITY AND FORTRESS DURING THE CAPTURE OF HAVANA BY THE ENGLISH. I push the heavy rotten wooden door. As I enter, the smell of shit and urine is so strong that it makes me recoil. Hold on, hold on, says a voice from inside, not so fast. We haven't even been here five minutes. Wait your turn—or go on out into the woods. . . . I descend over the boulders and come once more to the ocean. On the shore, jellyfish in bunches are dashed against the rocks. I contemplate them as they burst—swollen, reddish, some gleaming bluer than the ocean itself, they seem some strange enameled fruit, or shining transparent balloons. They're animals, Hector has told me; they're also called men-of-war. I climb back up the clinkers. I take the high rocky shore path lined now with fishermen. The ocean, becoming rough again, raises a crash of spray and a smell that pierces me through. . . . Above the highest breakers, on craggy boulders completely surrounded by water, on that ruined dock which no boat has moored to in decades—straddle-legged, arms outstretched, blackened by the sun, the nimble emaciated old men whose bones seem covered by a leathery skin like a breast-plate, the teenagers with billowing shirts, and flocks of children. They are all engaged in baiting the hooks, throwing out the lines, unwinding the cords, and spreading the nets, they are all partic-ipating in a kind of dance, a ceremony, a *fiesta*, a gathering—a rendering of homage inspired, sponsored, and received by the ocean. They are all ecstatic, fully immersed in this rite, gleaming in the evening light and accompanied by the pounding of the surf. . . . You are the only spectator, the intruder, the one who looks, scrutinizes, criticizes, with absolutely nothing to do with it, no hand in it. The woman who drives away lovers and fish, the woman who interrupts. . . . But no! No! No! I say suddenly, it isn't true, I can't permit, I cannot permit. . . . No! . . . Suddenly the ocean in one of its unforeseen dashes throws up a torrent of water that climbs the rocks and completely drenches me. So, soaked, I raise my head and see only the sun about to sink into the waters. Thus we will go, in just a few seconds, from day to darkest night. And I discover another ocean. A violet ocean churning into foaming waves, into spray, which is violet too and which swells, rushes upon the land, and then crashes down and shatters on itself—water on water, violet on violet. And now, not thinking of anything else, I begin to run toward the violet sand. I arrive. The color is getting farther and farther away. I run to try to reach it, but the violet shades run too. They are always a few steps ahead of me. I jump, and they jump. I try to catch them, snatch them, but they are quicker than I am. No matter, I tell myself, no matter; from way off there, where the fishermen are, everyone who looks this way will see a violet woman on a violet beach, walking over violet sand beside a violet sea. . . . I walk along next to the ocean, and it is getting darker. I walk along singing next to the ocean, and it is getting darker. I walk among the pine trees, walk across violet sand, touch with the palms of my hands the violet water that stretches before my eyes, the color that covers the entire ocean, and it is growing darker. I dance, I leap, I test the water, I splash in the water, I touch the water, I caress the water, I swim in the water, and it is growing darker. I walk along listening to the roar of the ocean, the murmur of the ocean, the whisper of the ocean, the mutter of the ocean, the din of the water; I listen to the ocean as I sing, and it is growing darker. I walk along making inconceivable gestures, I stretch out my arms, I breathe that smell of sea, this seascape, I am wrapped in the sea's violet, and it is growing darker. It is growing darker, and my voice echoes throughout the pine grove. It grows darker and the ocean flows timeless, draws away disregarding time and returns not remembering time. It hits the sand forgetting time, rises and collapses laughing at time, grows furious and once more calm mocking time. It is growing dark, and I am listening to the sea. It is growing dark, and my feet touch the ocean. It grows dark, it grows dark, and I am becoming one with the ocean. And now I can fondle the ocean's violet. It grows dark, it grows dark, and my violet foot leaves a violet print on the violet ocean's sand. It grows dark, it grows dark, and in these seconds the violet has covered the pine grove and beach, dyed the seagrapes and almond trees, changed cabins into castles, turned crabs into strange unknown flowers, permeated the earth, and it gleams on my hands and arms, my thighs, and on my face and eyes.

Night. I am walking slowly to the cabin. I cross through the pine grove, from which I seem to hear strange whispers (countless insects whistling) and see the blinking of thousands of eyes. I walk faster. When I come to the cabin, I am running. There is Hector, sitting on the porch, still reading—now in the light that filters through the open door of the living room. On the other porch—bright—the boy is whistling. We need to get a light bulb, I tell Hector. Huh? he says. Nothing, I say. . . . I look toward where the boy's mother's car was parked. It isn't there. No doubt she went in search of supplies for the boy. But how could she think of leaving him alone? . . . Late, I hear Hector say. What? I said it's gotten late, you must be cold, he says. I already ate and fed the baby. I hadn't noticed it was so late, I say, I didn't take my watch. I don't think I'm even going to eat. I keep listening to the whistles. I go in. The cabin will be full of mosquitoes with the door open, I say; you ought to read in the living room. But he seems not to have heard me. I bathe quickly. I slip under the mosquito net that he had already put up. The baby is sleeping. I wave at him from my bed, and I lie down. As I'm covering myself up I say to myself, What are you doing? Get up. Tonight more than ever you should be beside him. . . . But I cover myself up even more with the sheet, even pull it over my head. But I must get up, I must prevent, I cannot permit. . . . I throw off the sheet, and sit up in bed. This is the house, Hector says. This is the house, he says. This is what we got from the sale of our souls, we say to each other looking at each other, without saying a word to each other. . . . But listen, listen, the voices say to me now, from the pine grove, perhaps you really ought to get up. Listen to that whistling, listen to that whistle. . . . I hear the whistling, I hear those whistles. But I lie down again and cover myself completely. . . . The whistle floating, the whistle flowing. The whistle rising once more and entering suddenly, clear and unbearable, through the car window. I hear that whistling and know that he is hearing it too. I know that although he pretends to be driving calmly, he hears it, right now, just as I do. I know I should do something, that I should get up, speak to him, that I should help him. That I cannot allow, that I must not permit. . . . But What is it I must not permit? Get up, get dressed, go out onto the porch! But I'm so tired. I've walked so much, it's been such a hot day, and now night, that's long too, and if someone is whistling it is even worse. And him there, in the dark, pretending to read. But I don't want to think, I mustn't think, I can't think—even my fingernails hurt. It's better to keep on floating a few hours. A few hours? Or even not to return. . . . To float, through the calm that rises, through a nothingness, nothingness, nothingness. . . . They float, we float, I float. Behold, the house. Behold, the soul that floats. The house inhabited by dinosaurs, picture on top of picture on top of picture, dinosaur populations, cities taken over by dinosaurs. My belovéd, my lovely one, my dinosaur, has the summer truly passed? Has the season of rain come, the season of song? Have flowers truly appeared over the land? . . . The whistle, floating. I know I shouldn't have. . . . Floating. I am floating on my back on the ocean. At times the wind blows; I kick and am lost—I lose sight of the land, the pines; there is only the deserted sky before my eyes. Me, floating, my hands crossed behind my neck, the sun burning my thighs, my breasts, my face. Incoming waves dash themselves against my body. I don't know how long I've been floating on this water, since there is no longer time. Just ocean. Fish, wriggling, leap over my body, swim up to me curiously, feel me with their icy noses. The swollen body of a dead dog passes nearby. Above him travels a flock of seagulls that look at me and scream in laughter. . . . I go on like that, with no aim, no hurry. Midday cracks my skin. I, only body, alone, in the midst of that glare that becomes more implacable the more I go on. Out of that glare I hear now a sound like the deafening chanting of a choir, grown so loud that it even drowns out the roar of the waves. From over the ocean, out of the shimmering air, comes a strange procession. I raise my head farther out of the water and I can see perfectly who they are. The Virgin, God, and a host of singing angels are walking over the ocean. The Virgin has trouble keeping her balance—she seems to stumble—and sinks. Then the angels come to her aid, taking her up by her arms. The Virgin stands and begins to walk, her wet dress clinging to her skin. The angels around about her pluck off seaweed, shells, crabs, sponges, even a few small squid that have stuck to her hair and skin. God walks a few steps in front, so He seems not to have noticed anything; not even now that the Virgin sinks again (this time vanishing altogether beneath the water) does He look back. He gives the impression of being a solitary, bored old man. Once in a while, calmly and fastidiously, He waves a hand before His face as though He were shooing away a mosquito. But—I tell myself—It's impossible for there to be mosquitoes around *here*; we're on the high seas. Perhaps it's some flying fish that I can't make out from here, or one of those sea spiders that sometimes jump up into your face; or who knows but what it's a drop of water that splashes His face as the Virgin drops into the water like that. I go on watching Him. He is dressed in faded mechanic's pants that are too tight for Him, at His age. He is also wearing an old sportcoat, leather. I think He must be sweltering in this heat, or perhaps that is why He is passing His hand over His face. But why don't the angels try to make Him a little cooler? Apparently they aren't aware of Him. They're walking behind and have just (once more) pulled the Virgin from the water, gasping; while her hair trickles a stream of water a few sea urchins wriggle into the décolletage of her dress, which seems to be made of blue velvet—and although it doesn't gleam like God's jacket I think it must be just as hot. The angels, moreover, fan her while they talk among themselves in a strange gabbling like a kind of short trumpeting; but then I think that since she keeps plunging into the water over and over again, she can't be too hot. The skin of God and the Virgin is fairly dark—tanned by the sun, perhaps. Seen at a distance, anyone would simply think They were a family sort of tightrope-walking across a tree trunk in the water. But I know perfectly well it is Them—not by the great choral chant that now resounds again, not by the splendor that sometimes surrounds Them like a gigantic halo, not by that hard look of interminable suffering that moment to moment darkens the visage of the Virgin, nor by the way God sort of feels His way along—not even the choir of angels that surrounds Them is for me the most convincing proof that it is Them. It is the sense of solitude and renunciation They give, beyond anything my sufferings might conceive, that makes me know that those two old people, like two old fishermen, are God and the Virgin. It is Them. Besides, under Their feet there is no floating tree trunk. . . . For a moment,

I look at the angels. Most of them are men (that is, they seem to be men); few of them have a woman's figure or face, and even those are dressed in masculine clothing—long narrow pants made of rubber, shirts made of something like plastic. Not one of them is young. When they stop, God and the Virgin halt as well and seem to wait; the impression is that the angels are the ones who lead. Moreover, even when they pull the Virgin out of the water, I see no sign of compassion on their faces; they seem merely disciplined, doing a duty. Now they whisper among themselves. One takes out a cigarette and lights it. The procession goes on advancing. Now that they are near me I feel the splash of water when God strides the waves. They pass beside me. The bare feet of the Virgin are right in front of my eyes. I try to speak to her, to call her; I wave; with a strangled voice I begin to shout. But the noise of the chanting is so deafening now that I can't even hear myself when I call. So they go on passing, almost on top of my body, not hearing or seeing me, while the water they stir up splashes my face. I try to stand up, but I sink. I swim along behind them, calling them. The chant becomes more and more distant. Suddenly the entire procession stops; apparently they have heard me. Wait for me! Wait for me! I call to them and swim with all my might. Their backs are to me, motionless. Slowly, the Virgin's head begins to turn; at last she looks at me. Wait for me! I shout to her. Through the water I am stirring up I see the Virgin raise a hand to her mouth, as though frightened. Immediately she turns away from me and begins to walk. But all of a sudden she stumbles, falls, sinks again up to her neck. The angels, with tired fretful looks, but confident, raise her afloat. Two of them brush off her dress. From under her skirt little fish sprinkle out, and even a starfish falls and begins to scurry along like a water spider. Now the angels organize themselves into a long perfect line, as though they were going to perform a military exercise. The march recommences in that order. Desperately I go on swimming after them, though they are now almost lost on the horizon. The sound of a powerful engine is heard. From out of the clouds appear the wings of a plane that now, creating a huge waterspout, sets down. It is a brilliantly shining machine. On one side you can read, in bright red letters, an acronym, the mundane name of the airline company the ship belongs to. The door opens and a metal staircase descends from it. The procession is getting closer and closer. It arrives. God begins to climb the staircase. The Virgin (still dripping) follows Him with short steps. The chant can no longer be heard at all. The line of angels begins to ascend into the airplane too, as the waves wash heavy and slow against it. At last, everyone now on the boarding steps, they take out strange instruments. They are not palliums or crosses or any other kind of religious object. They look like pieces of wood that suddenly stretch out of all proportions, hooks whose ends open out into saucers, bottlelike things that end in crests, strange wheels, upside-down umbrellas that open just as they enter the ship, semi-amphorae, long jugs, something like a huge stewpot, and even a kind of enormous demijohn whose top part is a huge bulging neck. They are all inside. The stair rises automatically. The door is closed. Once more the roar of the engine is heard. The machine glides slowly over the ocean, leaving a wake of furious spray. Running in great circles, it takes off. When it passes overhead, its propellers unleash a huge whirlpool that drags me, carries me, into the depths. I try to fight to the surface, to stay afloat in this whirl of crushed grasses, mud, sand, and maddened fish. Don't leave me! Don't leave me! I try to shout, while once more the whirlpool drags me down and then impels me along in its current. Emerging on a wave I see the plane fall, sheeted in flames, at the horizon. Everything is illuminated by the brilliance of its blaze. The brightness is so intense that it blurs all contours. I feel myself diluting, disintegrating, in this immense blinding splendor. Don't leave me! Don't leave me! I cry again to the brightness that goes on drawing away. Here! Here! I shout as I swim. But now I am only a voice in the midst of this splendor, from which now begin to spring millions of little yellow planes, a huge swarm, that join together to produce an unbearable roar. I shout. But my voice too begins to fade away, dissolving, vanishing like smoke in the great brightness. When, at last, I open my eyes my voice is heard no more; not even I can hear it. I hear nothing, nothing in these seconds when my senses have not yet been able to settle down in this new reality. This is always the way it is when I wake up. I go through a kind of blank interval when I don't know really where I am—what town, what house, what part of the room, what position in the bed. I slowly begin to get my bearings, make things out. This time it is green, green, permeating, completely covering the morning. Within the green I begin to distinguish its infinite variety: the pines, the almond trees, the oleander

leaves, the tall waving grass beating against the cabin shutters. You have to get up. While I wash my face, trying not to make too much noise—Hector and the baby are still asleep—I avoid the mirror. You're all right, I tell myself. It's all right, I think as I put the milk on to boil. You're all right, I tell myself. And the milk begins to make little bubbles, although it still isn't boiling. I look at my skin. There are still no signs yet. My mother used to say, says, will say, that if you watch the milk it never boils; or it takes too long; that may be true. There are no signs. But there will be, soon. I turn my back to the pan. I feel my calves—no, no marks, and not on my thighs either. Just a second ago, when I looked at myself in the mirror, I didn't see any alarming sign either; it always terrifies me to think of the inevitable moment when I will go to the glass and find a wrinkle; then there will be no way out. I sit down. I look at my feet. They aren't big; the work in the fields hasn't made them ugly. I look at my calves—not too thick, not too thin. I caress myself. I go back naked into the kitchen and turn up the gas. I am a woman, I think for the first time—Mama has just told me so—I am a woman, my God, I am now a woman. . . . I go into the bathroom. I am a woman, I am a woman. Here are the down between my legs, the pains, the drops of blood, the chill that rises, that knots my stomach. I am a woman. The bubbles rise, cluster on the side of the pan where the fire is hottest. They accumulate, they become foam, they flow to the center of the pan. So this is what being a woman is, I think. Now the whole pan of milk begins to really boil; I wait for the rolling boil, I wait for it to boil over before I take the pan from the fire. And the worst thing is that there's no return, and like it or not you have to go on. I will not fall in love, I think at the beginning; I will not submit, I think, I will not allow myself such degradation, such humiliation, such submission. But he is there, in the bedroom without a door, reading those books I don't know how he manages to find; reading despite my mother's commotion—she now makes even more noise, just to spite him. Someone is behind me. I turn around. It's Hector, who has gotten up now. He has put on his bathing trunks and a shirt. He strokes my neck. I can feel his breathing, his body. Breakfast is ready, I say. I go into the bedroom and put on my bathing suit. The baby is awake now. I pick him up, I dandle him. "Come 'ere. Come 'ere." He laughs. The three of us sit down to breakfast. The ocean now is a plain; it looks as though you could actually ride off across it. While I eat I contemplate it and think that today I'll have to wash the dirty diapers. I watch through the shutters—the ocean gently rolls. One diaper after another after another—covered with dried excrement. I clear away the cups and saucers and carry everything to the sink; I turn on the taps. I'm going to try to find some liquor, Hector says to me, now at the door, his hand clutching the handles of the bag with its empty bottles. We two will go to the beach, I tell him. I see him go off. It's wonderful, it's wonderful. He turns and smiles and waves goodbye to the baby, who raises his hand too in farewell. Sitting on the porch (holding the baby), I see him fade into the oleanders, appear under the almond trees—it's wonderful, it's wonderful—walk toward the car, disappear along the pine-grove road. It's wonderful, I think, and behind me I hear a voice. Splendid, it says. I turn around. It's our neighbor, the boy's mother. Splendid, she says, we're going to have a glorious day. I motion for her to come over. You don't have to ask her twice. She almost runs up the steps of our cabin, showing her deteriorated thighs. Let's have a drink, I tell her. Terrific! she says, and laughs out loud. I laugh too. I bring out glasses, sodas, the little rum there is left. Did your husband go out? she asks me as she picks up the baby. Yes, I say, he went to Guanabo to get some rum. My son went to Guanabo too; he told me they were selling bathing suits and sometimes they even pull out ham rolls. I told him he definitely should go, he ought to eat all he can. . . . What a pity, I say (and Have another drink); if he had known it he could have gone with Hector in the car. It's true, she says and winks at the baby. I was going to take him myself, but he refused; he's an angel, he doesn't want to put me out, or waste gasoline, especially with this rationing. . . . *An angel*, I think, and look at the ocean, still gently rolling. We both smile and drink our drinks. How's your knitting going? I have it right here, she says and sticking a hand inside her housedress pulls out a ball of yarn and a half-finished sock. You've done a *lot*, I praise her; you've almost finished that sock. Yes, last night I knitted till late; I wasn't sleepy. I don't sleep much now. Must be old age, she says, but not dramatically or resentfully or sad—just with the tone of a person who accepts the normal, inevitable course of things. You aren't old, I say, and look at her hands. She's an old woman, I think, and watch her fingers among the threads of yarn. This keeps me entertained, she says. And perhaps without noticing, unconsciously, she begins to knit, does a few stitches and sticks it back in the pocket of her housedress; the baby sticks his hand in too. He's very curious, I say. It's natural, she says, mine wanted to know about everything too. At that age they're interested in everything; one day he almost poked out my eyes. God only knows what he thought my eyes were. Yes, it's "natural," it's "natural," I think. And there is the ocean, changeless. We should take a walk along the beach, I say. I'd love to, she answers, but I have so many things to do: cook lunch. My son won't be long. Yes he will, I think, and look at the ocean slowly rolling. But I'll go anyway! she suddenly cries, smiling and perky, as though this decision meant her liberation, her triumph, the permission that someone gave her at the last moment. But even so, she says, smiling and finishing her drink, I have to come right back. Don't worry, I say, we'll just take a little walk. Marvelous! she says. I even have on my bathing suit—and she lifts her dress—although I hadn't planned to go swimming. I put it on so I would fit in. . . . We get to the beach and sit in the sand. . . . I told him to take the cabin key with him, she says, but he didn't want to. Imagine, if he comes back now he won't be able to get in. . . . Poor woman, I think, her conversation has only one topic: *my son, my son, my son.* . . . Uh-huh, I say, spreading the towel and lying face up. . . . The sun doesn't burn yet and the ocean keeps on swelling and falling. Uh-huh, I say. Then I don't speak anymore. She doesn't need, doesn't ask, you to pay attention; she only wants to talk, and talk, and have someone, once in a while, look at her and, if they want to, agree, if only by nodding. . . . Because so long as you don't dream of scissors, my mother says, everything's all right. . . . The ocean rises and falls and at this moment Hector arrives in Guanabo. . . . The two of them walk together under the trees. But how could there be trees in those towns? A gas station, closed of course, a dusty marquee, a few squat houses, nothing more. . . . Because dreaming of scissors is death. . . . No. Not a tree, not a bird, not the least blade of grass is there in the vicinity of this shining highway down which we advance. Advance or retreat? How does one advance? How does one retreat? How can one advance retreating? Although we say—you have to say—that we are advancing, says Hector, while we keep pushing, making a way for ourselves through the esplanade where—at last—the great reviewing stand is, and the inclining white statue. And the mother smiles, and the ocean swells and falls. Perhaps it is the two of us, Hector and I (I think, while we go on advancing), who suffer most. For many people, perhaps, the situation is brighter. They define it according to the commodities they have lots or none of, according to what they can or cannot eat. This woman, for example, I think—*this poor old woman*, I think—and I look at her (smiling now, reddening, her forehead drenched with sweat)— for her, her worries come down to whether she will be able to get all the skeins of yarn she needs to knit a hundred pairs of socks for her son. But we, how will we be better off when all the goals have been reached—if they are reached someday? In what proportion does our happiness increase because they have increased our ration of rice? In what proportion will our happiness have increased when all of us women can show knitted socks? She will leave someday—if they let her, if she can take her son with her—and all her miseries will be over when she crosses the ocean and is able to fill her stomach and feast her eyes. But What about us? What about us?—and I look at the rocking ocean and feel calm, calmed—What will we be able to do? What can we do with our memories, with our hopes, with our emotions, with our desires, whatever you call them? And the ocean goes on flowing, and she goes on smiling and talking to me. And the pines now seem to exclaim, *Hurry, hurry, hurry! Make up your mind, choose your hell before it's too late!*. . . . Yes, it is late, she says to me, still laughing, I think I'm going to have to leave. If you want me to, I can take the baby. Take him, I'll be there right away. . . . But look, folks, look over that way and you'll see that that woman who comes along, walking and singing by the oceanside, is me. . . . She leaves with the baby. The ocean is taking on more color, intensity. Now it is blue, dark. I breathe. I lie down. Now, it is the clouds. The slow, swollen clouds, sailing against the ocean flow. The clouds, cathedrals, crumbling palaces, beards, flocks of sheep, strange beasts, bodies, hands, flowers, testicles, pebbled skies. . . . I turn over. Two women sit chatting on the sand. They wave their hands, gesticulate. What are those women saying? Of what importance is the life of those women? They don't wonder about it, but nonetheless they know. They speak: they don't even suspect that time is escaping, escaping. *Soon your eyes too will be sunken, you will show the world your fallen breasts, your thin and thinning hair.* I raise my head. It is the cicadas saying those idiotic things. But I cannot lose my calm. I lie back once more. Two swimmers, an old man and a young one, are approaching. The older one begins to talk to me. Those foolish, clichéd phrases they always use to strike up a conversation leading, or so they hope, to "better" things—the sun this, the heat that, the weather the other, and, naturally, am I alone? And the damned cicadas go on with their litany. My God, what was the first time I felt, discovered time? The older man leaves; perhaps he feels put down, or perhaps he is leaving the field to the youth. The young man drags himself closer over the sand and stretches out next to me. But I can't remember, however hard I try, I can't remember how I lived before, before I knew that passing. . . . So pretty and all alone, I hear him say. I look at him and smile. The poor thing, the same words, the same technique. Encouraged by my smile, he moves even closer, rubs his feet across the sand. And what did I feel at that moment, when I realized that you had to grow old, to die—that is, that we are always growing older, dying? . . . I have a cabin rented, he says mischievously to me now, staring at me; my friend and I have a cabin right nearby. Then he says something about "sharing," even mentions the word *loneliness* and showers another broadside of insinuations on me. I smile and look at the ocean, which has begun to slap at the shore, a little roughly. The man still more confidently brings his feet close to mine and goes on spinning out his line. And time passes, and time is passing. And what remains? Nothing, Hector says to me, beside me—and now, since gasoline rationing, we almost always take a bus to work—not even the memory of an intelligent conversation, not even the gracefulness of instructive, halting speech. Nothing! Just vulgarity, irritating mediocrity. I don't answer him, I look anywhere but at him or at that woman in a red dress with her hair in a high bun who looks at me as though she were shocked—she might have heard some of our conversation. Finally the crowds and commotion of the buses become intolerable. Hush, I say to Hector, who goes on with his litany, I'm not even listening to you. But he goes on muttering, mumbling, complaining—and *The weather, the weather, the weather,* the cicadas cry, the pines, this immense brightness which besets us, this glare which drowns, paralyzes, burns to cinders, and scatters the ashes of ideas. . . . And the nonsense goes on, the profligacy of his pauperized bullshit, the sentimentalism larded with *sweethearts, loves, romances,* and other truly unbelievable things. I look at him, smiling. He turns toward me; he has the nerve to show me how aroused he is; he rubs his legs across my knees. I laugh. He laughs too and triumphantly attempts to take my hand while he looks down the beach, no doubt searching for his friend so he can boast about his "conquest." I stand up smiling. The poor thing, I think. I run to the ocean. I dive in and come out far down the shore. I take the avenue of almond trees and come finally to the cabin. There she is, the mother, with my son, on the porch. I took longer than I ought to have, I tell her, apologizing, and take the baby. Not at all, she says, I'm going to make lunch for my son; he ought to be here any time now. I run down the steps. I go to the bedroom and put the baby to bed. I slowly begin to make the other beds. I straighten the mosquito net, fluff up the pillows, pull the sheets tight. The beds are made, I say softly, so as not to wake the baby. A fly—I don't know how it could have gotten in through the screen—buzzes around his nose. I shoo it away. It takes a short flight and lights on the sheet, rubbing its two front legs together as though in training. I start making lunch. Hector should be here any time now, I say, peeling some plantains; he'll be here any time now, I say then, starting the onions and peppers and garlic to season the meat—the plantains are frying in the skillet. He'll be here right away, I tell myself, as I finish the salad and the whole rest of the lunch. But he doesn't arrive. I go out onto the porch, I stand next to the porch rail, in the immense glare of the day, looking at that great brightness. Peace has flown, I think, although the ocean goes on flowing. . . . What peace? What peace? the seagulls ask me as they fly over the pines. I look at those gulls, I look at the landscape; it shimmers and bobs; I look at the dinosaurs once more dying of laughter, leaping over the ocean off there to one side. I might start reading now, one of those novels you brought, I might even just start singing, or lie down on my back on the bed, or on the sand, or on the ocean; I might, simply, go into the cabin and serve myself lunch, but Listen to me, listen to me, none of that will keep you from seeing the dinosaurs leap, leap. . . . The illustration (*picture*) is there, in the middle of an old magazine, in a trunk full of cockroaches. . . . But I haven't discovered that magazine yet. Outside that trunk, inside this house there is nothing that has any mystery to offer—nothing can comfort you or amuse you, in this house in the country, in this grass-roofed hut, this *bohío*, as the others call it (the ones who don't live in it), where you can stand in the doorway and see it all, all at once: the living room with its parlor table dead in the center, the two bedrooms at the sides, with their doors open, the kitchen with its rickety stove and the table, and then the back yard. Listen, standing like that in the living room door, you behold your whole known universe, your whole future. In a house like that, there cannot even be memories, I think. The bathroom is four walls without a roof, so the sun comes in; the toilet, four walls without a roof with a big box with a hole in it. . . . Look, now, from the living room you can see the hen that preens her feathers in the back yard. . . . But there is a trunk; *there* is the trunk. While I rummage through the yellowish papers, while I take out and put back the empty bottles, nuts without bolts, rags the lizards lay their eggs in, a doll's arm, old shoes, a pair of underwear (I don't know how it got here), and faded photos, I think, Behold, this is your comfort, this is your consolation. And when I discover this pile of magazines, I think, Happiness, sheer happiness! . . . Flipping their pages I come to this animal with a long neck, sad eyes, and gleaming rib cage, with his back arched and his tail erect. And I am utterly grief-stricken. I look. Slowly, slowly, I enter the landscape; slowly, slowly, the figure begins to come to life again. His heavy legs begin to stir, he raises his head a bit more, his great sad eyes turn on me, staring. . . . Looking at him, looking at him close up, I can hear the slow roar of his breathing. . . . Looking at him, looking at him so close that I am virtually under his huge eyelids, I feel a sort of secret communion between two solitudes. Looking at him this close, I can see a kind of mutual curse between us. Looking at each other, utterly alone on this background land-

scape, between that strangely dark, confused, faded land and sky—
as though the scene belonged to a lithograph, or etching, or drawing, or whatever you call it—for the first time, I think, I think I
have found terror—that is, *truth*. . . . I discover it and can do
nothing to avoid it, to convince myself that I haven't discovered
it. I can do nothing to keep that immense sad animal from looking
and looking at me with his immense sadness. We can do nothing
to stop looking at each other. When my mother comes, there is
no longer any salvation. What is it? I ask her, trying to find a
response to this fear, this interpenetration. Nothing, some kind
of prehistoric kind of animal, she says. . . . At last I pull my gaze
from the figure watching me, now, I think, a little mockingly.
And I look at the sea—one o'clock, I think. I look at the ocean—
two o'clock in the afternoon, I think. I go into the cabin and
begin to set the table. The two chairs facing each other, and even
the tablecloth that we still hadn't used. The embroidered white
tablecloth that my mother offers me now, in the season of reconciliations. My mother. . . . My mother arrives. She comes into
my house. The white tablecloth she embroidered herself. Thank
you, I say, but why have you gone to all this trouble? And I think,
So old, she's so old. . . . Now with the tablecloth on the table I
begin to put out plates and knives and forks and napkins. Three
o'clock, it's three o'clock. I look at the ocean. Slowly the dinosaurs on their hind legs fade out above the clouds. All it needs
is a candle, I think. A tall blue candle to place in the center of
the impeccably-laid table. But there aren't any candles, and I
think, moreover, that there's no way in the world to get any
around here. I sit down. I place my two hands on the tablecloth
and smell the food. I stand up and go out onto the porch—four
o'clock, I say, it's four o'clock already. The beasts have flown,
the evening goes on rising, like the ocean, but the sun still is
gleaming over the pine trees. It isn't going to rain today either,
I think. Far off there, across the glowing pavement, comes the
boy. I will stay here and wait for him; I will wait for him to walk
in front of the cabin, and I will say hello; and my greeting will
be like a warning to him. . . . Now the suntanned figure, dressed
only in shorts and a white shirt, crosses the avenue of oleanders.
The mother, exactly as though she were moved by instinct (or
just because she was peeping out from behind the blinds perhaps),
appears on the cabin porch, her face beaming. I look at her and

she smiles at me. There he comes, she says aloud, as though in a cry of triumph. What? I say, pretending not to understand. Him! she says; it was late, she had been worried, he almost certainly hadn't been able to get a ride. . . . It's true, I say, looking at the boy coming closer to us, passing before me but not looking at me, and climbing the steps. The mother welcomes him home with a hug. The poor thing, I think, if only he'd looked at me (if only his mother hadn't been on the porch), perhaps I might have been able to do something for him. If only you'd seen his eyes, his dinosaur eyes, you would have started packing everything up; yes, and when Hector comes in you would have said *Let's go, this very instant!* to him, and although he wouldn't have wanted to, I would have made him leave here. . . . But he didn't look at me, he didn't seek my help. He thinks he's safe. Sure his adolescent hair, his adolescent body, his adolescent face will save him. Poor boy, too much sureness. Poor Hector, poor me, poor dinosaurs. . . . They go in. She talks and laughs, triumphantly shutting the door. The mother and son are now together. Outside, the ocean goes on, constantly changing key—now dashing once more over the shore. For a moment the whistling of the cicadas is also deafening; but it wanes, it wanes. I go into the living room. I put the food in the refrigerator; I put away the plates and knives and forks; I pick up the tablecloth and napkins. I go into the bedroom. While I look at the baby, who goes on sleeping, I say aloud, *Now Hector is parking the car at the bend in the almond trees; now he is closing the door and starting to walk toward the cabin.* I go to the bathroom, pick up the comb, and begin to comb out my hair. My face slowly grows disfigured, in step with the swelling of my womb; the veins in my legs are swollen, and my belly grows and grows. It is the baby. Within you you hear him jump, quick, quick. . . . But I turn once more to my face now completely restored, to my waist without a sign, without a bulge; I look at my legs, I look at my breasts. I have not succumbed, I have not succumbed. Oh, God, I have not succumbed! While I powder my face with the puff, I say aloud, *Now he's crossing the paved walk, he's coming to the cabin, climbing the steps, opening the door.* . . . He comes in and I cannot say to him *I've been waiting for you for hours,* because you arrive and nothing but your arrival matters, and any explanation, any apology, would be absurd. He sticks his hand into the bag, takes out a bottle, and waves it in the air, immediately fills two glasses. At a signal from him we clink glasses. For a moment, I believe, he makes a move as though to caress my face, although it doesn't go beyond the intention (perhaps not beyond my imagination). He looks at me, widens his mouth to smile, but doesn't quite make it. Perhaps, I think, he's making fun of me. He raises the glass again and we both drink. He fills the glasses again, spilling the wine in a puddle on the table. I sip, sitting while he looks down at me with his mouth widened but not quite achieving a smile. Let's go out onto the porch, he says, and fills the glasses again; he takes the bottle with him when he goes. We sit in the midst of the brightness, in silence. Just drinking and looking at the sunlight that pours over the tiles of the floor and over our legs. The *noonday* sun, for though it is afternoon, with the change of hours it turns out that as far as the weather is concerned it is still midday. . . . Because nothing can be left alone, nothing can be left as it is! They fiddle with everything, change everything, even if it's only to spite you, to make things worse than they started, until un- bearable things pile up to the point that it's actually boring to talk about them—even though everything, on the other hand, leads always to the same topic, the only topic—since everything, even painting your nails or cutting your hair, is directly linked to the system and must have its approval. . . . And we have al- ready talked so much about the same thing. We've criticized the same thing so much—in whispers—that now I don't know when he's talking and when I am, that now I don't know whether I am thinking now or talking, or whether he is thinking or talking and I am simply listening or assuming. . . . Yes, until angry, critical, resentful, desperate words emerge as though by spontaneous gen- eration; they dance on every lip, automatically, and from being repeated so often they start rhyming with each other and lose all their meaning, their power. Yes! Yes! he says (now I am certain it is him talking). We have come to this, to losing the urge to protest, to complain! And now he's ready to leave, his white shirt buttoned to the very top button. We just have to close up the house, go off to work. When I turn my head, my eyes stumble on the cabin next door, bathed like ours in sunlight. But I drink, I drink again; I force myself to forget about the boy, the mother. But Why didn't she find herself a husband? A man who'd hit her or tolerate her, a lover, a "suitor" as they said in her day, whatever. Why invest so much tenderness, so much need, all your time in a poor seventeen—did she say seventeen?—year-old boy? Enough! Enough nonsense! Shoo! Not another word about her son. I know it all: he's perfection itself, openness, purity, an angel come from heaven. But excuse me, listen, you are making a grave mistake, you are committing a crime with that creature. Raise him another way. Tell him *Son, show what you're made of, show your claws; look, that's life.* And point anyplace, anyplace will show him. But I don't say a word and she talks on and on. *My son,* she says, *my son,* she says. . . . Enough! I cannot bear. I cannot bear. . . . And it is Hector who is looking at me, it is he who is questioning me. Yes, because I have spoken these words out loud, without realizing it. He fills the glasses again, raises them, clunking them violently together in a kind of toast. Yes, he says now, I understand you, I sympathize. . . . But listen, you don't understand a thing, you don't even know what I'm thinking about. Who *can* bear it? he says. And drinks. Really, he says, and raises his hand. Really! And puts his hand on his knee, his fingers spread, clenching. Unbearable! Unbearable! he says with a thick voice, his tongue clumsy. Don't you think everybody sees things exactly like you do? Don't you think everybody feels hounded, baffled, dead? Of course! he exclaims, answering himself. And now he raises his hand, opens it in the air, as though approving. . . . Everybody! But there is the *fear.* There is so much fear that no one even dares show it. The worst thing is, he says—and fills up the glasses again—that everything has been so twisted, mixed up, poisoned, polluted, confused that now you can hardly tell where good intentions end and the con job begins. Because don't you doubt for a second that we've been conned. And how! And *how!* So much so, he says, now raising his voice, that we have only the foggiest idea of the macabre machinations they hide behind. So much so, that if you managed to understand it completely, you would go instantly crazy. So much so, he says, and now his voice is a hoarse shout, that if someone dared denounce, or simply point out, that con job, there is yet another humiliation awaiting him. The plans to feed us will not go well (they're not interested in their going well), but the plans to put you down, to keep you on a diet, to force you to say *yes* even if you die of hunger or rage, are making excellent progress. There is no way out; it looks like everything has conspired to drown you, and they're watching, constantly checking, investigating. Ah, and so you think "over there" you can breathe, huh? Well, *bang!* They slam the door. Die, suffocate, and sing, sing, sing. . . . Hector, I say. Hector, I say, hush. Sing! he says, even louder. And I look over toward the other cabin, afraid I'll see our neighbor peeking through the shutters. . . . Sing, for this is happiness, this misery consuming you is happiness. Sing this never-ending degradation, sing. Yes, yes, it's all forbidden: *No Thinking, No Saying No, No Shouting.* But listen to me, once in a while you *have* to shout, protest, even when you're not right. But it frightens us, and you know it. . . . He puts a hand across his eyes, as though to protect himself from the sun, and drinks again. And goes on. Have you ever, ever heard of a sign with the order *LIVE?* No! They say WORK! LEND A HAND! HELP! KEEP WATCH! GIVE! SIGN UP! SACRIFICE! Or they threaten you. But they don't talk about life. . . . Hector, I say, and put my hand over his. Hector. . . . But he fills the glasses again. He stretches out in the armchair. It is just unbearable, he says, as you said very well a second ago; it is just unbearable. Hector, I tell him, let's go inside. It is just unbearable, he says. Slowly, stumbling and lurching, we go into the cabin. But what do you expect? he says, opening another bottle, what can you expect from a country that has always lived in slavery and under-the-table arrangements? What do you, *you,* do to survive, not to draw attention to yourself, to imitate everybody else? Take on their language, their manner-isms, exaggerate everything so they don't find you out. What can you do? What can be done? . . . Drawing near the table, he gulps down the whole glass in one swallow. Perhaps, he says now, they are more intelligent than I am—they fake it better than I do. You never know. . . . Hector, I say, and try to get close to him, to touch him. But suddenly he shrinks away, jumps, and begins to shout. And the triumphant words, he says laughing, will they never sound? And now he roars with laughter. Hector, I say, and go after him, trying to control him. You know, he says stopping, sometimes I think it's all the same to them whether the fields are planted with coffee, strawberries, or parsley; they just want to control us, and not leave us time to think. Hector, I say. He stops me again. You know, he says, what the punishment would be for saying publicly what I'm saying now? And he looks at me crazily, questioningly, seizing me. Death! he says loudly. Death!

he says shouting. And I hear the shouts of the baby too, who has been crying since who knows when. I go and pick him up. Rocking and whispering to him, I go back to the living room. Death! Hector shouts at us, pointing at us like a judge who has just handed down the sentence. The baby lets out a scream. Be quiet, please, I tell Hector, you've frightened him. Let new generations come to drink from these springs, he says; he grabs the baby from me and lifts him up while he goes on shouting. Come, frustrated youth, noisy mediocrities, menopausal professors, come and take on the high and mighty airs of the progressives here, come tell how wonderful, wonderful everything you see here is! You have the full support and freedom of the State to support the State, you have complete freedom to say *There is freedom* here. You know the rules—applaud, applaud. The most comfortable hotels (only for foreign "guests") are paid for with applause. . . . He waves the baby in the air again, and me after him, trying to control him, to talk to him. . . . Applaud! Applaud! And keep on applauding, don't ask about the dead, or about the jails, or about the slaves, or about hope. Just keep on applauding. . . . He raises the baby again, who now is crying, truly terrified. Hector, I say, but he goes on staggering about and stomping through the living room. Now he begins calling cadence to himself. Left, right! Left, right! March along with your lips shut tight! Now look to the man on your left! Your left! And look to the man on your right! Your left! If he's talking you'd better think twice! Your left! Report 'im at once—now that's right! Your left! For all you know he's a spy! Your left! And he's talking to trick you—that's right! Your left! Sound off! One, two. Sound off! Three, four. Sound off! One, two, three, four, sound off! That's *right*! Suddenly he stops, at full attention. . . . But isn't it a contradiction, respected guests?— and he bows deeply before me, holding the baby with only one hand—Is it not a contradiction that in a place where supposedly life is what the struggle is all about, instead terror reigns, and the cult, the obligatory adoration of a single person, is raised to dizzying heights, and persecution and absolute enslavement are the order of the day? . . . Step right this way to the marvel! This way to the wondrous creation! Give me your attention, please, dictators of the world, hurry, hurry, hurry! Step right this way! . . . And again he raises the baby, who goes on screaming. Hector, I say, clutching him, please, give me the baby. He looks at him and smiles, and keeps him in his arms. You! he says to him. Why are you crying? Does not great happiness await you? The perfect future? The shining paradise? . . . Hector, please, I say to him. . . . Suddenly he begins to sing. He sings hoarsely, as though he'd been up all night, while he walks about the living room. And the triumphant words? he says. And the triumphant words? he says singing. And then suddenly, behind him, without knowing why, I start singing too. The two of us, accompanied by the crying of the baby, skip all around the living room of the cabin, stumble against the furniture, knock over the wine bottles, an ashtray, and sing. *And the triumphant words?* says Hector, aping the gravelly voice of a baritone. *And the triumphant words?* he says, we say. . . . He falls onto the couch still singing and holding the baby. Triumphant words! Triumphant words! I go, singing too, over to where they are. I collapse between them. Instinctively I put the baby between Hector and me so he doesn't fall to the floor. I pass my sweaty hand over his face, slowly, slowly, to calm him. I feel a terrible urge to vomit. The feeling rises through my stomach and reaches my throat; then, unstoppable, it makes me retch. Finally, while I caress the baby's face with one hand, I pick my head up off the couch and vomit on the floor. The baby's crying isn't so loud anymore. Not much, not so much, almost not at all. I lean back next to them, calmer. I go on touching his face, not so much, not so quickly, less and less, more slowly, more—like his crying, that you no longer hear. Nothing. Who said, "Meatballs!"? Who said, "I prefer meatballs"? Who said, "As far as I'm concerned there's nothing like meatballs"? Who? . . . What surprises me the most, I say then, raising my free arm and pointing toward where the ruined city was, is that you don't hear any trumpets, nobody is announcing the end; perhaps, I say, and my other arm is falling off, that could be our comfort—it's not quite going the way we'd always thought. . . . And a pain, that I suddenly cannot locate anywhere in my body, begins to awaken in me. I open my eyes. Everything is white, shining in the evening light. I close and open my eyes again. It must be clouds, I think. Sometimes it happens like that, my mother tells me, it's the play of light on the clouds; it's a sign of rain. Look at the rainbow, look at the rainbow. That too is nothing but a play of light. . . . At last I identify, locate, the pain—it's in the arm Hector has trapped under his body. I try to get free without waking him. But he opens his eyes, Hector white. He closes his eyes again. The baby is still sleeping, lying against his throat. The baby white. At last I manage to free my arm. I open the refrigerator. I eat a little of the salad, using my fingers. This is refreshing, I think; maybe it'll get rid of this lethargy of mine. The smell of liquor permeates the cabin. I'd better have a bath. I undress. I get under the shower. The first stream of water is really cold. But as it falls it grows warmer. Without soaping myself, motionless, I let the water fall over me. The water falls. I feel the water fall. It hits my head; it slides over my shoulders; it rolls down my body, runs down my legs, and slips across the floor. At this moment, I think, it's getting dark. At this moment time is passing, time is passing. But the water goes on falling. I am taking a bath while night falls. I am bathing. Through the bathroom's high window, through the screen, I can see the sky taking on, as it always does, the intense violet of this time of day. The sky and the smell of time, the smell of leaves, the singed smell of earth that was waiting today too for a cooling shower, for rain. Perfume. The smell of trees that take darkness as a comfort. The smell of ocean and pine trees, the imperceptible fragrance of oleanders, the smell of almond trees. The smell of the ocean. All the odors of earth wash over my naked body the water is falling and falling on. I look at my dripping body. I look at my body. This is my body, I think. My God, Holy Mother, this is my body. The smells begin to fade. The violet disappears too. I go on bathing, in near darkness. I go on feeling the water falling over me, running over my body, caressing, caressing, caressing. Water.

But how do you describe that—what it feels like to bathe in the dark, when all the perfumes have faded, though we know such smells never were; how can you *say* that, that in the dark, stung by the spray, a woman is nothing but a shivering body that needs and cries out and sometimes pleads; how to express the numbness of this flesh still young for a while, but mark my words, only for a while. How can one express the anguish of knowing that besides this body you have nothing, and nothing will last, and nothing will belong to you; and this body not even a cause for happiness but simply the place where once in a while other passions, unsatisfied too, try to find satisfaction. . . . My body becoming a fantasy too, not *being* any longer, refusing to be simply a body *per se*. How it needs you, no one knows how this flesh needs you; poor conquered, conquered flesh. How can one express to someone else that there is not just one meaning of the word *conquered. Conquered*—not only by the habit of centuries, by brutal customs that perhaps, someday, I'm not sure, may be overcome, but also by the irrevocable condition of being a less highly developed force, vigor, by the condition of being hole that submits and not protuberance that penetrates. How can you explain—and I turn off the shower and begin to dry myself off although I didn't soap myself down. Now I discover, now I fully know, that we women are not their object, that we have never been, or will be, that the ideal object does not exist, that the body truly longed-for does not exist and that that is precisely why they come to us. We are simply the ones in charge of keeping the perpetual hunger within bounds; we are the penetrable shadows of a nonexistent ideal—and if it did exist, it would be they themselves, they themselves, who don't use themselves because they can't penetrate themselves. Listen, listen, then perhaps it would be better that way; perhaps it would be, is, better for them to come to an understanding among themselves; at least that way, perhaps, they might get closer to themselves, closer to finding themselves, might even be satisfied one day. . . . I get dressed, turn out the bedroom light, and go out onto the porch. There is Hector, quiet now, playing with the baby. I go back into the kitchen, pour a little milk into the bottle, attach the nipple; I go back out onto the porch. I take the baby and begin feeding him. He takes it without a peep, starving. Hector is still sitting with the radio on the arm of the chair, but not turned on. The ocean goes from dark blue to gray, from gray to black. A few lights begin to come on far away out on the water; they go out, come on, wink on and off sporadically. Everything in these seconds is somehow suspended—quiet, breathing slowly, enjoying a respite that will not last, in fact sometimes doesn't come at all. The whistling of the cicadas stops. From the darkness the sound of the waves and the breeze through the pine grove begin to whisper. Once more the fragrance of night envelops us. The last swimmers leave the beach. Somewhere far off, a cow moos, or someone makes a sound like that. A woman carrying two jugs walks in front of our cabin. Hector turns on the radio. The music swells and subsides, floats and falls, like the ocean. I listen to that music and look at my hands. Nothing out of the ordinary, I think; it's nothing that should move me, I think, and yet I know that I am trembling. I look at my hands again, my body standing out against, floating in, the darkness. For a moment I think once again that we still haven't swiped that light bulb. I look at my hands again, my arms; I listen to the music that seems to fade away from time to time. It always happens to me—any song at all, some popular song, heard in passing as I cross a street, ride in a full bus, will strike me suddenly, startle me. One hears that music and wonders, But why, why does everything have to be like this? And there is no answer. And for the few moments that the song that surprised you goes on flowing, you travel as though against the current of time, as though ignorant of time, asking yourself troubling questions no one will ever answer. Then, when it's all over, you're puzzled to find yourself in the place you are now. . . . Until at last you recover yourself a bit, get your bearings again. . . . But now the music flows, floods the darkness, while I look at my body. And the questioning begins again. And the music goes on. But What is it that you would have different? I ask myself. Where is the error? Because there must doubtless have been some error, something at the beginning or very close to the beginning must have gotten twisted, gotten broken, and since then we have gone along disoriented, not even knowing the origins of our misfortune, not even knowing what our misfortune really is. And the music ripples, subsides, floats and flows, like the ocean. I look at my body again, I look at the night again, the pine grove that is now just a wide silhouette melding into the darker silhouette of the ocean. My body grows paler, floating. . . . There are the grains of sand, still under my nails—my nails, white too, floating. I look at myself, sitting, here, while the baby goes on drinking in my lap. I look at him, at the baby. And the music goes on. I look at myself, all of me, with the baby on my lap, sitting on this porch in the darkness, and I listen to the music rising and falling. *Seated Woman with Child.* Do I say that? Does Hector think it? Did he think it and I say it? Did he say it and I repeat it? *Woman with Child. Mother and Child.* . . . And suddenly I feel that it's all just too much, and something starts coming over me. Take the baby! I shout to Hector. I stand up and almost throw him into his arms. And I run between the cabins, toward the pine grove. Goblets! Goblets! Goblets! I say laughing, as I cross the avenue of the oleanders. Goblets! Goblets! Goblets! I love the word *goblets*, and I go on repeating it and running and roaring with laughter. Goblets! Goblets! I repeat over and over as I run along the shore, and I feel stones pierce my feet. Goblets! I say and run into the bogs where the seagrapes grow. Goblets! And I run in and out of the fortress where at this moment the English are disembarking. And I go on—goblets!—and here are the fishermen—goblets!—carrying out their old mission, here the stones—goblets!—I run across without feeling them—goblets!— the outcroppings the ocean crashes against, and here the sea urchins—goblets!—that stab my knees and the soles of my feet, here the lush jellyfish I squash with my feet, my elbows, my hands—goblets!—and with my face. But I stand up—goblets!— and go on, walking; I cross the pine grove once more—goblets!— the avenue of oleanders—goblets!—and go up the steps to the cabin. I go in. Hector doesn't say a word to me—goblets!—he seems to have understood everything. In silence I put the baby to bed—goblets!—fix our bed—goblets!—put up the mosquito net—goblets! We go to bed without speaking. For a few seconds before the light is turned off, I see Hector's body—goblets!— Hector's waist—goblets!—Hector naked—goblets!—lying face up. Hector pretending to snore beside me—goblets!—me, the one who's exhausted. My God, the diapers! Today I had to wash the diapers! . . . Goblets! Goblets! Goblets! When, when . . . When the first *clang* sounds we both stop biting our toes and crying and we go out onto the shining esplanade. Stepping over the skeletons of men and animals, pushing our way through bones that at times pile up into real mountains (such have been the hunger and the plagues), we go on, sweaty, and now take our place in the great line for bread. At that moment sounds the second *clang*. A woman whose face has been eaten away by worms (or perhaps she herself has torn off the flesh) tells us *I was last.* And she looks at us with furious flashing eyes; she breaks into a harsh laugh but instantly brings herself under control and looks daggers at us again. Hector and I are in our place. People keep making their way through the moans and cries and curses, taking their place in the line. The end of the line is lost now in the farthest ruins of the city. The sun, implacable, rises in the sky, snorts, stops at the zenith, and sets in to fry us to a crisp. This line, like all of them, follows that customary pattern. A woman pulls out her hair while she kicks a young boy. You wretch, she says, I told you to come earlier, look at the place we've got. . . . Two other women, older, begin to argue loudly. . . . An old queer three or four people away from us starts talking to the boy ahead of him while gazing at his fly; the boy seems to ignore him completely but then, casually, begins to pay him a little heed. The old man goes on talking. . . . Water! Water! a man cries hoarsely. Water! he says, jumping up and down with his fists raised. Suddenly he turns to smoke. . . . The woman beside him begins to swell up, roars, keeps swelling, starts to boil, and at last pops, spewing streams of boiling water that carbonizes several people and blinds many others. She deserved it. She was hogging water, some people whisper. . . . The murmur swells, becomes daringly loud. . . . Thieves who have infiltrated the breadline fill their pockets with arms, fingers, pieces of ass, and even the heads of their victims. I look at Hector and tremble; I think that the person behind him could be a thief waiting for just the right moment to pull off some part of his body; but fortunately it's a woman, and she is looking at Hector with what appears to be a very different intention. I don't say a word, I look straight ahead and study the line, which winds and doubles on itself—I watch the people who violently enter it, those who want to butt ahead, those who utter threats, and those who utter death rattles. Situation normal. . . . I lean back against Hector. I look at the woman ahead of us and I see her suddenly blanch. From the line there rises a deafening scream that silences all the other screaming. Everyone points toward one side of the esplanade. Immediately there reigns the silence of the grave. The soldiers in charge of keeping order are appearing, bearing shining spears and swords. Now a third *clang* sounds. The mob is frightened and everyone huddles together in the line; some people groan softly, others hold their breath. The soldiers pass slowly in review. Water! suddenly shouts a woman, and vanishes into thin air. Silence, or you die! the soldiers order. One single line! they repeat furiously (raising their swords), although we are all already like that. Nonetheless, from time to time, perhaps to show how serious this operation is, they kick or decapitate someone. Now a handsome, dashing soldier takes out a knife, goes up to a child crying softly, cuts off one of its ears, and puts it in his pocket. At this moment they pass by Hector and me and they look at us grimly. I feel an immense relief (almost happiness) when I see them move on, cursing at an almost imperceptible sway in the line. *This line must be straight!* one cries; *if there is another curve we'll straighten it out with our bayonets!* And suddenly all the swords and spears turn into long rifles with bayonets fixed and gleaming. The line becomes so straight that not an arm or leg of those in it sticks out. It is a line on the sizzling earth. It's so hot, complains Hector, taking advantage of the soldiers' distance from us. Uh-huh, I say, and watch the old fag still chatting with the boy. The boy, with a mean face, says a few words to him too; from time to time he puckers his lips and spits, but it evaporates before it hits the ground. The two old women are arguing louder now; sometimes they raise an arm or fist threateningly at each other. The line begins to come alive again. The woman with the rotting face lifts her hand to the level of my eyes. Look! she says, and her finger-nails begin growing; they reach the sky and descend again. This is for you, she says, and roars with laughter. I look toward Hector, but Hector at this moment is watching the old queer and the tough-faced boy softly talking together. The woman's fingernails begin to grow again, descend. The stinking gas from the bodies of all the people and the animals killed by us or by the plagues (or by both at once) suddenly blows over us and bursts into flame, killing several people. Immediately the crowd, who can no longer be controlled, throw themselves onto the victims. But the Reserves, watching from parapets high on the roofs, are quick to the moment and kill the mutineers, make a huge pyre of the bodies, and set it afire. Calm returns. At this moment the fourth *clang* is heard. When will our turn come? I say; it doesn't look like they've even started to give out the first crumb. The woman with the fingernails looks at me disgustedly; then she begins to cry; then she roars once more with laughter. A soldier comes up to a very old lady next to her, grabs her by the neck, and throws her onto the flaming pyre. No doubt he thought it was the old lady who had laughed. Now everyone holds his breath. Only the crackle of the earth and the burning bodies can be heard. The young soldier with the impenetrable face reviews the line once more. Suddenly he stops before a girl standing a few people away from us. The heat is unbearable. The soldier yanks the girl out of the line. At once he unbuttons his fly and takes out his already erect member. Suck it, he says to the girl. She falls to her knees and begins to suck it with soft moans and whimpers. The impassive soldier looks straight ahead and orders the girl to hurry—if she doesn't make him come in ten seconds he'll throw her onto the fire. The girl gobbles at the soldier's great length, strokes it with her lips, tries to swallow it and retches, coughing and sobbing. *Seven!* the soldier says now. The girl clings with both hands to the soldier's hips and bobs her head rapidly over the head of his member. *Eight!* says the soldier. The girl runs her tongue all around the soldier's phallus, tickles him with her teeth, slowly, tremblingly caresses his huge testicles, takes the whole length of it down her throat. *Nine!* the soldier says, casting an impassive, imperturbable glance of hatred at the girl, who is now groaning and gasping as she rubs the gleaming member across her eyes, her hair; she strokes it with her hands, she begins to kiss it desperately. As she is about to gobble it down again, the soldier says *Ten!* and kicks her violently away. The girl struggles; she tries to seize the rigid phallus again. One second, she says, one more second and you'll see. . . . Her last words issue from the flames. The soldier, annoyed, stuffs his member back into his pants but then looks at the flaming pyre and begins to masturbate to the rhythm of the cries of the roasting people. Now he is utterly absorbed in his task. The line, which during these moments has been terrified, becomes a little more animated. The two old women argue loudly, the old queer rubs the tough-faced boy's fly, the tough-faced boy puts his hands in his pockets. I look toward the front of the line lost in the distance. It looks like today, I say without anger (almost resignedly), we won't get our ration either. Exhausted, I lean once more against Hector, who is watching the flaming pyre. The soldier's masturbation ends. The semen sizzles as it sprays over the flames. The heat grows worse. Another woman begs for water, lets out a howl, and evaporates without even giving the soldiers time to burn her. A man who still has one usable eye begins to read. Two soldiers come down from their parapet, grab the book away from him, and thumb through it a second. Man and book cut down the glare of the flames a bit as they fall. The woman with the fingernails looks at me again and lets out another peal of laughter. You son of a bitch, a counterwhisper-trained soldier says to a boy near the woman, you know you can't laugh here. Before the accused boy can defend himself he is thrown onto the fire. The woman howls with laughter again, turns, and looks at me in silence with her flashing eyes. This time the soldier blames it on a young man, who is also thrown to the fire. Cocksuckers, the soldier now yells, cupping his testicles through his pants, one more laugh and I'll have the whole line machine-gunned. Instantly the sentries' rifles become gleaming machine guns. The new weapons are aimed right at us. Silence returns. I look at the rotten-faced woman. She looks at me too; she raises both her hands. Her fingernails once more reach the sky. As the fifth *clang* sounds her nails begin to shrink. The soldier gazes fixedly at us. The old ladies who were arguing stand rigid and silent. The old faggot, his eyes half closed, looks like he's asleep; the boy, beside him, still has his hands in his pockets and the stony expression on his face. I look furtively at the woman behind us and see her caressing her thigh and looking at Hector. The soldiers walk away. Now the woman looks somewhere else (she has no doubt given up on Hector); she begins to chat with the man behind her. The man wastes no time and begins brazenly to massage his member. The woman, now delighted, goes on talking and watching. The line begins to stir. Smoke from the great pyre totally envelops us, the foul dust of the esplanade blows over us in gusts. Some people take advantage of the soldiers' absence to cough; others relieve themselves. The old women argue in raised voices now; the old queer now caresses the mean-faced boy's bulging pants as the boy stares straight ahead and casually whistles. Everyone chats or hurls insults at each other. The couple next to us begin to screw, moaning and gasping frantically. I look at Hector again and see that he is very pale, so pale that I fear he is about to evaporate. But I touch him. He is here, I say, and listen more calmly to the constantly rising hum. The bodies squeezed together go on screwing. The soldiers, now with their backs to us, talk in pairs on the high parapets; perhaps they are having lunch. . . . At times a cloud of dust blocks my vision; other times, I seem to see only a single confused body. The sun is still fixed in the center of the sky. The sixth *clang* sounds. Suddenly the woman with the changing fingernails writhes, rips off one of her breasts, stands on tiptoe; she takes a deep breath. *Chevrolet!* she cries in a voice that thunders over the murmur. We are all paralyzed. Fornications are suspended, arguments hang in the air, crotch-rubbers stand with motionless hands, insults go unspoken, blows are checked. The counterwhisper-trained soldiers also stand fast; others, awaiting orders, seem turned to stone as well. *Chevrolet!* the woman repeats; she jumps out of line and plants herself on the crackling earth behind the flames. *Air conditioning!* she shouts now, in an even more powerful voice, and rips off her other breast. A hum begins to surge from the line. The reviving soldiers, although still ash-pale and confused, aim at us from the parapets; the others follow suit. *Silence,* cry loudspeakers that rise up suddenly all along the line. But the woman, now almost in the midst of the fire, this time yells, *1969 Oldsmobile,* and rips out her throat. The hum grows louder again. *Hi-fi's!* she shouts from the blaze, tearing the skin off her face. The roar becomes deafening. While I think, with alarming certainty, that any second they are going to start firing on us, the piercing scream of an old woman is heard. *Singer sewing machines!* she yells in a voice that makes the whole crumbling city shiver. *Singer sewing machines!* she repeats as she rends her chest with her fingers, pulls out her liver, and throws it onto the fire. *Singer, Singer!* she cries as she expires. The murmur rises instantly. The soldiers stand pallid and unmoving once more. A wild-looking woman howls on all fours. *Electric washing machines!* she cries, and throws her head onto the pyre. For a second the flames seem to go out. *Taca T-shirts!* says a tall crippled man now. *Taca T-shirts!* he cries and at the same time takes a long nail from his tattered pants and begins to plunge it over and over into his forehead. *Taca! Taca! Taca!* becomes his death rattle. *Chevrolet! Chevrolet! Chevrolet!* cries the woman with the fingernails, leaping among the flames. *Chevrolet!* she exclaims, smoldering as she jumps from the flames, reinspiring the crowd. For a moment I see her nails pierce the sky again. *A pair of roller skates! A pair of roller skates with rubber wheels!* cries a boy striking his chest and hopping around the woman with variable nails. *Lilly dolls!* shouts a little girl in the midst of the glare as she bites at an old lady's ankle. *Ingelmo shoes!* says a respectable-looking but unkempt man, hopping barefoot on one foot and slitting his throat. *La Española chocolate!* enunciates the cultured voice of a pale thin girl. Immediately she opens her bag, takes out a bottle of gasoline (kept for who knows how long), sprinkles the fuel all over herself, and strikes a match. *La Española chocolate!* now says the ball of fire as it vanishes into the ruined city. *Ham! Ham! Ham!* the two old ladies scream at each other as they yank each other's ears and kick each other in the stomach. *Pitusa Pants!* proclaim several teenagers as they beat each other to a pulp. *Jockey shorts!* says the tough-faced boy and wrings the old faggot's neck, who expires repeating, *Pond's cold cream, Pond's cold cream, Pond's cold cream!* . . . *Coca-Cola!* cries the thundering voice of the woman with variable fingernails, and, dancing beside the fire, she pulls out her hair and peels off the skin of her stomach. *Coca-Cola!* shouts the mob in a frenzied chorus. They stumble against each other, hit one another, begin to devour one another. Meanwhile, the seventh *clang* is heard. For a while the battle goes on like that—everyone devouring everyone else, rhythmically, as though they were performing a prescribed series of gymnastic exercises. I look toward the man and woman behind us; they go on screwing while at the same time biting out chunks of each other's faces and gobbling them down. The eighth *clang* sounds. The soldiers manage to recuperate from the impact of all this and unleash their weapons on the crowd. (A hot stream of blood spatters my face; it's from a man who was crying *Siré cookies!* while he ate his own hand.) The first discharge of the machine guns wipes out a third of the members of this frenzied line, that is to say, of the whole world. Multiplying loudspeakers cry out for order and threaten to repeat the attack. No one listens. The clatter of the machine guns is heard again and another third of the line, which was chanting *Chocolate malts! Vanilla malts! Strawberry malts!*, falls to the blitz. The survivors, repeating *Velveeta cheese!*, immediately begin devouring the victims. The voice over the loudspeakers sounds stern: *We will be forced to use tanks!* As I attempt to free myself from a woman trying with all her might to cut off one of my arms, I see the gleam of hundreds of tanks in the distance, coming toward us, stirring up dust, human remains, stones, and banners, drowning out the noise of the crowd, which is crying *French fries!* as the woman with the fingernails leads them in their chant. The tanks are now upon us; they take aim. The ninth *clang* sounds, and a quarter of those left in the line are shot down. But the survivors, now not even pausing over the dead bodies, advance on the tanks to cries of

French fries! The struggle takes on unimagined proportions. The cannons, out of control, fire into the air, into the thin clouds, shatter the loudspeakers, tear the high parapets apart. For a moment only the fury of the tanks attacking the reddened sky is heard, and the havoc of the surviving multitude, who scramble over the tanks to the cry of *French fries!* and strangle their drivers and set fire to the complicated machinery. *If order is not restored,* now shout the loudspeakers from the monument in the Plaza Cívica, *we will be forced to use more advanced weapons!* But not only does the disturbance not calm down, it actually grows worse. The plaza begins to boil. The battle is taking place amid the flames. The survivors devour the soldiers who cannot escape. Suddenly I make out the woman with the variable fingernails on top of the National Library. *Bread!* she cries in a deep voice that silences the noise of the battle—and with that one blow the building begins to collapse. *French bread!* she cries from atop the ruins and leaps cleanly onto the Armed Forces building. *Sugared anise rolls!* she roars as she reduces the huge plate-glass windows to shards. *Party buns!* she shouts, and reduces a whole terrace to rubble. *Sandwich bread!* she shouts, and kicks down the reception hall. *Corn-flour muffins!* she clamors, and levels even the foundations, leaping clear to the Ministry of the Interior. *Crescent rolls!* she shrieks, and attacks the antennas, towers, and windows of this building too. The feverish multitude contemplates her from the scalding plaza. *Black bread!* she says now, destroying the Palacio de la Revolución with a single kick. *Chala bread!* she clamors, and knocks down the Castillo del Príncipe prison with one blow. *Bread and butter!* she shouts and pulls down the Granma newspaper building. *Sesame bread! Braided loaves! Thick graham cookies!* she cries over the screams and loud sobbing as she methodically destroys the CTC Theater, the Palace of Justice, and the Olive Green magazine building. *Raisin bread!* she clamors, running and reducing El Morro prison to rubble; from there she springs to the Hotel Nacional. *Italian bread!* she shouts, and we all watch as the old building collapses into the streets with a crash of bricks, glass, furniture, concrete-reinforcing rods, and bugging devices. *Whole-wheat bread!* she exclaims at the top of her lungs, and with an extraordinary blow of her fist topples the Foxa Building, the tallest in the city, which creaks painfully as it goes down. *Pound cake!* she says now, shouting, taking flight and destroying all the buildings, the most elegant houses, the statues and official monuments. The mob, screaming *Bread, bread, bread,* runs through the city and begins destroying everything, even picking through the rubble and reducing it to dust. One commission, repeating *Nut bread!* over and over, takes charge of obliterating all traces of the parks with their police stations in the middle; another, shouting *Rye bread!,* eliminates the public buildings that are still standing; the third group, crying *Toast!,* destroys official vehicles (which are the only vehicles left). *Crullers!* shouts the fifth commission and sets about pulling down radio stations, airports, printing presses, and military bases. And thousands of smaller subcommissions (to one of which Hector and I belong) have as their mission pulverizing the rubble and throwing to the wind everything that can't be put to the torch. So gnashing our teeth, devouring ourselves (for we cannot control ourselves either), we take over the entire city and spread disaster everywhere. Now the tenth *clang* sounds. The sky clouds over with aircraft. Their roar momentarily drowns out the cries of the various commissions smashing and destroying the city. Then bombs begin to fall. The untiring throng, kicking and biting, runs through the ruins, topples anything that has miraculously managed to remain standing, even picking up stones, and hurls it all to smash against the airplanes. The air darkens with bones, heads, and fragments of columns, statues, and banners. Below, the chase intensifies. The crowd goes on moving through the debris. A woman seized with labor pains lies down in the dust. The chorus of children eagerly waits for the baby to come out so they can devour it. Let me eat my mother! shouts a mortally wounded man pursued by the unwearying chorus. I was just about to grab her, I was right beside her! he says and expires, without satisfying his desire. The chorus of children gobbles him up with real gusto. The two old women who were arguing in the line pass before me; they are torn completely to pieces but are still wrangling with each other. The aerial loudspeakers go on threatening, but you can no longer make out exactly what they are saying. Deafening explosions come from one side of the city. Amid the explosions and the rising smoke, dust, and shards of glass, I make out the woman with the fingernails, shouting *Rye bread!* and pulling down even the most distant suburbs. . . . Two soldiers are ripping each other apart in the rubble. At last the battle seems to get organized. The pursuit seems to take shape, be ruled by some mysterious law. Each person hunts down a single adversary (no matter who), who also hunts another victim, who in his turn hunts the next. . . . When two people, hunter and hunted, come together, the rest go on with their objectives, their goals, without taking part in the feast. The children begin to hunt each other down too, making the battle even noisier, even fiercer. You can hear explosions closer now. A distant tower, still miraculously standing, suddenly disappears in the burning air. Through the crash of the battle I make out the woman with the fingernails, almost totally flayed but still haranguing, speaking now in a thundering voice, naming thousands of products whose existence we had completely forgotten for years and years. Brand names of TV sets, curtains, styles of houses, clothing, records, butter, travel agents, kinds of beans, brand names of cigarettes and beer, names of distant beaches, perfumes, titles of movies, books, plays, songs, magazines, and symphonies, kinds of mineral water, rugs, carpets, umbrellas, hair dyes, innerspring mattresses, medicines, belts, hammers, flashlights, light bulbs, handkerchiefs, and handbags. . . . It is all listed in an incredible roar, with implacable power, above the explosions, above the constant crashing, and across the utter desolation. Mutilated bodies fly through the air, blood flows, horrible insults are heard, the most startling commotions, the most shocking screams; but over the crashing blows, the gnashing teeth, the piercing shrapnel, the smashing fists and dying bodies, over the whole erupting city turned to whirling dust, the woman with the fingernails is heard displaying her seemingly infinite vocabulary. She now goes through an immense catalog of home products: *pressure cookers,* she cries, *aluminum pans, enamelware, plastic pails, fans, plumber's helpers, stainless-steel washtubs and stainless-steel spoons, pot scrubbers, corkscrews, clothespins, table lamps, crystal glasses.* . . . And she goes on and on, like a professional orator. She leaps over the last debris, dances over the mutilated bodies; transformed into a talking tornado, she whirls above the dust; she appears, she springs up, she fades echoing away; she cracks like a whip and revives the din everywhere, drowning out the latest warnings from the loudspeakers, the latest *clang*. While I, we, listen to that voice now reciting every single variety of deodorant the world has seen, I look skyward and see the jets. And all of a sudden there is a great cloud of dust, the final bang. An invisible fire begins to cover the city, melting the electric fences that surround it so no one can leave, spreading through the air to the last whisper-detection and threat-spreading installation. The invisible fire reaches the ground; the battle freezes. Hair, eyes, skin, flesh, all melt away. In an instant the city fills with skeletons, and then those melt too. Unable to shout, scream, I watch my hair flow down across my eyes, watch Hector fall to pieces; both of us, using all our strength, putting on one last effort, begin to run through the rubble and shards of bone, toward the ocean. We come to the Malecón and manage, to the sound of death all around us, to scale the promontory formed by the wall. Without the strength even to throw ourselves into the sea, we look back at the ex-city in ruins—ruins which now disappear themselves, becoming emptiness. Then we turn toward the ocean. From the water spiders begin to emerge, and then hens, crocodiles, rats, deformed fish, turtles, parrots, a huge golden shark, a boy's mutilated body, snakes, crickets, Indians in loincloths, lizards, enraged old sirens, crabs, suits of armor, a dog that doesn't bark, screws, dinosaurs, and animals and objects I cannot name. They all dance maddened on the surface, try to escape that boiling pond, grunting as they try to climb up the boulders, but finally they too fall apart, dissolve. I turn my head toward the destroyed city. For a second I think I can still hear the woman with the fingernails, now naming every kind of canned meat placed on the market shelves of the world during the last year. . . . But it is all a great silence. I feel, now with no pain, one of my arms falling off and see it rolling toward the seething water. I turn and see Hector, silent, losing his extremities too. What's strangest of all to me, I say then, waving my only remaining arm toward the place where once the city was which now is in ruins, is that there are no trumpets blowing, no one is announcing the end; perhaps, I say, and now my other arm is coming loose, this may serve as a comfort to us—It has not quite come to pass as it was promised. . . . The pain in my arm returns; once more the consciousness of pain, which I now locate in my arm, returns. Once more Hector, without realizing it, has lain on top of me. I open my eyes. It is still night. Everything is clear, but it is still night. I can make out, through the mosquito net and the shutters, the glow of dawn; I can even see, if I raise my head from the

pillow a bit, two or three stars twinkling, and the moon. My God, because I can hardly believe it, the moon still exists. The moon in transit, floating behind a thin curtain of transparent clouds—as light as this mosquito net I have just awakened under. I watch that glow fade into the more implacable glow of day and I think, Somewhere, someplace in the world, someone is waiting for me, someone needs me. Somewhere there must be more than this violence and loneliness, this stupidity, laziness, chaos, and stupor which are killing us. . . . Somewhere someone is waiting for me. Someone like me, seeing time pass, hoping. Perhaps the object of that hope is me; perhaps he is the object of mine. And while he waits and hopes, there, we are both growing older; while we both wait, not coming any nearer each other, we are aging and dying. . . . And thus, while we are slowly dying, everything is held in abeyance, in waiting. And we are living—that is, going on— doing all the things we do, as though this life, as though these things, were not really reality, as though the meaning of life, its end, its very motions, were other, which we could not manage to glimpse but that surely, we suspect, is not *this*. . . . But then, I say to myself, What is it, what is it? What is the meaning behind all these gestures, these actions (repeated a thousand times over, and a thousand times over ineffectual), behind this show of reality? . . . No one is waiting for me, I think; no one—anywhere— awaits me; but nonetheless time (that glow, that sense of being cheated, this stinging that doesn't seem to come from anyplace in particular) passes, and while I gather up the dirty diapers and throw them in the washbasin, while I turn on the tap and start soaking them, I grow older, and he who might have been waiting for me, he whom I don't know, he who doesn't exist, somewhere else, doing useless things too (as I am doing now), other disgusting things (as I am doing now), grows older too, is dying too, little by little; perhaps at this very moment he has just gasped and stiffened. . . . But listen, listen, what are you thinking? What do you solve with these flights of imagination? . . . I scrub the diapers, rubbing the heels of my hands together in the water, scrubbing the excrement from the diapers. *Mother Washing Her Months-Old Son's Shitty Diapers.* Behold a true action, from which a product, an end may result: the washing of the diapers. Limit your hopes to that, to the possible result of possible efforts; to the outcome of actions dictated by custom and habit, sanctioned by repetition. I have not seen, nor have I heard, him who awaits me; he has not sent me a sign. Therefore, he does not exist. Or perhaps the one who waits for me does exist, but I am not interested, and as I am not interested I pay him no heed, and as I pay him no heed it is impossible for me to catch his signals. Perhaps the fact that he is waiting for me is all it takes for me not to be interested. I think, I reach the honest conclusion: Hector is the only man who really interests me, the only man I really wait for, the only man I wish were waiting for me some(nonexistent)where. But, I think once more, the fact that I feel passion for him makes him feel less than even concern for me. Because listen to me, listen, if there's anyone not waiting for you it's him, I'm certain of that. He's not waiting for anyone, and there is no communication possible between us; we are no more than the excuse for a conspiracy. We use each other to conceal our shortcomings. I make him into the object of my love; he makes me into the object that holds him back, maddens him, defines him, and protects him. But I am sometimes also the object of a sacrifice on his part, I also demand that the game be played out down to the last move. And the rules, sometimes, are observed: He is then the object of my desire; I, his outlet. But perhaps, I think, and raise my arms toward the sun, and wring out the now white diapers and hang them on the clothesline behind the cabin, what is most terrible and frightening is not that state of things, but rather the fact that we are conscious of it. And I contemplate my work (the diapers hung out to dry) in the sunshine. The sun, I say, and I think, Our relations have reached a point of no further evolution, no hope of change (and I wave to Hector, who is watching me from the bedroom door), because before, listen (and I go into the bedroom and pick up the baby and give him his milk), before, you had the consolation of ignorance (and now the three of us head for the beach), the consolation of ignorance, the consolation of ignorance. . . . The three of us on the sand, contemplating the ocean. *(The consolation of ignorance.*) . . . What is the ocean to a few-months-old child? How does he interpret the ocean? What might the ocean be for him? How does he feel the ocean? Hector, lying in the sand, throws him up, catches him in his hands, and he laughs deeply, delightedly. I look up. The white ocean begins to turn yellow; the yellow ocean takes on a pink tinge; the pink ocean throws off that color and turns white again, bathed in a leaden light. The clouds retreat; the pines are reflected on the water. The ocean is now infinitely green. Who would imagine that only moments ago it was otherwise? Who could imagine, looking at that stability, that firmness of color, that the ocean had ever been a shade that wasn't green? I turn over, knowing that for a time, perhaps all morning, it will not change. Over there under the almond trees, near our car, I make out the mother and the boy headed down toward the beach. Hector goes on throwing the baby up in the air. The brightness intensifies. The glare now penetrates the balcony, strips the furniture of its least shred of comfort, the most insignificant mystery, all sense of intimacy, familiarity, pity. Attended—flooded—by the brightness, I go out onto the balcony. Here the brightness becomes even more intense. *Summer will come,* I think. *Here is the summer once more,* I say aloud, from the balcony of the house, looking at the ocean, all one sparkling, beating blue. The racket of the street—motors, horns, squealing brakes, shouting, even the bang of a tire that just blew out—suddenly grows louder: *Summer,* I say aloud to myself. *Summer.* . . . How is it possible for me to be alive if summer is here once more? If summer is always here? What have you done with the time? What have you done with your life? Summer. . . . I feel, run my hand over, my growing, growing belly. And how could I have imagined what it is like to have such a belly? How could I have imagined, if I never had been one, a big-bellied woman's terror? How could I have imagined that this wouldn't work for me either, that nothing would be kept at bay, that nothing would bring us closer? I turn and leave the balcony, thinking, *Ah, summer once more, once more this glare.* . . . I go into the bedroom. I look at myself for a long time. My face has slowly been covered with smudges as though by a vague shadow, my legs have swollen; my stomach has grown so large I feel deformed. The two of us sitting by lamplight in the middle of the living room, without saying a word to each other, after dinner. He is reading and I feel the baby kick inside me. Listen, I suddenly say, and take Hector's hand and place it on my belly; he feels the throbbing and we look at each other and smile; then silence returns. We live now as though everything had already been said, as though there were nothing left to discover between us. We live now as though we bore each other only with great difficulty. Making an effort not to make each other angry, not to explode. He comes in. I serve dinner. We sit down. We eat in silence or, worse, speak without saying anything to each other; and I have a feeling that behind his simplest words, behind his silences, there is a kind of violence, a kind of accent or shade of insult, a kind of old resentment, a kind of desire to object, which dissolves into accepting monosyllables. But what is the cause of this? I say to myself. And the baby jumps, kicks within my womb. My step becomes heavier and heavier, my figure more and more grotesque. The baby inflames my knees, disfigures my neck, covers my face with blackheads and my stomach with blue veins, gives me dark bags under my eyes; it arouses an uncontainable voracity in me. I go back to the mirror, go back to examining my body. And what have I solved? I think, and touch and pinch my shadowed face; I examine my hands, their swollen joints, and feel the throbbing, throbbing, throbbing inside myself, devouring. . . . Oh, God! And this thing throbbing in my womb is the product of our desperation, our cowardice. For Hector, a definition; for me, a measure of security. But listen, listen, that thing throbbing in your belly is first of all a human being, a thing that will demand, cry when it's hungry, ask for and be satisfied when you give it attention. And I go on thinking that, more and more every day, we are being destroyed— in order to live we renounce our freedom, compromise ourselves further and further, we stop being alive, grow more and more guilty, contributing to this state of things. Because this throbbing thing will be a man. It will suffer—and suffer, endure, as well— of course, provided it isn't an idiot; it will feel hounded, harassed, out of place, malcontent, alienated, left out—will feel too that there is another reality, the real, hidden, unreachable reality behind the seeming. . . . And this thing throbbing here will be one more anguished soul, filled with desires, hungers, maladjustments, humiliations, but that will, at last, also grow old and die. My God, and I'm the one to blame! I will always be the one to blame. It's as though I were now carrying within me the prolongation of this hell. . . . Someday, yes, he will call me to account, will claim his right to protest, to detest me. . . . My love, we are going to have a child—in a time so hard that not even horror hews to fixed principles, when there are no laws that justify it or control it. My love, our child will come into a time when opening a newspaper renders us paralyzed not because of what it says but because of the infamy with which it hides the truth. . . . My love, one more slave will bend over the land, one more slave will seek the meaning of everything, without finding it; and the answer he will receive, if he persists in searching, will be a kick in the ass into a cell. . . . We go on in silence, or speak only to criticize other people, politics, the times, the weather. We take advantage of the horrible state of affairs to avoid our own horrible situation. We speak (very softly, very softly) about the concentration camps so as not to talk about our own despair; we denounce the implacable censorship so as not to discuss our own silences. Little by little, as the terror grows, our terror, our own special terror, grows as well; our relations grow more intolerable. And the child stirs, kicks in my womb. . . . And the worst thing is that the relationship between us is not (or does not become) violent. We sit, eat, talk, and yet the fury is present, the violence which never boils over still is simmering, and while he says Good morning and kisses me, I feel that he is shouting, How I detest you, can't you see how I detest you? . . . My nails grow bluer, the veins flow like dirty rivers all over my skin, my waist disappears; I am a formless mass shuffling heavily through the furniture. Thus I gradually discover—in the midst of this summer, in the midst of this sun—looking out from the balcony at the ocean struggling to jump the wall, always looking at the ocean, trying to find . . . what? . . . in the ocean—that I have never been even the object of your sudden whims, that you don't need me. . . . For a time I live with the foreboding that something is inescapably about to happen, going to break out, not around us, not just over us in particular, but all over the world. I go out onto the balcony, I look at the ocean, I look at the encroaching brightness, and I think, *Something is going to happen, something has to happen.* I lean my heavy body out over the railing. I see the street full of people, see the flow of people going in and out, walking slowly, running; some afternoons I see a warm mist begin to fall, the mist changing to a rain that soaks my dress; I see the water beating against windows, see the water flowing along the now-deserted streets, see people squeezing in under doorways waiting for the rain to end; I see lights come on across the city, the ocean become a dark echoing emptiness, and I think, *Tonight, tonight, tonight the world will end.* . . . But nothing, nothing! . . . Another day. Lunch has been more or less the same as always; the words, the same. In the afternoon we go out walking. We have a date. After the movie we come to the Almendares River Park. We take a seat in the boat, cross the river. As the boat full of women and children glides over the quiet muddy water, I think *Now, now.* . . . The rickety ferry comes to the mouth of the river, turns around, and takes us back to the park. We buy a couple of paper cones of peanuts, get in line for soda, cross the bridge, and still have time to go to the zoo. A woman, already middle-aged, perhaps a widow, perhaps an old maid, perhaps abandoned, heavy and sad-eyed, dressed in black, watches us. How happy they are, she probably thinks enviously, looking at us walking under the park's big trees. . . . And nothing happens. We get home at night. I make dinner. We eat. We talk about how bad the buses are, how impossible it is to get a glass of water. And nothing happens. Now late, even though we have to go to work tomorrow, we go to bed. I will cough, you will pretend to be exhausted. The night is passing. And the heat and darkness of the night are the same as always; our aloneness and our misery, the same. Perhaps they are a little worse, but anyway, nothing happens, nothing occurs; no gigantic shadow comes in the window and smothers us, no fear incarnate in something now inevitable arrives and in one blow destroys us, no immeasurable explosion comes about. And the waiting for the great collapse, the certainty that something extraordinary is going to occur, the comfort that the world is going to vanish in the wink of an eye, becomes one more of the many speculations of the imagination, one more absurd whim, perhaps utterly selfish, of a woman almost eight months pregnant. Thus I gradually discover, in the midst of this summer now hounding us, in the midst of this sparkling sun (looking at the ocean, looking at the ocean leaping without reaching the top of the wall), that it is not hatred you feel for me, that I have simply never interested you. And now feeling the baby kick within my womb, knowing now that no catastrophe is going to come to pass, I see, clearly, that I am just a front, something that must be accepted if you are not to perish, one more tradition (*duty*) imposed by the implacable system, a hypocritical rule that may not be transgressed. . . . The advantages, moreover, of coming home and finding everything done, the advantages of having someone to talk to if you wish, or not talk to if not; someone to exhibit when it's prudent—*essential*—to do so, someone to talk about when one is among official friends and to forget about among real friends, are considerable. Now I understand your silences, your contained violence, your late comings-home, your constant reading, your boredom disguised as tolerance, pity, love; I understand why you always seem to be somewhere else and, perhaps, the reason for all the scribbled, torn-up, hidden pages. . . . And the ocean goes on pounding; it rushes in, springs, and crashes against the wall, sometimes sending waves flowing into the street. Listen, listen, so when once I know I'll never be the object of your desires, you become for all time the object of my passion. What about the life I glimpsed once, guessed at, saw from afar? . . . The whistle of a siren—a boat coming into port—comes out of the darkness. I leave the balcony likewise in darkness; I go into the house. Hector has come in from work. I put out the plates. He enthusiastically remarks on how delicious dinner was—because today he is happy. Then when we've done he asks me to the movies. The way I am I don't even dare show myself on the street, I say, thinking, That's what you want to hear. He kisses me and leaves. I don't go out onto the balcony since if I did I wouldn't see the ocean, I wouldn't see anything. And I understand, as I pick up the china and carry it to the sink, that real disaster never comes suddenly, because it's always happening. He won't abandon me, I think, because he doesn't even hate me. That is my punishment. For after all, I am the one who brought this situation about. It was I who went into his bedroom, it was I who cried with him, and not exactly for myself, either. *But I am young too, do you hear?* I now say aloud, and put the dry dishes away in the cupboard; I have a right to demand too, to desire. And suddenly I look at my body, swollen now, my hands, deformed. I pick up a plate, I walk slowly out onto the dark balcony, I clutch the railing, and I hurl the plate into the emptiness. I hear the crash of the china as it hits the pavement. . . . I go in, pick up the book I read sometimes, move my eyes across several pages. I lie down. And now to have to have this baby, I say, pressing my belly. My God. Where am I? What have I come to, having a baby? But I am young! I repeat. I cannot permit! I say loudly; I cannot permit them to make fun of me! And as I end the sentence I suddenly feel—just that quickly—that a tear is rolling down my face, my red face, disfigured by this monster that throbs, throbs, throbs. . . . No! I cannot permit such humiliation, such ridicule. I stop crying and get up. I dress. Who does he think he is? I say, packing my suitcase. There's a limit. If he at least spoke to me, if he at least said something to me. But I don't have to let on that I have figured out, understood, what he hasn't talked to me about, what he hasn't wanted me to understand. What does he expect? For me to play his game? For me to be his mother, his friend, his confidante? No! I am first of all his wife. I am a woman. First I insist that he treat me like a woman. And I start crying again. I cry as I close the suitcase. I open the dresser, saying to myself, *I am a woman, I am a woman.* I take part of the money we had saved for when the baby comes. Now ready, shouting *I am a woman* in fury, in sadness, in grief, I close the door. Shouting in shame, in disgust, *I am a woman*, and crying, I go down the stairs. I wait for a taxi. At last one comes by. To the station, I tell him, and now I gradually feel calmer. . . . Where to? the woman selling tickets asks me. I suddenly don't know what to tell her. I look at the sign with the names of the different towns. I choose one with a short name, so she won't notice how unsure I am when I speak. Somehow I must get free, I think, putting the ticket into my purse. When the public address system announces my bus's departure I am drowsy, I almost regret having left home, but Listen, listen, I tell myself, furious at myself, do you prefer humiliation, is that it? Do you prefer to play the game? Would you prefer him to go on using you, and you not even letting on that you know? The people at the station crowd up to the gate. I show my ticket. Do you prefer to stay with someone who's not interested in you? For once in your life—someone helps me lift the suitcase; thank you, I say—at least for a second act like a human being, that is, like a person who knows there's no leniency and that therefore you don't have to show it for others. Bear your solitude for once, because you cannot permit—the bus crosses the dark city, takes to the country—because you cannot permit him not even to take into account that you are a human being, someone who needs at least a glance of contempt. . . . I feel the silhouettes of the trees that pass, I feel once more the throbbing (that *kick*) in my womb, and unable to help it, almost without realizing it, I am sobbing loudly. Someone calls for them to turn on the lights. Somebody's sick, I hear them say. Two women come over to me and look after me. Gradually I calm down, little by little. What a thing to do, traveling alone in this condition, one says. She must be going to her parents' house, says another voice. And I begin to sob again. Someone gives me a pill, a glass of water. I control myself, I pretend to sleep so they'll leave me alone. In the morning, when I open my eyes, I am already in the little town I bought the ticket for. An employee carries my bag to the little wooden station. I see his ironed, faded uniform and an inexplicable sadness comes over me. He puts the bag on the bench in the station and looks at me, friendly but not quite smiling. Hasn't your family come? asks one of the women that looked after me and who apparently has gotten off to buy everything they sell. No, I say and watch her, staggering under a load of wrapped slices of pound cake, bags of candy, crackers, bottles of insecticide. . . . She buys up everything she can to take to her people, I think. And once again the sadness comes over me. But why do you have to be sad about *them*? I sit on top of my suitcase. For them, after all, there is a certain logic; they, even living within the same horror we do, have principles, habits, secret laws. They will certainly last, resist, a little more than we—I—will. They will stand more . . . As far as they're concerned, when you arrive somewhere someone should be waiting; if along the way there's something for sale (no matter what), you have to buy it on the spot to present to the person waiting. There is an invisible current, a tradition stronger than any law, that protects them, that identifies them and groups them together and saves them, that is, keeps them alive within the holocaust. . . . Watch how they recognize each other right away, watch how, without knowing who a person is, for no other reason than that chance threw them together in the same bus, they talk to each other like old friends. But I am free, I think. . . . With complete naturalness I ask the lady working in the station where the nearest hotel is. She looks at me surprised, perhaps even shocked that I asked her such a question. My God, I think (while I stare at her, while we stare at each other), how long has it been since I've been outside Havana, how could I have forgotten how people in the interior are, how could I forget how my mother still is, my whole family? For this poor woman it's so strange that I, alone, big-bellied, should inquire about a hotel. The most surprising thing for her is no doubt my belly; without it everything would be clearer: whore. But in my condition, the logic is a bit more complicated. The bus left me here, I smilingly explain to her, I'll spend the night here and go on tomorrow. She calls another employee then, who gives me directions to the town's only hotel. I thank them and pick up my suitcase. Once in the street I feel so weak that I have to sit down on the curb. A group of children come up to me and ask me if I feel all right. I'm going to the hotel, I tell them. And now they all squabble over the suitcase and take me there. I give my papers to the clerk at the hotel, show him my worker's card. He looks at me surprised but respectfully. Finally he collects for the room and hands me the key. Once on the stairs I send the children away although they insist on carrying up my bag. I go into the room, close the door. It's a big sad room. Made not to welcome, not to shelter, but to demonstrate how an iron bed, four walls, a bathroom with no curtain, a chair, and a table with a drawer can be all the world's loneliness. I go to the only window and open it. There is the sun, bouncing on the pavement—not a tree or the ocean on one side of this desolate shimmering highway, not even the consolation of an ocean breeze or the sight of a seagull flying. I light a cigarette, inhale, and now it is the little towns we pass through in the opening and closing of an eye, towns you pass through before you can finish a cigarette, ugly, ordinary towns, wadded up and thrown down throughout the length and breadth of the island. How many times, in our outings for work on the farms, for anywhere, from a truck bed, from a train window, from a rackety bus, have I seen these towns that leave nothing in the memory, not even the evidence, the contrast, of a distinctive ugliness. Low, stunted houses shut up, made so rainstorms, the sun, robbers can't get in—windowless houses with straight walls, houses like coffins, with their doors stained reddish from the mud that even cakes on the walls, houses squatting in the glare, with no gardens or sidewalks or the tiniest porch; perhaps a drainpipe opening onto the street through which all the filth escapes to the outside—dirty water from the laundry, dirty water from the bathroom, dirty water from the kitchen and sink. Horrible towns that don't say a word, that don't point to anything, that don't announce anything, that don't remind you of anything, that don't awaken in you anything but the instinct of revulsion, the urge to abandon them on the spot. These are towns with indefinite personalities but terribly concrete in their buildings, made solely to support life badly, made for missheltering—a bed, four chairs, and a table—and so the people in them die slowly for thirty, forty, fifty years, shut up in unplastered cinder-block walls and low ceilings, looking out through the window's fixed shutters from time to time to a street that offers no landscape, only another house identical to the one we inhabit—as though we were standing before not a window but a mirror. Loathsome towns. A billboard on which is stuck a name—the name of the town—shrill, coarse, bombastic; a gas pump (where there's no gasoline); a shop with a counter of wood or bricks; a drugstore with burglar bars; and the mass of houses crumpled together in the sun; at last, perhaps, a tree—which if left standing must serve as a hitching post or bulletin board. . . . Once more a gas station (closed), some traffic sign marking a curve, a grade, a repair that is never completed, and the town ends just as it began, without even having justified its existence with some original mark of desolation. Another sign, another dusty tree, another housing project thrown down in the implacable sun. . . . Are we entering? Are we leaving? Are we always passing through the same town? How can pity, love, beauty, exist among these crude houses, among these people of impenetrable angry faces, in this environment where drinking a beer, or simply not being asphyxiated by the heat, is the fundamental reason of life? How can any respect for privacy or imagination or dreaming be conceived here if every tree is an enemy to be brought low on the instant, if a river (if there is one) is the place to dump feces, urine, dirty water, if finally it is misery and helplessness, the pressure to survive, which rule all actions? Towns that aren't even by the ocean, that don't even see the ocean, people who hate the ocean. Oh, God!—but enough naming God!—and we are in His hands, we are in His hands. . . . While the car goes faster and faster, while we pass through these rigid cadaverous housing developments, stripped of all mystique, I think that the damnation is total, there will be no salvation; I think, mark my words, that there's no use your accelerating, that however fast you drive we will run up against (*we are headed only for*) another town of ordinary houses, utterly devoid (*justifiably*) of pity. There is no transcendence here, everything belongs to immediacy here, to the pressure of weathering through. And what would *they* say if suddenly we stopped the car and began scolding them? If suddenly we spoke to them in this language we think in? *Look at them*, they would say, *criticizing us, how dare they, who do they think they are, at least we know what we want, or what we hate, at least we cooperate, we aren't stumbling blocks, or full of resentment. Ah, and we don't consider ourselves superior. Who do they think they are? . . .* Or perhaps the insults would be worse: *How dare they criticize us, that pair of dummies, monsters, sick beasts, criminals living at the expense of our sweat! Who do they think they are? What country do they think they're living in? Philosophizing here, where the only question is planting a potato and picking it, eating it if you can, if the international market doesn't need it. It's shameful, it's dirty, it's high treason! We can't tolerate it! . . .* Yes, they would speak like that, or perhaps the language would be even fiercer, perhaps the words used would be so strong that I couldn't say them, or even understand them. Or perhaps not even that—perhaps they would look at us like scum, they would come up to us and squash us like you'd squash an insignificant but still disgusting cockroach. And then would come the roars of laughter. . . . A dusty tree, a sign announcing another town, a (closed) gas station, an empty store, a group of houses baking to bony whiteness. And the car goes on, goes on, and the towns, the nearer we come to Havana, become more frequent, dizzyingly alike. . . . I light another cigarette, look straight ahead. I want to look only at the highway, I want to contemplate only these frightful little towns, I want to stop, to stay in this horrible landscape, because what I don't want (and here are the voices, here now are those unbearable whispers, those threats, those groans, those cries) is to see her face, see that woman's face, see the way that woman jumps up and down, see that face deformed by shock of that woman jumping up and down, jumping up and down, jumping up and down and shouting and banging her fists against her head . . . a dusty tree, another billboard that announces another vulgar name, another store where the only product you are certain to find is a bottle of insecticide, and you have to present your ration card to be allowed to buy it. We drive on;

although the landscape doesn't vary, we drive on. . . . Useless town, I say; I've ended up in one of so many useless towns, I think, and throw out the cigarette (luckily there was a pack in my purse), close the window (I don't know what time it is, nor do I care), and lie down. I stand up, open my eyes; there is Hector—splendid—with the baby, on the sand. Once more he's a boy, I think; and I hear his laughter beside me, as young as the real boy beyond, on the sand too, resting on his back, his hands over his face, his fingers open a little over his eyes, allowing him to look about discreetly; his mother beside him, although fortunately she hasn't discovered us (she is so engrossed in her knitting). . . . I hear Hector's laughter as he plays with the baby. Does he pretend? Is he pretending? Are we always pretending? Is there for you nothing but a perpetual stage where truth is hidden, where anxiety is hidden, where desire and fury are hidden but lie in wait? . . . But no, no (and now I address the voices, the pines), I am not going to allow anyone to ruin this peace for me, I cannot permit my few, only days of peace, of rest . . . I lie on the sand. I think, *Now, now I really will be able to sleep awhile. Today I won't make lunch.* . . . When I open my eyes I gradually recognize things. Today it hasn't happened like before, when I woke up not knowing where I am. Here are the discolored walls of this hotel room, the chair, the suitcase lying on the table, the toilet, a few nails in the bare wall. Thus, still in bed, I think that although no time has passed (since nothing has happened) I have been in this room for three days, that I have only left this room two or three times to eat some disgusting food, that on top of everything I'm about to give birth and no one will know about it or come to help me; I go on thinking that the end has come, that I have been the catalyst for the end, that I have always only been good for hastening an end. But why have I never been intelligent enough to understand that the last thing you should do is surrender and that, given that you have, the worst thing then is to show it? Why have I never been intelligent enough to tell myself, You are in hell, like everyone else, but you will be shrewd enough to pretend that you don't feel the fire, you will be shrewd enough to find a place where the flames will not destroy you? I should have spoken to myself like that, as others (I am sure) do; somehow they survive, somehow they do not destroy themselves like I always do. Then you think they are happy? Idiot. They have simply been shrewder than you, have understood where they are better than you, and they have occupied, have staked out, the safest refuges. But *I*, if I got up right now, if I took two steps in this horrible hotel room, I don't know what would become of me, perhaps I might even go mad. But no, I know perfectly well I couldn't even aspire to that. I can analyze it all with relentless lucidity. I can run over again those moments when the horror has seemed intensest to me, I can live those moments again; I can do all that. All of it. But what I will never manage is to go mad. There is no comfort in that for you. Lying on my back in bed, I hear all the sounds of the town growing; I hear the voices, I hear the rattle of the wagons drawn by horses; I hear the evening, the murmur of night now washing over the walls. And I don't go mad. I hear now, in the darkness, the sound of a record player, the voice of an American singer on a miraculously preserved record—the privilege of a town in the interior, I think. Lying in bed I hear the racket of that foreign music, the scratched, exhausted sound that comes from the record; I feel my belly. And I don't go mad. Still not dressed, I hear now the little murmurs given off by the dawn, a church bell, an animal's hoofbeats, the conversation of two women walking along the street. How I envy those women. Either one of them is better off than I am. . . . I imagine what the life of those two women must be. They surely have their immediate problems, their fixed habits, something to tire themselves out with and yet not think about. . . . Brightness comes again through the window, the day arrives once more, the morning noises, and although I know that whatever I do will be futile, although I haven't eaten in many hours, although I don't know what I might expect, what I might do, or how to (or *why on earth*) go on, I still don't go mad, I still don't go mad. . . . Lying in bed, listening to the crackling of noon, a pain sluggishly begins flowing through me, coming from I don't know where in my body, and takes possession of all my senses. Almost happily, as I bite my knuckles, I feel myself growing faint. I think that at last someone has taken pity on me, that at last Death, the real, true death that does away with all the others, is now soothing my rages, is now eliminating all this weariness. At this moment the rattling of a jackhammer begins pounding outside. I go to the window. Construction workers are breaking up the street right in front of the hotel directly below my window. The noise mounts until it is so constant and so deafening that I think that it is all just a joke, played expressly on me, that otherwise it is impossible for everything to be so ridiculously grotesque. Now it is not just the noise of the jackhammer but shovels too and even the roar of a concrete mixer. And I begin to howl with laughter, completely conscious of what I am doing, knowing that I will stop within a few minutes but that the roar of the jackhammer will have to go on. And then I will begin to yell, to yell not because I have gone mad but simply because I have an urge to yell, and because I know that with that racket going on down there I won't be disturbing the peace, since no one will be able to hear me. . . . Just as I had planned, I yell; I go on yelling, almost as loud as the racket of those engines tearing up the street; I go on yelling as loud as my body, which has gone days without eating, will allow. Loud, loud. In spite of all. Until suddenly, a noise outside the plan interrupts my immediate intentions, which are "go on yelling." Someone is knocking at the door. My God, they may have been knocking for minutes! Perhaps, in spite of the jackhammer, someone heard my screams. What am I going to say? How will I explain? . . . Instinctively I jump out of bed and open the door. Hector is there before me. He comes into the room; I sit down on the edge of the bed. The noise that breaks up the street and the glare of the day make everything unreal to me. For a moment we are both silent. At last it is him that speaks. How do you feel? he asks me loudly so I can hear over the noise from the street. Okay, I say loudly too. And I stare at him, in the midst of the brightness. He's an old old man, I think. I couldn't get here sooner, he says now, as though apologizing, bathed in the glow of midday. I don't answer him. It took quite a little effort to find you, he says and keeps aging. At first I thought you'd gone to your mother's house; I sent a telegram. And he looks at me guiltily. It doesn't matter, I say. I didn't get an answer, he says; communications are so bad. And he goes on talking, rationalizing; as if he were the one who had to justify himself. And the brightness goes on deforming him, and the hellish noise continues. While he slowly tells me what he's been through these last few days, in a loud calm voice—his inquiries from town to town, station to station—I see him, little by little, becoming young again, once again becoming just a man, then a young man, then a boy, and when he is finally done—with the deafening background of the jackhammer—he is a baby. And how innocent, how helpless he looks now, as he tells me how he lighted on my whereabouts, how he followed the trail, how happy he was when he saw my name on the guest register, and he even smiles. And suddenly I feel as though I'm about to start screaming again, that I won't be able to help myself. And thus, as he goes on talking, saying things there really is no reason to say, I discover how much he needs me, and how much I need him. And now, telling me clumsily how happily he climbed the stairs, the worry and happiness he felt when he knocked at the door, the worry that obsessed him through the whole trip, thinking that something could have happened to me, his voice seems to grow gloomier, deeper, hoarser, as though he can't control himself either and is about to cry too. That noise, that noise! I say, making a gesture against the brilliance, and I run to him. He is unable to go on talking. Hector, I say, and I squeeze him. Hector, I say, bathed in tears. And he, sobbing too, embraces me. And now only the sound of the jackhammer is heard, down below. And I understand that Hector and I not only need each other, we love each other, we really love each other even though neither of us knows how, knows what kind of love it is that unites us. . . . The fact is that we will never be able to be apart. Hector, I say. Hector. And even when I stop talking, when I stop sobbing, he goes on crying, holding me. How could I never have realized before how much he needed me; how can I have been so cruel? And I seem to understand everything, although I don't think I will ever be able to explain to myself why I understand, although I don't believe I will ever be able to explain to myself what it is exactly that I understand. . . . Let's leave right now, he says, pulling himself together, and the roar of the jackhammer takes possession of the whole room once more. I hurriedly dress and close the suitcase. I turn in the key to the hotel clerk and speak to him in a firm, almost proud, voice. We go out into the brightness and cross the street, now almost completely destroyed by the jackhammer. Hector opens the car door and helps me in; he closes the door. He starts the motor. I look at him. At this moment he is still a young man, almost a boy. Do you feel all right? he asks me again. He puts a hand on my knee now; he looks at the baby asleep in the back seat; he goes on driving; he speeds up. Yes, I say. And now he's an old man. . . . A dusty tree, a metal sign, a deserted gas station. We go on. . . . We arrive in Havana as it is growing dark. A neighbor comes out to greet us. How is your mother? she asks me, and I understand that Hector has arranged (*foreseen*) everything. Fine, I say, and go into the house. Hector turns on the lights, I go out onto the balcony. I go up to the railing and look at the great expanse, now almost black, flowing in silence. The table is ready, he calls me. I'm coming, I'm coming, I say loudly too and look again at the water flowing, slowly, unhurriedly, beating against the whole length of the Malecón. Suddenly the pain comes over me once again, the pain here, in my very womb, a dull pain, a prolonged throb, a blow to the stomach. Hector, I say with a still louder, clearer voice, now we really do have to call the doctor. And before he can run to help me, before he can come, worried and happy, and hold me, and take me to the bed, I look toward that dark expanse that flows invisible and I wink at it. . . . Hector is still beside me. Hector, I say, and half asleep he turns over on the sand; I feel his warm skin brush against my side. God, I say, it must be really late. I pick up the baby and we stand up. Let's go to the restaurant, I say. I fell asleep, Hector says, and brushes the sand off his legs. At this moment, I see the boy again. He is coming out of the ocean, running along the beach toward us; when he is close he stops, looks straight at Hector, and goes back into the water. We take the paved path that leads to the main building. Hector plucks a reddish oleander and gives it to the baby. The baby brings it to his nose, smiling, as though grateful. We watch him and laugh too. We go into the dining room. The hostess tells us that it's too late to have lunch and that dinner doesn't start till six. She refuses to wait on us. Hector pleads with her, flirts a little—he really acts like a boy. The hostess, a middle-aged woman, is seduced; looking cautiously around, she lets us in. Hector reads the menu. "Croquettes and rice!" he says, speaking deeply, like a distinguished headwaiter naming exquisite delicacies. Second dish, "Spaghetti and rice!" Third dish, "Green peas and rice!" he says, acting the perfect fool. To cap the performance, the waitress says we can only have the first dish. While she writes down the order, Hector expresses amazement that she still has blank pages in her order book. The waitress looks at us somewhat confused and a little insulted, but since he goes on smiling, she finally laughs. Oh, and if by chance there's any water left, bring us two glasses, please, says Hector now. We are served, we eat. At least noon is past, I think as we are leaving the restaurant. The mother and her son are on the porch of their cabin. He is dressed all in white, with tight pants and a full shirt, tennis shoes. The mother, in her gigantic housedress, is talking; she seems to be giving some advice, some ideas. He lowers his head, his hair falls over his forehead; the tanned, dark skin of his face contrasts even more strongly with his white clothing. Seeing them in those positions, mother and son (son bowing a little, in silence, mother talking), a kind of fear comes over me again, a kind of strange, perhaps foolish worry. If only the picture would stay like that, if only nothing would change. If the five of us could only be frozen like this forever: Mother's and son's heads lowered before the falling splendor, Hector, the baby, and I sitting in chairs, watching, without really seeing, the ocean. . . . But what I would really like to preserve, have, is exactly that which vanishes—the brief violet of evening on the water, the last gleam of the pines, the moment when a yagrumo leaf flutters and falls, a smile of my mother's that I never saw again afterward, Hector entering the house when he came back from the Sierra, the perfume of the night-blooming cereus flooding my room, a fragrance that comes only rarely, only from time to time, and only when there has been a shower. . . . Things that fade and die, scenes that have changed in the blink of an eye, vanished forever; and later one wonders whether they ever really existed. . . . The baby begins to whimper (perhaps it has gotten too much sun), Hector gets up and goes into the living room, I wave at the mother, who was waving at me a moment ago. The moment has vanished. The scene perhaps didn't exist. The mother will start talking to me, the son will start whistling. She enthusiastically declares how much good the dips in the ocean are doing her. (I hear the whistling.) She gives me another detailed account of all her illnesses, tells me what she's been through, and is still going through, to get medicine. Some of it, she explains to me, is from abroad so you never see it. How many people have died, she says to me tranquilly, like a woman holding a conversation a thousand times repeated, like a woman stating such an ordinary truth that it is really uninteresting; how many people have died because the medicine they needed, some little pill, a shot, something so you can breathe, couldn't be found. . . . Uh-huh, I say to everything she says, and go on looking at the ocean, changing now second by second. Not even it can offer me a fixed image now, a still picture on which to rest my eyes and say, *You are there, you are there, I can stop looking at you, I can stop keeping an eye on you, because I know that you are there and will not change.* . . . The ocean is at one moment flat, then the blue forms a heap of glittering shapes like cans; now it is a huge rolling sheet, then it ripples and a convulsion throws off the slightest hint of red; it is transformed, it is transformed now into a still green lake, utterly transparent. . . . He's going out, she says—and although I haven't followed the thread of the conversation I know she's talking about her son—tonight he's going to Guanabo, she explains. She says he gets a little bored at night. Even though the buses are so terrible. He says he can walk, but how can he possibly; it's more than ten miles. . . . Uh-huh, I say. And the ocean now looks old, tired, an old man with wrinkled gray skin, hardly able to breathe. . . . Perhaps he can find something there, she says; I hear people have gotten tamales. Tamales! Today lunch in the restaurant was so bad. . . . Yes, it was, I say. And the baby in my arms has fallen asleep. As she goes on talking I stand up, tell her I'm going to put him to bed—I'll be right back, excuse me—and go inside. Hector is sprawled across the bed. His legs, tanned too, stand out against the white sheets. I lay the baby down. I wash my face, comb my hair; I put on perfume; I sit on the bed next to Hector. Today he's hardly read at all, I think; this morning he flipped though a book and put it right back down. Today he hasn't had to take shelter behind a book. I contemplate him again. Little by little I slide to the floor, I kneel beside the bed, bend over, and kiss him. Since it is still hot I decide to stay, on my back, on the tiles of the floor. The coolness of the floor is something of a comfort. Through the partially open shutters a few rays of sunlight filter in, no longer so fierce. A mosquito buzzes around my head, hovers, and dives at me. I sit up swatting. As I abandon the cold tiles I seem to abandon calm. For now I hear the baby crying. I listen to him jump, the way he constantly kicks in my belly, rending me. Hold tight, says the doctor, breathe deep and push. And I groan, scream. It's like having a flame in the very center of my belly, as though I wanted to expel that flame and couldn't. It is a pain, a burning, a feeling of suffocation so unbearable that at times I think I must be different from other women. Hold tight, says the man's voice. Push, a nurse says, push like you were urinating. I feel as though I were breaking apart inside and while I feel (know) that my blood now is gushing out, I think, My God! This too, this calamity too is reserved for us women! . . . And with my screams there is suddenly another scream, a yelling accompanied by mine, in the midst of a pain so deep that it ceases to be pain so as to become a kind of swoon. And I see the baby, the baby (that the nurse is now lifting up by its feet) crying, terrified, wrinkled all over like an old man. He's so ugly, I think, telling myself, Now I have a son, now you have a son, woman. And I cry again, but no longer screaming, no longer loud, no longer from the burning I still feel between my legs. I cry, I cry slowly, sadly, with an inconsolable weeping not of pain but of resigned defeat; with a weeping that could go on infinitely, that could last my whole life, without my going crazy from it, being harmed by it, or for that matter experiencing any relief, either. . . . No one understands anything. I go on crying. And no one understands a thing. And it's best that way. It's over, woman, the nurse says to me, showing me the baby, now powdered and wrapped in soft cloth. He had to kick like that, it's healthy, look at him. And I look again, through my tears, at that little baby with his face still grimacing and wrinkled. And I go on crying softly while I stroke his blue head. That little mass of flesh, that little mass of flesh. . . . I pick him up slowly and bring him to my breast. I walk him, rocking and cooing to him, through the living room and bedroom of the cabin. You'll wake up your father, I tell him softly; hush, I say, kissing him slowly. He has stopped crying. I look at him there, in the crib, as I lie in bed too, resting, here in the house; Hector is at work. Little by little, the wound is closing. I can go to the bathroom already without feeling pain, I can walk, as I do now, already without any pain; little by little, I think, while I look at myself in the mirror, now holding the baby, my body is getting back the shape it always had; in fact, I might say I've become more attractive, my skin softer, my eyes brighter, my lips fuller, even my hair blacker and with more body, my face more serene, smoother. A kind of plenitude seems to have taken hold in my face, my whole body. Sometimes, just for the pleasure of looking at myself, I spend hours on end before the mirror that reaches almost to the ceiling in our bedroom. I take advantage of the respite, the maternity leave from work that lets me rest. Outside the roar of the street continues, people shouting and calling, the hubbub of the lines and the packed buses that creak past; but I am suspended in another time, on the margins of all that. . . . Here, in a married woman's, mother's, bedroom, I begin gradually to recognize my face again, to rediscover my beauty. . . . Outside the uproar of people continues (there seems to be some kind of disturbance in the line), but I am quiet, holding the baby, staring at my own face, my body growing thin once more. And once more I feel its throbbing (my body's throbbing), its call, an indefinable thing rising. . . . And the ocean goes on swelling, like a heavy, silent film of metal. The brilliance and the smell of the ocean wash over the balcony and flood the house. . . . One by one I am trying on my best dresses (which now are few); I comb my hair, I pluck my eyebrows. All decked out, I pause, pose in every nook and cranny of the house, contemplating myself. I spend whole afternoons before the great mirror looking at myself, trying out various ways of smiling, growing somber, walking, looking at my body arrayed in finery, saying aloud, not worrying about waking the baby, *You're fine, you look terrific, you're really splendid-looking.* The brightness creeping farther in, the smell of the ocean climbs over the Malecón, over the avenue, floods the balcony, permeates the whole house and envelops me. . . . Hector comes in and I serve dinner. I light a candle and put it in the center of the table. Today's a red-letter day; the baby is one month old today. I go to the bedroom and get him. Hector kisses him, kisses me. We eat dinner. He asks me whether I feel all right, whether I still have any pain. Oh, God, and how do I tell him that waves of ocean smell are coming over the balcony; how do I tell him that the days are clear, that soon my maternity leave will be over. How to explain to him— with words I cannot find either—this feeling of wanting to run, sing, dissolve in it? . . . When dinner is done, he picks up the plates—he helps me with everything—and says to me, Don't move, I'll make the coffee. Holding the baby I go into the living room; I sit down and turn on the radio. Hector brings in the coffee. I say, at a moment when the music is slow and we can talk without raising our voices and the beating of the ocean against the Malecón is almost inaudible, Yes, I'm fine, nothing is wrong with me, I just feel a little tired. We go to bed. Tonight, as on so many nights in the last few years, he slowly strokes my hair, and

I let my hair take the shape his hand gives it; he rolls slowly over my body and I let his body gradually enter mine. Tonight, like so many others, it is not pleasure I feel but resignation and a certain grief at thinking, It isn't me he's thinking about. . . . We finish. He rolls over and goes to sleep. I go to the bathroom. I come back, cover Hector with the sheet, and lie down beside him; I put my head in his hands. I think How much I love him, how long I have waited for this moment to come, how many days, how many nights in silence, without giving the slightest indication, waiting for him to decide, and now that everything has come to an end, has been made real, I discover, like always, that it has only served to reawaken, even intensify, my aloneness and to make me feel more despairing. . . . The night's many shadows file through the bedroom, and I begin to brood over justifications: Perhaps marriage is just this, is like this for everyone, a kind of shadow, a sort of ghost, of what we really desire; perhaps the best thing about marriage is having someone you can ask to turn on the light when you're afraid and to blame, once in a while, all your accumulated frustrations on; perhaps its greatest comfort is having someone you can always go back to without having to make a lot of explanations. I, like everyone else, must have little modest dreams, even without thinking they can come true. . . . I must accept my existence, as others accept an incurable disease, enjoying its letups, those moments the pain is not so great. But perhaps even the fact of deeming my life a kind of misfortune is no more than a show of pride, a show of that vanity of mine that makes me think I'm better than other people. . . . I must bear my life unprotestingly, put all this feeling of discontent aside; I must become a simple woman, and think no more that that would be a contemptible thing to do. . . . But morning comes. The smell of the ocean rises. Nothing has happened, I think; I have not changed one whit, I think. And no disaster has made me succumb. And here once more is the brightness, once more the inexplicable feelings, the urge to go, to want to go, beyond. Once more I am before the big mirror in the bedroom, looking at my body, my white flesh, my young thighs, my breasts which still give no sign of sagging. I must demand, there is no reason why I should accept humiliations; I must have great dreams and above all always satisfy my desires. I must demand, I shout, and the baby wakes up. I must demand, I repeat loudly as I go over to the crib and pick him up. I must claim. . . . I walk back and forth in the living room holding the baby. *Demand*, I say, and I go out onto the balcony. . . . The ocean. Waves crashing, bursting into sparks. I go in and put the baby to bed. Now, bathed and dressed, coiffed and perfumed, I sit down in the living room to wait for Hector. He will come, I think, and nothing will have changed. He comes in. Everything happens just as I had thought. Just one little change in the calculations: When we finish eating, he pours me a glass of water and I, seeing the water falling into the glass, feel pity for that water, so docile, poor water, so soft, so tame, so obedient; I cannot conceive that this water that is now in the glass, taking on the color and shape of the glass, spilling from bottle to pitcher, from pitcher to glass, I cannot conceive that this little bit of water has been part of a river, has crossed the land in great torrents, has sailed through the sky, has been ocean, dew, torrent, cloud. And now this is all it is. Looking at it without being able to bring myself to drink it, I lay my head on the edge of the table and begin softly to sob. Hector stands up. What's wrong? he says, and puts his hands on my shoulders. Are you sick? Oh, Hector. Oh, Hector, I say. He sits down in front of me again. I raise my head and he appears, through my tears, drowned, as though we were separated by a curtain of water. And I go on crying. Don't you think we'd better send for your mother? he says to me, but not as a question or a statement, just to remind me. And suddenly I think of her. My God, how long has it been since I thought of my mother! And I say yes, send her a telegram with the money for the trip. Perhaps everything that happens to me is just because I want to see my mother, I think. . . . Poor Mama, I think, while I rock the baby and begin to feel calmer. I croon to the baby, who little by little is falling asleep again; I put him to bed and go out onto the porch. The mother and the son are still there. The boy is sitting on the wooden chair, lazily, his legs spread, his arms dangling beside him. The mother, as soon as she sees me, grins happily and picks up the conversation again; she doesn't even give me a chance to apologize for having taken so long to come back out. Why don't we all go to Guanabo together tomorrow? I don't know, I tell her, and look at the ocean. I'll ask Hector later; he's asleep now. She goes on talking while I go back to the ocean, until at last she jumps to her feet and says she's really sorry, she has to go and get dinner, her son—*my son*, she says—wants to leave early. . . . She goes smiling, skipping like a mouse, into her cabin. The boy and I are alone, he on his porch and I on mine. Each pretending to ignore the other's existence. But I know you, I think; don't think you're fooling me, I think. And I turn and look directly at him. He remains motionless, sitting in his chair, looking at nothing, whistling. But What if this is all in my mind? What if this were all in my mind? . . . We remain like that (now me not looking at him), profiled to each other, trying to reciprocally ignore each other, feeling haunted by each other's presence, and trying to seem indifferent. . . . We remain like that, like two soldiers in some strange battle whose victory will go to the one who resists most without attacking, who bears up best without seeming to bear up, without exhibiting the least sign of weariness, or hatred, or irritation, or bother. . . . I hear Hector's voice at my back. He has taken off his bathing suit and is dressed like the boy and I—all of us in white, as though the three of us (secretly) had come to an agreement. Want to take a walk on the beach? I hear him say. And now we go, with the baby—whom I've also dressed in a little white suit—toward the ocean. We tread the dry leaves of the almond trees, we cross the pine grove. It didn't rain again today, I say aloud, gently pulling away the baby's hand, which is squeezing my ear. He's got that obsession lately, I tell Hector. I think all kids go through that stage, he says. And now we are walking on sand. The baby waves his hands, flaps them, as though in a funny tribute to the ocean. The swimmers are coming out of the water. The dripping bodies still gleam in the light of the setting sun. A group walks by us laughing. The din of the cicadas sounds monotonously now; it is a high, cold sound, perfectly regulated, and it seems to come not from any animal or insect but from electrical equipment, high-precision instruments. Yes, since now I know how to distinguish their various rhythms, their various sounds, the music of the noise. . . . Little by little, once I have lost my provincial accent, my country girl's way of walking, my bad taste in clothes, I learn other things as well, enjoy other things, suffer from other things, feel other things. I go, with Hector, to almost all the concerts, I read a few books, we go to the movies to see the films he wants to see, we attend a lecture from time to time, a few in which someone truly intelligent knows how to get around the muzzle and talk about what really is, about what remains. Things that at first seemed absurd or boring to me take on real meaning. I also discover true solitude. The song I am listening to at this very moment, what is it if not as well the manifestation of pain, of a deep way of feeling loneliness? Not that loneliness that goes away when physical company arrives, but the certainty of knowing that even when we have a loved one who loves us too beside us, comforting us, understanding us (everything is so difficult, so impossible), we are at the same time irremediably alone. That song I am listening to now, that music floating above all our heads, flooding the theater, that symphony that according to the program notes is "one of the greatest artistic monuments of all time" (and which can easily do without these program notes)— what images it brings to me, what impressions it makes on me, what new suffering it wakes in me. . . . That music I'm listening to makes me yearn for something I never had, see people, trees I lost without ever knowing. . . . That music echoing now throughout the neighborhood awakes in me the sense, the *certainty*, that something we don't have (and how we treasure it, how we need it!) is constantly slipping away. . . . That music that now falls, now slows, now whispers—as it flows great veils seem to lift; windows open on nonexistent fields, and landscapes dominated by castles appear, vast panoramas crossed by a river—a river we will never see—and, beyond, a house blurred by fog. . . . The sound transports us to seas at perpetual floodtide. Hunters returned from the glade with their quarry hung from long poles; red paths bending away around the inlet of a lake. The music transfigures the ridiculously dyed heads of those old women into objects worthy of veneration. Sounds which make us forget ourselves and sympathize with, respect, love, the whole world. . . . I come in from compulsory labor. We have just finished a long stint of farmwork. It is Sunday. We bathe, dress hurriedly, and run to the theater. We enter. And the orchestra breaks out on the instant. The music swells and takes us, transforms us. It still exists, I think. It still exists! I think. Although it must surely disappear as well, I think. My eyes are fixed. Tears roll down my face. And my handkerchief is dyed, stained a little by these dirty tears. In my haste I didn't even wash my face too well. . . . That music, that whisper, that roar, that fall, that soaring, that harmony, makes me think, suspect, that we do not belong to this reality, this world—that we are here, suffering, by some mistake, by some accident (*cosmic*, perhaps) that threw us by chance into this place, onto this planet, which we are strangers to. Because this yearning for something we have never known must have some meaning, this nostalgia for a time we cannot find in our memory, this sense of being not in reality but on some sort of stage, this suspicion (this *certainty*) that our actions, our motions, our words, all of it is nothing but a pale glimmer of what we really desire. . . . Where am I, where am I? Where should I be but am not? Where do I remember having been but have never been? Where to be? How to be? How can I get to the place I will never be but must be in order to *be*? . . . The last notes quiver, the applause explodes. Once more we are here, unreal, unrecognizable, irremediably alone and pathetic, vulgar, and now with no sense of that other imbalance, now with no suspicion of a trail to follow, of a justification, of a hope. . . . But how, but how, how to get there? What can I do? And what about Hector, how must Hector feel? I think, and look at him, walking ahead of me, up to his ankles in the water. He is worse off still, I answer myself. I at least have my goal. I know, if not what I want absolutely, at least what I cannot stop wanting. He doesn't even wait for (*suspect*) anything, I tell myself, while we walk away from the beach. We walk along in silence, he in front, along a little-used path that also goes to the cabins. Suddenly we stop. We both stand still, looking at a bone riddled with holes, an eroded, crumbling white bone (some animal's) among the little stones. There is such desolation in that simple bone (a jawbone, a shank, I don't know), it has such a terrible peace about it, an infinite disconsolateness, that we stand mute, lost, contemplating it until the darkness gathers. It's the femur of a horse, Hector says now, with an almost professorial tone, and his voice is like the signal for us to go on. I give him the baby and walk off toward the pine grove. I'll go get dinner started, he says, the baby piggyback on his shoulders. . . . With my arrival in the pine grove the whistle of the cicadas diminishes, as if they were frightened or were watching me. Under the trees there are two empty chairs. I sit down and look upward. Not a cicada can be seen among the branches. Little by little the violet color informs the whole landscape once more. I breathe. The violet makes my arms glow. The cicadas draw out their curious silence. A seagull rises and drops over the ocean.

The calm persists, mysteriously. All at once there is the splashing of suddenly dusky waters. There are two boys on the beach. They shout, play, maneuver in the peaceful water. Now one jumps on top of the other. Now the dripping, glistening body of the other surges and dives. Now they both emerge shining. They float on their backs together. They rhythmically cut through the still waters. Rising, sinking, paddling the water into splashing spray, they romp, shriek, shout in who knows what barbaric tongue. They float along together while violet spouts erupt from their mouths and scatter in the air. They fill themselves again and float along like strange fountains. The violet water again falls over their darkening bodies. Now they laugh. Now I hear their laughter. I hear their laughter. And mine.

I lean over and pick up, at random, a piece of broken comb, a smooth little stone, and a pine nut. I go farther into the pine grove, headed for the cabin. The cicadas have still not resumed their litany. When I come out from among the trees, I see the boys wrapped in towels running toward the nearby cabins. Now it is totally night. I arrive and sit on one of the porch chairs. I discover the stone, the piece of comb, and the seed still in my hand. None of this is worth a thing, I say aloud and sit up to throw them over the railing. As I raise my hand, the door to the cabin next door opens and the boy comes out. I can hear his mother giving him some piece of advice; finally part of her body sticks out. Luckily she hasn't seen me. The boy bows his head and walks down the steps of the porch. As he passes in front of the cabin he sees me with my hand still in the air. For a second we are both startled, looking at each other. But he, immediately, sticks his hands into his pockets, stares straight ahead, and keeps on walking. Since he is dressed in white I can watch him through the darkness. He crosses the avenue of almond trees, passes next to the oleanders; the whiteness of his clothes still floats in a way, almost phosphorescent, when he goes into the pine grove and takes the little wooden bridge that leads to the Guanabo road. Making a great effort, almost imagining it, I still make him out at the bus stop. The bus comes. Its lights illuminate him from head to toe. The door opens; he gets in; the bus lurches forward, growling. I stand up and finally hurl the piece of comb, the seed, and the stone off the porch. Immediately, the din of the cicadas from the pine grove and a swarm of mosquitoes hanging around my head force me inside. Hector has already put out dinner. We sit down. I tell him how much I like the food, which otherwise we eat in silence. We finish. I take the plates to the sink. Hector puts the baby to bed. We both go out onto the porch and sit down. There are the lights of the Coast Guard, symmetrically spaced, flashing, blinking into the darkness. At least they serve a specific function: to remind us where we are and, should we not wish to remain here, to eliminate us. Slowly the pitch of the cicadas rises. I smoke. The outline of the pines, the silhouettes of the trees and the cabins begin to stand out in the gloom. To one side of the ocean the moon, swollen and enormous, is rising. Looking at that immense face, a kind of dull pain rises within me. I close my eyes; I stand up and go inside the cabin. . . . Calmer now, I go out to the back yard and begin to take in the diapers. As I feel the cool contact of the white cloth, I am completely bathed in moonlight. I turn and see her, La Luna, high and huge, a little mocking, somewhat compassionate, looking at me with my arms full of diapers. What loneliness, what great loneliness. . . . And I look at myself, foolish, loaded down with diapers, here in the back yard of the house, as she calls me, as she calls me or mocks me, as she questions me and stares at me, calling to me. . . . If only he'd arrive, if only right now that man that has never existed would arrive, if only he'd descend and arrive, then all this, suddenly, would be just a dream, a nightmare I would occasionally remember, something to tell, but something no one could bear— that no one could understand, that no one could even imagine. . . . *Woman with Diapers. Woman with Months-Old Baby's Washed Diapers.* I run, I run inside. I close and lock the door, quickly make the bed, and lie down. Go to sleep, go to sleep, I tell myself. *Run* to sleep, because perhaps, because perhaps (because *for sure*) you will awake in another world. Yours. . . . I close my eyes, cover my head, pull the pillow over my face; I hold my breath, stretch, yawn, squeeze my eyes tighter closed; I cover my eyes with the pillow. I hear, nonetheless, Hector come in; I hear him slide in next to me. Sleep, sleep, I order myself. And I squeeze my eyes tighter shut. I pretend again not to hear, not to feel anything, that the brilliance doesn't reach this cabin. But it is impossible. It is impossible to stop seeing that blinking of lights, stop hearing that beating of drums, that laughter, that applause, those echoing snare drums that make you wiggle and tap your feet. Through a peephole in the curtain I look at the hall. All the seats are filled. A few boxes are occupied by dinosaurs who slowly raise to their mouths some strange kind of candy; others are occupied by women, children, men, a whole audience stirring and shouting—*clamoring*—for me to come out; and the music, that uncontainable rhythm, that beating of drums, becomes more and more driving, more demanding, more contagious, more infectious, more delicious, more persistent. I cannot control myself. My feet move all by themselves, my body sways, shimmies, twists and jiggles, wiggles its hips. I look at myself in this bathing suit covered with sequins (this outrageous bikini made of things like sparkling fish scales), and I can't control myself. I move my legs, move my belly, shake my hips and my shoulders, waggle my head. And the racket of drums and maracas (for there are maracas now) becomes ever more overpowering, hotter, the rhythm drives fiercer and fiercer. I'll split my sides. I'll split my sides, I say aloud. And I go out there. In the midst of a muffled ovation the curtain rises. I'll split my sides, I'll split my sides! I shout, wiggling to the rhythm of those drums. Everyone keeps applauding. Viva! Bravo! they shout. They cheer me, they stimulate me, and I am whirling, doing outrageous contortions, bumping and grinding half naked in the middle of that great runway. What lights, what colors, what music. . . . And my elastic body like a snake, coiling and uncoiling, leaping and swaying in the midst of the roar, to the rhythm of the roar, more, and more, and more and more rapidly. . . . I'll split my sides! I shout, raising my arms, swiveling my waist, shaking my tits and ass, ever harder. And the dinosaurs bellow, stand in the boxes, and begin to fling their teeth down at me. A hail of dinosaur teeth falls on my naked dancing body. A rain of feathers, a rain of warm water mixed with horseshit, hair, claws, and insect wings fills the stage. And I, never stopping, bumping and grinding, pick all that up and fling it by handfuls into the air. Wings, feathers, teeth, claws—I begin to wallow in the midst of all that. And then, to the sound of that music, to the sound of that roar of drums, I strip off my scanty garb and throw it into the audience. Shouts and whistles and frenzied clapping—while I whirl stark naked. I look toward Hector and see him wrapped in a sheet behind the curtain, hidden, shy and thin, but now discreetly swinging his hips. I wiggle over to him, to the rhythm of the noise, and take his arm. He is rigid now as I insist on dragging him to the center of the runway. The audience, now seeing him, explodes into even more frenzied applause. The music becomes even catchier, more insistent. Right on! Get *down*! Get *down*! I hear them shouting—there's nothing I can do but go along with it. I drag Hector by the arm and push him to the center of the stage. I never stop dancing. I'll split my sides, I'll fall apart, I'll come unjointed, I say to Hector, bumping and grinding. I'll spill my guts! I cry impetuously, and in a fit I strip the sheet from him with my teeth. He is completely naked too on the great stage. The roar of the crowd grows more and more deafening, more throbbing and rhythmic; it becomes a kind of measured frenzy, utterly synchronized with our blood. The applause and the roar of the dinosaurs is also a dull frenzy, one single ovation issuing from one gargantuan throat. I'll split my sides, I'll split my sides, I whisper to Hector as I overwhelmingly bump and grind, and I yank him about by the ears, press against his crotch, rub my breasts against his naked body, and wrap him completely in my lengthening hair. Spinning my hands hypnotically I feel his whole body; never stopping my dance I bend, fall to the floor, and writhe in frenzy as I bite my toes; I jump up, dancing, and press myself against him; wriggling and nipping at him with my teeth I set him in motion, make him spin. He too begins to dance. We dance. The two of us writhe now in a schizophrenic dance. We tangle and merge, wriggling and shaking, we move apart, bumping and grinding, we watch each other feverishly, and we never stop swaying. We bump again, rubbing against each other (a beating of ass cheeks and eyelashes) with more and more rubbery motions, more and more rhythmical grinds, more and more dizzying whirls. We fall to the ground, we stand. He takes me by the waist and lifts me; I whirl in his hands now, I glide across his shoulders, I slide between his legs and come up gleaming, sweaty, and naked, astride his hips, moving in rhythm with his unceasing, ever-wriggling body. . . . Parrots, millions of rats, rabbits, a two-headed dog, a one-eyed horse ridden by a "toucan or royal bird," and a million brilliant monkeys shrieking begin to pour out from the wings. . . . While I embrace him, while I put out my hands to squeeze myself, melt myself into him, dancing, the dinosaurs begin to crowd around us, to the inflamed beating of the drums. Now, rearing on their tails, their huge members swaying, driven by the monumental beat, they improvise a chant, which drowns out the drums, and ejaculate over our bodies. Making a wall of their bodies, they surround only Hector, who disappears among their huge legs. Once again I hear the sound of the stroking and the chant. Desperately I draw closer to the cliff face the animals form—and which he is behind; I tug at their huge tails, I kick at their flanks. But the wall is impenetrable and the only reply to my shouts is the wailing of the chant growing louder, until I can't even hear myself. . . . Hector! I go on calling. Hector! I continue to cry, running around and around the promontory. Hector! I say, but I cannot get to where he is. I cannot manage to touch his body though I stretch out my hands. Hector, I call again and look all around me. The moon's brightness filters through the blinds, illuminating the mosquito net and the bed. I find that the roar is just the buzzing of a mosquito, now trying to light on my arm. I get out from under the net. I turn on the light. Hector, I call, thinking he must be in the living room. He isn't in the cabin. Although I know he is not going to answer me I go on calling him. You can hear the baby's crying. Hush, I tell him, going closer. The mosquito has lit on the wall now. The baby goes on crying. I try to swat the mosquito with my palm, but it takes off and lights higher up, almost at the ceiling. I pick up the baby, who finally goes back to sleep, lay him down, and go out onto the porch. Such silence. Only the sound of a sheet of zinc almost falling off some roof, stirring slowly, since there is no wind. I can hear my own breathing, I can hear the beating of the breeze in the pine trees. I sit down on the porch, and I wait. Hector, I say aloud, calling him once more, thinking perhaps he's behind the cabin, perhaps he went out for a minute to get some air. I look up. There, up there she is, the moon, in the very center of the sky. Idiot! she says to me. Idiot. . . . And I see in that huge face a kind of pained look of compassion. Idiot! I say to myself, and suddenly, almost running, I go up to the cabin next door. I knock. I knock hard and wait, thinking I cannot wait a second longer. The door opens and the haggard, expectant face of the mother appears. Oh, it's you, she says. And although she smiles she can't hide a certain disappointment: It wasn't him, it wasn't him, her son, that was knocking. . . . But listen, listen to me, What if it's all just a stupid fear?

Perhaps, *surely*, he is asleep, and the mother's expression of surprise is simply at my unexpected visit. . . . I'm sorry to disturb
you, I say, I have a terrible, terrible headache and I've run out of
aspirin. Oh, come in, she says, looking at me, and suddenly, now,
I find that I'm in my underpants. She smiles at me, using the
words she always uses, not even letting me get a word in to
apologize. It must be late, I say. Four o'clock, she says, I just
looked at the clock. My God, I say, and look at her again. But
she doesn't say a thing to me, doesn't mention her son. But She
was awake, I think, she came to the door instantly; she's waiting
for him. Poor thing, I think, perhaps this is the first time he's
done this. And, suddenly, I feel pity for that old fat now frightful
woman poking nervously through a cardboard box. . . . Here they
are, she says, here are the aspirin. I thank her, thinking Poor
wretched woman, wretched woman. But listen, what if all this
were just your imagination? What if *you* were the abandoned
woman, now upset, haggard, not *she*, and her son were asleep in
the same bed she sleeps in—obviously he isn't in the living room—
and she seems nervous because *you* so obviously are? . . . I think
I'll take it right now, I tell her. Could you give me a glass of
water? And she, always helpful, but something like terrified, as
though in me she, too, sensed a danger, as though she saw in me
something dangerous she dared not tell me, runs to the kitchen.
I hear her running water. Without wasting a second, I push open
the bedroom door and stick my head in. I see the beds (just like
ours) tumbled and empty. I jump back and am already at the front
door to the porch, saying to myself Idiot! Idiot! . . . Here's the
water, the mother says, holding up the glass. I take the two
tablets; I thank her once more. She—constantly fearful—smiles
again. You're welcome, it's quite all right, I hope you feel better.
It may have been the sun, I say, unable to bring myself to leave.
Because, listen, the son might have been in the bathroom; when
you stuck your head in he might have been going to the bathroom;
or perhaps he was in the kitchen, eating something. And that is
why she's up, getting him something, a piece of pie, perhaps, a
cup of coffee. . . . Kids that age are voracious. No, no, if he were
in the kitchen she would have mentioned it to me at least ten
times. She's always talking about him, I don't think she even
realizes it, instinctively; if she isn't now it's precisely because
she's avoiding the subject, because she's keeping hold of herself,

with great effort. . . . And she gives me a whole package of aspirin. I think two or three are enough, I tell her. Oh, no, I brought a lot, keep all of those. I take them and suddenly, now, I realize that she is using the formal *you* with me; perhaps without her realizing it she wants to impose a distance, at this moment, between us. . . . For a second I think I hear a sound in the kitchen. Your son, I say, looking at her fixedly, did he get home from Guanabo early? She looks at me now as though confounded by the question and as though she had just discovered in my face the sign of some curse, some jest, some conspiracy. . . . Well, no, he still hasn't come in, she says clearly, I don't know what could have happened. The buses, I say (saying to myself Idiot, idiot, you're an utter idiot. Did you really need to bring this woman into all this mess? Now at least try to comfort her), the buses at night are impossible, worse than during the day, which is saying a lot, since sometimes it's four hours, or more, and the bus still hasn't come. Uh-huh? she says, and her face seems to glow. Oh, yes, I say, don't worry. And I say good night, trying not to show interest, not to give the matter any importance. I go into my cabin slowly. Idiot, I say aloud to myself, stopping furious in the middle of the living room. And I stay like that awhile. Then in the bedroom I think, with real terror, that now perhaps things are getting serious, that the moment has finally come, that my premonitions were *not* wrong. Other times it hasn't even bothered me that Hector comes in late; I have never been concerned to know where he was; what's more, it has almost always been me who wanted him to go out. . . . But if you did, mark my words, it was because you knew there was no danger; he is not lonely, I would tell myself, he is alone; therefore no one can keep him company; he will never leave me. He needs no one, and I come before all those people that hang around him, that surely hang around him. I even see, with no fear whatever, some of them come up to him using some excuse or other (a match, the time) and begin to talk. And me smiling and thinking They're wasting their time, he isn't interested in anyone, not even in me. Finally, seeing Hector step away, I take his arm and we continue walking. He is such an egotist, so alone, I think, that if he needed anyone it would be him himself. And I go on secure, clasping his arm. . . . But with him, with that boy, with that poor woman's son, I feel from the start that this time may be different. He too has the mark not only of being alone but of being a loner. In that adolescent body, behind that casual walk, in that overflowing indifference, brazenness, toughness, or mockery, in that whole front of his, there is hidden, I feel, I see, a real terror, a sense that he knows that for him there is no salvation. From the first moment, from the second I find Hector peeking through the blinds, I see in the road next to the car, in the face of the newly arrived boy, the mark of damnation, not the superficial sign of a person who considers himself different by the fact of his having certain tastes or affected mannerisms—it is the look of unbearably knowing oneself to be lost, different, utterly and for all time. . . . I watch the boy open the car doors, I watch him, now with the suitcases, look blankly toward us. This is the sad part of it— there was somebody just like him, there was another one just like him. . . . But that isn't true, I tell myself; it isn't possible, I say to cheer myself up, the only thing Hector has is his solitude; he's too proud to give it up, to give himself up. But Listen, listen, the voices tell me, if the other is he himself, nothing is lost. . . . No, I answer, it is precisely now that he must demonstrate to himself his contempt (his knowledge, his mockery) toward everything, including himself. . . . But listen, but listen—Enough! I shout, and try to soothe the voices: If anyone knows him, if anyone knows anything about him, it's me. And I know it will be as I say. . . . To end the dialogue once and for all I slip under the mosquito net and pull the sheet right up over my head. The din subsides; I hear the sound of the water, the banging of the sheet of zinc on the roof, the unreal and remote sound of the cicadas, and, at last, someone's steps coming closer through the cabins. I slip quietly into the living room. Along one side of the pine grove comes the boy. He is walking slowly; his white clothes seem to float through the darkness. He stops and looks back. It's dawn, I think. The sun will be up soon, I tell myself, and go on waiting. . . . Hector will come in soon, I think, lying down again, there's no reason for him to be long now. Although perhaps, although perhaps. . . . But Listen, listen, whatever deduction you make, whatever conclusion you try to arrive at will be utterly worthless and, no doubt, wrong. . . . The cabin door opens. I hear Hector come in now without turning on the light. I pretend to be asleep. I hear him undress, slowly, noiselessly, and slide in under the mosquito net. I listen to his breathing. His body is resting now at my side. Now I can sleep easy, I think. Slowly, as though I were sleeping, I draw my head toward his hands. I put my face between them. . . . Poor thing, I think, he's had to come back and lie down beside me. The tears come slowly, sluggishly, with so little strength that I don't have to worry about their reaching his hands. . . . But what excuse, what extenuation can be offered in defense? the judges, ensconced behind the great table, question me as I go on crying. Instantly, still crying, I try to lift a hand, but it turns into a chortling turtle, and as I raise my arm it gives me a terrific bite on my eye. The guffaws of the whole audience flood the hall. As I touch the wound that has cost me an eye I understand that I have committed a horrible crime, that I have killed someone. But whom, whom? . . . And I look at myself, utterly guilty and foolish, sweaty and with all this ridiculous makeup all over my face like a whore, and wearing this sequined bikini that, to top it all off, is coming apart on me. . . . I look toward the judges again and see now, on the great table, the long cadaver covered with a sheet. I also find her, Helen (attired in a billowing judicial robe), looking like a shocked matron, looking at me with real contempt. . . . State your excuse! the judges challenge me again, looking at me with severity. I try to speak, but when I do a large toad comes out of my mouth and falls to the table, bringing a hysterical scream from Helen, whose wrinkled hands fly to her equally wrinkled throat covered with necklaces. The laughter of the entire audience is now a unanimous roar. One of the judges picks up the toad, lights a bonfire right on top of the table, and, making a grill of his potent hand, fries it. He takes a bite and offers generous helpings to the other judges. Helen, now calmer, making a million senile gestures of flirtation, tries it. It's delicious! she says to the judges, then looks at me again appalled. I think that there will be no escape for me. The crime is horrible and the court implacable. I look at them. They look like professors, perhaps heads of some Basic Secondary School or of some farm, militants from some civic or patriotic organization, that is, sinister, evil people. . . . They finish gulping down the animal and point at me again, to demand an explanation. I try to speak, but now I begin vomiting up parrots and other noisy fowl; even a tiny cow falls swishing its tail onto the great table. One of the judges milks her. He drinks the milk and, once satisfied, invites the others to drink. The hysterical laughter of the whole room echoes. I raise my other hand to cover my ears. I find my ears have turned to pieces of wood; now, riddled through and through by termites, they disintegrate into two little mounds of sawdust. The din of the laughter is deafening. I try to take a step but my feet have grown together, have become one great sharp blade, a stinger, that threatens to pierce my womb. The laughter and stirring in the hall is unbearable now. I try to speak but only manage to emit dry leaves. It is a storm of great leaves— green on one side and white on the other—that flutter through the hall echoing (now even louder) with laughter. I try to point to the cadaver, try to ask them (by way of signs) to uncover it. My fingers turn into corncobs. Looking at them sadly I feel I cannot bear this not knowing, this feeling of uncertainty and guilt. So I try to hop forward. I use my stinger like a spring, a pogo stick—torrents of laughter, my lower parts covered now with scales. Dragging along my various appurtenances I reach the end of the table where the cadaver is lying. Panting, I take up one end of the sheet with one of my claws and jerk it back. It is Hector, hacked to pieces. I look at that bleeding mutilated body and it suddenly acquires my mother's face, and now be- comes a teenager, and I understand (now fully) that it is I, it is I who have killed him. . . . Raising my claws to my head, which is a strange crusty thing, I begin to scream; strange fish come out, birds that sometimes have spurs instead of wings, bats, thou- sands of crabs which now begin devouring the mutilated body. The torrent of laughter reaches a peak now. I scream. I go on screaming as I change into an oozing hole, oval and violet-colored, fringed with hair; I am now a hairy wetness running, opening and closing, showing its little throbbing reddish pip. . . . Like a desperate hairy sea urchin I run, I run under the seats, between the feet of the judges and the audience, who try to stamp on me with shrieks of glee. Don't let it get away! Don't let the crazy cunt get away! I hear them shout and see them rush toward me. I keep running and screaming, leaving a wet trail under the pews. Now just a tiny mess of terrified runny hair, I see the judges, now once more at one end of the great table, and Helen with them, pointing implacably at me, offended and condemning. While the whole audience prepares to squash me, I sob and try to melt into the floor, keeping even closer, tighter to the freezing tiles. I go on sobbing, until I feel a hand touching my hair, tangling in my hair, softly stroking my head. It's him, it's him, I think. It is Hector. Until, at last, ashamed and confused by having allowed him to hear me cry, I draw away and turn onto my back on the

sheet. Whirlwinds of ashen fowls falling over the waves. Hundreds of seagulls rising, falling, diving headfirst into the water. Hundreds and hundreds of seagulls that seem to have found a school of fish, having a feast on the ocean. I see them flashing in the light and realize it must be late. I come out from under the mosquito net and go over to the baby, stretching out his arms, but I don't pick him up. I go into the bathroom and close the door. Now I hear the baby crying, but his cries come distantly through the closed door; they don't disturb me. He stops crying; Hector has no doubt taken him into bed with him. I brush my teeth, comb my hair, leave the bathroom, and prepare breakfast. Breakfast is ready, I say aloud. Hector, already dressed, comes with the baby in his arms; as he feeds him I think, The baby gets along better with him than with me. He doesn't whimper or kick. . . . Little by little, I tell myself at the beginning, I will get used to this. Little by little, I would tell myself, I will grow used to playing this new part that I will have to go on playing for years. But no, I think as I put the cups into the dishwater in the sink, you haven't gotten used to it. And I let the running water wash the dishes. Slowly, still maimed from the delivery, I walk with the baby all through the house; I go to look out the door, I sit with him on the balcony; but I don't get used to it, I cannot get used to it. What will happen, at last, is that I will have to come to some definite conclusion, some effective destruction. . . . Several times I've thought seriously about it. Sometimes, mornings, when the brightness begins invading my bedroom, and you feel that the sounds of day have taken over everything, and you already know exactly what you will do all day, and you know how the day will end, and what the day after that will be like, and all of them—at those moments when, still lying in bed, you see your skin look almost transparent in the glow, you see your body somehow parked, utterly given up, between the sheets, you conclude, Everything is futile, everything is just absurd and futile. . . . Then, for a few seconds, there is such desolation that I don't even have the spirit to bear it, to get out of bed, I don't even have the strength to go on thinking about the desolation; I am empty, without memory, waiting, from moment to moment—once more, once more—for the end. I close my eyes. *Here it is, here it is.* But it is not the end which comes, it is the sound of engines in the street, a dog barking while two women talk, and, now, the clang of a pot that just fell in the kitchen. I get up and as I dress, as I sweep the floor, as I clean off the table I forget that a second before I got up I had a moment of lucidity. . . . I finish washing the dishes and place the cups on top of the refrigerator. Hector in shorts and with a towel over his shoulder is talking with the boy's mother on the porch. She greets me enthusiastically, although I stand for a moment looking at the ocean. She is talking now about her son, about how hard it was for him to get back last night, and even about a certain resemblance she has just seen between him and Hector. And Hector smiles and goes along with it all as he plays with the baby. Finally the two of us decide it's time to go down to the beach. And she, always thoughtful, today happier than ever, I think—because last night she knew uneasiness and so now she thinks she's secure—asks me whether my headache is gone. I say yes, I'm fine, and a little splash in the ocean will finish the cure. Hector stands up. For a second I think the boy's mother even looks at him admiringly, proud that her son has something of Hector about him. And now, truly enthusiastically, she pleads with us to leave the baby with her, she'll take care of him, her son is asleep and she doesn't have anything to do. I'm about to say something evasive, but Hector gives her the baby before I can speak. And I even seem to see a kind of smile, a sort of mocking look on his face. The two of us walk toward the beach; we come to the ocean, which is completely transparent and, when we take off our shoes and sit on the sand, totally green. I think, looking at that yellow ocean, that this is our last day on the beach, that tomorrow our time is up and we have to leave. Now more than ever I wish not to think about anything, not to talk, not to see anything. . . . The baby isn't here, Hector is still lying beside me, resting, listening to the feeble sound of the cicadas. And what if all this were only a dream? But Listen, listen, that does it! We cannot abide such cowardice, we are certain you know how to distinguish your real nightmares from the other ones. Your ridiculous dreams, those grotesque, grandiloquent dreams of yours that even—what a laugh!—Helen of Troy her own sweet self appears in, they have nothing to do with this patent reality, though come to think of it perhaps it too, like the nightmares you wouldn't dare tell anyone (would you?—tell the truth), is good for nothing but making you the butt of a joke. . . . Yes, yes, you're right, I say, using the same language as the voices; but sometimes when I wake up I feel the sheets, afraid I'll come across the bone of some prehistoric animal, or a gigantic nut and bolt, or some outlandish species of scorpion still alive in the bed. I run my hand under the mattress. I search through the pillow, thinking in terror, *Here it is.* For a few seconds the fear is unbearable, since I am certain I'll run into some gigantic spider that will chew off my fingers. But I find nothing, touch nothing strange. . . . The sound of the cicadas keeps falling, making us drowsy. . . . Then, without having received the extramundane prick, without having stumbled on the harsh rough skin, I sit on the bed, confused, asking myself where all the vermin have gone, since if there's one thing I'm sure of it's that if I turn off the lights and get into bed, I will feel them again, scurrying about under my body. . . . The roar grows even softer. A single cicada settles into tempo. Suddenly it's the music of a radio Hector had brought without my noticing. A *danzón.* But I don't want to hear anything, I don't want to have anything to do with that music at all, I don't want to remember or imagine anything. . . . For a time I see a dog under my bed. It's no ordinary dog, it's more like a cat in the shape of a dog. I peek under the bed and see it looking unwaveringly at me. What most frightens me is that it doesn't do anything—it doesn't growl or show its teeth; it looks at me steadily, cold, sure of the horror its coldness inspires. Now as Hector, lashed by the sun, turns over and the *danzón* flows on, I see the dog once more, watching me quietly from over there by the ocean. For a time I think that these "visits" are not just mine, that certainly other people see the same things I see so clearly. A dog, a dog! I cry, calling my mother. She runs in frightened, with the broomstick. But that is only for two or three days; then, when I scream, if she comes running with the broomstick it's to brandish it over *me.* Poor Mama. We've never been able to understand each other, never been able to talk awhile, no longer like mother and daughter *(which is impossible),* but simply like two women. Poor Mama. She is there on the porch, looking not toward the sea but toward the brick wall that separates our building from the one next door; or perhaps not looking anyplace in particular, simply standing on the balcony. How old she looks, I think, she already looks like a woman sentenced to death. She is bent, her face is vexed, as though offended. . . . We have never been able to understand one another. Nor has she ever known how to confide certain things in me, troubles, just to unburden herself. But nonetheless I can imagine how much she must have had to suffer! I know she was widowed when she was young, that she couldn't bring herself to live with her family—which they never forgave her for. So much work, so much solitude—in return for what? . . . I come close; I'd like to speak to her, touch her; I wish that though she didn't unburden herself to me I could unburden myself to her. But I know it's impossible. For a time, when we hated each other (everyone always called her "Obnoxious"), I thought her coldness, her fierceness, her silences were directed against me. But now that she's come to help me, that she's deserted her hometown the moment Hector sent her the telegram that I had had the baby and wanted to see her, that she has even given me a tablecloth she embroidered herself, now, watching her all these days, seeing her take care of me, wash diapers, cook for us, I understand, not from the work she's done but from the expression on her face as she's done it, from her cold discipline, that her hatred is not directed against me but is part of her personality, of her deepest self, and it comes out against the diapers she washes, the floor she scrubs, her hair when she combs it before the mirror. The fact is that she doesn't even know herself who it is she hates. It may be that she is not even aware of her own unhappiness and it is simply from instinct—because she has never seen anything but dirty diapers, pots to be put on and taken off the fire, floors that have to be swept—that she understands that everything is horrible. Poor Mama, I think, there she is, my God, growing old, and what can I say to comfort her? . . . Now she's in the kitchen making lunch; I stop at the door and look at her. She asks me how I feel. I tell her fine and look at her hands, sort of smoke-colored, whipping egg whites. For a while we remain silent. Sometimes I'm a little sad, I say now. Sometimes I don't even know what I want, I say. She looks at me now in surprise, as though I had all of a sudden insulted her. Without stopping beating the egg whites, she speaks to me. I don't understand what's wrong with you, she says. You have a house with all the comforts; Hector seems to be a good husband, he has a job, he earns good money. What more do you want? I have never in my life had a kitchen like this, she says loudly, suddenly, but still not angry. Don't you feel well? And now she comes up and looks at me closely. I see her worn face, I see those big veins that emerge from her throat and vanish into her collar. . . . Oh, Mama! I say, and leaning on her shoulder I begin to cry. She strokes my back. Do you want me to ask Hector to call the doctor? I gradually calm down and tell her he doesn't need to, I just feel a little depressed. And as I say that last word, she looks at me, confused and upset again, once more offended, as though that word were unnecessary, or it were not normal to talk about it. And I think that indeed it was a mistake on my part. Now she'll never stop watching me. She looks at me without caring whether I notice or not; she follows me to the door, stands watching me as I go out onto the balcony. If I stay too long, she comes up to me—as she does now—to tell me the air is bad for me. Sometimes while I see her fearfully spying on me, as though she were afraid I might do some harm to myself (or to her), I feel the urge to laugh; I feel the urge so strongly that I can't take it anymore. So I do. She looks even more startled. Do you feel all right? she asks loudly. Perfectly, I say, looking at her and thinking Poor thing, I'll have to be more careful; if I break out laughing she'll think I'm crazy as a loon, maybe even try to get me in a straitjacket. Poor woman, I think as I watch her suspiciously sniff the air of the balcony, all her hatred, all her frustrations might have ceased to exist if only in her youth she had had a magnificent stove like mine. . . . In one of the many books Hector recommended to me—and now on the sand I see him stretch, put his head on his arms, speak some unintelligible words, and go on sleeping—a character tells how his mother would talk to him sweetly about the time when his grandmother was younger and she gave him the *Arabian Nights* for his birthday, telling him lovingly that even though he wasn't working, at least he could read a little. . . . I wonder, looking at that woman with her rigid, sullen face, looking at that damned, loved face, whether those mothers that spoke sweetly of other times and gave copies of the *Arabian Nights* as gifts, that sympathized, discreetly, with our weaknesses, ever really existed. . . . At the end of the week,

Hector and I go with her to the bus station to say goodbye. I try
to give her a little money. She refuses, insulted. Finally she gives
in to my pleading and takes it. As I watch her put the money
away in her purse, a terrible sadness, a terrible sense of loneliness,
of guilt, comes over me once more. . . . The departure of the bus
is announced. We see her disappear among the people and then,
now at the window, look steadily at us. She detests us, she must
hate us, I think, as I wave goodbye. But Perhaps I am mistaken,
I tell myself, and sit down in the sand, Perhaps it is just that we
live in a certain comfort, so she can no longer have much sym-
pathy for us. . . . The ocean is so very still that it reflects the
flight of a seagull. The boy passes before us now, turns, looks at
Hector, no longer caring that I am beside him. He goes on walking
along the shore. Hector is still drowsy, looking nowhere; I turn
off the radio. For a while I just stand there at the oceanside, letting
the water bathe my feet. Hector comes up to me. We swim out
to where the ocean becomes dark, forming wide bands of deep
blue. From here you can't even hear the cries of the bathers. From
here no one would hear my cries. . . . I see Hector come smiling
up to me. Now he will kill me, now he can get rid of me easily. . . . He comes nearer through the whirl of dark waters. He
reaches me. He takes me by the neck. The deep murmur of waves
coming in from the open sea is the only sound. While his wet
hands press my skin I feel my terror turning to happiness. It is
joy I feel, perhaps, at knowing that the moment of our liberation
has arrived. . . . His hands slide, squeezing, across my body. They
slip down to my breasts, slip and touch my thighs, come together
behind my back, and hold me in an embrace as we sink. As we
descend locked together, I think It was all nothing but a trick to
drown me without frightening me. Once more the feeling of
definite liberation comes over me. . . . But we return locked together to the surface and I, dazed, even confused, feel his stiffened
sex liberated from his shorts rubbing against my thighs. I push
his body away; I dive again, swimming toward the shore. Before
I come to the coast I open my eyes. I see the shining white seabed,
my hands just above the bottom, and between my hands and the
bottom hundreds of gliding leaves, rolling softly, some of them
brushing against the palms of my hands. . . . Twice this week, I
think as I come out of the water, I've seen the yagrumo tree of
my childhood. It has looked so close, the coolness of its leaves

has been so close that now no one will be able to tell me it didn't exist, that it didn't exist even though it didn't. . . . Hector comes out of the water too, picks up the radio and the towels. We walk unspeaking to the chairs under the pines. He sprawls in one of the chairs, stretches out his arms and legs. The sun dries our skin, making little clumps of salt all over us. From time to time I raise my head and see the boy, swimming now out where the ocean is darkest, exactly where we were. He swims rhythmically, with style, sometimes floats, letting himself be carried by the current; other times he leaps and plunges, bursts out, his shoulders and belly gleaming. He goes on swimming like that near us, diving, resurfacing, noisily beating up the water, calling attention to himself. . . . At last Hector begins talking without opening his eyes. Slowly, softly, he begins pronouncing the same old words, the same old offensive and offended discourse, in which nothing, not even ourselves, is saved. Now he *is* going to shout, I think— looking fearfully around us—now he'll begin, angrily, to put down the system. What he is about to say no longer has any interest for me. I'm just worried that somebody will hear him, that one of those countless informers hanging around everywhere will hear him. But he doesn't raise his voice, doesn't shout. He goes on slowly with his eyes closed; the words flow in a monotone, pitched calmly, tiredly, as though he himself understood that getting worked up can't really so much as make you feel better, even. . . . And even when he names again almost every hardship—hunger, torture, censorship, persecution, prison—I seem to hear an oration recited from memory, to keep a tradition whose origin is no longer remembered. And now, when he prophesies the future—prison, persecution, censorship, torture, hunger—his voice has the resigned tone of a man classifying, enumerating, talking mechanically about an assortment of things which are insignificant, impersonal. He goes on like that, making a kind of inventory of calamity. I, resting by his side, my eyes closed too, wonder What will happen? What can it be that's happening now? What can be happening between us now? . . . We remain in the same positions, moving just once in a while to shoo away an insect or pick some pineseed fallen from above off our bodies. One hour, two, and he is still talking, not altering or raising his voice, while in the water before us the boy keeps appearing and disappearing, floating and diving. We remain like that while midday passes, only standing up from time to time to drag the chairs out of the sun. But even when we perform those motions we are still stuck in the same lethargy, him talking, me listening and ignoring, trying to ignore, that figure cavorting before us, wanting, obviously, to show himself off. . . . The bathers go in to have lunch. The hot afternoon breeze begins. Now there is only one cicada sounding through the pine grove—perhaps it is the same one as a few hours ago. For a while we keep our silence; that is, he stops talking. Both of us listen to that high, unvarying whistle. Little by little I come back to life, wake up (although I haven't slept), emerge from my lethargy, and as we drag the chairs back again I am surprised to hear myself asking Hector whether he plans to start writing again, whether it wouldn't be good for him to try again. But now, once I've said it, and I see him sit down beside me once more, I think that I shouldn't have, that there's never any excuse for mentioning that—I think I've just lost everything, even, as of late, the calm of no hope, even the sad condition I'm in of always being the one that listens. Now he won't even go on talking. He has never liked being asked how what he's writing—*was* writing—is going, he has never shown me anything. . . . But I do hear his voice again, just as the noise of the cicadas revives, though it is distant and monotone, as though they too were tired, worn out from their futile efforts. . . . What can be written in these times? he answers without looking at me, his eyes half closed, and with that cold, impassive, sort of distant tone. . . . Any story you tell becomes a cause for conflict simply by the fact of its being told truthfully; and if you make things up, if you use your imagination, if you create, it's even worse. . . . He falls silent again. The ocean takes on a deep blue over which the boy goes on paddling furiously. . . . It is horrible, Hector suddenly says—and I say to myself, Now surely he will shout, now he will start up his resentful, angry diatribe, but his voice goes on so muted and low that at times I have to strain to hear it, and despite everything I lose some words in the creaking of the trees and the whistle of the cicadas—It is horrible to live in a place where the notion of "productivity" (a productivity that, however, no one benefits from) reigns so supreme that the creator, the artist, is considered ornamental, useless, or parasitic if he goes along with it all, and a fiery-eyed, bloodthirsty enemy if he objects to any part of it. It is shocking to think that the act of cutting two hundred fifty pounds of sugarcane is much more important than that (impossible, anyway) one of writing a good book. . . . The cicadas have fallen dumb. The heaviness and heat of the afternoon grow. The ocean can be heard crashing rhythmically and, over that sound, the boy's splashing as he swims near the shore. A swarm of mosquitoes suddenly moves from one place to another in the air, settling into a motionless cloud. . . . And if you want to survive, comes the voice of Hector again, you must fall not into simplicity or even into silence (which don't exist here anymore), but into vulgar fawning, into the elementary vulgarity of praising and buttering everybody up because they don't even believe in themselves. Write an anthem, a cantata, a hymn, if you don't want trouble. But a poem, your poem, poetry is now an old-fashioned, reactionary, foolish, counterproductive, dangerous emotion here, precisely because it tries to keep being new. . . . His voice is pitched so low that if I weren't seeing his lips move I might think he hadn't said a word, he wasn't talking, and that I had thought these last words, that I had been influenced by his previous conversation. But he goes on. I hear the same old words filing past, shoved along by his loathing. At last they dissolve into the whistling of the cicadas and the beating of the waves. . . . A gust of wind which seems to have come from the beach itself creates a column of sand that whirls into the pine grove and falls over us. Sand covers all the trees now. . . . And how can one give a vision of all this? says Hector more clearly, but still in a monotone. And suddenly I think, He's taking me seriously now, he's using me as a sounding-board, not just to let off steam like before. He's spoken to me, he's speaking to me, he's asked me a question; he needs to, I think joyously as I brush off my bathing suit. And this is just the beginning. He'll go on talking; he'll tell me everything, and I will understand. I'll make him see that I understand, and I will comfort him. And his confession will be the tie that binds. . . . Our tie as lovers. . . . Then what secrets, what excuses, what shapes, what hells will be able to part us? . . . And I think, reason now (as he goes on talking), that this conversation is a reconciliation, a recognition, a *rapprochement*. . . . And What must those people be thinking—I think now—as they leave the beach now and see us here? What can they think but that he is declaring his love for me? What can they think but that we are two lovers talking

softly and waiting for the beach to grow even more deserted? . . . And perhaps they're right! Perhaps they aren't mistaken. . . . And how can one give a vision? How to give that vision?
he says now, and I think that that heavy woman looking at us
as she stands up must be thinking, *Now he's making a confession
of his love, now he's telling her he can't live without her.* And
for a second, looking at that woman with her deformed body
covered in a billowing wrapper, walking off and looking at me
with a certain envy, I can't keep from smiling. . . . You flirt, you
flirt, the woman is probably thinking. . . . How can one show
proof of all this, he continues, how can one show, demonstrate,
to those who live under order, those who are sheltered by tradition, those who know what civilization is and are able to call
on its laws, to count on the logic of reason if they make plans,
expect recompense if they make sacrifices—how can one communicate to those people, how can one make them comprehend,
see, what absurdity really is, what injustice really is, fanaticism,
poverty, repression, terror. . . . No book, no word, nothing will
make people who don't suffer those things understand that
dreaming and thinking are foolish, even dangerous in a place
where getting a can of milk is a task for a hero, where being
friends with an artist is enough to make you considered an enemy.
Who do you appeal to for justice? . . . And he sort of waits, waits
for someone (perhaps *me*) to answer him. And I think, looking
at the ocean rising as the boy rhythmically cuts through it, looking at the ocean becoming mountainous waves, He is drawing
close, he is drawing close, he is drawing closer and closer to me;
soon he will let all this resentment be, and start speaking to me
of himself. . . . How can one communicate to those young people,
tourists—well fed, decked out in the latest fashions, exercising
their rights to make demands and to protest in their own countries—who come here to praise the abolition of those rights; how
can one make them see that once that "new system," which they
have the right to lobby for in their own lands, has taken power,
then simply going out into the street decked out like they are
now will be enough to be booted into jail on their asses without
any preliminaries? . . . Another group of bathers passes before
us. . . . I hope they manage to learn the jargon they'll have to
repeat day and night when they get what they want, he says now,
slowly raising his voice. And I tell myself, This is just a round-

about way of beginning a real conversation, a confession. But he remains quiet. Now he seems to be listening abstractedly to the sound of a cicada chirping among the pines. A lifeguard, coming down from his perch, blows his whistle. The last bathers leave. At last the boy goes off too. . . . Hector and I, both motionless, listen to the hum of that cicada as though it were the only thing in the world that mattered. It finally stops. Only the roar of the ocean, truly enraged, is heard . . . No book, says Hector, now with his eyes completely closed, will ever be able to express what you feel when you pick up a machete and start cutting sugarcane, and you look ahead and see another man, with another machete, cutting, and you raise your head a bit more and see nothing but machetes rising and falling. Hunger, thirst, weariness. You ask, secretively, what time it is and it turns out to be seven o'clock in the morning—and every day like that, month after month, your whole life—and there's no choice in the matter. The swarm of mosquitoes shifts slowly in the air, gradually floats off until it disappears among the branches. Another cloud of sand whirls in from the beach, dissolving before it reaches the pine grove. . . . Faced with all this, says Hector now, as though coming to a conclusion, you must flee this place, you must try to escape. Then, if we can, we will think about the rest of it. A sound like footsteps crashes over the trees. Both of us open our eyes and then feel the first big drops of heavy rain falling through the branches. We are caught so off guard that for a second we are paralyzed. Then, already soaking wet, we grab the radio, the towels, and dash through the pine grove, which booms as though up there somewhere a gunfight had been unleashed. We run up to the cabin. The cloudburst completely swallows the almond trees, batters the dry leaves off the trees, bends the oleanders double, and falls on the thundering ocean, which seems to reject the water, sending it bouncing off once more like an inverted storm of huge drops. The beach, the road give off little clouds of dissolving steam. Standing behind the shutters, I smell that smell of drenched trees, drowned earth. . . . It goes on raining, the rain goes on pecking like a mad hailstorm on the roof of the car (now it will start raining every day, I think) and although the windows are closed, dampness filters in, and with it that strange sense of yearning, of remoteness, of grief, and that urgent desire (that *need*) to find refuge, to run to someone. Hector drives attentively now, never taking his eyes off the road, absorbed in the wet highway. The baby, lulled by the rainstorm perhaps, has gone back to sleep. Hector speeds up and, although his face has not changed, there is some imperceptible sign, some look, which makes me think that the rain has affected him too. He too has perceived *(is suffering from)* this sensation of being alone, listening to the rain fall, listening to the wind and thinking No one will come to rescue us, no one will make it through. And the torrent goes on, stronger still. The headlights have to be turned on. . . . The rainstorm batters the oleanders to the ground; it covers the entire pine grove like a mosquito net. The rain pours down, the rain is pouring down, and I am running from one corner of the house to another; I hear the water splashing on the rain gutters, on the palm-frond roof, and I watch the golden shower fall like wine into the barrels. The rain pours down, the rain is pouring down, and Hector and the rest of the cousins and all the boys from the neighborhood and I go out into the yard bleached by the rain; we leap around in it, we splash about and dive in the lakes forming all through the garden; we listen to the water popping on the tamarind tree; we build quick dams across the streams that surge across the yard; bathing ourselves, we watch the nighthawks up there (bathing in the downpour too), screeching happily, drenched. . . . The rain pours down, the rain is pouring down; it falls on the breezeway that cuts the house in two, it rings on the sheets of zinc, it makes the sharp leaves of the grass in the yard gleam, it batters the buds of the marigolds, it maddens the pansy-orchid vine which flails its branches and scatters its purple flowers, it paralyzes the cattle huddled under the flamboyán. . . . And there we are in the yard, jumping, and dancing, and paddling in the streams running through the gutters and downspouts and now overflowing the barrels. The rain pours down, the rain pours down. It echoes dully on the roof, it rumbles in the rain gutters, sheets down the sides of the house, flows between the tree trunks, and now forms a broad pool next to the mouth of the well and out by the remaining stands of thorny, troublesome wild pineapples. There we are! There we are! Dancing, jumping, running, whirling through the reddish water and shrieking with delight. . . . It falls on the avenue of oleanders, on the car parked under the trees, on the pine grove bending under the weight of the water, on the red flowers that break off, crushed and battered, and on the sopping land that now begins to reject it. . . . It falls on the cement roof and begins to leak through the roof tiles—and Mama and me running with pitchers, pails, buckets, wash-pans, and we put them under the drips, we roll up the mattresses, close the windows, cover the mirrors. Sit down, she says. And we sit down, our feet on the crosspiece of the stool, not touching the floor so lightning won't strike us. . . . It falls on the ocean that shakes itself and draws itself up and charges upon the Ma-lecón and tops it and spreads out along the street. It falls on the street, on the soaking-wet, scurrying people; it falls, between flashes of lightning, on the towers and the few umbrellas. A gust of wind suddenly penetrates the balcony and bathes my face. It brings that smell of water, the smell of dampness; I feel that urge *(once more, once more)* to do I don't know what, to be I don't know what, to run suddenly through the streets, dive headfirst into the gutter, and rise, disappear, merge, upward, upward with the hawks. For a second I sense someone has knocked at the door. *He comes in the rain, he comes with the rain, he comes from a distant place with the rain.* I run to the door and open it. A deluge sweeps in, stirring the curtains. I instantly close the door. Hector finally stops reading and turns. What happened? Did a window break? he asks. No, nothing, I say. And lightning strikes close by; it is breaking over the whole city, but not here, not on us, where it should strike. . . . It is raining now less violently, more rhythmically, professionally, you might say. Hector is still lying on the sofa; he hasn't taken off his shorts. I am sitting beside the table listening to the shower. Suddenly, in the same sudden way it began, it stops. The clouds disperse; the pine grove takes on a deeper green now; the ocean changes its gray for a thin smooth blue. The cabin is filled with the smell of wet earth. When I turn around, Hector is beside me, brushing his body against mine. I'm going to get the baby, I say, and get up. Then on the porch of the other cabin I think I hear sobbing. I call. The mother opens the door immediately. You don't know how much we've enjoyed having the baby, she says to me; you can leave him with me a little longer if you want to, he already took his milk. I say no and thank her. She opens the bedroom door and picks up the still-sleeping baby. The boy, beside him, covered with a sheet, looks like he's asleep too. My son played with him a lot, the mother tells me. If you'll stay a second I'll make coffee. I make some excuse again, thank her, and say goodbye. She, talking all kinds of nonsense, goes out onto the porch with me. As I go down the steps I seem to hear the strange moaning again. I listen, but now I hear only the ocean, and now the radio Hector has just tuned in: *Tomorrow the big province-wide potato harvest begins!* Hector, without saying a word, turns off the radio and lying back on the sofa closes his eyes. The afternoon sun sifting through the blinds bathes his face, falls lightly across his body; for a while, as the light slides down his legs and off them, and now washes over the sofa, I go on watching him. The silenced radio on his chest. His closed eyes. The still-moist shorts clinging to his body. Once the brightness slips off the sofa and makes a little shining circle on the floor, I stand up; I go out onto the porch. The door of the cabin next door opens and the boy appears. For a moment, surprised, we look at each other again. He is once more arrayed in white pants, tennis shoes, and the same shirt as yesterday. Disconcertedly, he takes a few steps across the porch. Then immediately he goes to the door, doubtless to say goodbye to his mother. Now he passes before me, not looking at me; he crosses the paved path that connects both cabins to the avenue of oleanders. Suddenly, now seeing him cross the almond-tree grove, I think about those sobs I thought I heard; I see Hector lying on the couch, once more talking softly, to himself, so I can't understand what he's saying; I see the smiling face of the mother holding the baby, I see the baby playing with the straps of my bathing suit; I look at the boy again, walking into the pine grove, and I feel I must catch up with him, I must run after him, talk to him. I go into the cabin. Take the baby, I tell Hector, who's now absorbed in inspecting the palm of the hand he's holding up before himself. I head for the beach. The boy, walking slowly, crosses the pine grove, goes up the beach near the promontory where the fort is. It is hard to follow him, but I am going to wait until I get closer to call him. Wet leaves cling to my dress; mud covers my shoes and spatters my legs. The cicadas' whistling now sounds muted. The boy skirts a little bog completely covered with blue flies; he crosses, bent over, through the stand of mangrove trees, comes out onto a part of the shore where there is no beach. I pause, watching him. He comes to the ocean. He pauses too. The smell of damp earth and the whistling of the cicadas from the pine grove now beat against me. The boy, without un-dressing, advances, wading into the water higher than his knees. Then he bends over and seems to observe the water at great length. He puts out a hand and drags it across the water, making a thin wake of spray. Dripping water, he comes out and stands on the rocky ground. He looks all around. He walks by near me, as I watch him from behind the trees. He goes again into the stand of mangroves, taking a muddy track clogged with plants and vines. He stops and looks up at the mangroves, as though orienting himself. Now he goes on faster. I follow him, stooping so much that sometimes I am almost crawling. The ground be-comes even swampier. I don't think either of us will be able to go on. But he goes on, hanging onto tree trunks, grabbing onto branches. I follow his example. The afternoon brings a gloom to the floor of the woods, though the tallest trees are still shining. The swampy ground ends; we come out onto an escarpment covered with dry tree trunks from where you command a view of the entire ocean. The boy, running now, crosses the clearing, comes out on the other side of the mangroves, and climbs the first cliffs made by the rocks. He goes on climbing fast, while I, not worried now about his looking back (knowing, at any rate, that he won't), follow him closely. The climb ends. He takes a few steps over the almost smooth surface of the top of the boulder. He pauses. I, gripping the cracks, still climbing, watch him. He walks to the edge. Down there, the ocean seems to flow slowly, majestically, turning to spray as it crashes against the rocks. He runs all around the promontory now. He stops in the very center. He begins to take his clothes off. He slowly unbuttons his shirt, peels off his pants, kicks off his shoes; he takes off all his white clothing. The brightness bathing part of the boulder shines on his naked body now stretched out on the stones. He has just come for some sun, I think; it would be absurd for me to show up now. It would just inflate his ego. He no doubt would think . . . Anyway, although I think I have to talk to him, I don't have to offer him the chance to insult me, much less to be able to think I'm interested in him. . . . He has just come to doze for a while in the sun, I joyfully think again. What he wants is simply to be alone. I'll wait for him in the pine grove, I'll run into him "accidentally"; I'll talk to him there. I will help him, I tell myself, and think again of the moans I thought I heard in his cabin. Ready to climb down, I contemplate him. But now one of his hands moves slowly down across his chest; it stops at his crotch. He begins to caress his sex, stroking it slowly; he strokes it frenziedly now as his other hand goes to his lips. The din of the cicadas suddenly comes over me so near that it seems as though they were all concentrated on this very rock. I climb down carefully, trying to escape his notice. I run across the rocky clearing, stumbling on tree trunks, hounded still by the cicadas; I run across the stand of mangroves, the pines, the avenue of oleanders, the paved path. I run up onto the porch and go into the cabin. You're just in time, says Hector, now dressed, I've just finished making dinner. But where in the world have you been? You look like you fell into a mudhole. . . . Everything is wet, I say. And we sit down at the table. When we finish, he picks up the plates, telling me to sit still, it's his turn today. I sit on the porch. Once more darkness breaks across the ocean and falls over the pine trees, and as it wraps them it fuses them into one enormous tree. Once more the darkness makes the snaking paths and the cabin roofs gleam, makes the ocean an invisible murmur, a throbbing, a call. Hector, pulling a chair up near me, sits down. . . . Where am I? On the balcony of my house? Beside the ocean? In my mother's bedroom in my hometown? In the country, hearing a familiar sound but awaiting a strange apparition? What darkness am I in now? . . . Woman, for you there is only one same gloom, that which you yourself exhale, that hangs about you. . . . I feel something coming apart in my arms; I look down, and it's the baby. When did I pick him up? I begin to get my bearings. I begin to get my bearings. I am on the balcony of my house, in the darkness, with my baby crying softly, I—I finish getting my bearings—I hear Hector's voice, I feel Hector's hand, he. . . . Are you tired? he asks. I'm tired too, he says. We need to rest. Get away. Disappear for a few days. I'll ask for a vacation tomorrow. Even if it's just a week. They can't turn us down. We'll go someplace peaceful, near the ocean. . . . I hear my breathing grow more serene. . . . I hear his body enclosing me. I hear the murmur of darkness, the murmur of oleanders and the earth. I hear the night in waves, in muted gusts coming up to the cabin porch. I also hear the footsteps of someone approaching, the firm tread and whistling of the boy that make themselves heard as he passes before us. The boy goes up the steps of his cabin, still whistling, and is greeted by his mother. The mother's voice: "You've been gone so long! I'll heat up dinner." And she goes on talking, happy, going inside with her son. . . . Listening to darkness, listening to the slow creak of darkness, looking at those unmoving lights twinkling on the horizon, those lights telling you, *You cannot, you cannot, don't even try* . . . I lay my head back against the chair. But now my neck does not touch wood. Hector's arm is there, awaiting me.

Hearing about us that confusion of thousands of cries, whispers, tiny whistles that make up the night here, that vibration, those flutterings in the darkness, we remain together, quietly, a long while. When I look up, I see the boy on the porch of his cabin, wearing the same white clothing, sitting in a chair, contemplating us. . . . Darling, says Hector now, bring the glasses and bottles and come sit here. I go inside, put the baby down, and come back with the bottles and glasses. Darling, says Hector now, go see if there's any ice left in the refrigerator. I go, thinking, It's just an excuse to be alone on the porch, for each of them to be alone and look at the other. . . . Oh, his voice calls from the porch, bring cigarettes too. Uh-huh, I say, and take longer than necessary, letting him understand I'm giving him some extra time. . . . I go back. He's in the same position before the view, utterly remote from the boy (who is still staring at him), unaware of his presence or, simply, pretending not to have noticed it. I approach and place the ice, the cigarettes on the side table. I will not want. I will not want? No, I hear Hector say. What? I say. Nothing! Nothing, he says, and drops the little pieces of ice into the glass and begins drinking again. We go on like that, the two of us together but distant, chatting about the heat, the mosquitoes, without saying anything. . . . Darling, let's go to bed, he says now. I gather everything up, we stand and go into the cabin. Listening to the distant sound I straighten the sheets, put up the mosquito net; we undress. Now in bed, Hector turns out the light. For a second we are both still, listening to that throbbing, out there. . . . Until Hector rolls onto my body. His legs squeeze my thighs, his sex brushes my belly, his mouth nips at my face. Hector, I say. Hector, I say. And all the sounds disappear. And there is only us, our aroused breathing, our sweaty skin, our bodies joining, our gasping darknesses. Hector, I say. Hector, I say, and see him fade away, on a stick horse, through the cassia thicket. . . . Hector, I say, as we return to the sense of fusing. Hector, Hector, I say, and I am now just hands to squeeze, mouth to moan, something that dissolves and surrenders, receiving, and thinking, faint, Afterward it will be even better, afterward, when I remember it, the pleasure will be absolutely mine. . . . Hector! Little by little I stop moaning; my calls, my whimpers grow more quiet. I descend heavily, I submerge. I come out. I come out to hear the dull murmur of rising water. I hear the wooden walls of this house begin to creak now. Now it is my mother who approaches me. She is black from head to foot, carrying a pot on her head, with the baby inside it. My mother speaks to me. Waving her arms about, she pinches my neck and yanks my ears; she points to the baby clinging to the lip of the pot. She asks me, through wheezes, bellowings, and blows, to get out of this place. But I pay her no heed, and as she goes off cursing, I take a pair of huge shears and begin to cut off my eyelids, finally pulling out one of my eyes. *Banzai, banzai, banzai!* I say, showing my eyeball in the palm of my hand. I am in one corner of this immense house listening to the roar of rushing, rising water and cutting off my fingers. Suddenly a dog is born from one breast; from the other a colored bird. They both quietly beg me to leave this place. The dog bites one of my ears, the bird pecks at my empty eye socket. But I pay them no heed and go on saying my favorite word and cutting off my fingers. Now it is the yagrumo tree, covered with leaves and lizards, that approaches me. In a voice which seems as if at any second it were going to fail, it begs me to leave this place. As the tree pleads, the lizards are aroused and begin crying disconsolately. Their tears fall on the leaves, and the tree, shuddering at my refusal, lets fall a heavy shower of rain. At last it begins to beat me with its branches; it whips my face, my mutilated hands, my head. The lizards climb all over my body and begin to bite me. But I feel neither the lashings nor the bites, and go on saying the word *banzai,* firm in my resolve not to move from this place. . . . I am in this closed-up house, flaying my skin with scissors. (The roar of the inevitable torrent is closer now.) River rocks, round and shining, hop toward me. Go! says the biggest one in a hoarse voice; go! says the tiniest one shrieking hysterically; and it hops around, landing several times on my big toe. Go! says the biggest one in a hollow voice and, starting up with two or three little hops, jumps and suddenly penetrates my sex. Once inside me it begins to whirl and leap about. But I pay no heed to those shining rocks, and as the blood streams down my legs, I go on working with my shears and saying the word *banzai*. I am in this immense house, in this pile of boards, palm husks, and fronds that the wind and sun have bleached, under this ceiling so high that it is almost out of sight. Now I hear the rushing of the madly stampeding mob. Get out, they all say gravely, surrounding me. Get out! they tell me menacingly. Go, quick! begs a boy kneeling before me. Go, my daughter! two old women holding hands and dancing about me say. Leave, madam, please, a heavy woman supplicates in a terrified voice. They all crowd around to expel me. But I pay them no mind and finish peeling my skin off to the bone. The old ladies give me a couple of whacks, a man takes out a jackknife to attack me; a baby begins gnawing on one of my legs. I brandish the shears and screaming *banzai! banzai!* I drive them all away. . . . I am alone in this immense house, slitting my throat. The water now breaks through. In a blind rush it smashes the old palm thatch, the palm boards; it surges and swells into the house. I'm not white anymore, I'm not white anymore, I say as I am swept up by the waters. I feel myself impelled upward. Dead rats, cockroaches, empty cans, furniture legs, bottles, pieces of excrement, corks, a caster off some sofa, a trunk, an aluminum pitcher, almond seeds, a shattered doll, palm husks, all encircle me in the whirlwind that rises in a huge creaking waterspout. I'm not white anymore, I'm not white anymore! . . . My arms crossed, the shears on my chest, we reach the ridgepole and go through the disintegrating roof. We go on rising in an irresistible whirlpool sweeping along palm fronds, drowned bats and blackbirds' nests. Rising higher and higher. . . . I go on rising, in the very center of the waters, in the very center of this lake that once more fills all of space. Me, in the very center of this immense expanse of rising water, now covering everything, everything covered, now, but which goes on, grandly, ceremoniously, with me on top, avid to devour brightness, rising to the very sky. . . . In the midst of the splendor that grows brighter and brighter by the second, I turn over.

SIXTH DAY

Hector, lying on the bed naked, is the first thing I see. Hector naked. Hector's legs. Hector's face. I slowly turn my head and contemplate the length of his body. Hector. We look at each other. We both, naked, contemplate each other. Now, utterly white from the brightness, we begin to come together. Slowly he crawls on top of my body, presses my face. I slowly run my hands down his back. We give up being two, to become one single tense vibration. Hector, I say again. *Hector!* I say for the first time. And the mosquito net comes undone and envelops us as we collapse panting. Then, now, a scream is heard. For a moment we remain in our embrace, utterly still. The cry, a kind of wail, grows even more piercing. We look at each other. We leap from the bed, throw on clothes, and run out toward the cries. A crowd of people is gathered on the beach. The screams are clearer now. I think we both, at the same time, have just recognized them. We shove our way through. The naked, battered body of the boy is lying on the sand. His mother, with her housedress open, is jumping about him with her hands on her head, giving those horrible shrieks. A couple of men come up to her and try to hold her. She goes on howling as she looks at us with dry, bulging eyes. Hector and I draw closer until we are motionless beside the shattered body. He must have fallen from someplace really high, someone softly comments; nobody gets that messed up from just any old fall. Somebody saw him floating right by the shore, another whispers behind me. And the talk goes on. The people arriving begin asking what happened; everybody gives his own theory. I see them all circling the corpse. I see the mother, now tightly restrained but still shrieking. I see Hector. I see the ocean washing sometimes right up to the boy's crushed feet. And I feel, suddenly, a strange sense of calm, a stillness, an unbearable but imperturbable serenity. . . . The police and ambulance arrive together. They inspect the place and photograph the body. At last they signal the medics to put the corpse on a stretcher. They photograph it again. They cover it up. Silence is now almost total; you can only hear the soft moans of the mother—it seems she has suddenly gotten control of herself. One of the policemen gives a sign. The medics carry the body to the ambulance. The mother shrieks again. The police and some other people have to almost drag her to one of the cars. The ambulance door slams. The vehicles pull away. The people, speculating among themselves, disperse. A few swimmers go into the water, others lie in the sun. A lifeguard looks at us. He comes over to us. With his feet he scuffs out the marks the boy's body has left on the sand. We go back to the cabin. As we pass by the office, Hector tells the woman that she can come take her inventory whenever she wants. She shouts from her window that we can stay until noon. Hector asks her please to hurry. We go in. He picks up the baby and begins to feed him. I take down the mosquito net. I gather up all our clothes. When I finish I think I still haven't worn the pants I brought here especially to wear for the first time. I take them out of the bag, and take out the sandals too. I dress. I go to the bathroom. I comb my hair. Hector, still holding the baby, has made breakfast. We both sit down at the table. Someone knocks at the door. Come in, says Hector. It's the woman in charge of taking the inventory. Mechanically, meticulously, she begins to go over everything. We wait on the porch. The whistle of the cicadas rises in step with the brightness. There's an ashtray missing, the woman says to us now. It must be around here somewhere, answers Hector without getting upset; if it doesn't show up, tell us how much it costs. The woman refuses to take money. The Management won't allow it, she says, and goes back to hunting for it carefully. At last she finds it under an armchair. We turn in the key and leave the cabin. We cross the paved path; we come to the car. Hector puts the luggage into the trunk. Since the baby has gone to sleep we put him in the back seat. Hector starts the engine. Looking through the pines at the ocean, I light a cigarette.

The ocean, I think, and now we pass under the arch that marks the entrance to the tunnel where huge letters spell out ON-WARD, ALWAYS, TO VICTORY. The ocean, I think, and see Hector, growing old, speed up even faster as he takes the curve in the tunnel which carries us into Havana. The ocean, I say, thinking We will arrive, we are already arriving, within a few minutes we will be going into the house. . . . For a time—January, February, March, perhaps—the days won't be so fierce, we'll be able to get out onto the balcony once in a while; we'll be able, perhaps, sometimes, to go to the movies, in the evening, provided someone will stay with the baby; go to the movies, see a film we've already seen a hundred times. But Listen, listen—it will just be a little break. There will be the unending days of work in the fields again, the compulsory labor at the camp, the moment you'd give anything for a glass of water, the unbearable degradations, the hateful speeches that last a whole day and then are repeated—*oh, faster, faster*—until even you can repeat them from memory. . . . Perhaps you can have a new dress to wear once a year, go out once a year to a restaurant. But feeling real enthusiasm, joy, recompense, *that* you are not entitled to. . . . You will grow old, and all your dreams, and all your aspirations, all your hopes (all your *efforts*) to be something, not this thing we are, will gradually fade away, be forgotten, discarded in the face of the pressure to find a pack of cigarettes or a Sunday afternoon free, to sleep. . . . *Faster! Faster!* . . . We are now passing through the tunnel, accompanied by that din of nocturnal creatures, the shrieking of those voices which cut off further thought. *Faster! Faster!* they cry, louder and louder, until it becomes one great, single roar of millions of joined cries. . . . With the wind of that shrieking screaming past our ears, with that vast mother's shrieking resounding down the tunnel, we come out into brightness. The screeching dies away, the colossal howls of the mother fade away. Hector, an agéd man, drives even faster. There we go. *Hector, Hector,* I scream, clutching him. And still, through the wind and the wall rushing toward us, I can see, once more, the ocean.

PART TWO

The naked man sings his own special woe.
José Lezama Lima

CANTO ONE

The ocean
            now is muted tumult,
its outrages masked by quiet
whispers.
            The ocean
writhing cry,
ruffled instrument
over which all terrors
have glided,
above which all fanfares
have resounded.

                    The ocean

a gust of raucous laughter,
a relentlessly stalking fury,
a luminous death rattle.

                            Summers.

Like a fag in heat
rushing through the streets,
hoarse, possessed by a fury,
eager and damned;
thus the ocean bleeds and writhes,
strikes, trembles,
arches, returns,
and ends up lashing itself
with its own abstinence.

Like the adolescent boy in school,
a scholarship boy
who awaits the precise moment
(the single instant)
to throw himself on his phallus
and perform the epileptic
jerks—
rapid and rudimentary—
furtive and trembling,
swooning and scared,
yet still gasping and stroking;
thus the ocean strokes,
with timeless indignation,
the dirty seabed where
shining ships bob and sway
that in times gone by
trafficked in hope—
                    the seabed where
ironwork, stones, and
rings,
bones and coins and rotted flesh
and titles
tickle and bite.

Summers.

A woman
in rising menopause—
                    ay, the poor thing can't take it anymore—
seized by a fire that aches like a bruise,
unscrews the water-pump handle
(the thick haft of ancient wood)
and buries it within her, out behind
the farm-machine shed;
afterward she lies spread-eagled, bleeding and spent,
gasping yet still ungratified.
Thus the ocean lies spread wide,
like that sad shafted woman.
Thus the ocean rends and whips itself,
like that sad queenly fag.

Thus the ocean strokes itself
and vomits,
finding
no comfort,
like that racked boy
jerking off
in the latrines
of the new monasteries.

                                     Ocean of Fury,

hear now the cry
of this desperate son,
for I am certain they
won't give me time
to cry out again.
                 Radiant Ocean,
hear now this hurried account
of those infamies most memorable;
let me
number mine,
for I will not be able to tell
over the whole wearying inventory.

             We will drive along through
the pine grove's shade
but the din of the cicadas
will not drown our common
din.

                                     The ocean.

            We have driven already
through the orchard's shade
but the crunching of the leaves
adds nothing to our common
crunching.

                                     The ocean.

            We have already driven
down the avenue of oleanders—
                  still hanging on, still persisting—

but the constant bursting of the crabs
under the car
means nothing to our common
bursting.

                                        The ocean.

We have already taken the highway
but the insult of that brightness
filled with billboards
adds nothing to our constant
insult.

                              The undulating ocean.

"High and alone, high
and alone," I hear you say.
                A few hours ago, it must be now,
I too thought of saying lovely things.
Worms came out instead—amoebas—
old queens skulking
in sewers,
        urgent
adolescents aging under the first blow,
blazes,
wild little gods
snarling at each other over hunks
of excrement,
howls,
crowded vessels embarking,
vessels shelled and fired upon,
files of innocents tearing out their eyes
quite sure
(as the latest directives proclaim)
that they will see better that way,
exquisite sentimental swishing fags
longing for the "gold of olden times"
or "days" (I forget)
and desperately waiting for the visa to come
that gives no sign of coming;

Catholic campy gays who curse
(more bitterly than the son-of-a-bitch demi-god)
the Bitch-goddess his Mother
who now sends them off to a work camp where
they raise hemp plants.
Hounded, harassed queens.
University graduates metamorphosed into gay day-laborers
(and all because their hormones got mixed up?)—
fags picking tobacco
under a hellishly hot canopy of acres of mosquito net,
still thinking of the distant, pale façades
of the cathedrals in Murcia.
Fags who wanted to keep their secret
but "The Party had a talk with their parents."
Fags slitting their throats.
Fags throwing themselves headfirst from the seventeenth
        floor
of a university dormitory.
                    Fag after fag after fag.
All trying to fly the coop.
All in the throes of death (snorting, stamping)
and dyeing their frayed shirts
with gentian violet
or hanging little cards in the European style,
made from the flyleaves
of manuals on Marxism-Leninism,
around their necks —
JE SUIS FROID, *I am hot.*
Fags collecting anxieties and polished colored stones
on beaches kept under surveillance.
Fags—whom two thousand years of persecution
(now intensified)
have imbued with that air of a hawk
in flames,
the desperate look of a rat caught by surprise
in the middle of the women volunteer workers'
bunkhouse.
Fags who have seen the creases of their asses wrinkle
                            from harassment.

Sad Weird Sisters, beached, cast away,
on the shores of the nine oceans of infamy—

                        Ocean of Harassment
                        Ocean of Blackmail
                        Ocean of Misery
                        Ocean of Abstinence
                        Ocean of Damnation
                        Ocean of Impotence
                        Ocean of Desperation
                        Ocean of Forced Labor
                        Ocean of Silence

and the little seas
of day-to-day fury,
of day-to-day insult,
of day-to-day weariness.

                                        Undulating.

Friezes
columns
marble statues
trees   palaces   and castles
waving grasses   walks   tablec
loths unfolding   laughter   freedom
of expression   freedom of movem
ent   freedom of elections   freed
om to loathe those palms
against the sky   dreams   wor
ds   words   words   words
                                                                        words
images which shatter
against the great signboards recently erected.
            But you will sing,
heed me well;
you will wring the peacocks' necks
and piss on the chaste trees,
you will stuff the ice-cream man's Sunday tinkling
up his ass,
you will feed arsenic to the survivors of the family
of "Old Hope,"
you will toss Martí's "little pink slippers"
onto the burning bush.

You will denounce that woman to the Coast Guard—
            that one there,
fishing in the sea (ah, madam, if they should see
you shift your substantial body onto that bobbing spar,
not giving a shit for the laurel crown, fleeing in darkness
from intransigent vulgarity, yearning
for the vulgarity of hard work! I fear under these circumstances
you would not be able to compose your sonnet
"On Parting"—"Pearl of the ocean, star of the . . ."];
you will masturbate over the "prodigious flood"
            (now, now, while nobody's watching me)
and stand in line for the hooves (the rest
goes to the Soviet Union) of the bull killed by Heredia in 1832
with forty hendecasyllable lines,
your purr will burst their eardrums—
those people who still dream "dreams of glory engulfed, lost
in the deep night of Time."
You will expose the bullshit that always hides
behind divine rhetoric.
You will teach distrust of big words,
big promises,
big heroic charades.
Your blasphemies will poison the city that smothers you.
    Or
you might simply say
            A military post
            A shimmering highway
            A glare shaping mirages
                    the pavement dissolves into.
            A military post
            A dry hillside flayed of green
            An ex-fruit stand
            An ex-restaurant
            An old sign peddling
                    soft drinks
            An old mansion inhabited now by cows
                    and great white birds.
            A military post
            A military post
            A military post

Or will I say
          Historical fatality,
and accept the diverse shades of horror,
finding, like a good militant, a rationalization
to fit every terror?
     Will I say
          It's true, there's no place to sit down,
but it was terrible before, too—and with those words
will I beatifically sit my ass down
on the burning Island?
     Or will I say
          Everything is awful, but if you learn to bear
and to fake, if you learn to lie, perhaps they'll finally let
you in, and they'll repay your obedience by raising
your rice ration and lowering
the quota of prescribed kicks which are stipulated
for you, a petty bureaucrat?
     Or
will I murmur nothing, ask for nothing, and,
unaccepting but unprotesting, burst
in silence,
like these sea nettles and men-of-war that waves tug at
and driftwood destroys?
          What shall I say?
          What shall we say?
          What will I be able to say that somebody—
besides ourselves in our historical complicity, in our common
hell—
may understand?
          I do say   What do I say?
          I shall say   What shall I say?
          I am saying   What am I saying?
          I can say   What can I say?

At dusk, whirls of fiery water flowing.
At dusk,
          will there already be a solitary adolescent
flaunting the outrageous insolence of his beauty?
                                   No, not yet.

_____

At dusk,
          will there be a warm stretch of sand
where for six days we can appease our furies?
                                        Now, now.
At dusk,
          will the dining room on the beach be open? Will there
be a line? What will there be to eat?
                                        Lentil soup.
At dusk,
          will there be a dance of dinosaurs, a woman
lamenting woman's old fate, a baby still too young to talk
who awaits the truncheon blow and the chance to heap scorn,
a respectable family?
                                        Naturally.
At dusk,
          will the din of cicadas give us any chance
to hear, really hear the sound of our own lamentations?
                                        No way.
At dusk,
          will there be a bottle still corked, a table
under the trees,
two towels, two inconsolable bodies polishing the tarnished
rhetoric
of the domestic ritual? The galling mask,
tradition, the state, good habits, the family, Party morale?
                              Always,
                                   always,
                                        always.

     At dusk, whirls of fiery water flowing, whereward, where-
ward. . . . At dusk, whirlwinds of birds, flames, fluttering feathers; the headlong scrabble, over still-shining sand, of creatures
most ancient and persisting—creatures made for escape, for opening holes and disappearing before the foot falls and squashes them,
before the crack of the stick crushes them, before the roar of an
infuriated wave bears them away; creatures that have been forced
by a history of threats and harassment, of kicks and contempt,
by a life of "kill it, it's so creepy," to take their eyes and project
them above their bodies—eyes like uneasy antennas, revolving

radar, instruments uniquely suited for detection and salvation. At dusk, the scurrying of crabs covering the whole extent of this beach gilded for an instant, which is still miraculously given me to see (just for a little, just for a little while);
the slithering of bellies seeking the millennial hole, certain that nothing has changed; the headlong creeping, the frantic dashing and skittering, the nervous rattling and fading away, seeking some temporary safety, the scant protection of the few places still silent and dark. And meanwhile,
a whirlwind of light falling on the ocean. Whirls of violet water. The pine grove taking fire, the flock of gulls gliding in formation, whereward. . . . Ah, my organdy sweetheart, my hysterical skunk in those prehistoric dresses of yours, worn now for the first time, rustling. Ah, anonymous porpoise in your shirts just now dyed, here is the ocean. Ah, mother, pathetic whore who tries to console me with fond monochord letters—*Tell me whether you're eating, tell me whether you're sleeping, tell me whether you're still alive.* . . . Ah, my pathetic whore, hellish creature, virgin and martyr, old fire-tending beast with grease-spattered face. Ah, hidden womb you opened only twice—to lodge and to expel. Ah, forever sacrificed, ah, slut, ah, mother most beloved in spite of all, here is the ocean your eyes will never be able to understand. And the sorrowful lot of the poet—those essences everywhere that beckon and madden you—inevitable lot of the poet forever gagged by the men who buy and sell happiness. The ocean. . . .

Ancient and Splendorous Ocean, the Countess, a whore to the tips of her toes, crossed you not to admire your gleams but to see what she could make off with from this Island—where, according to her (such worn-out romantic boasting), a drop of rain fills a glass, a seed becomes a tree as it falls upon the ground. . . . The Countess, desperately looting. Her pimp is named Charles; he is a professor of philosophy (such bad taste). Ay, Mercedes, what demands the pimp makes. Ay, my poor menopausal María Mercedes—more plucked than the parrot in the tale.

Come, venture out onto the sea, let's dance on the ocean (did Christ perchance do a few steps on it?), let's plunge into the ocean, or write a book about the ocean, put Paula Avenue to some use, limn the Pier of Light, but hurry, for the pimp grows more and more pressing—here is his last letter: *Write, write,*

write. Stretch that paragraph, ask Mérimée to check your spelling, dedicate the book to His Excellency General O'Donnell. "Permit me, General, to place this book, conceived out of the patriotic sentiments of a woman, under your protective aegis."* Ay, General, screw me with your acgis, toss me a few more little pesos for this miserable paragraph. Ay, General, ay, General. Ay . . . Island. All daring shatters against you. All miseries have grazed on your so-vaunted greenness, and now they have settled in, and it looks like they're here to stay. Smugglers and adventurers have sung your praises, as an exotic harlot possessed in passing in a warm distant city is praised in after-dinner talk. And so, while they cursed you because they found nothing in you, they also bestowed on you, in passing (one must always think of History—perhaps Moreno Fraginals will read these notes), a spray of stars, adorned your coasts with the nonexistent brilliance of a fish likewise nonexistent. Ah, ocean. Ah, ocean—no one has cast you pearls (save perhaps Martí's mad Mooress) but everyone wants to get them back again. Libations, sacrifices, and offerings, and now these skillful fornications and this muted machine-gun clatter—have they raped you? Do those frenzied frictions, those bursts arouse you? Or is it the golden nates of adolescents plunging straight down to brush against your bed that make you lose the beat? Perhaps it is more than you can bear, and so you boom. You crash against the wall from which I contemplate you—are you always bursting and I alone divine it? You convulse, bellow, erupt—are you always aroused and I alone divine it? When you moan, pale under the reflection of the stars—can you bear it no longer and I alone divine it? When you lie motionless and your still surface only gives me back my face—are you dead? Can it be that this verbal flood of mine has no interest for you whatsoever and that we contemplate each other, always unseeing, here, where all is silence? And when you throw off sparks and burst, bellow and rear like a crazed, hunted beast, as my fury does as well—can it be that only we alone, the two of us, are left to tell the tale? The two of us, living among ruins and petrified, venerable banners? If we suffer—have we died, or are we the last two left alive? Tell me, if we suffer—have we died? If we suffer—

*Mercedes Santa Cruz, Condesa de Merlin: *Viaje a la Habana* (*Voyage to Havana,* a nineteenth-century travel narrative originally written in French).

are only we left to go on alone? Tell me, tell me, for the afternoon only dazzles, it does not console; the pine grove whispers but does not make sense; the wind only carries the cry, it does not soothe it; and the sand receives our body in impersonal embrace. Tell me, since no one any longer holds back the terror, and it spreads over the Island walled in by banners; it claims, in high-flown communiqués, all the farms and even this stockaded beach where it plants its military units, its Coast Guard. Ah, ocean, ah, oh shun this place!, though you be the rhythm of our dis-concert. Ah sea,
swish away, oh ocean, shun this place!, swish gaily away

so you may

see.

Words

     words
words now only thought,
sometimes murmured, but
fearfully, almost silently.
Incoherent—words spoken under the breath. Words
which cause a man forever to forfeit love, the soothing habit of walking through the streets and talking to strangers as though to old friends, the leisure for listening to others, any chance (how-ever remote, anyway) of a trip to the "developed countries," the pleasure of sporting a well-fitting shirt, the privilege of eating a grilled fish, the walk under the trees, the roar of the ocean. Words someone was forever condemned by, someone fried to a crisp with. Words with which someone mysteriously suddenly contracted cancer. Words always spoken in the certainty that then comes the hatchet. Words spoken in fury and hunger. Words which deny or doubt but do not supplicate or obey, words which reject institutionalized crime and the imposition of a law on the creases of an ass, the imposition of a hymn on all the schools, of a jargon, of a cuirass over the heart, of a lie on all men. Words which refuse to accept the happiness that great theoreticians have made plans for, as glibly as they announce a grand pork plan to be implemented throughout the nation. Is anyone dazzled by the polished harshness of their Thou Shall Not's? Is there anyone

who hears those voices? Is there anyone who catches the cry in the faces of those who seem to smile? Is there anyone to halt the march of the new rhetoric which annihilates as well? Is there anyone to feel the fury as his own? Is there no one who retains a memory outraged, proof against the stupefying mottoes and the spanking-new threats? Who picks up that roar? Who sees beyond? Who suffers suffering?

> Who turns back the terror?
> Who eats shitmeat on his feet?
> Who swallows the fool's drool?
> Who fingers the fusty spinster?
> Who licks the fetish's dick?
> Who lights up the rancid night?
> Who hears the hitch in the pitch?
> Who washes the horse's watercress?
> Who takes the snake up with a rake?
> Who's touched by the heat, jumps up from his seat,
> and steals a feel on the keel?

I mean,   Who climbs the coconut tree when it's hot
            and picks his nose and eats his snot?

> *You do! . . . You mean,*
> *you do not!*

A cicada grates out its persistent sound. Whirlwinds of lights and roar of water briefly violet. Whirlwinds of birds. Flash of a wave. A cry. An erupting ball. Children leaving, children running under the pines. The sudden restlessness of a whirl of rising paper—whereward, why. . . . Boys moving away. Demons moving away. The racket of cicadas in rhythm suddenly ceases. The crash of furies. The golden crash of water. Someone's voice rings out; a woman's ringing call. The voice of a woman ringing out. Your woman (ah, wedding-be-ring'd) whose call rings out. The image, violet too, of a woman whose voice rings out your name. Of a voice in flames? Of a woman ringed in flames? Finally, your woman (be-ring'd) ringing you—in flames.

At dusk, whirlwind of violet light, violet crabs, violet birds. Calling you. Noise, slaps of water, voices ringing out to you,

voices ringed in flames. Someone who comes touching the ocean,
the violet ocean. Dusk. Voices, voices, but no heart that hears?
                    Can it be true?
                    Can it be true?
                    Can it be true?
                                The barking of a dog.

On the earth
there is a place in flames
against the place in flames   the ocean beats
Beside the ocean   a house.
Or no, better yet:
              The earth
                      a place in flames
              The place in flames
                      an island
              The island
                      a hulk the ocean hits
              The ocean
                      September
              September
                      a house
              The house
                      a mosquito net
              The mosquito net
                      a cell
               The cell
                      she and I
              She
                      I
              I
                      she
                              Behold, the earth.
                              Behold, the place in flames.
                              Behold, the cell.
              Who holds the key?
              She?
              Me?
              Sleep?

She: "Sleep?"
Me: "Sleep?"
        I

        Behold, loathing.
        Behold, insomnia.
        Behold, the fear
        that she will insist.
   Under the mosquito net
       closed eyes
   Under the closed eyes
       wakefulness
   Under the wakefulness
       desire also

Toward her?
By her?
For her?

        Behold, the earth.
        Behold, the place in flames.
        Behold, the longed-for silence
   in which great fears, glowing, graze.

By her?
Because of her?
Because of her beseeching?

        Behold, the place in flames.
        Behold, the first yawn.
        Behold, the third mosquito

biting me and I have to pretend I'm asleep.
Is this her fault?
Is this for hatred of her?
Is this to keep her?
Is this just for her?

        At last
     The delirium of colors
     The delirium of interrogations
     The delirium of images

Does she appear?
Is she, too, delirious?
Is she speaking?

And that fondling
And that work camp
And that book
And that sobbing
      Are all grieving women
passing their hands
across my crotch?

CANTO TWO

A line of strange monsters passes
playing musical instruments.

(Marxism erupting)

The brief coolness of dawn passes.

(Marxism erupting)

Pass by,
never-halting hope.
Hope plucked of feathers, pass by.
Shattered, dusty hope,
pass by.
You pass by. And what remains behind?
You pass by. And what savor, what breath?
You pass by, and what of it.

Marxism erupting
like an intoxicating metaphor
in naïve men's heads.

I'm leaving.

One must always leave.

I'm leaving.

One must always grab one's stuff, pack one's duffle,
and beat it.
One must always choose again the sad road of the
sad (the honest, the insolent, the true) men who have
gone before us.

I'm leaving.

But one must always leave.
One must always leave.

All the heralds of night pass.　　　　　　　And
a bird, they say, shrieked in the air.
A bird, they say, beat its wings against the half-
closed blinds; beat against your dream.
　　　　　　　　　　　　A bird, they say.

I'm leaving.
　　　　　But
one must always leave.
You always have to take off running and get lost.
Panting, you've got to wipe out the last remnants, destroy
the last dreams,
and run out naked, as though fleeing a crime,
silently flee,
flee screaming silently,
and enter the darkness silently.
Flee the darkness and silently enter the darkness.

　　　　　　　　　　　　　　Island,
on you all flights of daring crash, and burn.
You are sad, like the letter from a friend in exile,
like the figure of an old fag
with dyed hair,
like the voice of a man calling to the creatures in the garden
of his childhood.
With your year-round meadows where a starving cow grazes
on your monotony, you are sad.
With your houses built for other climes,
with your over-seasoned seasons,
with your avenues, shorn of trees and hedges,
which once had signs and now have slogans,
with your women now strictly imbecile
　　　(bovine, oxlike),
with your cynical rumba-ing men
　　　(big kids),
with your exhibitionist youth,
with your philosophy of bread-and-guava for everybody,
with your grab-assing and backside-swinging,
with your crushing collection of shrieking fags,
with your immense dusty summer

with your single river
your single highway
your single product
your symbolic tree
your highly touted *joie de vivre:*
                                    You are sad.
    And yet this is the place you love best—
more than anything else in the world.

    And yet this is the place that will haunt you forever
and that you'll always want to hold. . . . What has come to pass?
What always comes to pass? (Did Rodrigo de Triana really pass
this way?)

    A mosquito buzzes past my ear.
A car passes (the sound of a car)
and stops before our cabin.
I pass my hands down over my body,
I slip from under the mosquito net,
I slip through the passage and
pass into the parlor.
                        Who said: *Living is watching things pass by?*
It might be watching that boy pass by,
that boy getting out of the car,
elastic,
bouncing now on the path.
Living
like a little turtle lodged in an outhouse full of roiling worms.
Living seeing life pass,
getting nothing out of it but a bunch of standard insults
or a mess of nontransferable promises.
Living always waiting for someone else to decide,
determine, do with us what they
will
        (a blade of grass stuck in a pile of foul shit always waiting
                                        to be plucked out).
Living
seeing pass by
—and only once in a while, at that.
                                Which is older?

Damnation or desire?
Or are they simply one?

                                                            She comes
sulking and silent.
She, the sufferer,
poor wet rat, comes in like one of those people who don't even
dare to say excuse me.
Her image passes
behind my body in flames.
We are informed that they've been married ten years
(exactly).
We are informed that they fled their hometown.
We are informed that nights
We are informed that afternoons
We are informed that mornings

                                        We are informed that he goes
                                        out alone

and visits a depraved beach.
        As for that which pertains to the female spouse,
we are informed
                that she is silly
                that she is foolish
                that she loves him.
                                And he turns and looks at her.
And he looks at how she looks at him,
and he knows, when he looks at her,
that she too was looking where, at whom, he looked.
She knows that the two of them looked at each other.
                                And that they're waiting.
And he lowered his eyes before her gaze.
He contained his fury.
He said not a word.
                        (Were seagulls passing? Were seagulls
                        flying by? Were the seagulls shrieking?)

Your eyes have gazed at me
with such muted sadness
that for a moment there awoke in me
the now obsolete feeling of pity.

Your eyes have gazed at me
with such quiet desperation
that for a second you re-awoke in me
my now withered tenderness.

Your eyes have gazed at me
with such silent pleading
that they managed, briefly, to stall
the iron gears of this curse.

Your eyes have gazed at me
with such desolate intensity
that for a second I almost blessed
tradition's poor, dying light.

Your eyes have gazed at me
with such helpless questioning
that all words were rendered futile.

Your brimming eyes have gazed at me
with such irresistible compassion,
with such despairing love,
that for a moment I thought I'd glimpsed
the aching (terrifying) face
of complicity.

                                    The yellow ocean.

The sea
murky
ochre
and tranquil.
The sea gray as a ce-
ment slab.
The ocean
like an old prophecy
which will deliver up to us
only its outward sense.

                    The ocean
like an iron fence across which gossipy old charlatans are reduced
to gesture.
(But they gushed forth.)
The ocean like a lowing in the fog, like a gurgling
through
the murky air,
like a meaningless roar.

(Could he be the chosen one?
Chosen for what? Chosen by whom? —Fool,
no way.)
For in these miserable towns, you say, I say to myself, I say,
I make you say, looking out into the intractable brightness, intractable green,
not even the promise of an unlooked-for rapture
can shake us;
everything is so bright, so elemental, so coarse and
emphatic.
Everything is known before it comes to pass, everything is told
before it occurs.
Therefore the victim never is caught unawares
by the knife; he carries it with him always. And even terror
itself perishes, pulverized by the methodical whispering in
back yards crossed and recrossed by that one same sun of fire,
and that age-old frustration, that weariness, that
                    t   e   d   i   u   m.
Don't you see those long hands of his? He's a cretin.
Don't you see that long pale face? He's a snob.
Look at the way he bobs up and down when he walks.
What a hick!
Oh, look how he lowers his eyes and hunches his shoulders. He's
one of those queers, they must have missed him.
                    Plunging
into a yellow ocean.
                    Entering,
with his fists out,
a yellow ocean.

_____

                                    Go
                                 f
                              a
                              r
                                 f
                              a
                              r
                              a
                                 w
                              a
                              y
                                          on a yellow ocean. . . .

In the house
aunts,
in the house
cousins,
in the house the old dressed-up Sunday creatures,
the cry of unsatisfied women,
grandfather and grandmother who never get sick, burying
the hatchet
in your back. And the feeling of never-ending ennui,
your fate
        (awaiting you)
in the tiny mounds of dust left by the termites,
the dust your hands scatter
when you unconsciously lay them on the sill
of that window
                that opens on nothing
        (silently stalking you, imagining you).

And the ocean
whirling yellow
became the wheels of the carts at the harvest
of the corn.
                                The myrtles flowering.
And the rhythmic, musical sound of the winter rain
announced the coming
of Christmas Eve.
                .   .   .

Throughout the stands of wild pineapples—bells.
On the air, in the mares' hooves—carols.
Arrival of the relatives
(they gushed forth).
The splendid cousins display their impressive
familio-phallic specimens.
High-breasted angry women.
Round-assed women.
Women with lips that flap like sheets
in a heavy gale.
Women always about to be shipwrecked on the beaches
of some fly.
Women of shrill, rare, and dizzying verborrhea.
Women.
And splendid cousins.
They all arrive and hover around you.
    (Behold, music.)
A cow has gotten lost, but I won't go looking for her today.
Today I'm going dancing.
Today I'm going looking.
Today I'm going to suffer.

                              Back of the thicket
in pairs,
                    cooing and laughing.
Back of the orchard
in flocks,
shrieking and holding
hands.
                              Back of the orchard,
spreading thighs.
And them steering the course of things.
They are supple and assured,
                triumphant,
screwing.
                The
                big
                meal.
Them groping under the table (you, drinking).
The big
            meal.

Them bursting into laughter and snorting with pleasure (you,
    wolfing it down).
The big meal.
The women clucking, breaking dishes, and dancing. (You,
fleeing.
The prickly stands of wild pineapples offer you
        their mocking, invariable shelter.)

When you dived
you touched the seabed
and the waters were no longer yellow.

Sand covers your eyes, you hold your breath;
at last, you shoot to the surface, to machinery's echoing sound—
                ga-ga-*boom*
                ga-ga-*boom*
                ga-ga-*boom*.
                        The Advance of the Revolution,
and him living in a house
falling to pieces, doomed,
among unsatisfied women
and lecherous old men.
                        Advance of the *R*

and him hearing the rumor
of furtive suicides,
boasting about the
inconclusive resolutions he made,
his postponed resolutions—
clumsy, unjustified post-
ponements.
                        Advance of the *R*
and him sitting in the living room
watching two lizards
who, if they aren't in love, at least
certainly have the hots for each other.
                        Shots,
and him watching the bustle
of happy vermin.
You'll die of hunger as others die

of fear or heroism, or
of colic nephritis—pointlessly.

                                Advance of the *R*
and letters from his mother
typical motherly letters
typical letters from a poor countrywoman
clumsy loving
and alone
who after working for twelve hours
in a factory
in Florida (Wait a minute! Didn't they tell me
she was taking care of somebody's kids?)
still has the spunk to write
Dear son. . . .

                            Who comforts us then,
who scratches an ear and tries to protect the son
from bad weather,
from lascivious words
spoken greedily (ah, how they lure you).
Who protects you from so much harmful protection
Who from the men's rooms
Who from the cousins
Who from the downpour seen through the window
Who from the conversation of unsatisfied women
Who from the soap operas and bloody handkerchiefs
Who from an old woman muttering curses
              at the head of the table
Who from the shut-up cunts running the house
Who from the excessive chatter
Who from the excessive sewing
Who from the excess of foolish loving letters
Who from the sewing machine
Who from the games of chaste women
Who from that smell
Who from your cousins' boyfriends
Who from the kith and kin that kiss you
Who keeps down your cousin
Who from the secret sweating
Who from so much white, white,
white.

And the death of his mother.

"Just look at this. He killed his mother again. This
is the third time he's buried her."

"Yes, sir. Don't believe a word he says."

"But it's really true" says the obnoxious aunt, "and after
his mother died (or rather, after he killed her, because she died
of sadness), he came to our house, for a rest. Or really, even before,
he was almost always here. He slept here, ate here every day.
Here! Those other bitches never cared what he was doing. That's
something that needs to be said. And also . . . !"

When you come
to the surface, far from shore,
when you look at the water flowing away,
when you look at those distant bodies that seem to flash
in the sun,

has the moment come?

On your back,
the waters which looked yellow carry you away
and follow you,
a flooded place, an empty echoing realm.

Can you not live without the
word?

When bats burst out into the half-light
of your woman's restless sleep,
when you hear the hysterical, rhythmic echo
of a million enslaved, degraded creatures
suffocating—
Who do you love?
Who do you trust?
Who are you waiting for?

Confronted with the firebombs of September
and the other 11 hells,
confronted with the armored shore and the ocean that now flaunts
only the outrage of a new fanfare—
Who do you love? Who do you trust?
Who are you waiting for?

Confronted with the din of the forks,
and the forced, compulsory stints in the fields,

the heat, the hoe bogged down, an anthem you must intone
that says you are grateful, and absolutely free—
Who do you love? Who do you trust?
Who are you waiting for?
      Confronted with that firm teenager's body that offers up
its brilliant insolence to the sun—there, there, there he is—
confronted with the boys' salacious gestures
traced with casual (terrifying) innocence;
      confronted with the rudeness of the waitress
      and the half-done croquettes,
confronted with the thousand futile gestures which,
obligatorily,
you must make day after day,
confronted with the thousand futile slogans which obligatorily,
optimistically,
you must repeat day after day—
Who do you love?
Who are you waiting for?
Who can you trust?
      Confronted with the shameful present decked out in
gaudy tinsel from the shameful past,
confronted with the trashcans full of medals
that wall in the future,
confronted with the lack of water and of faith,
      confronted with the unerring possibility
      that they'll shoot you
if you manage to print what you think,
confronted with the possibility that you'll disappear in that ocean
that condemns you, excludes you,
      confronted with the possibility that you
      (and everyone with you) will disappear
      into this land that curses you and excludes you,
or confronted with the possibility that they'll make you
a laborer in the van,
worker emeritus, hero, candidate to the Party,
model youth chosen to visit the friendly tombs
abroad—
Who do you love?
Who do you trust?
Who are you waiting for?

Against frustrated pride, against perpetual cowardliness,
against the loneliness of exile, against the possibility that they'll
reduce the size of your cell; ah, against remote dignity, against
distant rebelliousness,
and against the permanent terrors against which there can be
no possibility of rebellion or of truce,
     the burning pain in your back,
     your hair falling out,
     the afternoon that once again comes and drags out
     its passing and stamps another line of weariness on
     your face;
ah, against loneliness and impossible desires,
against the crumbling afternoon,
against the crumbling life,
against that beat and beat again of the water,
and against the growths a little above your navel,
against the lubricious sidelong glances of the women
who desire you, and
(once more)
     the young man in the long white shirt who aims to
drive you mad—
     What do you throw up to protect yourself with?
     How do you protect yourself?
     What do you do to protect yourself?
Against the way the Grand Inquisitor tugs at his ear,
standing now on the reviewing stand toward which we march
to cheer him,
   against the makeup clotting the eyelashes of the woman
   who pours our water
   (after we have finished eating),
   against the neighbor's laughing and interminable chatter,
   against the bitter face of the militant gay,
   against the vacancy of memory and the eagerness
       of imagination,
ah, against being rejected and having a pass made at you—
       what secret, intimate terror, all your own,
unique, nontransferable, sustains you?
Against the first body
felled by the volley (and revolutionary justice)—
What high ideals, or what resentments,
immunize your vision?

. . .

The March sun.

March afternoons
when silence
was not just an occasional comfort
coming like a pleasant surprise,
but a quality of the weather,
a natural thing.

The March sun.

March afternoons,
the wind and smells of
March;
      the walk
            and March returning,
and the varied colorations of the sun like an inexhaustible
sphere
         revolving;
the river through the leaves, through the seasons,
a mirror of white river through leaves, turning,
the warm lighted earth, wheeling, seen from the window
of a moving train,
         revolving.

     No.
Don't stop, don't
stop, go on, go on, don't
ever
stop.
           Scratch my cunt, crun, cran, crack.
Scratch my crorrk, cros, cros, crossk.
Yell at the dogs, turn up the radio.
Sing, sing louder,
         crawk, crac, crawc.
Bark, bark, bark
drop to all fours
bark, bark, bark
        phonyosfrasf, phonyosfrasf, phonyosfrasf.
Do you like it like this or do you want it with a little turpentine?

Do you like it like this or with hendecasyllabic enjambment?
Do you like it like this or with plain Vaseline?
Tell me how you like it
so I can always say it to you another way.
Bread?
Broth.
Cassava?
D'you pronounce that *garbâzhe?*
Was that a cat meowing?
No, a dog barking.
Is that a dog barking?
No, a hundred or so cats.
Is someone singing on the hill?
Yes, they're standing in line for the dill.
                              But
                                    they
        sprouted forth.
The beloved in profile
                    ha ha ha:
                              the beloved in profile.

Midday does not flow by, we flow
through it.
In the bright light of day,
with a book in your hand,
what's most important is to run away,
don't look at that face
don't let yourself give in.
Wait, while everything dissolves in the heat and the glare (the
popular song fades away, the baby has gone to sleep). Before us
the boy now passes in his white garments.
He passes. He has passed.
He passed. . . . He is passing.
                    —Cozzen the cousin before she kisses you.
"But above everything, the calm," you say.
I close my eyes: a dance of vermin.
(Lovers washed out in the glare of the pine grove.) I open them:
glassily they collide, they hover over my eyelids.
                    You
are in the same old bedroom
        (organ music)

in the same old hail of grumblings and threats;
you hear how she is stirring in the other room—
(outside, the era's standard adornments—bombs, shots,
arguments, shouts, threats, torture, humiliation, fear, hunger),
and you too stirring up the unspoken things that stick in your
craw.
You are on the porch of the cabin ten years later
    (military music).
You hear her typical nervous longing breathing,
there inside—(outside, the era's standard trappings—
arguments, shouts, threats, torture,
humiliation, fear, hunger).
You are at the Sunday dance ten years ago
    (organ music),
standing there while everyone else is dancing,
and she jabs you with that look of hers, like a sad pitiful dog.
And you in another world, absent, drifting.
And she is so noble, sweet, and all she wants
is for you to want her.
She is so tender, so unbearable.
                    And *You are so cruel*, says the *danzón*.
    She turns the other young men down,
ignores the offers of splendid suitors,
pats her hair and looks at you. And you're so sweaty-handed;
oh, you're so few-worded. And she comes closer. She looks,
she hovers over you;
she brings you something to drink, and she shadows you,
she grovels after you,
she admires you. She is so sweet, so attentive, so . . . quiet,
so unbearable.
                    And *You are so cruel*, says the song.
    You pull your body away,
you turn your face. She
tries to touch your face,
tries while you dance to make you hold her tight.
She gathers the sweat that runs in torrents
from your hands.
                    And *You are so cruel*,

    says the song.

You hold her. Your soaking hands
clasp her. Your cheek lies against her cheek. Her hair
falls over your face. Warm sweat bathes her back,
soaking the crushed crepe dress she had to
wear for the first time, for you, especially for tonight.
Bumping against each other, you come to the center of the room
flooded now by your hands.

                              And *You are so cruel,*
says the song.

                    Swimming, you come to the shore. You sit down
by her side. You contemplate her.

                              Her hands in the sunlight.
                                                  Her
hands
and the car seat from which they rise; am I chaste?
Her hands in sunlight.
Your son and your wife in the sunlight,
the family in the sunlight
and the cluster of sounds swirling
in the golden goblet of the palms.

                              Is someone returning?

Who in the hot springs' murmur
offers you his delicious body
with a quick virile gesture?
The sand where athletes left no marks
and, beyond, the roar of the water.
Who is returning?

                    Liter
                    ature
is the consequence of a traditional and well-established hypocrisy. If man had the courage to speak the truth at the moment
he feels it, face to face with that person who inspires or provokes
it—when he talks, for example; when he looks at you, for example; when he humiliates himself, for example (for it is then,
at that very moment, that one feels how much one suffers or is
inspired); if man had the courage to express day-to-day beauty or
terror in his conversation; if man had the courage to say what

is, what he feels, what he hates, what he desires, without having to shield himself with a riddle of words saved for later; if he had the bravery to express his unhappiness in the same way he expresses the desire for a soft drink, he wouldn't have had to take refuge, seek shelter, justify himself, behind the secret, heartbreaking, and false confession which a book always is. The sincerity of one voice speaking to another has been lost. Did it once exist? We are ashamed to express the revulsion (or temptation) which the unknown produces in us. Out of cowardice (in those places where the law fosters imbecility) and out of fear of ridicule (in those places where tradition imposes stupidity) we make compromises with the here-and-now, and then, secretly, in fear and trembling, ashamed, embarrassed, we attempt to make up for the betrayal of our life: We, traitors, write the book. Thus the expression (the manifestation) of beauty has been left to pages and letters, dead hours, moments of respite. Feeling pity, joy, terror, longing, rebellion is circumscribed within the writing of a text which may be published or censored, which may be burned or sold, cataloged, classified, or ignored. And so the real man (the man who still feels remorse) feels himself obliged to scribble over thousands of sheets of paper so he may leave witness that he was not just another shadow that choked down his old unease and sensibility with sighs, idle chatter, and base sensation. Is every work of art then an act of remorseful rebellion against original betrayal? And is every man who does not leave the testimony of a work of art a traitor unreborn? Is every work of art then the brazen, beautiful invention with which a coward tries to justify himself? Is every work of art then the payment of an old debt a man bears to the truth but which he dares not assume every day? Plenitude, the moment of inspiration, the poem's arrival—what are they? Perhaps the worn-out boasts by which a timorous person, yet now invested with temerity, would rationalize his simple, splendid, and stereotypical human condition.

The age of Pericles,
the feasts of Dionysus.
The days
passing by imperturbable.
The divine hours
and the painstaking preparations

for going to see tomorrow the last 4 tragedies
of the intimate of Herodotus.

> The tears of Antigone among the muted whisperings of the
> earth.

> The caresses, the prints of naked boys on the beaches of
> Khios.

> Elms beside the river.

Walks through venerable spots
or the chance of a delicious, disorderly encounter on the paths
of Decelia.

> Everything, everything, is it all no more, then, than a false,
> glittering invention

with which disconsolate men have forever
tried to allay their uncertainty?

> Is nothing, nothing, any more than the cozy, nonexistent
place always invented
by men who loathe the place that is?

The last swimmers abandon the shore. The brief opulence
of sunset crowns the prickly wings of hungry birds. The rustling
of leaves is now an honorable sound. They all return. The oleanders infuse time. The day's last brightness plays among the trees
and over the arms of the chairs that someone (gaily) drags toward
the ocean.

This is the moment when things are gathered up and the
burgeoning of time breaks the rhythm of breathing. This is the
moment when, if we leaned our head against the back of the
chair, the weight of memory and affliction would change us into
loathsome sages.

This is the moment when the yellow leaf that flutters toward
our feet becomes a bright omen, a decorous (tenebrous) metaphor,
a philosophical system whose overwhelming neatness, if we tried
to interpret it, would annihilate all the useless, convoluted verborrhea of all the philosophers who have gone before us.

This is the moment when a footprint in the sand or the brief
luminous path that disappears into the ocean topples all the books
ever written or yet to be written.

This is the moment of confrontations, the awesome, unique

moment when the two most implacable and unavoidable questions of all come back to us, and strike us—

One goes, but where?
One lives, but for what?

One goes

out onto a burning plain
which you can't
stay in, or
stop in, or
leave,
even for a
second.

One lives

struggling desperately
to make them let you go out
onto that plain.

One goes

to a village
where the shriek
of wheels and pulleys   (ga-ga-*boom*)
is its only
music.

One lives

to attend those wheels
and pulleys.

One goes

to a place where, they assure us,
there is justice, where there is mercy
and truth on earth.

One lives

to flee, terrified,
from that place.

One goes

into a line for bread
where it turns out that
all there was was paper clips and "We just ran out,
friend!" . . .

One lives

to stand in that line.

                              One goes
to a beach
where the waves rhythmically vomit up
a young man's drowned body.
                                        One lives
remembering that beach.
                                        One goes
to an emaciated sea
where a marmoreal marmot murmurs
myriads of mistreatments.
                                        One lives
to be able to sail across that ocean.
                                        One goes
              to one of the camps where they till the land
              (from which one never returns, or can)
              located beside an earthen dam—
              where an ugly, skinny, wizened band
              of incarcerated ogresses dances maddened
              in celebration of the making by the hand of man
              of an ever-ready ogre like a great African
              who stands there smiling, licorice stick in hand.
                                        One lives
beside that dam.
                              But one goes
              finally to the finest fuck-up of them all
                the great floating flophouse where
                  a phonograph forever flutes
                    its philanthropic fluff and
                  an   unphotogenic,
                      fetid,   syphilitic,
                    aphonic mephitic
                       proffers   us
                       frothing   at
                       the   mouth
                        his   furi
                       ous phys
                          iog
                          no
                          my.

                              _____

My, mi, meeeee

                                    Someone is singing

Aee, aeee

                                    Is someone singing?

But what of that vast serene flowing water? And the solitary
spots where a pine tree touched by flame announces the rhythmic
roar of night? And the walk in calm along the deserted shore
where the ocean soothes? . . . I will never be able to communicate
those states of quietness. I will never be able to put down that
beauty, peacefully, without betraying myself. I will never be able
to list the colors of the sunset without my words having throbbing in them the imbalance of an anguish that comes, well, from
who knows where? . . . And what of the glow of night on the
sand? Of the blinking lights that might be distant fires and not
signs of surveillance? . . . But listen, you too will sit up a bit and
hear the lamentation of all those who have been destroyed simply
because they desired what you desire, simply because they conceived what you no longer even dare to mention. They too wanted
the ocean to carry only the murmur of waves, the wind only the
rustle of leaves. . . . You will rise up a little, mark my words, and
you will hear the unending lamentation of those who always
perish because they allow themselves to dream, imagine, invent—to be free. . . . Well then? Should *I* be able to speak of
moonlight and the little boat flowing toward shining places? Should
I adorn with lovely, pious lies what is no more than a realm of
echoing groans?

17

swallows were gliding
fornicating above the ocean
and a bird (a *Bird of Paradise* because he wore a Manhattan)
gobbling down his own eyes masturbates with the hand of God.
God, said the blackbirds, banging flagpoles to the beat of the
choral chant of the dead cousins who fell over the area, unan-
nounced by the one-legged prestidigitator with the big beard (but
bald on top). Thanks to the secret sale of the beams of the convent,
Clara Mortera passes out cheese to the rats in the baseboard—
their tails tickle her fancy. Eight sparrows show their teeth and

coo among the leaves which once henscratched over had to be hid up in the attic (it was all so futile). Maltheathus, the most coveted queen that frequented La Concha beach, took Coco Canijo at last up on his offer—and he, when he was bestowed with the big black bugger's masterpiece, burst with his pure contralto voice the timpanum of a prominent lady loaded to the lips with contraband necklaces—everybody said it was all on account of Marta Arjona. In the palm grove, a penguin strutted—delight in that well-dressed breast plastered over with medals, enormous eyebrows. While on an ice floe the firebird Quetzal teetered.

Who were those arriving people?

Who was it that kicked down the door?

How many were hanging, naked, there on the threshold?

Uncategorizable
voices,
melancholy shudders,
stubborn be-ring'd figures
ejaculating in single swoon
kept me from getting a good count.

But they

gushed forth.
I
    T
   R
    U
     L
      Y

       B
        E
       L
       I
        E
         V
         E

        I
        T
       !

They gushed over the wild crags, gorges, and chasms, over the abysses, unbound boulders, and rock rubble about to avalanche; over shockingly unsupported outcroppings, rust-streaked and teetering, and—can you believe it!—in the fire-shorn, sunburned, ashen clearing, waste, overwhelming, numbing, and alone. And here, where a bed of bones bleached and jumbled by the continual inhuman hiss of surf struck the viewer by its stunning staggering lumber. . . .

For the craftiest accomplices there was chick-pea soup; for the others, just the scraps of new gaffes, flagrant villainies, foul chronology, vile files cheek by jowl with malfeasances compiled upon signboards which divulged that here we were mired in delight. Even the hope of perishing as the prisoners of this particular oppression was a thing of the past, now past and gone—disparaged, pooh-poohed by the news (Big Mama bellowing) of the new reinterpretation of history and the autos-da-fé.

But they still were sprouting forth.

There was a trashcan full of medals. A dog, mesmerized but authorized, scrabbled in the gleam. . . . Deft and parsimonious, glorious and decorated, the patriotic rehabilitated experts (ex-putas) were operating the powerful computahs that at a gesture from those ex-putas computed the number of parasites and prostitutes (still putas) that were to be precipitously precipitated from the gibbet.

As had been foreseen, lights artificial were beamed, and the sandy expanse—Old Ocean—sparkled. TO INCREASE YOUR CHANCES FOR CONSUMPTION DECREASE THE NUMBER OF CONSUMERS, the electric signs, feverishly waved by the regrouped hordes, screamed.

They, the couple, walked out toward the infinite plain of sparkling sand. They saw the swaying fossils—nothing could stop moving for a second; they saw the enemy fallen to dust. And like everyone they heard the glorious anthems and contemplated the undulating ocean of new banners waving in the air. And to her, One and Only Mama, already plugged in, tuned in, and turned on, obstetric and electric, came the roar of the anthems—but, set, calibrated, and breath-bated, she thought she heard something contradictory under the sound of metal and voices. The couple went on. . . . Whisperers, the machines that controlled the compulsory recess, flew over the city, hastening the last hastening passers-by's passing, those picked to promenade. The sky—covered with artificial heavenly bodies which explored, stood surveillance, investigated, sniffed out, denounced and took depositions, spotlighted, and detected (*they were springing up*)—descended to save the expense of those profligate protectors, which were constructed and kept up with the support of heroic and ongoing sacrifice on the part of all generations, even those yet unborn. They, the couple, also descended. They slipped in silence through the rocks, carefully creeping round a weapon, a detector, an electric inspectic eye that could pick up, catch, the merest twitch, the imperceptible but compromising movement of the lips, the unexpected, quick palpitation, any blink outside normal blinking, which the potent registers, regally manipulated by the dedicated ex-putas, rhythmically registered. Any little detail might bring on the conflagration. Once on the shore of Old Ocean, they sat down. Some birds—exact copies of the ones forever made extinct by the building battalions—thunderously passed over. The two of them, then, hastening on, fled even the outskirts of the city. COSMIC ALGAE WILL FEED US. THE SUCCESS OF THE EXPERIMENTS IS COMPLETE. NO ONE WILL STARVE. A WELL-FED, WELL-INDOCTRINATED, WELL-ORGANIZED, WELL-AWARE, WELL-DISCIPLINED, WELL-MILITARIZED PEOPLE GREETS THE PRESENT AND DETESTS THE PAST, brayed the communiqué sprayed out, unanimously and monotonously, by the automatic monolithic loudspeakers linked to high-voltage lines, and which continued to blare in the ears of sleeping men, menacing sleepers' subconsciousnesses, as well as those who were awake—that is, they were heard by every inhabitant, save those two who flew the coop and who now, throwing caution to the wind, cross the clearing of unalloyed aluminum that is there, forever, to split space, to stop the escape of those (like these) that have not been doped up enough, given hope enough, made model men—that is, been *fully integrated*. But they did cross it, and come miraculously now to the Region of Glittering Whispers, where the fear-dealing heart-freezing anthems are hymned, horrifying and petrifying. THE WALLS ARE OF FLAMES. THE WORDS OF OUR COMRADES ARE OF FLAMES. THE BODY OF THE TRAITOR WHO DARES TRESPASS AND SO SULLY THE DIGNITY OF THIS PLACE—WILL BE FLAMES! But they trespassed across it. BEHOLD THE RUIN

OF HIM WHO IS RULED BY AMBITION! said the huge letters strung on a high-voltage line. BEWARE! But they went on. The Great Mother, exasperated, chrome-plated, militant, bad-mouthing, bejeweled, and mewling, leaves her many-pillowed seat and screams at the rooms of adjoining computahs to get the slivers of metallic sleep out of their rheumy eyes. Rearing up to her full height, she rains down threats; pissed off past words, she thunders the word: AFTER THE TRAITORS! There follows a precise and precipitous precipitation, galvanization; her voice is multiply-heard, echoed in the roar of electrostenographers. All astral communications instantly stirred to her considerable sobs, for the conscious computahs of the subconscious, catching the order, worked it over, looked it over, polished it over and over again and transformed it, unaltered, into a sob. The sob, exactly as she proposed, filled the sleepers' store of fury—a store which by central order is always left open so that even in sleep "active awareness" may be kept up and "repressive anxieties" erased. . . . The Mother, monumental, martial, dyspeptic, and eugenic, arrayed for urgent action, frothing and prepotent, came out onto the Court of Curtsies. The pursuit had still not been mounted. So that, neurotic and exalted, grim and bimbombastic, truly enraged and scathing, she cranked up the metallic machinery with the sound of carpenters banging and pounding. Tense and tendentious, her automated shrieks resounded. The radio transformed them into deep sobs. The stores of fury filled to overflowing. *They were sprouting.* A jet-claw, bought from the enemy at a staggering cost, took off like a karate chop straight for its mark, veered, disappeared among the highest constellations, dived. . . . Sheering from their course, the stars shattered.

The thunderous regular tramp of the feet of a metronomic anthem was on the march. . . . It was morning, confected by a kick from the Mother, who, freshly plugged in, spun now from one to another of her shining plastic intangible inconceivable mirrors, in which was reflected even the tiniest trajectory of a certain brass ant—a strangely constructed mechanical artifact that the Mother left lying about at the door of her room. The chosen one caressed the curious custom-made artifact and gazed into the sphere that gave her back her outraged self. *The Earth, this heart-stabbing sphere, the Earth, a wheeling orb of horror and fear*, she, multicolored, thought she heard someone about her say; then, martial and multitudinous, marmoreal and emulsified, swollen, apoplectic, but unpoppable, she issued new irreversible orders; she convoked a plenary session and, with the flat of a sword, flatly, fully unfolded her plans before the plenum. . . . Mechanical and ccumenical, colossal and calling on all the Muses, unique, rare, and wondrous, thunderous, she passed out the prospectus and with just two bashes inspired the masses with euphoria. RALLY, RALLY IN HONOR OF HONOR! TRACK DOWN THE TRAITORS! WASH AWAY THIS DISHONOR, HEED THE CALL OF OUR GREAT BREASTPLATED MOTHER! Thus jangled the jingoistic calls, and to the beat of that native clamor the multitude danced and stamped.

In a rage, the legions of heroes that came before they were called, that were ready for action before being alerted, spread out through all parts of the land.

The couple went on fleeing, and crossed now the field of scattered mines. The Mother, planetary and patrician, stomped her feet, patriarchal and procrustean, on the platform of prominent promises and purposes, threatening to unleash a cataclysm.

The legions departed toward every chasm.

The rampant birds returned, returned the exterminating frogmen, the circling peripatetic platforms commissioned to beam back even the eentsiest eddy in the concatenation of the circulation of the infusorians and the holothurians. Sizzling with fury, even the flames that flare before the gates of the future (those queens of obscure night) returned.

All of them bowed, contrite, on the concourse floor of the foyer before the greatest teleprojectors. None brought news of the traitors.

There was hell to pay.

Steely and stern, armed, alarmed, and alembicked, she, unfortunately fettered to the farrago of fatidic information, ochre, jaundiced, and partial, inoxidizable yet infected, yoked to all the creaking gewgaws, stubborn and screwed, autogenous and authoritarian, cut to the quick, emphatic and lymphatic—unable to conceive such an escape—took up the map of strategic meridians, the sphere and the quadrant, leaped up, and now before the popular projector, proclaimed, athletic and eclectic, equine and epic, through a snort of pistons emitting whizzes of lightning, her rotund yet multifaceted fury. . . . It was now useless to pretend. Useless now for the officious officials and ex-officio trans(in)formation officers to display their famed efficiency, striving to turn curses into big moving tears. . . . Autonomous and Napoleonic, she, leaping pneumatically, cacophonic, truculent and virulent, drastic and sarcastic, acoustic and elastic, trotted bustling about.

Grim and bimbombastic, with a clink of its sparkling spurs, the Sizzling Legion departed for North Desolation; her fear-dealing circuits shuddered and the Crackling Legion departed for South Desolation. I mean, uniformed, with a unanimous thunder as of tightening tourniquets, she threatened to strip them of their stripes, a threat meant to sway them, those who had not yet dedicated themselves to unceasing search. The artificial officials took note of the eminent pronouncement of Her Eminence, and, in an instant, impatiently and unstintedly, shaking off all traces of laziness they buckled on their blazing bronze breastplates. But still more stubborn, she cried out even louder, and wicked and witty, cacodemonic and cacophonic, covered with medals, at the apex of craftiness, she spunkily clucked, and it all came about as her crackerjack quibbling skull had calculated.

There was flaying and fleecing. A wave of atomized fury covered the countryside, keeping any antipatriotic port or anthill from fostering the fugitives. The thermonuclear carriers combed the land, and the squeak of every scream was painstakingly peeked at, screened, and miniaturized. Likewise, every scintilla of seismic action of every miasma they abysmally fathomed was resorted, re-sieved, and (once inspected) sent out again.

Meanwhile, the Mother, irked and murky, lugubrious and abbessaical, deformed and forever uniformed, on the very last platform, waited and watched, without winking, the Unfathomable. . . . But they crossed the watercourses and the reichs-watching machines, past the officiousness of the officered moats, the many-phased howitzers, the howling undaunted dogs of the K-9 corps, past the sterilizing turrets, terrified. Before the before-mentioned Mother, who militant and blitzing meditated on the scene of explosions, a rocket zipped across the sky, sought through seven galaxies, and shattered in a flash of shrill frustration. Before her who, inclusive and hallucinatory, lethal and fatal, was about to let loose a shriek from the monumental platform whereon she struck sparks with her spurs, a green-eyed weapon flew furiously into infinity and reduced it to a rain of meteorites. Before her, thundering and at the brink of bursting in rage, a drilling iron fist filled with immense energies splintered a million planets which like a brief shower of Roman candle sparks sprinkled her breasts and scattered into the abyss, making milky clouds in the Milky Way. . . . Oh, yes, there *were* dogs. The trees had already been wiped out, struck down not only in the precincts of the real realm, and in photographs, but as well in the conservative country of memory—such a reactionary mechanism. Trees, insects, all natural green, natural soft sounds, in fact. But because of a ministerial resolution passed in plenary session of the world council and even acceded to by the reigning ideologues of the enemy camp, the dog (*blesséd be the dog!*) was considered the immortal symbol of what, in social terms, was called the "great garrotte of the universal system." The dog (*blesséd be the dog!*) was to be the model that we all should follow: the dog (*blesséd be he!*) always licked the foot that kicked him, the dog (*praised be he!*) with a rope around his throat was happy, hitched, to keep step with whoever walked him. The dog (*glory be to him!*), if he was led to an artificial tree to be hanged, humbly wagged his tail. The dog! The dog! LET US ALL BE LIKE HIM! the great interplanetary electro-billboards hymned, blotting out the brilliance of distant constellations. LET US BE LIKE HIM! the shining heavenly bodies spelled out in fluorescent letters, infinite in extent, above which was limned, happy, submissive, optimistic always, the gigantic figure of the dog (*immortal be he!*). The ideal to which we all should aspire! The final goal for all those who trust in the great love of the three-engine Mother:

1. Mother Prenatal
2. Mother Artificial
3. Mother Fundamental!

The searchlight of a concentration camp, which was now converted into a concentrated campground, slithered across the feet of those who were fleeing. But it didn't pick them up. He looked at the city in flames; she, at his blazing eyes. . . . But behold, the Mother, mechanical and ecumenical, that is, Copernican and Averroean, thermal and epidermal, fondles the handle of the Incinerator of All Hope and then, dynamic and administrative, grim and gruff, scourges the vast already-calcined camp. They, seeing the desolation trampling down their treaded prints as they fled, also heard the howling of the Mother, who, riotous and raunchy, bovine and bullocklike, however epical and prudish—typical—pleaded, screaming, for their capture, never ceasing to shriek; then . . . *But what is that roar? that racket? that terrible narration, that strangled fury-filled creeping, that fevered reiterative advance, those cries, those flutters, that awful way of reciting a tale—could that be, perhaps, what is to remain?* . . . This exasperating palavering reached her ears, and she, the nonpareille, loudspeaking and spunky, Mama Begewgawed, guarantrix of our gravitation, sole expert in body odors, first lady of frogs in throats, found this whole situation stuck in her gullet, so she gargled, and her incandescent gurgling reverberated repulsively. Torrid and torrential, tempestuous, jealous, and sinuous, lowering and deluging, she eliminated esplanades, holes in the ground, ditches, canals, battlements and buttresses; she leveled towers, headlands, and pebbled stretches. Unparalleled parametrix, she made everything the same. And, uniquely wondrous winch, she increased, with a creak of her crankshaft, just in case, the chase, by changing the quotient of the High Crackerjack Commission on Weeping and Illegal Laughter. And thus, oligarchic and oligophrenic, uniformed, centripetal, rectilinear and lapidary, autonomous and thermodynamic, but stunned and tomtomthundering, she bursts into the Palace of Projections, sees the wheeling of the fire-dealing ships, and orders the destruction of half the earth; she also orders the moon rendered cinders and the extinction of the eight artificial satellites created for publicity purposes during the Year of Interplanetary Peace and Harmony. . . . At a snap of her fingers, the stars whistled and vanished into smoke. Then, amazed and earthy, she peered into the atomic spheres and saw the raving multitude, in the midst of the blitz, who were still cheering her and pursuing the traitors. Collaged and colossal, cylindric and alembic, huge-assed and hallucinating, but brusque and mystical, still adenoidal and mafiosal, she went once more, obese and possessed—filled to the brim—into the Hall of High Chastisement. And she gave orders. A thousand claws were mobilized and carried the command. A thousand experimental ships prowled the vast sidereal realms. And a thousand glowing telegrams were graphed back across the artificially oxygenated sky:

WE STILL HAVE NOT DISCOVERED THEM

At which, iridescent and omniscient, but now gripped by an obscure terror, all at sea, at bay, bewildered and bombastic, most expert in ballistics, she delved into the Chamber of Strategic Weapons. For an instant she was rigid, infinite and plenipotentiary; then creaking and incandescent, stunned, left speechless, bent out of shape, she stops in the center of the atomic quadrant, takes up, abrupt, the control board, and opts, epileptic but still optimistic, to send slithering out the skyscraping (scratching) icosahedron of acoustical threats. There, multifaceted, since eclectic, though dogmatic, pragmatic and melodramatic, scholastic and plastic, she hears, squat and stocky, through convulsions, the concussions of her detonations. But still she sees the same telegrams, sending back once more the same report:

THEY STILL HAVEN'T SHOWED UP

Boreal and hyperbolical, hypertrophied and hybridized— bearded, after all—she laughed. And all the while, a great one for the rumba, she shook, shimmied, whined, cried, and commanded—and through the air flew metals most costly, as she, villainous, slow but alert, managed the controls. New constellations were extinguished with a squeaking weapon that she, exulting, invented in an instant. The pursuers, not pausing for a second, or lessening the proportions or productivity of the pursuit, on guard on high, applauded with fulsome display the aplomb with which she'd invented the armament, acclaiming it for what it was—a triumph of science and epitome of imagination. New pennants were instantly printed up. And whoever didn't help out was hanged. And anyone who might have a doubt about it was garrotted. And anyone who smiled was smitten and exterminated, and anyone who blinked, even for an instant, was electrocuted. But anyone who merely batted an eyelid when the condemned were consigned to death was dealt with lightly, and only sent off forever to a forced-labor camp. . . . Then, toward the end of settling the score on the finis of the defamers and the infamous fugitives, diaphanous and farcical, fulgurous and filled with vanity, vaunting like a little cornet in a fanfare without end, she enunciates, frenetically and in unbridled fury, a brief resolution, to be signed by her herself, which commanded that the quota of chickpeas will be cut to a third so we can afford to construct a counting-and-accounting-for-scrutiny-computer for minor contradictions. Automatically, all the world ante'd up for it and clapped. The shining machine, built in an atomic blink—that is, even before the project was begun—paraded through the city in ruins. Many of the donors for it were destroyed, even as their palms were applauding the arrival of that just-invented fury. The machine itself, so presumably precise in its perfect machinery, was just about to be betrayed by one of its bobbins, badly discombobulated . . . *But that music I think I sometimes still can hear, sometimes still have heard! That smell of ocean, murmur of sea, the roar of the ocean, and, above the waters, that distant sound, that rhythm that suddenly casts its spell! . . . That smell of cool earth, of trees I have never seen; that pine grove I sense but have never glimpsed, and know never existed! Land running with water, flowers bursting into bloom! A song that floats constantly through the air! A ship hung with ribbons, laughter, sailing to the warm sands. . . . Whereward, whereward! . . .*

Battered by those murmurs, she revolving and counter-whispering barked out new orders. A balloon filled with intestinal bacteria floated bloated away and laid the obverse and reverse of the universe waste. An electrified needle shot off straight for the Unending, and the death ray was installed in all the infinite ends of space. . . . *Toward a feeling of waters flowing, toward the flutter of moist leaves, toward any place where dreaming is no longer a crime. Something tells us we must go on, something tells us we must not surrender, give up, that after the defeat the real battle commences. We want the memory, at least, of a past that did not happen but that would come to pass there with all the possibility of occurrence. . . .* Furious and funereal, the Mother hears again that distant rumor, without doubt given out by the fleeing betrayers, so that with bangs and thuds she sets sail shielded and anti-soft-spotted-in-her-heart, talkative and ovaloid, investigating and exterminating. At last, having found nothing, she, swiveling and swearing, terribly serious and unyielding, decides to make, once more, her big sensational appearance before, and once more speak to, the faithful multitude. Thus, gussied up in her finest for the occasion, she sets out—wave after wave of applause—for the Universal Circular Quadrant. . . . Regal and rumbling, armored, stuffed and stubborn, scrappy, magnetized, turning over in her mind the ideas for her discourse, she martially marches.

Over her eyes, mirrors bifocal; through her nose, the ring communal; in her hands, the scepter universal; in her anus, the plug monasterial; over her pubis, the chaste chain mail; on her chest, the ribbon transversal; at her throat, the unequaled collar; on her belly, the vest antinuclear; binding her breasts, the bra Wagnerian; on her belt, the pistol marsupial; on her finger, the great state jewel; on her wrist, the order rural; on her arms the escutcheon three-dimensional; on her forearm, the pennant patriarchal; over one shoulder, the emblem equatorial; on one earlobe, the great order multinational; on the other, the medal doctoral; on her back, the mantle of a general; on her forehead, the star colossal; on her chest, the great order municipal; on her skull, a helmet of metal; on top of that, a military beret; on top of that, the tiara superpapal; on top of that, the crown without rival; all around, a glow episcopal; at her sides, a march as to war; at her feet, the carpet incredible; in the air, the "Internationale." . . . Thus, omniscient and iridescent, to the tune of cornets but stumbling on her corns, thunderstruck and tropical, she arrived, tweedling, at the colossal tribunal.

Once there, whirling with rage, babbling and emboldened, bovine but always troublemaking, jinxing and hexing (though still scientific), thick and specific, shoving and pushing, pejorative, she got it all off her chest, she said her say, she told them she was pissed, she rained down a hail of onomatopoeia. . . . Bravo! Bravo! Brilliant, beautiful, cheered and bruising, thermal and epidermal, fluorescent, strident, excited though somewhat battered, hydraulic and hydrocephalic, brazen still though almost beaten silly, wheeling and ejaculating into her own mane of hair, and weaving a warp of intrigue, she, trilling, all woolen, all thrilling all over, such a captivating bird in a wired cage, crippled, chanting. . . . Cutting short that great state text, she spent only forty days and forty nights delivering the diluvial burst of words: The General Rationing Law was abolished and the Law of Total Abstinence passed. Thus all *basic* foodstuffs (for all those not basic, by not being, it goes without saying, had long been abandoned) were forbidden so that the result of that unequaled abstinence would be the construction of the Ideal Weapon for capturing that diabolic duo.

The most faithful subjects immediately began to vomit, so that they would be absolutely purified; the others, unfaithful, were destroyed for the crime of BASIC INGESTION OF REPAST IN THE PAST AND PRESENT. Thus arose the new capital offense of BASIC NON-VOMITING, which everyone unanimously approved. . . . *History, a macabre microbe. History, a lesioned lesson. History, a huge quantity of compromised promises.* . . . But she, in a trance almost of death agony, intransigent, both entering and exiting fixed in her resolve, not hearing that great ovation but rather this last whisper sighed without doubt by the bad, bad fugitives, befuddled, leaves the roar of that occasion as though she were deaf as a post, intent on naught but the pursuit of the naughty escapees. Although the fugitives have not appeared, she announces, approves, and signs the writ of execution. Thus, turgid and liturgical, orthodox in her excesses, and somewhat self-appeased, she proclaims them deceased, ordering the chief of the Dysfunction Bi-Section to draft the act of the defection and decease and de-exist of the fugitives, since though they are still alive, they have been driven from the bosom of the glorious nation and therefore no longer reside in the heart, under the wing, of her love. But monolithic and megalomaniac, touchy and alert, testifying, she calls vessels, vassals, to the witnesses of the text and she herself, nodding, makes the supposed testament her will, all the while cupping her (no, no such) testicles. Once drafted it is immediately submitted to the mass, which exulting and emotion-filled frantically applauds such an appalling resolution. *Life, the feeling of something we lost without ever having; a light tremble, a rush, a dizzying fall. Always all one?* . . .

Impossible! It was impossible! Above the uniform clamor of idolatry she heard them, she could hear them. It was them, all right, the deserters, who kept on, stubbornly, growing more distant. Then she, supreme, Super Leader, declared the Universal Thousand-Day War. All forms of locomotion, all precipitations and resolutions, all passion and repulsion, placed themselves at the service of the heroic pursuit. Even the dogs, those final relics, the glory of the homeland, in which reposed all conceivable confidence—truly they were an institution—ran out baying. . . . From afar they, the couple, saw that barking advance, contemplated that bustling and scurrying about the mobilized city. They even wondered whether all that hustle and bustle was over them. While so many instruments were perforating, drilling, annihilating with pops and backfires, half the earth was covered with a dense, foul-smelling cloud in which they, the couple, sought refuge. And that advancing cloud brought back to their senses a great percentage of the enslaved masses who, disoriented and persecuted, suddenly became aware, and wondered, and finding no sense to that persecution, but no possibility of salvation either, slit their own throats.

Chorus of slaves slitting their throats: In the foul-smelling cloud howls a mastiff, a slave slits his throat, and your dark, violated life passes rapidly by.

Aggrieved and apocalyptic, radical and radioactive, the Mother, seeing that her plans did not culminate in the glorious results she had planned, submerges, still all decked out in the motley of her frippery, meditating. Then, gaudily jeweled and Goyaesque, striking flint before the self-slitters, gravel-voiced and whiny, dressed for the battle, looking so bonny in her bodice of vicuña, shouting out Shit and balling her fists, grows suddenly glum, and groans, and like a woman who does a derring-deed, scheming, splenetic, and hermetic, plunges incautiously into the jungle of the great control panel and all its adjoining underpanels and underpinnings. . . . To swell the already ample terrors, a ship set sail for the center of the earth. There it inflated and burst, bringing down all the interior strata of the deteriorated planet. Fevered, the subterranean seas seethed and sizzled into smoke like the formless blowholes of furious volcanoes.

Chorus of high officials seeking refuge in the midst of the slaughter: In the crackling, sizzling night, the oft-scourged flanks of the earth collapse.

But they, the couple, kept running. They saw abominable exhalations spreading across the earth. They saw the glowing dog, the great monumental billboard, disintegrating and wafting away in a cloud of smoke, when the mocked and mocking Mother, miffed and peremptory but still fixed up in her finery, persuasive, still sponsoring, ministering, minimizing, that is, still meddling and mongoloid, commanded, though they scoffed at her, total destruction, but no capitulation, never. They, the fugitives, stubborn too, decided to perish but not to surrender, never. BUT WHETHER YOU DISOBEY OR BURST, then said Robot in Charge of Dispassioning the Passionate, that ultimate weapon for annihilating misfits, WHETHER YOU PERISH OR WIN, WHETHER YOU ACCEPT OR REJECT, DON'T YOU FEEL A MEASURELESS LIE FALLING ALWAYS UPON US? AN ANCIENT INCOMPREHENSIBLE LIE! resounded the voice of the Disillusioning Robot. MORE ENDURING THAN ANY COMFORT OR TRIUMPH! THEN WHAT ARE WE TO DO? WHAT ARE WE TO DO IT FOR? said the deceiving high-frequency voice. THEN WHY GO ON LIKE THIS, PERSISTING, LONGING, STRUGGLING? . . . Meanwhile the Mother, worn out but cheered up, stirred, feeling how the ungraspable pair grew despairing. But at that very moment the fugitives' fingers brushed against each other. He stretched out his hand and took hers. And they saw that it was good. Then the Mother, surly and sulfurous, vast and stammering, seeing that the detectors still did not announce the disappearance of the objective, ordered the Discourager of Courage to be burned. With a great shudder the Disillusioning Robot disappeared.

They stopped in the midst of the rubble and boulders. She sat down and beheld the handsome, heartbroken body of him who was with her. He, standing above her, discovered her gazing at him. But no computah, however skillful it had been made to be, could register that sensation, for it was still unknown in all the universe. . . . He bent and passed his hand over her singed hair. She stood and placed hers against his breast. . . . The Mother, ignored and immoral, martial and marmoreal, still high-falutin' and high-pitched, stomped across the glass carpet, calling orders. The world, incredibly, was bursting apart. But this time neither one of the two paused to see. She began to shed her clothes. He trembled. She drew near him. He drew her to him. She gave herself up. He gave himself to her. He laid her body on the pulsating ground. She felt his body lying over hers. He took her. And the two became as one. Meanwhile the Mother, steely and fearful, faded, pale, roared. But now for them there was nothing but a measured, rhythmic stirring, a murmuring frenzy from which all other sound had been banished. At last he burst within her. And she felt that bursting. And the two of them went on to completion, fusion. The Mother, demoralized and red-eyed, stuttering and staggering, rickety, but still shrieking and stubborn, made one last fulminating gesture. With the tip of the quadrant she shifted the disintegrating lever. In an instant everything came unglued. And everyone thought—so the radiant waves indicated—that the world had finally come to an end. *But they gushed.* . . . At first, such had been the gladness that the two themselves did not notice. *But they gushed forth. They were not splendid, not considerable; they were not yet fit to adorn vases, urns, arcades, salons (things at any rate nonexistent). They were not yet intoxicating. But they sprang forth. . . .*

The Mother, atomized and autopiloted, vanished. She saw that springing forth and, fulgurous and furious, she desired to wipe it out, but the superpolice and the computahs, the gears and levers, and even the most mysterious ministerial regions of the realm were invaded, covered, by that burgeoning advance. They, the couple, still sheltered from the curse of the persecution, made love again. This time they spoke to one another. Your chest is a wall, she said. Soft is your voice, said he. At your beckoning I will throw myself to the ground and give myself to you, she said. At your sign I will rend my body and feed you, said he. Even if you deliver me to abomination, even if you kill or betray, I will hold you in my arms and press you to my heart, she said. Even if because of you I must defend infamy, or even contribute to it, I will do all that, said he. And I will sustain it, bear it, if you order me to, she said.

Chorus of vermin (hooting with laughter and disappearing): That's the way love is! That's the way love is! There's nothing like it!

He lay down on that carpet (now intoxicating) which was growing at his feet. She bowed down, kissed him, cooed to him, adored all that shining body. He drew her to him again. Once more they joined and burst. At last, locked in each other's arms, they fell asleep. . . . The Mother laughed and laughed, dexterous and sinister, whipped into waves of arid fury, irritated, delirious and destructive, torrid and horrid—as she dissolved she was still laughing. . . . They awoke and began once more their praises. I like your body, he said. I wish yours were always on mine, she said. In that way they went on lauding each other—with simple language. For simple are the words needed to confirm gladness. Simple? No, *unnecessary*, he thought, and fell silent, contemplating. And for a second, while the dream came to an end—that is, while they dreamed that they escaped, that they outwitted the fury of Great Big Mama, and, finally, that they found themselves in a place where flowers gushed forth like springs of water—they thought, for now they awoke, that it would have only been right that that dream, for having been so much dreamed, should begin to come true—so they thought, as they dissolved, disintegrated, and vanished.

(Simple, simple . . . oh, and self-contradictory.)
But they gushed.

O
  F

     C
    O
      U
       R
        S
         E

          T
         H
          E
          Y

            D
             I
              D!
                Flowers poured forth.

Aiee, aiee,
        it's him whistling once more on the porch.
Why don't we go for a walk,
      my love,

let's go out for a walk.
We can visit the great wall
where, in golden letters,
the names of heroes
are carved.

                        They used us.

Why don't we go for a walk,
        oh, love,
let's go out for a walk.
We can go into the libraries
where, in golden tomes,
the history of great
leaders and great times
is told.

                        It is all a lie.

Why don't we go for a walk,
        oh, love,
let's go out for a walk.
We can visit the mass graves
of the martyrs.
In unidentified tombs
the bones are jumbled.
        We are there,
        oh, my love.

                        We are there.

*If they live on the other side of the river, we
will take a boat and throughout our passage
we will admire the gleaming snow which melts
at once in our hands. No shade of white is
truly white against the snow; it makes even the
wings of swans seem gray. Out to infinity
the countryside is a bowl of milk.
    At evening the clouds disperse and in
the pure night a magical, lovely setting of
jade appears.* *

*Anonymous: The Magic Mirror (a collection of Chinese poetry from the Ming
Dynasty).

Aiee, aiee

                                        H
                                    T
                                R
it's him whistling Once more on the porch.
                            F

                    G
                N
            I
        H
    S
U
G

CANTO THREE

I get out of bed and only see sheet lightning, streams of harsh light, great rings of flame falling, coming in, gnawing, destroying, ringing me, about to strike, making me get up, making me look, like this—stuck here, naked, useless, impotent, and infuriated, a castaway on white, white sheets, in the midst of the brightness. Look at yourself, look at yourself. Here, there, confronted with this reality that is not reality but unhalting incoherence, eternally unchanging inconstancy. . . . I get up; I get up, but I can't get up so I stay here, gazing at this rigid extension of solitude, my body. Gazing on those thin walls which dissolve, these hands reposing, like monsters, on the white cloth. I get up, I don't get up, I get up without getting up. And the what have you done, the what are you doing, the what are you going to do torture me like this lightning that keeps me from taking a step. . . . How, how in the world abandon this place, where only the not-made-clear exists (the what-might-be), the certainty of constant uncertainty? How abandon our definite purpose, our timeless desire, our yearning to remain at least in the tattered memory of that person we do not know and who yet will sustain us? "Poor people, how they suffered. Look, it says so here; someone was able to say it, not without difficulty and truly dire problems, not without having to abandon his whole life, and even more, as forfeit for it." . . . And the sun begins to throw its same old light: *Give up, give in, succumb, don't say a word; dance, dance, dance in my splendor. Listen only to the rustling of creatures that run, thanks to me (and I've only barely risen), to find shelter under a rock, in the*

elemental dark and wet; or that seem as if mounted, stuck with
a pin, dazed, weak, truly mechanized within my rage, under my
light. . . . Listen, listen, look at them writhe, look at them merge,
twisting, revolving, look how they turn pale, then transparent,
until they form a formless miasma; look how they give in to the
drowsy, overpowering unanimous repetition of the fixed night-
mare of the tropics. . . . You've gotta get up, you've gotta get out;
you have to give in. Come, everything is rustling. Come, everything here is so vibrant, so bright, so ineluctable, so brazenly
shrill and dominating. . . . Come, those desolate, immediate silhouettes are calling to you. So much stupidity, so much sadness.
So much desire and so much impotence. . . . Get up. Sheets in
brightness; windows onto brightness; ununited bodies rendered
up to brightness; bodies that display that agony of being just a
copy of something that melted away long ago. And yet, the pain
is the same, the oppression of the light on your skin is the same;
the same, the sensation of futile burning, now, this instant, always. I get up, I get up. . . . Do I get up? Nudged along by the
light I am now walking. Go, rinse that face, clothe that body;
have a seat, get comfortable, stand up, run for cover. . . . From
one wall to the other, what a distance. From one armchair to
another, what certainty we'll never make it. Raise an arm, stretch
out a hand, pick up the soap—the most heroic of exploits. Pa-
jamas, rags knotted around a body; body hair sprouting out like
a grotesque forest, like a dream within a dream in which big teeth
gnaw, with a strange gnashing sound, at either end—with us in
the middle. . . . Start walking, start walking, as though every step
decided a continent's—or a distant planet's—destiny. Rub your
eyes, thus. Walk. I get up, I get up. With the first cigarette lust
sets in, and then—now—there is no more salvation. I get up and
keep lying there, looking at myself; looking at my self. I get up,
I get up. Pushing a way through the brightness, I walk; disintegrating from so much light, I am outside. I smoke another cigarette. My tongue, stung by a million little stings, trying to find
who knows what strange comfort, stirs within its vault; the vault,
by definition unsatisfied, folds in its walls, compresses; that sense
of pressure between palate and tongue, that dripping wetness—
a *get up and go,* a *go look,* a *go by God or bust,* but not in a little
while—*now,* right now, not later. . . . The smoke drifts off, the
smoke goes in and out again; the smoke, within, shapes a body

that dissolves as I try to imprison it; the smoke, without, forms
a face, two legs, an insolent magnificent gesture that dances, *thus*,
that stares like *this*, that beckons—with such looks!—that beckons and leaps. You step forward, and the smoke (that figure we
yearn for, that sketch that lingers, that challenge) retreats a little,
a little above your lips, almost allowing itself to penetrate your
nose. *Follow me*, the smoke keeps saying. More smoke within.
My tongue—pursued by, pricked on by a sense of desire whose
name it does not know and which therefore it will never be able
to satisfy—makes a desperate sally. The darkness opens, the darkness closes; the smoke, imprisoned, proposes a battle. The smoke
which emerges again now, runs riot across my view, displays its
warriors. The chief of them rises up. He comes in shorts. I light
another cigarette. Let's go! . . . And great projects collapse—for
there is smoke. And grand purposes dissolve—for there is tongue.
The great projects take on now the shapes of absurd ladies "in a
doubtful state of piety"—for there is sunshine. . . . Homer is vanquished by a girded pair of shorts. By a *look at me, come to me,
here I am, here I am.* . . . Oh, a temperature truly overwhelming.
Let's go outside.

The ocean

yellow.

The ocean

clumsily outlining a stretch
of anonymous sand—for there is no history.
    Let us go, then, down to the ocean.
One must speak. Let us say then: *Along about here, I think,
there are not so many rocks. Did you bring the thermos bottle?
We didn't forget the matches?* . . . Let us think then,
remembering I don't know which half-read book
in the clutching mob
of a bus: *Along about then
a plague wiped out the working
population.*

Sand falling

on bodies spread in the sun.
Mother.
Father.
Son.

Falling sand.
Branches, behind; the wind and
                    the ocean
no longer yellow.
Your face, your face
yet young, falling sand.
Your body, your body
doubtlessly still admirable, falling sand.
The delicate little hands of one
who still retains the right
to silence—perhaps to ignorance—
his eyes that stare at us,
the plant that protects us,
the truly approving, even
envious comments
of ladies, parents, and other
                    domestic
artifacts.

                                        Falling sand.

            Sit down here, right here, protect us,
make a wall with your body
                    (you say).
Look how he's fallen asleep,
look at him wake up,
look at him look at us
                    (you say).
What shall I make for lunch?
Where would you like to go?
What time is it?

                                        Falling sand.

A few seconds ago,
a few hours ago,
I felt—I thought I felt—
(the texture of the towel,
the plant's shadow
surely contributed to that
sensation)
an inexplicable shudder of pleasure,
almost painful, at *being*.

The wind, which was not too strong,
the cloth, and the tree
took part in this
revelation.
You are, quite simply,
he who lies on the ground
and watches.
You are, quite simply,
something that is there
and feels.
Preserve yourself from the body
that desires you most;
the chosen one is to be the one who tolerates you.
Think that it is a privilege
just being here,
like this, lying on your back, in the sun, suffering.
Use that air that strikes you
without violence.
Touch a branch.
Lie back a little more.
Close your eyes.

                                             Falling sand.

Tap that natural pleasure,
that minute you will never recover,
and is almost yours,
this silence.
Remember, life is nothing but concession and yearning.
Think, now you are lying in the sun, you are breathing.
Remember, life is nothing but stupor or renunciation.
Think, now you are lying in the sun, you are breathing.
Remember, life is nothing but whispering and betrayal.
Think, now you are lying in the sun, you are breathing.
Remember, life is nothing but thirst and resentment.
Think, now you are lying in the sun, you are breathing.
Remember, life is nothing but muzzling and meekness.
Think, now you are lying in the sun, you are breathing.
Remember, life is nothing but extortion and silence.
Think, now you are lying in the sun, you are breathing.
Remember, life is nothing but slavery and applause.

Think, now you are lying in the sun, you are breathing.
Remember, life is nothing but fanaticism, or the knife.
Think, now you are lying in the sun, you are breathing.
Remember, life is nothing but risk or abstinence.
Think, now you are lying in the sun, you are breathing.
Remember, life is nothing but recantation, or the fire.
Think, now you are lying in the sun, you are breathing.
Remember, life is nothing but deference, or the abyss.
Think, now you are lying in the sun, you are breathing.
Remember, we are instruments of a thing we don't control, but
        that watches us.
Remember, we are nothing but some passing terror, an angry
impotence, an insatiable, ephemeral flame.
Think, now you are lying in the sun, you are breathing.
Think, now you are breathing, but not a
moment ago,

         but

         not

         but no more

         but—

            no more.
Tell me I'm not going anyplace,
and without a doubt I'll go on.

                 Once—how today's misery

exalts him—
he knew the secret
that each tree trunk hid.

                 Once—how today's misery

enlarges him—
he protected the night
with his solitary devotion.
Evening.
He sang to himself on the grass.
He writhed in ecstasy on the ground.
Each stone, a symbol.
Each blade of grass, a message.
Each tree, a castle.
Each morning, a new song
made up on the spot,
an offering.

Run.
Jump.
Find a place to hide.
                    But he comes out of the ocean.
He comes toward us,
he lies down over there,
so close.

                    And
                    Homer is
                    forgotten about completely. He
                    picks up his staff and swings off
                    for all anyone cares
                    ·to the moon.
(She. . . . Has she fallen asleep? . . .)
                    Sunday.
                    Sunday.
The holy family is about to depart.
The carriages at the door.
The castle in the distance,
investing the landscape
with the classical austerity of an old
etching.
                    Now they return.
Him in front.
Him, distant, embracing everyone.
Setting them down here and there, placing them,
scattering them;
                    at last
erasing them.
                    The bottles ("Cologne 1800,"
"Florida Water," and
even old flasks)
lie buried in the grove.
That jar of "Golden Sun" brilliantine was a queen. This one,
long and green, the mud has clouded, was
the prince.
                    Night
                    night
                    (cave
                    arcade
                    thicket)

what have you left me?
>   Lips,
            calves,
            thighs,
            there, too, over the shorts, fine dust,
            little grains of sand,
            reminders
            of the spray,
                  strategically
            taking up position.
            Dripping hair.
                                          The corpse washes ashore.
(She. . . . Has she fallen asleep?)
                        Budding tree,
            buds that were birds
            birds, ships
            delirious fire-ant colony that was a
                                          well.

            Regal parapets,
            battlements and crenellations
what have you left me?
                  Let us bury our offerings
            out in the thicket of wild pineapples.
            The rain will make those glass shards shine.
            The seeds they made of coins
            will surely sprout.
                  But look, look, there's a tractor over there
breaking up the ground
to sow—
                  what?

                  And
Homer
is most definitely vanquished by the looming figure
of that teenager
who once more gives the sign
                  and passes
so close to us.
                        Poor devil.

_____

Let's all sit
here
under the almond tree
—this one is not like the others.
Let's squeeze each other tight amid the leaves,
which will scrape our clothes and chafe our skin.
Let's play hide-and-seek, or follow-the-leader.
I'll tell a story.
Remember, this is what's important.
Remember, this is really, really
the only thing that's any good for anything. Remember,
beyond, beyond, we know nothing, yet
I feel that it too is
horrible.
Speak,
say
anything at all, laugh,
hush, listen, don't move.

Falling sand.

The family bench,
soup set out already,
and dogs, hens, other
dear creatures under
the table, waiting for the offering.
How pleasant, how nice
to be here all together, like this. Out there,
the lantern, marking the boundary of
this domain.

Falling sand.

First one to touch the ground, loses.
First one to the column on the porch,
wins. Whoever's not hid by 30
can't hide over.
You're it.

Falling sand.
Falling sand.

"He's crying because he doesn't want to
die,"
says his mother, who doesn't know.
(He's now eight years old.)
                    Advance of "reality": victory of *R*.
My God—
            (invoked to fill a gap)
You are no longer a man who calls things
by their name—
you blaspheme.
You are no longer a man who laughs—
you jeer.
You are no longer a man who hopes—
you mistrust.
You are no longer a man who loves—
you accept.
You are no longer a man who dreams aloud—
you are silent.
You no longer sleep and dream—
you are sleepless.
You are no longer one who is wont to believe—
you consent.
You are no longer a seeker—
you hide

                                        (not 30 yet!)

My God
            (or something along those lines)
                    And not to be able to get away.
                    And not to be able to say this that I'm
                    saying.
                    And not to be able even to scream NO.
                    And not to be able even to stop going on,
                    going on.
                    Not to be able to resign yourself or to
                    resign.
                            Not to be able to scorn.
                            Not to be able at least to burst.
                            Not to be able to desire or
                            stop desiring.
                            And not to be able to forget.

On
skin
that lays all philosophy waste,
on time that shrinks
dreams into slogans, on
hands that do not desire what they might
have, that sweat,

                                           falling sand.

On
the soul
which though not eternal,
not even existing, weighs
on us so,

                                           falling sand.

On
noble ambitions,
on ambitions which even
when they aren't so noble, aren't grand,
how heavy they are.
On our pride and on
our fury
and on our pure secrets
(ah, he can, he can)
and on our inconfessable stupor
(he can't)
and on that memory, surely unreal,
of the garden and the sun,
and us, them,
under the tree,

                                           falling sand.

    This is the house.
Let us go in—
                Every door a dozen smirks.
                Every window a hundred curtsies.
                The price of the sink—never to write the poem.
                Squashed dignity is overlaid with porch tiles.
                The wall, the bookcase are applause.
                A wineglass is a wink of assent.
                Every chair, an act of cowardice.

This lamp is something unsaid that needed saying
desperately.
In the living room, the other rooms, is our soul.
Don't mention that wood-fired stove to me—
more than an arm and a leg,
it has cost us our whole body.
You see—
The ensemble is the shape of the renunciation
of noblest things, that which doubtless we never had,
but which justified us.
                    And after all, we have been lucky in having our
                                                      products
accepted—others have offered more and they are still living
under a bridge.
                    (A thousand years, a thousand years. Now he is
                    a thousand years old.)
But the boy turns around.
She. . . . Has she gone to sleep?
I get up.
                    (Homer and all the treatises that preceded him
                    have fled.)
                    He walks among the others and he
                    stands out; he does not turn, knowing
                    that I'm following him.
                                        (No longer.)
                    And he begins to walk away slowly,
                    knowing I'm following him.
                                        (No longer.)
                    He walks along the highest part of the
                    beach. From a distance he seems to
                    walk even more slowly, firmly, as
                    though not to be confused with the
                    others. His body, tanned and slim, his
                    white shorts, his legs inexorably ad-
                    vancing give life to the landscape.
                                        (No longer.)
                    That heavy young woman turns and
                    stares at him. This married couple
                    seated on an imported towel—they're

officials—turn as well; each one, sepa-
rately, clandestinely, watches him.
There's something almost of cruelty in
that walk. Something that commands,
pulls, inspires adoration or destruction.

(No longer.)
I know that, I know it. And that all
this is ridiculous—I know that too. But
he has gone into the densest part of the
trees, where there's almost nobody. . . .
In the sand the print of his naked foot
is unmistakable. "If you seek," say the
trees; "if you seek," say the trees. . . .
And burst into laughter. "If you
seek. . . ." And burst out laughing
again.

(Right now, right now.)
They shade his body. They bathe him,
they touch him; they caress him with
a trembling circle of light, which the
wind disposes as it moves the
branches.
Now he walks over the dry pine
needles. Knowing that I'm following
him. Proud. Assured.

(Then, then.)
He leaves the pine grove. Skin and
shorts shine again in the glare of noon.
As though carelessly, randomly, casually, he strides now through the rocky
ground with scattered sand, pieces of
wood, and broken shells cast up by the
waves. For a moment he halts, gives
his thigh a sort of light slap—perhaps
just to swat a mosquito. Without turning, he goes on.

(Now, now.)
He walks slowly, without seeming to
care whether he is noticed or not—nat-

urally, because you have to walk, because you have to follow him who, at
his whim, commands it. I halt.

(Then.)

Now into the mangroves, he halts
without turning around. He bends over
as though studying something beside
his feet. He goes on. Without having
made the slightest sign.

(Then.)

In the mangroves everything is moist
and warm. The ground is spongy under
our feet. Above his head a swarm of
mosquitoes glides. He stops next to a
huge mangrove trunk, a tree. He goes
on. He pretends to be looking for some
specific thing—he is assured, alone. He
takes a little trail and comes to a path
narrower yet, bordered by sand and
grass. Once more he emerges into the
light. I halt.

(Then.)

He too halts in the splendor. *He,* that
irreverence in the light, that don't-do-a-
thing-and-still-dominate. He stands
there inevitable in the brightness, van-
quishing it, conquering.

(Now, now.)

I sit down at the edge of the path.

(Then.)

I lean back in the grass.

(Now.)

There are the trees, letting swirls of
blue glint through sometimes, closing
then, casting a trembling circle of light.
The cicadas, silent until now, sound
clearly. There must be ants in the
grass, I thought, looking up at the sky
dappling down through the trees. . . . I
placed my hands behind my head and

closed my eyes. I thought, He's still
walking, he thinks I'm following him;
by now he's probably disappeared.
That's the best thing.

(Now, now.)

I thought how pleasant it was to do
this once more, lie back, feel nothing
but the sun dancing, fluttering over
me. I thought too about a barn with a
hole in the roof where, so they said, a
bat would sleep. I thought about a
nook with the soft wan light throbbing
through it. I thought about a kind of
sadness, resignation, joy, revelation;
about a song under a tree and this very
brightness. About no real place.

(Now, now.)

I thought it was really laughable to
have come all this way following that
boy. I thought, Why do you think it's
laughable if you want him? I felt a
slight stinging along my legs. I
thought, Sure enough, ants. I thought I
had no doubt stirred them up. I
thought perhaps it wasn't ants, but
rocks, or the grass itself, or sand. . . . I
thought about the way an enormous
tree made a roof you hung upside-down
to nap in. Strange and not unpleasant
figures were dancing; one passed over
slowly, throwing a shadow across my
face. . . . I don't think I slept more than
a few minutes. The sense of annoyance
brought on by the heat, the rocks, the
sand, or the ants woke me. I thought it
was time to go back, that she would
certainly be waiting for me. I open my
eyes. There he is. He is standing before
me, watching me, neither pleased nor
upset, with the distant serenity of an

animal in his natural element just
studying you—with a certain curiosity,
with a certain irony perhaps, and,
above all, with that indifference, that
assuredness.

                                        (Then.)

I think I fell asleep—
I say, yawning.

                        He doesn't say a word.
                        He stands there staring at me.

I get up and sit down
on the edge of the path.
I take a cigarette. I
offer one to him.

                        No, he says.

I light the cigarette. I let
the smoke escape. . . . It
must be late, I say.

                        He doesn't say a word.
                        He stands there staring at me.

        Along the path a funny
        noise can be heard approaching.
        It's one of the swimmers
        with a portable radio. He's
        coming toward us, apparently.
You know this place
pretty well? I ask.

                        He doesn't say a word.

        The man with the radio comes
        up to us now, holding a
        cigarette. He asks him
        for a light.

                        He doesn't move.

I hold out my box
of matches to the
intruder.

        He lights his cigarette. He
        speaks to the boy once more.
        He talks to him about the heat,
        the sun, the people on the beach,

the nice quiet place he'd like
to find.
                          He doesn't answer.
Finally, the man leaves us,
with a smile of complicity.
We both watch him as he walks away.
Once into the mangroves, he turns.
Once more, he smiles.
Why didn't you go
with him? I say.

                          With who? he says.

With him, I say, gesturing
toward the man; at least
he had a radio.

                          I don't understand, he says.

You wouldn't be bored.

                          I'm not bored.

Sit down, I say.

                          He sits down.

Are you going to be here
long?

                          Fifteen days, he says.
                          Well, thirteen,
                          we've been here two already.

You must be a good student.

                          Like the rest.

If you're like the rest, why
didn't you go with the guy with the
radio? It would have been fun.

                          I don't understand, he says.

If you don't understand, do you
mind telling me why you're
chasing me?

                          For a while he remains
                          silent. Then—I was going
                          swimming on the other beach
                          now. There's another
                          place around here. If you
                          want to, we can go.
                          He stands up.

No, I say. And once more
I think of an enormous tree.
And of me walking upside-down toward
that brightness, toward that
soft green foliage.

We have a radio
like his too,
he says now.

Oh, really? I say,
falling out of the tree.

Expensive. My mother
bought it on the black
market.

Oh, of course. . . .

But there aren't any
batteries for it, so I
didn't bring it—

It's strange you didn't bring
a friend, I interrupt.

I don't have many.

No? Everybody has
friends.

He doesn't say a word.

If you'd brought somebody
you wouldn't be bored now.

I don't get bored, he says.

So what do you do, then?
     The cicadas begin whistling again.

He goes on standing there
among the undergrowth
that hardly reaches his knees.

Well I get bored quite a bit,
I say. . . . And I'm even
running low on the liquor
I brought.

He lies down face up on
the grass. The sun shimmers
across his face, his chest,
his throat; then it goes
back again. He

                              picks a blade of grass and
                              brings it to his lips.
                              Always at once rather
                              distant and sure of him-
                              self.
           The sun dances on, rises, falls.
I go on squatting,
staring at him.

                              The shadow of his eyelashes
                              falls a little longer. He
                              has closed his eyes.
                              The long thin blade of grass
                              comes and goes, slowly, from
                              his lips. One of his legs,
                              stretching, touches the edge
                              of the walk.

           The cicadas fall silent.
I light a cigarette.

                              The sun bathes his entire body.

It's late, I say. My wife's
probably worried, I add,
and instantly feel
utterly ridiculous.

                              He doesn't respond. He goes on
                              slowly chewing on the blade
                              of grass.

Listen, I say all of a sudden,
if you don't have anything to
do, find a friend for yourself, or
two, three . . . your own age. Go out
with them, take off with them.
There'll be plenty of them for you.
I guarantee it. And you know it.

                              He makes no response. He's
                              still entertaining himself
                              with the grass. His eyelashes
                              throw shadows across his face.

I rise. I'm going, I say
aloud. And that statement

sounds counterproductive,
utterly stupid, even to me.
               Suddenly, the statement takes on
               the shape of a depraved old maid,
               winking and grimacing and making
               horrible gestures, nudging me toward
               that reclining body.
I'm going, I say now,
louder.
               And that statement (the nasty old
               maid) breaks out laughing and beckons,
               making signs with one of her
               greasy fingers to several other
               old maids, a divorcée, and a
               widow, who instantly begin shrieking.
I turn my back on them all
and begin to walk away.

                              In Guanabo the booze practi-
                              cally comes out of the water
                              taps, he says then.

I turn around.
               The dreadful women have fled.
               There is only the young man's
               body, lying on the grass.

                              That's what my mother said,
                              he says. She wants me to buy
                              her a bottle of good dry wine.

I stand there,
staring at him.
               The old maids and the fat widow are off
               there at a distance, making affectedly
               horrified gestures and fleeing with
               exaggerated skulking strides.

                              He goes on just lying there.
                              The sun dances now across the
                              blade of grass he holds up
                              between his fingers. Some-
                              thing, a tiny stone, a leaf, no
                              doubt deliberately placed,
                              shines on the skin of his belly.

The heavy black dress of the widow
tangles in a tree and rips off her.
The old crone shrieks and runs on.
Tomorrow morning,
I say to him, wait for me here
and we'll go to Guanabo.

                              He doesn't say a word.
                    Run, crones, run!
I walk away
through the pine grove.
                    The cicadas begin their whistling once
          more.
                                        (Now, now.)
What a laugh!
What a joke!

                         In
                        the
                    THIRD ACT
the mirror is an accomplice in our lewdness.
                              (What a laugh, what a joke.)
Sir, dinner is served.
                    In the Third Act
blind fish (eyes usurped by gloom, head
guided like a torpedo) come to the surface
to not see
to not see.
In the Third Act
          blind fish
          light falling on balcony and sea.
          Her, always sticking her nose in.
In the Third Act
          figures at the mirror, shaving, shouts, sun-tempered
          skin, tribute, homage!
          And summer devouring transcendent ambition.
In the Third Act
          (Unruly old sun! Let's move the chairs.)
          before you come to the ocean, the landscape dissolves
          in shimmering light, the light devours the enchant-
          ing wood,
          the cicadas skim over the glow,

the glare creates a sinuous mirage,
a repeating image that swells and, repeating, reflects
even what has not been.
Let us stop here, now (though it is no longer possible,
though it is never possible). Remember that there is
nothing like that vine which for its never having been
we love so much. Remember that I am alone and
suffering and I know there is nothing. . . . There's just
no way:
                    The
stroking goes on more and more dizzyingly—ha
        ha—the
food is getting cold.
Ha ha—and the
                        food is
                                getting cold.
In the Third Act
            morning unfolds like a curse,
            the angry serpent slithers in his absurd constellation.
            The swans' necks have been wrung.
            A pair of swelling shorts at last makes the bower
            burn, the beams, the zinc passageway, the palm-leaf
            roof. The house and all
            in flames.
In the Third Act
            nothing is blue anymore.
            The keyboard breaks off its angry tune
            under the ocean's uncontainable—unconfessable—
            gesture.
            In the holy vault, stained-glass windows exude irony
            and lust.
            In the ashy clearing, promises shape unavoidable gal-
            lows. . . . *Oh, God, I will die in this harsh land where
            people communicate with phallus-blows and shame-
            less gestures.*
            The rain holds off for the fifth straight day
            but the revenge for something—the curse of being
            alive (a rancid croquette,
            rolled-up shirtsleeves)—takes on quite an allure. . . .

Oh, God, I will die in anguish, longing for those
gestures.
Mercy is now the only way to speak of the horror.
In the Third Act
In the Third Act
> Is there anyone who doesn't know his part
> Who can stop
> Who can leave the stage
> Who doesn't foresee the dénouement and yet goes on
> standing in the dark, watching,
> or in the space bathed by light, acting it out
In the Third Act
> The instruments play or don't.
> The song, the key, is already known—
>> Oh, come embrace me, oh, come swal-
>> low me up
>> oh, come slap me. Oh,
> quickly. Don't go on,
> let us not go on,
> for all that is not trivial is damned and,
> as we all know,
>> we must pay for it with our lives.
> Good evening, you look divine in that dress
> (as of course you know.)
> Forgive me for using such obvious words—it is
> impossible for me to speak.
> Jesus, and reeking of perfume (or was that tomor-
> row?).
In the Third Act all the rules are ignored.
> Authenticity—that system of "logic" native to this
> place—takes over the domains so long usurped
> by good judgment.
> The fact of being alive asserts its fundamental insult
> (so long waiting, so long waiting)—
>> Oh, come push me.
>> Oh, come lend a hand.
>> Oh, come and blow me away.
>>> The fish are smashed to bits,
>>> battered, furious.

The sand follows the course
   his feet traced.
            Letters
            interviews
            memoranda
            condolences
            general meeting
            preprojects and
            projects
            laws.   ·
      Seagulls above the ocean.
                        And in the sand
                        the print left by
                        his feet.
Soon.
Soon.

               Soon night will come
and you will face reality alone—scorning it, scorned by it.
               Soon night will come and you will be a
gesture in a time that detests you.
               Soon night will come and you will be a
mere storm of unanswered questions,
a string of tragic assertions,
painfully but unerringly conceived.
               Soon night will come and you will be a
mere conjunction of bitternesses,
an incoherent thought,
a widening solitude which, however, cannot expand any further.
                  Soon night will come
                  and you will be only
the slow burning of a cigarette in the dark, the stupor
of being alive in a place which embraces and withers you.
                  Soon night will come
                  and you will be alive,
                  beside the prison of the sea,
perceiving, if that, the buffeting
of that alien wind,
a bird's shriek, its now absurd fluttering,
the shape of the dark melding into the dark.

Soon night will come
and you will be alone,
thinking
thinking

INTERLUDES

Man
is a deplorable freak
for though he has a soul, at the same time
he has an eight-hour shift—
which no lower animal
suffers.

Man
is truly a shocking hodgepodge
for though he lives alone in order to be free
he may not set one foot from the spot
which is most loathsome to him, a thing
even the stupidest beast
can do.

Man
is indisputably a fiendishly conceived calamity
for knowing himself mortal, that he will grow old
and be food for worms and then, dust—
which, they say, no animal can foresee, conceive—
he must nonetheless seek, in pain and
sweat, day by day, his sustenance,
as other animals must,
though man with much
more
work.

Man
is truly a product of Machiavellianism
distilled, for knowing that infinity exists
he is yet the only being who knows
himself finite.

.   .   .

Man
is of all vermin the most loathsome,
for convinced that all things
go to irrevocable death,
he kills.

Man
is of all disasters the most lamentable,
for having invented love he only fully reveals
himself at the level of
hypocrisy.

Man
is of all insects the most disgusting,
for producing the same slimy excretions as all
other beasts, even those which
are filthier still than he, he builds
vaults and roofed gardens
to shelter them.

Man
is truly a piece of work that deserves our
deepest amazement, for knowing
that beyond death is death
he ceases not to pass
resolutions which
restrict his
ephemeral
life.

Man is of all monsters that which must be handled
most distrustfully, for though his intelligence
does not avail him to overcome his monstrous
state, it does aid him in
perfecting it.

Man
is without doubt the most alarming of all inventions—
made for thought, he never comes to

a definite conclusion which might save him;
made for pleasure, he persecutes and condemns
all those things which might
bestow it on him.

Man
is truly a thing which deserves
our most scrupulous condemnation—
having suffered every
manner of disaster
he does naught
but repeat them.

And
the man of our times, the oldest yet known,
is yet the most abominable and pathetic freak, for feeling
the same desires, the same emotions as the pagan, he yet
decks himself with the inhuman feathers and beads
of Christianity and Marxism
even though they weigh him down,
that is, even though
he does not believe
in God
nor has read the writings
of Karl Marx.

Ah, man,
a doubtful, laughable thing
that merits our most suspicious
observation—having invented God, philosophy,
and other punishable crimes,
he feels obliged to withdraw into his cabin,
for a mosquito buzzes
around his nose.

Soon.
Soon.
Soon it got dark,
and the two of them went into the bedroom.
Soon they put the baby to bed,

undressed, turned off the light.
Soon he closed his eyes
and pretended to be asleep.
Soon she placed her head in his
hands
and slowly they grew moist
(both of them went on ostentatiously breathing quietly).
Soon the cabin became a spot made whiter by the night.
Soon indefinite persistent creatures filled
the night.
The swarms grew and grew—
cries
flutters
cunning slithers
pendulums crashing into each other
hops
heavy thuds of soft bodies
cavernous wails
gnawing
whispering
disemboweled things
blows resounding like the tolling of bells under water
desperate whirls
shuddering searches for love
the death throes of some indefinite creature—toad, rat, dove—
trapped
by the sucker that chokes off its air
a creeping thing, a thing which alights, which bumps, and hops,
gurgles, wriggles, swishes, rubs
Grapack
Grapack
Grapack
            Or this—
    The lovely night keeps us from sleep. The cricket chirps,
the lizard warbles, and its choir answers; even through the shad-
ows one still sees that the mountain is formed of monkey-goblet
and avocado trees, the short pine rising into the sky; little ani-
mals fly slowly about in the air; from the strident nests of birds
I hear the music of the forest, measured, soft, like thinnest
violins; the music rises and falls, weaves and ravels, spreads its

wing and alights, tinkles and swells, always subtle and pia-
nissimo—the myriad ways of this fluid rhythm—what wings
*brush those leaves! How Soul makes the leaves dance!**

       Aie, aie,

                         T

                      I

                    G

                 N

it's him whIstling on the porch, once more.

                 D

              O

            O

          L

        F

*José Martí: *Diario de Campaña* (*Campaign Diary*, written in Cuba, 1895).

CANTO FOUR

Who will begin the canto? Some queer confined in perpetuity to a farm camp for having—damnation—greedily stared at the despot fly of a cop disguised as a country boy? The ex-minister reduced to four walls and a desolate memory? A draftee who was blinded in one eye by the point of a cane leaf and so imprisoned for negligence? An ex-pimp with philosophic pretensions, now become President of a Committee for the Defense of the Revolution? The refugee couple who pine, from "over there," and chant "the gold of the days"? . . . Ah, who will begin the fourth canto? A salaried worker who's supposed to double production for free on his days off? A suicide frustrated in his attempt thanks to the poor quality of today's barbiturates? A dawn-singing lyrical skunk sentenced to provincial ostracism because, though it won him a literary prize, his book did not find favor with Rolando Rodríguez, the Torquemada of today's *cubanis letris*? A shipwrecked castaway drifting forever through the Gulf Stream on a truck tire and two boards, futilely fleeing this "paradise," knowing he'll never arrive, anywhere, but fleeing? A quadrille of mute poets? The man who, for having talked about one of the latest outrages, was put to vile torture, and who now suffers the even crueler torture of having recanted? Ah, who will begin the fourth canto? A teenager with all his hair cut off? A homosexual led to the firing-squad wall? Ten million people enslaved, gagged, yet forced to applaud their slavery? . . . Ah, ah. Listen to those cries. Listen to those cries. Be still, be still. . . . A grocer accused of robbing the country because—so they say—he had a few beans in his boots? A writer locked up in the dark after having been forced to swallow every page he had written, plus the shit that came from them, and so on, through three recyclings? . . . Ah, but who will begin the fourth canto? A child forced to repeat "Patria o muerte, patria o muerte," even before he can talk? An ex-whore made superintendent of a cabinet-level department? (Listen to how eloquent she is.) A currently practicing whore who gives herself—and so eagerly—for the remote promise of a pair of stockings? Oh, tell me who shall begin the fourth canto? A combatant sentenced to thirty years of prison, or to death, since he understood, understandably, that he was to go on fighting? An angry queen? An embittered cook? A cunt locked up and therefore patriotic? An immortal painter gagged? An old lady even the memory of whom they have interdicted, so she won't tell it aloud? A member of the Interior Ministry with Freudian dreams? Somebody to whom they gave a doctorate in Political Science for climbing Pico Turquino, the island's highest peak, twenty-five times? A mother seeing her son go off again to the work camp— shovel, pick, mud, Lenin? A playwright silenced to the saddest silence of all, drilling oil wells for a macho lieutenant of aberrant opportunism and physiognomy, the president, naturally, of the National Board of Culture? Oh, who will begin the fourth canto? What angry, anonymous voice? What throbbing shrunk to stone? What great passion drowned in resolutions? What heartbreak smothered in anthems and affronts? What unceasing, alert sense of a blazing bonfire? . . . Listen, listen to their shrieks. They're all trying to talk, they're all desperate to be heard, so they're shouting; they're telling all their horror and outrage as fast as they can talk. Hush! Hush! Good lord, what a racket! . . . Calm down. Stop hitting each other like that. . . . Ow, leave me alone! Let me talk, goddammit! . . . Shh, don't yell like that, stop cursing, lady, the Committee can hear you. . . . Just get in line, stay in line, for God's sake; everyone's case will be analyzed, one by one. . . . Hey, no hitting! . . . Good lord! They're beating down the door. Quiet, quiet. Wait your turn, please, wait your turn!— Lady, for Christ's sake! . . . Ow, what the hell has Christ got to do with it!—Lady! . . . Leave me alone, you assholes!—Lady, please! . . . Aiee, assholes!—Lady! Good lord, they're tearing this place apart. . . . Aiee, boy, sweet fucking Jesus, you better leave me alone, goddammit!—Christ look at 'em banging. . . . Aiee, goddammit, open up!—Okay, okay, it doesn't matter who starts. You go ahead.

Ow, aw, shit. Finally. Oooh. . . .

Oooh, well, mine is such a tragedy, so hard. Oooh. So hard. Aw, you just cannot imagine how it is. Aw. But here!

Look here—this old woman you see here is me! This old woman with her hand up, here, I swear!

Ow, this hassled, humilified woman. Yes, humilified. I don't know if that's the word, but humilified is what I am. Goddamned humilified. Ah, me, so humilified, I can't win for losing. You can't imagine what this has done to me.

Me, a good Catholic. Me, a good Catholic mother. Yes, young man, and I've been a good Catholic since the day I was born.

Me, a respectable woman—I went to the Franciscans. Ungh, me, a Catholic, a lay sister and everything.

Me, after all those Sunday chats and coffee and walks. Me. —I had all kinds of lace and shawls, and I wasn't so fat then, either—all that slop has made me lose my figure, you can imagine. . . . Agh, me, a *lady*, stuck on that orange grove in the middle of the swamp. A *prisoner*, do you hear, a prisoner, *locked up* in there! . . . Well. . . .

Me, from a good family, one of the best. Ugh, me. . . . Aagh, look at me, young man, in this work camp, with all this sweat, this canvas, this stink. What a stink! My God, me on this farm waiting for my exit visa so I can get out of this country. A visa that doesn't look like it'll ever come, to me or anybody—and meanwhile they've got me weeding all these orange trees, acres of them! Agh, me, a good, honest, self-respecting woman—I mean, you know, really—well, I had my self-respect, aaaagh.

But that's not the worst—the orange trees—because everybody has to do that these days. No, listen, come a little closer, come here, listen. . . .

Listen—it's all women here—*whores*, every one of 'em! Oh, Lord, *whores*, filthy.

Me, a filthy whore, oh, God, oh, Holy Virgin—oh. . . . At first it wasn't like that—No! At first, when I first came here, I

just let it roll right off me—water off a duck's back. . . . I was
respectable, and I let them know it. I was a respectable lady,
goddammit. Ungh.

But it's so *hard*, it's so hard to know your place, I mean keep
those whores in their place, in a place like this place is. What a
place, Jesus. What a place. Do you hear that, listen, do you hear
how those women talk—

> *You mean that old woman doesn't do it!*
> *You mean that old woman doesn't suck!*
> *You mean that old woman doesn't fuck!*

Oh, my God!

And so me at first covering my ears up.

Me, with my head buried under a pillow.

And them up there wiggling and shaking their backsides.

My God, I even got out a book—a little prayer book, Jesus—and
started reading. Angh, but good lord, you cannot imagine.
Agh. . . . Comes nighttime—dark, dark—

And the whole orange grove is like stuffed with screeching,
> bawling, whinnying—yes, *whinnying*, because the
> men come on horses—and what language!

Comes nighttime, my lord. . . . And from afternoon on, they're
> all getting themselves up—taking things off and
> putting things on, gussying themselves up, smearing
> themselves all over with rouge,

swinging their hips and shaking their behinds and, oh, my
> God, saying such indecent things—you cannot
> imagine— so nighttime comes.
> The horses nickering and whinnying,
> the nickers horsying, and up there on the beasts,
> the men, whinnying themselves, the beasts.
> Oh, my God! Aagh. . . .

Hicks and hayseeds, draftees, mechanics, tractor drivers,
laborers, the guards from around here, all of them—
all that drunk carrying-on, all that garbage, that scum,
it all shows up here.

Aagh, and you ought to see them. You ought to see the things
they say, how they come. See how they come, supple and so
brand-new, dashing, those sons of miserable mothers, those
thieves, those rogues. Ungh, aagh, there they are. . . .

And me with my prayer book, my God.
Lying there on my cot.
Crying to heaven, but hearing not
a thing but that racket in the orange grove. Ungh,
                                                    my God,
and them, those whores—
> The old bag could still find something,
> for Christ's sake, they say.
> And The old woman could still suck one
> if she wanted to, they say. And even
> The old woman—like that, always old
> woman—
> The old woman, if she just looked for it
> > a little, all she'd have to do is
> > come to the door, they'd have her
> > on their stick quick enough.

Ungh, they talk.
> And The lay-dee, if she'd just let her hair
> down a little, she'd get screwed before
> you know it.

Aieee.
And me, praying my way right through my prayer book.
And thinking about my daughters, good lord, over there, abroad.
Even about my grandchildren. But that racket, oh, my God, that
racket.
And the men.
And horses. And whinnying. Oh, my God, and those whores,
aagh,
the way the whores were screeching.
Aagh. . . .
And now comes the heat. And the downpours, aagh, and the mud,
and this sweat, and all day that constant droning from the whores.
That nonstop gossip passing from mouth to mouth
about the machos—Oh, Jesus, deliver us.
Aagh—from mouth to mouth—
> And That other one, the dark one, quite
> a number, huh?
> And Did you see the way he came? Sharp.
> Aiee, he almost split me in half.

Aagh, and orange tree after orange tree after orange tree,
          here, here, all
around me, waiting for me to weed them.
And mouth to mouthing
young men. Jesus, deliver me. What I have
come to.
          And once more comes nighttime.
                    And once more I hear the humping out-
                              side the barracks.
And once more I hear them coupling like beasts
against the orange trees I weeded.
Oh, give it to me, give it to me, one of them cries.
Oh, quick, hurry, I'm coming, says another.
          Aagh.
And such heat.
And this brown canvas cot.
And this low concrete ceiling.
And these mosquitoes, my lord.
And this itch.
          Aagh!

          The old lady ought to doll herself up,
               get a new coat of paint, have a
               little renovation.
          Just yesterday there was this farm boy—
               he was so cute, he had such
               a hard-on, and he kept running
               from one tree to another,
               like crazy.
          Everybody was all paired off already,
               and this poor kid was just
               running back and forth. The
               poor thing, he came all by
               himself, all over a tree.

Aagh!

          If you could have just seen him—
               he was neighing like a horse.
          And what he had—like a hunk of
               salami. Like a horse.
          And so cute—just cute as he could be.

261

Aaagh. . . .

My God, my God, Lord, Our Father, Holy Father—this is really too much. Me, a respectable decent woman, with children over there, and grandchildren. Me, a grandmother. Aiee, a grandmother, listening to that ruckus all that running back and forth all that squeezing and hugging—that never-ending scuffling and talk and the way the whores wiggle their backsides.

Jesus, almost without noticing it, as though it was nothing at all, here I am saying *whore*. Agh, deliver me. Ave María Purísima, deliver me—I'm picking up those whores' vocabulary. Aagh, there, I did it again, like it was nothing at all.

I said *whore*.

        Ah, Jesus, deliver me.

      But

look here,

look

here

comes nightfall.

We're into June.

We're into November, we're into September.

We're here. Filth, boots, mud, dirt, heat,

heavy food (Russian beef), aagh, like lead. Agh. And the

                    visa is a thing so far away.

      My grandchildren are so far away.

      God is a thing so far away.

            You mean the old lady doesn't screw?

            Well, what's the old lady waiting

                for to get screwed?

            You mean the old lady doesn't see it's

                easy pickings?

            And such pickings!

      Aaaagh!

And that—that's so close at hand. . . .

      But look.

      But look here—

            Today we filled 20,000 sacks of dirt.

      But look.

      But look here—

            Today we filled 30,000 sacks of dirt.

      Aieee!

May,
June,
August.
          The air is full of that horrible glare, the dry grass
we walk on crunches, squeaks, rustles. The trunks of the
orange trees begin to ooze a thick resin. Even the shade
of the trees is a fixed circle of shimmering light.
          And God farther and farther away.
          And this crackling in the air
                              —right over there—
Holy Virgin
Holy Virgin
          Once more it is nighttime.
          And I am covering my ears, my eyes—and my body
                is soaked with sweat
                against the canvas.
          36,730 orange trees weeded by us women today.
Oh, my God, I'm saying *us*. Aagh.
Aaagh. . . .
          And now, under those very trees, they are shrieking.
          Jesus, such screeching. Such panting. Jesus,
          such gasping. And such
          language!
          Ugh!
                Listen.
                Listen.
                          And no one sees this.
                          And no one is capable of stopping this.
          Ay!
                Listen.
                Listen.
I throw on my nightgown—or what's left of my nightgown.
I go outside.
                Such noise.
                I run, holding the nightgown to my body.
                I run away, finally.
                I leave this hell. I run.
Aagh!
                From one of the trees a naked young man steps
                out and beckons to me. Aagh, but I run.

Run, running away.

From another tree someone calls to me. But I go on running; now I am running through high grass. I go on. I go on, wheezing, running from that hullabaloo, always holding the nightgown to my body.

Oh, Virgin,

Now I cross the hedges, the windbreaks. Now I hear the voices of all those whores—wallowing under the trees, calling me. "Well, old lady, finally, you've finally come out to fuck!" they screech.

Aagh!

But now I streak by like a flash. I run, deserting the field. I jump embankments, I run across meadows, through the grass; ungh, I slip, I fall; I get up again, still clasping the gown to my body, and I run.

Aagh!

Now I arrive. I come to the main street. Men passing by. Men, looking at me. My God, such looks. They look at me. Young men who bring a hand up to their pockets, or closer to the center, and stare at me.

Aagh!

But I keep running. I leave the main highway and run. Now I cross some rocky ground, running. Such shouting. How they pant. My lord, I hope nobody sees me leaving, running away; ungh, sees me finally leaving this shrieking brothel. Oh, grandchildren, aaagh, daughters, aagh, God, look at me running, running away. I'm coming to you, still clasping my nightgown to my body.

Aagh!

My nightgown is in tatters by now. I sweat and run. I come up out of the rough. The barbed-wire fence. I run! Run, run! Angh, always clutching my ragged nightgown, I run away.

Ay!

There is the soldier. His rifle beside him. His legs spread. Watching me run, and masturbating; hearing the sound of all those people wallowing around on the mountain.

Ah,
He stares at me. Now he is really staring at *me*.
He's discovered me, running away in the middle of
the night. But he goes on masturbating and watching
me. His legs spread wide, his rifle far away on the
ground. Why doesn't he stop me. Why doesn't he
shout at me to halt. Why doesn't he fire at me. Why
does he keep doing that, staring at me, staring steadily, metallic, shining and sullen, and stroking himself? Ah,
staring at me.
I pause a second, waiting for him to stop me. . . .
I run, run, run . . . desperately.
Aagh!
Finally I come up to him. I fall at his feet, panting.
Furiously, I strip off my nightgown, I get up onto my
knees.
I clasp his thighs. I begin
kissing and caressing him.
Ay,
    Ay,
        Ay,
            now I arrive.
          Here my running ends.

This has been, then, an edifying story. The high-born old lady
finds, thanks to the R (privileges of the system), her *authenticity*,
her true native self, and finds how it fits her for *here*. "Better late
than never, granny," sang the chorus of eroticized women from
the orange grove. From that moment, she danced and sang and
wiggled her ass. . . . Oh, I forgot to say that she was a widow and
she never managed to get out of the country. Finally, she "embraced" Marxism. Now she is head of the camp and works in the
orange groves day . . .
and night.
        And meanwhile . . .

The pure contralto sings in the organ loft,
The married and unmarried children ride home to their Thanks-
    giving dinner,

The gatekeeper marks who pass, the paving man leans on his
    two-handed rammer,
The convert is making his first professions, the President holding
    a cabinet council is surrounded by the great Secretaries,
The city sleeps and the country sleeps,
The living sleep for their time, the dead sleep for their time,
The old husband sleeps by his wife and the young husband sleeps
    by his wife.

SERVICE CONTROL SHEET
OPERATOR: JOSÉ RODRÍGUEZ PÍO

Marital status	—	Married, 3 children
Physical status	—	23 years old, up-to-date health card
Result	—	Negative
Attitude to TC	—	Arrives at assigned time or before
Attitude to TV	—	Goes to agriculture work every Sunday
Attitude to DC	—	Keeps guard duty
Attitude to LPV	—	Has performed all pertinent tests
Attitude to BOM	—	Responds to all calls
Attitude to CDR	—	Performs all work, keeps all guard duties
Attitude to SMO	—	Performed with distinction
Attitude to UJC	—	Disciplined and proper
Attitude to CSO	—	Proper
Attitude to PCC	—	Defers to all advice
Attitude to EJT	—	Attends all called meetings
Attitude to MININT	—	Obedient
Attitude to FMC	—	Cooperative with comrades

Attitude to FAR	—	Respectful
Attitude to UPC	—	Cooperative with "little members"
Political attitude	—	Cooperates harmoniously. No one has ever heard him speak badly of the Party
Social attitude	—	Does not receive visits or phone calls of a personal nature or family members not directly related by blood. Keeps normal hours of sleep. Donates blood quarterly
Peer attitude	—	Greets everyone
Attitude to Social Security	—	Short haircut, correct dress, never seen with antisocial elements or predelinquents
Attitude to Labor Security	—	Takes charge of all appliances, gear, and tools necessary for the maintenance of his equipment
Attitude to State Security	—	Positive in all checks and pre-checks
Friendships outside the Center	—	Blood-related family members of first degree—wife, children, wife's relatives (mother and grand-mother)
Collective attitude	—	Goes to national festivals, funerals, emergency meetings, and sporting events
Color eyes	—	Brown
Color hair	—	Dark brown
Distinguishing marks (interior or exterior)	—	None
Mental state	—	Normal by RRATT standards (secret)

Technical prepara- tion	—	That necessary for performance of his job
General culture	—	Reads *Granma* magazine and books the Circle recommends to him
Technical improve- ment	—	Takes all mini-courses recom- mended by Center
Morals in and out- side Center	—	Proper
Special vices	—	None
General vices	—	Smokes after lunch
Family	—	Father and mother dead
Religious ideas and other blemishes	—	None
FESE (secret)	—	(blank)
CACZTP (secret)	—	(blank)
RRTXZW (secret)	—	(blank)

Work performed: When he comes in, checks the general condition of equipment. Greases, looks over, adjusts, runs, loads, and unloads equipment. Supervises and maintains control of equipment during his assigned schedule. Clears the area of material not having to do with equipment. Performs lubrication of equipment. Checks exactness of flywheels and voltage; goes over carburetor and sets and supervises boiler clocks. Conditioning of equipment tanks and supervision and constant checking of areas near equipment. Opens and closes valves and watches the proper functioning of filter mats; supervision of gear wheels and timely lubrication of same. In charge of ladders, chains, sawhorses, tarpaulins, pails, sterilized blankets, and rectifier rods for equipment. In charge of watering cans, brooms, sponges, spare flywheels, nail-pullers, valves, and high-voltage wire circuits to equipment. Before lunch corrects equipment, making notes of all verifications in the pertinent schedule, leaving gloves, helmet, punches, uniforms, crust scrapers, and other work-related items in equipment booth. After lunch, re-sets equipment, reporting on it, putting all items in place. Afternoon duties arc like morning's, making the general daily report on the equipment. And finally, waiting, next to the equipment, for the change of shift. Performs inventory of damaged parts (bands, belts, rings, plugs, struts, eye-pullers), leaving all personal items (uniform, gloves, billy-club, helmet, raincoat, and protective glasses) in the equipment booth. In case of unforeseen emergencies—serious illness, death of family member, sudden illness— must report from equipment area, waiting for substitute next to machine. In case of foreseen death, may suggest operator who in his judgment would give best service with equipment. In case of sudden unforeseen death, operator on previous shift will stand in for him in equipment control, until hiring of new operator. In any instance of decease, firing, retirement, or work stoppage, all gear for equipment is to be turned in to General Control, including items related to dress, such as masks, glasses, hangers, as well as items of vigilance, maintenance, and working of equipment. In case of loss of reason, mutilation, or drowsiness while handling equipment, access to equipment should be withheld under strict monitoring.

Reasons for suicide　　—　Unknown.

　　　　　　　　　　　　Oh, Whitman, oh, Whitman,
how you exasperate me!
　　　　How could you have been so superficial,
optimistic, cowardly, and temporary?
How could you not have realized that you had to see, too,
the red tree of memory
plastered over with horrifying artifacts,
faded yet eternal,
　　　　　　　　bursting there, in the future, bursting
in the future?

                              Ah, Whitman, ah, Whitman,
how could you not have seen the hypocrisy
behind the mask of an act of mercy?
How was it you couldn't see the harrowing questions
time forever raises
(not to make us greater but to make us see
our misery, our impotence, our anguish),
the inevitable chicanery implied by living, by being alive—
the danger, the constant mockery that every act of ours,
even the most genuine, must bow to?
How could you not have perceived the dizzying void
looming before and behind this shadow of our being,
the brief cry we barely utter,
and no one hears?

                              Oh, Whitman, oh, Whitman
                              —you shameless old woman—
how you exasperate me, how impatient you make me!
Did you feel no indignation at misery
no powerlessness at crime
no degradation at vile acts
                and at that obscure, persistent, unending lie
humming always in the air, falling, falling
                upon us, and us humbled, grinning and bearing?
Was there no moment when you could feel that wearying
ennui, that repetitiveness, hear that futile noise
which announces, accompanies, and goes on long after
the most exciting
moments?

                              Oh, Whitman, oh, Whitman,
how you exasperate me!
How angry you make me!
                Did you never, at any moment, intuit that queer curse
that puts its mark on, weighs on, even the commonest actions?
                Were you never, at any moment, able to see that in
even the most casual one-night (or -afternoon) stand, there is
only defeat, that what excites you, provokes you most is not
what promises to satisfy you,
                but what gnaws at you, secretly,
                and impels you at last, dregs upon dregs, to seek
                one more momentary dreg?

                              _____

Oh, Whitman, oh, Whitman,
I refute your poetry with my sweaty hands.
I refute your poetry with a decayed, aching tooth.
I refute your poetry—oh, you, *fleshy, sensual*—
with a summer burning all coherent thought to ashes—
bare blistered feet skipping along across asphalt.
                    I refute your poetry with
your own rotting beard, your goddam beard full of worms
and vermin,
                    your bones which emit one last sarcastic
howl of laughter.
                    I refute your poetry with those strange eyes that
follow me.
                    I refute your poetry—oh, you, *fleshy, sensual*—with
the sound of a pot scrubbed furiously in the
afternoon.
                    —I tell you, I swear and can prove to you that that
sound is immortal. I assure you that it is great humanity who
makes that sound.
                    I refute your poetry by that single and singular eternal
disproportion
                    between what is possessed and what is desired.
I refute your poetry by this: *Toward the end of the twentieth
century a million adolescents were enslaved on a sugarcane
plantation.*
                    I refute your poetry with the rudeness
of a mosquito interrupting the poem and my meditations.
                    I refute your poetry with the plain, strict,
wearying fact of being alive.
                    I refute your poetry with the inevitable certainty
that after that fact, so wearisome, there only remains
disintegration through all eternity.
                    I refute your poetry with that look of that
sixty-year-old woman who devoted her life
to bringing up her son (and I quote)
"and just look what happened, he turned out to be gay,
and he's working in a forced-labor camp now."
                    I refute your poetry with the mute, angry,
incontrovertible

pain of that son.
                        I refute your poetry with a plate
of cold croquettes.
                        I refute your poetry with the unsatisfaction
of every encounter and the constant urge to have another.
                        I refute your poetry with the painted face
of an old queen
in a provincial cabaret.
                        I refute your poetry with the fact
that though your belly, your eyes, even your ass is full,
such emptiness, such void is yours
                after the rainstorm
or
before.
                        I refute your poetry by that violated,
secret canto,
that angry, melancholy plaint that is every real
man.
                        Oh, Whitman, oh, Whitman.
I refute your poetry with the newborn baby's eyes
looking steadily at me.
                        I refute your poetry with this deserted
highway
which doesn't go to or come from or lead anywhere and which
you have to travel.
                        I refute your poetry with the milky skin
of the grocer, exuding the smell of food and semen.
                        I refute your poetry with the smell
of wet sacks and a zinc-roofed passageway.
                        I refute your poetry with a tape recorder
in every public urinal (no water
in the private ones).
                        I refute your poetry with a strident
billboard.
                        I refute your poetry with the vision
of a crab on the sand.
                        I refute your poetry with the vision
of all those naked bodies—
even if you possessed them, one by one, it would only serve
to swell your desperation.

I refute your poetry with the certainty
that old age does not extinguish desires, it only reduces
the possibility of
quenching them.
I refute your poetry with the depths
of this hellish poem—which is life.

Look at those shrinking figures, march-
ing numbly from so much sun and frightful misery. Look at that
rough skin, that grotesque smile. Look at those people who only
see the ocean now as a puddle that's hard to jump, as a wall, as
this side of a barricade, of their loathsome prison. Look at those
bodies offering themselves to you in exchange for something to
cover themselves with, even if they seem to want you urgently;
look at that smile for sale, that treacherous friendship. You will
tell me that there are other things, you will speak to me (if you
are clever) of a mysterious rhythm, of a harmony *other*. . . . Ha
ha, how nice, how sweet it all looks, how pleased the audience,
there, watching, at a distance, from the plush box, or conversing
at the table after dinner with your folder of exquisite pages beside
them. Ah, how sweet the symphony heard among roses, gently
savored after lunch. Ah, such respect for that rhythm. But here,
come on, go explain to them, tell them what's behind it, what
images, what events nourished that harmony, how many figures
consumed, one after another, in return for one sound, how many
figures discarded, in spite of complicity—necessity—and desire,
in return for the harmony. How much loneliness, resignation,
desperation, fury, impotence distilled through cold unbearable
mornings, how many purposes rejected, how many sacrifices made,
how much cruelty, how much truth, how much pain, how many
secret and even familiar (intimate) confessions had to be cruelly
unveiled. How many blue (or pink, or brown) nights sacrificed
to the horrible, to the formless, to what might not be anything
at all or might be, simply, a monster; how much adopted uni-
formity (how much piety, how much hypocrisy) destroyed out
of deference to chaos; how many people had to be caricatured,
put down like that, like they are. . . . How many holy lies had to
be unveiled, how many prosaic truths had to be swallowed; how
many astonished eyes, how many foul-smelling hairy beasts, how
many animals of armored striations, how much shapeless,

shameless love, how many vermin are there, protecting that rhythm. . . . How many weaknesses, or noble souls, sacrificed, how much resignation, harriedness, madness and risk, selfishness, passion, and danger, for a simple cadence. How many adventures without recompense. How many signs and reckonings over the vast rough weather. How much desolation and how much dismay had to be suffered, discovered, demystified, assumed, and gotten around, so a man could take them up again and go on working. How many feelings had to be leaped over. How many souls, "charitable or plain," had to be tactlessly put in their place. How much revenge, mockery, impiousness, rigor, and unconfessed love are needed for us to come, at last, to the fitting, harmonious orchestral note, hard struck. . . . And then, after having shown all this, after having told everything that shapes it, take the still unpublished symphony. Put it into the hands of those gentlemen (and ladies) who are now savoring its most sublime refrains. They will rip it to shreds. It will never be heard.

Oh, Whitman, oh, Whitman.

And meanwhile. . . .

The contralto sings in the organ loft. Sings, sings. And a tapeworm begins to emerge from between her buttocks (oh, how bothersome these parasites are). But what can the contralto do but sing? For behold she is arrayed for the occasion. Behold—she is fittingly, elegantly attired—not to scratch her ass, but to sing. And the audience, in their classic finery and Sunday faces, contemplate her from their seats. The organ sounds; she is on the stage. And she sings, she sings! And the worm, the terrible worm, taking advantage of the situation, sniffs around the edges of her anus, and goes on nibbling craftily, but voraciously—stimulated, let no one doubt for a second, by that heavy, shiny, hot reddish-wine-colored velvet that torridly swathes the contralto's backside and falls in draped folds to the boards. . . . And the contralto sings, she sings (and the worm stubbornly nibbles the pucker of her anus) and the audience, entranced, is washed by those incredibly high notes, higher and higher. And the tapeworm now pulls half his cylindrical body out and examines the mountainous landscape. . . . Ah, how she sings, how she sings, how the contralto sings for this large audience. Listen to her yourselves. . . .

.   .   .

The married and unmarried children ride home to their Christmas dinner. Jesus, but this year we didn't get even one extra pound of rice, the mother mutters, and goes on: Jesus, don't turn the radio up too loud—they might think we're plotting something. Jesus, go to bed early, and be quiet about it, because since they abolished all the holidays, celebrating them, or even talking about them, has all those political implications.

The hugging and loving bedfellow sleeps at my side through the night. While they are sleeping, the woman in charge of the guard (fifty-ish, and naturally austere) called the patrol. They're a couple of fags! she screams. Now they beat down the door.

The boy's longing, his suffocation, his hesitancy in telling me his dreams—all that will appear in his personnel file, and in mine.

The farmer stops by the fence as he walks on a First-day loafe and looks at his oats and rye, plowed under one day by the wrath of the Prime Minister and First Secretary and President, who, so poly-faceted, is, of course, also the Chief Agricultural Engineer for the entire country. "And do you know why they plowed it under?" the countryman, now on the main highway, asks me. "To plant it with pigeon-peas!—and that's what they had plowed up before I planted the oats."

My friend *resting the chuff of his hand on my hip*—He stole my wallet!

The youth lies awake in the shingled garret and harks to the musical rain. And also, through it, to the steps of the police who've finally caught up with him—fled from a labor camp—"Army deserter" in official language. He envisions those armed bodies come closer. He hears that sound. He makes not the slightest motion to run or hide—where? why? Standing, he says *Here I am.* He sees, senses, beyond the brightness, the figures awaiting him, the fatality of that splendor and the relentless pursuit (the curse and the destiny—a closed, weathering plain, explosion, and fire)—and he knows it would be ridiculous to try to elude them, that. And he would like to embrace those bodies (although he

doesn't, perhaps out of shyness) which now, weapons in hand,
charge in on him.
                    And meanwhile:

The President is holding a cabinet council of great Secretaries.
The city sleeps and the country sleeps.
The old husband sleeps by his wife and
the young husband sleeps by his wife.
                              (Ha, ha—the young husband
                              sleeps by his.)
                              Oh, Whitman, oh, Whitman,
                    —*turbulent, fleshy, sensual*—
come here,
come here.
             Look at this magnificent prison in flames.
Come here.
Come here.
             Unscrew the locks from the doors.
Come here.
Come here.
             Unscrew the doors from the jambs.
Come,
come.
             Open your eyes if you can—open them wider,
                                        wider!
And look.

I go out into the street with nothing but breathing on my mind.
I walk, stroll.
The fact of being alive is like a natural insult
—it is the banal exaction of every day in hell.
I get on a bus full of people
—on every surface, photos of Castro, photos of Castro every-
where.
             And the stripling poem is pummeled, kicked to death;
The aggrieved Muse mutters curses at each laboring breath.
Youth passes you by, you are crushed by heavy bodies against a
                                        wall,
And the new caste's new cars down the streets seem to crawl,
Like vermin.

—————

Someone cuts the buttons rudely off my jacket;
Someone else, ruder still, stomps my foot—and I dare make no
                                                    racket—
Me—poor wretch—with no aim but to breathe, I can't
Do a thing but *see life pass*. That is the aim and the extent
Of my life. I pass confused through the hustle and bustle
And I know I form part of this hissing rustle
Of hushed whispers, one more voice muted,
As I pass before, beside them, praying only not to be gutted,
Passing through kicks and bruising vituperations,
With a book in my pocket, now ripped to ribbons.
I can pull, now, from the volume of vacant memory only empty
                                                    days,
While I seem to stroll, now, along—with the image of a noble
                                        Island set ablaze.
              Water! Water! cry voices which cannot, may not cry,
Water!—and they watch the Plenipotentiary Minister pass by.
Water! with lightning or with thunder, but let it, please God,
                                        rain!
But the sole sound heard is the rumble of an inclement train.
Toothless mouths, briefcases pursue me,
Huge radios, stinking armpits undo me,
Portable shrieks, unending idiotic words—
In the confusion, I am run through with a sword. . . .
              What are they saying, talking of, what does that
                                        gossip cry?
What secret nonsense is such senselessness inspired by?
What can they think of, good lord, how can they dare reason
When holy dogma's curse has rendered thinking treason?
Who analyzes, who, over all this, dares to meditate?
What is the word—we have lost—which could, might resuscitate
dead dignity?
                  Wailing voices, groans reduce all sense of wrong
to some macabre parody of some absurd love song.
Groaning voices, wails, shrink all sense of oppression
to the need, within horror, to find in simple sleep, cessation.
Wailing voices, cries, compress all thought of grandeur, olden
                                        glory,
to thoughts of how to lay hands on a bottle of icy Coca-Cola.
                                        Aiee,

Wailing voices reduce all sense of joy or happiness
to dread your name will show up on that blackest list.
Wailing voices, groans, reduce all sense of feeling in and for itself
to fear—in this prison they could clap you into yet a straiter cell.
Wailing voices are heard, which blot out all desire, all future
plan.
Wailing voices cast shadows over soul, poem, reason, the best of
man;
man's highest reach is by this myriad groaning drowned.
—Suddenly someone kicks me, once again.
I dive, descend—burning—but do not find a fairer place to stay.
Sundays, Saturdays, Wednesdays, Mondays; and nights lead only
to another day—
nowhere, no place, everything tells me, over and over again.
But as fall I must, descend, I go on falling, I descend.
And this I trail along behind me—sweat along the pavement;
and this too drag along—my faded sense of hope, though all but
spent.

Through the window overgrown with vines I think I see a leering
face,
hear howls of laughter (horrid Naturalism, passé literary phase,
banal tradition with roots now deeply set in place).
Behind the counter a mannish woman makes no bones of her
distaste—
"We ran out of Cokes, strawberry sodas, everything. There's nothing left today."
Houses with windows like ugly holes that fingers make in clay,
asphalt laid so skewed that over it no feet will ever stray.
Houses in a blinding glare of light so torturing, so cruel
that it will not be cleansing fire nor yet admit the cool
of green shade. A muted repeating monotonous drumbeat—Fool!—
the teenaged body, gravitational, working its inexorable pull.
Look how those eyes in every doorway follow as you stroll,
look at that faggot cruising every public urinal.
Man comes to resemble the tools of his trade—
in a while he'll become the bench itself, a mere hinge,
a blade.
Oh, run, for God's sake, while you still have time.
Run, before running is ruled a crime.

———————

Run before the wall grows too high to climb,
run before you sink hip-deep in this thickening slime.
Look how stern that guy is, with the poker face,
look at the face on that old bag with her skirts tucked at her
waist,
look at those hands, those eyes, look at that skin scorched by
the sun—
Look how they slip off, one by one. . . .
And our Island is made up of holes left by such flights, now.
All past degradation brought forward into the now
and onward into the future, and even beyond; harassment, now,
and pursuit handled so subtly in the present, and how
subtly lurking still in the future, and residing in every memory
now;
and lending its sallow complexion to our whole Island now.
Shirt, sweat, unruly uncut hair—
what soft hand walks beside you there?
What sweet body soothes your care?
What thought still comforting and fair
Still exists, that might allay your fear?
Ah, yes, let us parody the old soft air—
now that infamy, dressed as a new-come volunteer
teacher, can set its horrible, traditional snare.
The savior at last cracks his whip in the air
and the awesome drama ends with a cheer
for the farce—for that it is what it cannot help but be,
since it's all acted out where men take themselves to pee:
  Repeat, repeat that old refrain
  In a voice creaking and filled with pain—
    A tisket, a tasket, a bugger's bulging
      basket—
    I don't know if I want to kill or kiss his
      pretty ass-kit.
    I'm saintly, I'm sinful, I flirt with all the
      menfolk
    And then I EEK! and then I shriek, so
    now they're in the pen—Fools!
  Repeating and repeating the go-to-hell grin,
  Repeating the repeat of a distant chagrin.

Repetition, repetition of the repetition
Which began when somebody repeated the wrong
information.

Enough! Don't go on with this useless persecution!
Please! They just got in some more soda, this time lemon.

Come. Come. Come hear that harsh shrill sermon
which our whole tradition hangs on.
Do as they do, seek their solution—
look to the land.
If they speak of "evil," give them a hand.
If of "good," why, strike up the band
and chant the song of the War without End.
Repetition, repetition—here, there.
Repetition, repetition—hearty har har.
Repetition, repetition—repetition
is the Grand Solution.
I drag my body through the streets to the house
and find myself at the door at last—expressionless
smooth wood, final torment, gate to pass from passionless
defeated search to familiar conquered hopelessness.
The key turns in the lock, the feet advance,
the glare of the afternoon creates strange shimmering dance.
Body on the balcony forever awaiting me.
Stupor of *here* while *there* still is aching me.
A few steps, two voices—*G'afternoon.*
The whole world underfoot, overhead seems to burn.
Legs stretched at ease, a few words dropped, spoken
about the day—It's seemed like an oven.
The necessary pretense of "glad to be 'home' "
(with words like pulled teeth)—ah, to be alone.
I'm back, you see, I'm here again with you.
I lean back and say, "Such heat today. Whew."
The privilege of dying by inches by being here
and watching you slowly die as well, "dear."
As you go on dying, I feel double death, for
both dead, you and I, we speak about . . . the weather.
Dinner is served.
Mayonnaise traded for a jar of preserves

with the woman next door. Baked fish, green pepper.
I cut up my soul, take the last bite of supper,
chew. Ought I say, "Mmm, delicious!"?
Instead we silently do the dishes.
And go out to sit in the living room—
though as for me, it might be the moon;
for—son asleep in his bed,
man and wife at the holy tête-à-tête
talking about the traffic, the noise,
some common problem, impossible choice—
he is thinking, abstractedly—thinks of and lists them,
a few of the unique

PRIVILEGES OF THE SYSTEM

Writing a book on cutting sugarcane and winning the National
Poetry Prize;
Writing a book of poetry and being sent to cut sugarcane for five
years;
Dying utterly muzzled, exalting the "freedom" we enjoy;
Imbecility, machismo, and terror as methods of reasoning and
action, hypocrisy as the language of official life and
even among friends;
Concentration camps exclusively for homosexuals;
Forced labor, firing squads, torture, gangsterism, robbery, inva-
sion of privacy, and blackmail, all with patriotic ends;
Popular democracy in which no one can criticize, complain, leave,
or choose;
One sole owner, one salary, products terribly scarce and costly;
The substitution of *levels* for classes;
The black market managed by the Prime Minister;
The death penalty for teenagers;
Political poison as the foremost export, submachine guns as the
foremost import, constant retraction as fundamental
law, *mea culpa* as litany, the exuberance of anthems
as compensation for absence of water, food, and free-
dom;
Sexual relations considered political acts with serious conse-
quences;

Too much hair as counterrevolution;
The official use of the verbs *parametrize* and *purge* as a means
of implanting intellectual terror and wiping out all
true artistic activity;
Song festivals without singers;
Writers' conventions without writers;
School in the field;
University, automobiles, housing, beaches, and trips only for sub-
tly playing the game;
A tape recorder between breasts, mattresses, in urinals, tele-
phones, hedges, and other "strategic" places;
The child as a field of police experimentation;
History, literature, plastic arts, music, dance, etc., reduced to a
subsection in a department of the Ministry of the
Interior;
Tamarind trees felled to plant tamarind trees;
Betrayal of ourselves as the only means of survival;
The blank page as a matter for conflict;
The written page as a criminal offense;
The police as enemy and the friend as possible policeman;
Feudal legislation, slave production, capitalist trade, and Com-
munist rhetoric;
Even salt rationed.

Oh, but do you remember
that young girl who killed herself
leaning in her stupor against the window frame
that opens on noplace
or floating on a provincial river—
this new Ophelia whom no one will ever come to know,
who'll not appear even in the last act
of a mediocre play
written by a village queer?
Do you remember that face
in the window looking. . . . Where?
Do you remember her pallor,
her look,
that insult, that proffered virginity? Proffered to whom?
Privileges of the system—*Suicide as self-realization.*
And

the horrid beast turns.
Armor-plated it gazes on you, cruel and suffering it picks you up,
raises you, lifts you, hurls you, and lets you fall there,
here, where you cannot flee, where you *are*, already . . .
gazing at you. . . .

                  Privileges of the system: He, I

                            When I arrived, he was
                            waiting in the place we'd
                            agreed. Tennis shoes, shirt,
                            white shorts, and (like me)
                            a bag full of empty bottles.

I hope you had something
to drink, I say
by way of greeting.

                            He stands there, indifferent
                            and assured, as though he
                            weren't waiting for anything,
                            convinced that whatever he
                            craved would come along. . . .
                            And what's more if it didn't
                            come along he wouldn't be too
                            upset. He is holding, too, no
                            doubt to accentuate the gratu-
                            itousness of his whole attitude,
                            a dry stick he's swishing
                            through the grass. He throws
                            down the stick and walks off,
                            without saying a word.

               The grass, the sand, the pines
               seem startled in the brightness
               and the noise of the cicadas.

I guess your mother gave
you permission, I say,
trying to insult him.

                        He doesn't say a word.
              We leave the path. Leaving
              the pine grove farther and
              farther behind, we go on
              walking along the beach.

Hey, I'll say, are you
sure this is the way
To Guanabo?
                        He doesn't say a word.
                        He turns, supple, grave. He
                        looks at me. And keeps walking.
                The ground is now covered with pine nuts
                and pine needles. An empty bottle seems
                to absorb and reject all the brightness
                of this time of day.
I think it's better to take
the avenue, I suggest.
                The empty bottle cackles brilliantly.
Unspeaking, I go on
walking behind him.
                        We come now to a long file
                        of tents, made of blue canvas.
                                He stops. They rent them out
                                during the season, he says.
                                They're empty now.
I draw closer.
                        The wind raises little whirls of sand that
                        pitter over the canvas.
We'll be late,
I say.
                                He puts down the bag and
                                brings his hands up to his
                                waist. He seems rapt in the
                                contemplation of his feet.
We'll be late,
I said.
                        The cicadas once more take possession
                        of everywhere.
We'll be late,
I'll say.
                        The sun rebounds off
                        the blue canvas.
                                He starts walking.
You know this place
well, I say.

_____

                                        He doesn't say a word.
Do you like to read?

                                        He turns around. He looks at me,
                                        surprised and curious.
                        Hearing the chant of the
                        cicadas, I understand
                        how out of place my question is.
                                        Yes, he says. I read some-
                                        times, but not as much as you do.
I'm sure your mother
likes you to read;
and do sports, of course.

                                        Yes, he says. They're both
                                        good. I like swimming
                                        and baseball.
Idiot, I say to myself.
Of course, I answer.

                                        Don't you?
Yes, me too.

                        We cross the bridge; some boys
                        are skipping stones across the
                        water with keen concentration.
                                        We're almost there, he says.
                        Without speaking we begin to
                        walk along the shimmering high-
                        way. We cross the town's first
                        streets. A group of young people
                        in their summer clothes go by and
                        look almost familiarly at us.
Go with them, I think,
and say it, even, although
very softly.

                                        What? he asks.
Nothing, I say.

                        In front of the store there's
                        a crowd. As I try to figure out
                        who the last person is in this mob, I
                        observe them all—bones, bellies,
                        huge tits, bald heads, kinky hair,
                        buck teeth or gaps, broad and
                        narrow noses, red or green faces.

Too much, too little. All that
shapelessness in bathing suits,
to boot. . . . No wonder
they fall silent when he comes.
I hope we don't have to wait
all day here, I remark.

                    Sit down if you want. I'll
                    tell you when our turn comes.

I don't answer.
I observe the glance,
half ironic and half conspiratorial,
that a heavy gentleman
wrapped in a pair of huge
flowered shorts
bestows on us. I sit down on the curb.

                    A stream of filthy water flows
                    down the gutter. It's that same
                    water—sewer, washbasin, sink—
                    that runs down the streets of
                    every village.
                              Watch this for me, please,
                              he says, and gives me his bag.
                    He runs toward a great crowd of people
                    gathered at the corner. He pushes
                    his way forward. He is back, laughing,
                    carrying two ice-cream cones. Here,
                    he says, and holds one out to me.

Good lord! I think, and
say it, not too loud.

                              What? he says.

Nothing, I say.

                    And the man in the loud shorts
                    smiles at me brazenly now.
I throw the ice-cream cone
into the gutter.

                    He, not saying a word, throws
                    his into the stream too. The
                    ice cream melts instantly.
                    The cones float along the filthy
                    water.

I am in this brilliant light, in the midst of the crowd,
holding a bag full of empty bottles. What am I doing here
with all these bottles? I ought to break every one of them
over that old fart's head. I raise the bag. The old man's
expression is now leering.

                    Come with me, the boy says,
                    taking my arm. I got a place
                    at the front of the line. We
                    can buy the stuff now.
          We head back. The boys on the
          bridge are still engrossed in
          skipping their stones.
          We enter the pine grove.
It's noon, maybe even
later, I say.

                He doesn't say a word.
          We go on walking in silence.
Perhaps he expects me
to praise his cleverness
at slipping ahead in lines.
"Outstanding," "tough"—something
along those lines. I imagine
he's used to receiving
those glorious tributes
for even less effort.

          The cicadas whistle faintly, as
          though the very heat, the very
          brightness, were drowning out
          their racket.

                He pauses now before the
                same tent as before. He
                looks at me.
          We are both sweating.
                Let's go inside, he says.
          Inside the tent, the heat
          is even more suffocating;
          daylight is a yellow brilliance
          made to tremble by the moving
          branches of the trees.

                              He puts down the bag with
                              the liquor bottles and sits
                              on the ground, leaning his
                              head against one canvas wall.

It's even hotter here
inside, I say.

                              He doesn't say a word. He
                              slowly takes off
                              one shoe.

It's much hotter here,
I say aloud,
standing up.

                              Without saying a word, he
                              shakes the sand
                              from his shoe; he takes off
                              the sock, too, and shakes it out.

            The landscape outside, seen
            through the canvas, seems to have
            been set afire. An ocean
            in flames covers the parched shore.

I'm going outside before
I bake to cinders, I say.
We should have taken
the car.

                              I don't know how to drive yet, he
                              answers now.
                              My mother hasn't let me learn yet.

It's easy, I say.

                              She says it's dangerous.

She's very careful with you.

                              He doesn't answer. He stretch-
                              es out his legs across the
                              sand. He lays his head back
                              against the canvas.

She really loves you.

                              He doesn't say a word. His
                              face seems to darken.

I, here, on the other side
of the tent, squat on the

sand. I light a cigarette. Hey
I say aloud now, why are we
here? What do you want?

                He doesn't say another word.
                One of his hands rakes care-
                lessly through the sand.

I smoke.

                Sometimes people leave things
                they've dropped, he says now.
                Wallets, rings. When the
                season's over you can find them.

Bathed in sweat,
I stand up.

                He starts slowly putting on
                his shoe. Then, standing
                too, he turns to face me.
                He looks at me. He brushes
                the sand off his shorts.

I go outside.
        The cicadas receive me with
        deafening babble.
I wait outside.

                He comes out, slowly, still
                brushing off his shorts.
I start walking.

                He, behind me, whistles.
        The cicadas hush their babble.
                When I learn to drive, he says,
                we'll see who goes fastest.
Why do you think we'll ever see
each other again?

                He doesn't answer. He goes on
                whistling.
        We cross through the pine grove.
        We are now in front of the
        stand of almond trees.
Listen, I say to him,
stopping,
we'd better not go on

together. Stay
here and wait till
I get there.

                         Whatever you say, he says.
                And I see in his eyes, his
                lips, in his whole body
                a kind of triumphant scorn.
                         He hands me the bottles
                         of liquor he's carrying.
                         I don't drink, he says.

Take them to your mother;
didn't she send you for
wine?

                         No.

Take them to her
anyway. What will you
tell her if you don't?

                         I do what I want to, he says.

Take them to her,
I say to him.

                         Whatever you say, he says.

I walk away.
I come out into the light.
I stop.

                         He comes along, whistling,
                         walking slowly and staring
                         at the ground. He has
                         picked up the stick once
                         more that he had thrown down
                         on the path. Without opening
                         his mouth, he seems to smile.

Listen to me, I say to him,
don't ever use the formal *you*
with me again. I'm not
your grandfather.

                         Whatever *you* say, he says, smiling.

I keep walking.
I stop.

                         He has stopped too.

I go up to him.
I look at him.

He looks at me too.

Listen to me, I say to him.
Tomorrow night, in the same
place. Late.

He doesn't say a word.
All the splendor of the day falls now across his face.

There are bridges which are utterly flat, barely indicated by the spideriest of railings, steel suspended in a void, high, shimmering swaying piles which somehow, no doubt, testify to the "advance of civilization"; there are bridges of complex architecture, almost birdcages, soaring threads, cupolas climaxing in an interweaving of metal; birthday cakes, vines nourished on forged iron, rails which sustain and rock an enormous train through space; bridges which ape long sarcophagi, guarded over by monumental candles; bridges of undulating gray chains. . . . There are bridges which are mad spiderwebs, vertiginous arrows; there are those palisaded by rope and wood, fashioning medieval roadways; there are those so modern that they are unnoticed, so that we never know when we are really on them, or whether they are above the river or beneath its waters; there are those that sway, inflated like balloons in an infinite green; there are also those bridges serpentine and infinite—spans linked one to another, one to another, sometimes marked by enchanted lamps. There are bridges made entirely of black iron, like an upside-down train; there are those too woven of niches, galleries, and overhangs and apses—so you don't know anymore where to get on them or jump off them. There are those not for crossing but for parking on, or going backwards on. Bridges that chirp when you step on their rotting planks; suicidal bridges falling; drunken bridges arching, perhaps disgusted, too, by the filthy water flowing incessantly beneath their spans. Bridges that totter without quite ever toppling. Bridges that laboriously carry out their traditional mission. Bridges that open, bridges that close, bridges that dive, bridges that rise, bridges that move from place to place, bridges that roll, or even roll up; sonorous, enormous bridges like sopranos with girdled mountains, singing bridges, cheerful smiling bridges, bridges with rough flanks that flower when it rains; bridges a river has never flowed under; bridges just to be a bridge, just because; bridges of mud and straw, bridges of a single vine, village bridges, city bridges, interstate bridges, cosmopolitan bridges, existential bridges, Roman bridges and realist bridges, movie bridges, philosophical bridges, police bridges, slanderous bridges, childish bridges, lubricious bridges, Sunday bridges, business bridges, lyric bridges, Gothic bridges, effeminate bridges like a pergola and patrician bridges like a shield, medieval bridges, bridges for exiles and bridges for tourists, surrealist bridges and imperialist bridges, smoky bridges and schizophrenic bridges, ministerial bridges, municipal bridges, bridges for balletomanes and air-mail bridges, bridges for the "charter ferry" and bridges for the fishing fleet, structuralist bridges and hamlet bridges, senile bridges and burlesque bridges, Gothic bridges and agnostic bridges, picaresque bridges and tragic bridges. . . . Oh, but which bridge do you prefer? That one, praised by the poetess in constant uterine flame? This one, that fits so well? That one there like an odalisque? The one beyond that glimmers? Choose your bridge! Get your bridge here! Cross over the bridge! Look at a bridge! Pause on a bridge! Pet a bridge!

Jump off a bridge!

Look at those forking veins,
look at that alcoholic fuddle,
look at those hands.

And the triumphant words,
And the triumphant words,
you sing now.

Look at those eyes. Look at that body whirling now before you, crying out.

Ha ha— She thinks she's driven you mad
or vice versa.
Same thing.

Ha ha— She dashes outside.

Two hearses
Two hearses
pulling away, in opposite directions, in the
afternoon.

(Carrying bottles, rags,
scribbled banners,
I think even a baby and
some other stuff.)

                                            Two hearses
                                            Two hearses

toward terrors so vast
that who knows when they will meet again.

                                            Two hearses
                                            Two hearses

departing in opposite directions,
sure to meet again.
                          I will not go.
                          I will not go.
                                              Two
                                              Two

                Well,
she guesses that running is good for desperation, so she runs.
She guesses that returning is inevitable, so she returns.
She guesses she saw who can imagine what conflagration of colors,
sexes, and ships driven toward exuberant sea animals,
and she sees them.
The ocean guesses that it grows dark, and it becomes violet.
Time guesses that another day has gone by,
and it exhales some incomprehensible strange sigh.
Night guesses it's night, and it fills with mosquitoes.
The two people guess that the mosquitoes lash them,
and they go to bed.
They guess they have to close their eyes, they have to lie down.
                And they're already lying there.
He guesses that a sound, a beat, a movement (whistle, footsteps),
a body, a curse call him. And he listens.
She guesses she sinks, sinks, sinks. And she falls.
He guesses that he guesses he can guess what she is guessing
about him, oh, yes. And he guesses it.
                To free himself from so many guesses
he imagines he is not alone,
that no one is hounding him, that lots of people are waiting for
him,
                    and there he goes.
    Ah, he imagines that in spite of everything, or because of it,
there still exists, he in fact inhabits, a place where
horror and mystery seek, too,
like water and fire,

their place to spread,
where they can acquire resonance and shape.
                 He imagines that he can still express
what he yearns for or struggles against,
that he can still convey his vengefulness, his
desperation,
                 his truth,
                         that someone will pick up his words,
that no one pursues him,
                         that he is no longer an instrument, a
number,
a card, an enemy,
a project, a pompous phrase,
a watched contradiction.
   Ah, he imagines that in spite of everything (or because of it),
he still is.
                 And he composes.

MONSTER

   In that city there was a monster, too.

   It was a complex of suppurating arteries, tracheas pumping like furious pistons, coarse hair streaming over its head, warbling caverns, and huge claws communicating directly with its sinister ears. All the world raised its voice in praise of the monster's beauty.

   It would be impossible to name the odes composed, by all poets of renown (for the others could never even be anthologized), in homage to the delicate perfume its anus exhaled—actually, its anuses, since a single intestine would hardly have been enough for it, such was its capacity for absorption and swallowing. . . . What is there to say of the innumerable sonnets inspired by its mouth?—a mouth divided into several compartments. In one of them it saved the vomit that the monster disgorged in its moments of greatest orgy; the vomit lay in that pool undergoing a kind of natural coction, and the broth was rendered thus even more delicious to the monstrous palate. As for its eyes, always bloodshot and rheumy, the verses they inspired could not even be summarily enumerated. Of its body, made to measure from several deformed hippopotamuses, suffice it to say that it was the eternal source of creation, as much for the most fragile of damosels as for the most virile ephebes. Heroes, students, workers, soldiers, ministers, and professors learned to wax ecstatic before such a vessel. These little lines belong to Mirta Aguirre; from the millions that exist, chance placed these in my hands:

> Alto como el Turquino,
> Radiante como el sol matutino,
> Su voz no es voz, sino trino,
> Su paso no es paso, sino camino.

Though their music is untranslatable, perhaps the English reader may gain some idea of them from the following unworthy translation:

> Tall as a mount in Himalay,
> Radiant he glows as the first fires of day.
> His voice is not voice but thrilling neigh,
> His footsteps leave not footprints but broad highway.

There is no doubt that in that city everyone loved the monster.

When he sang—so they called the havoc that issued from his throat—what multitudes, gathered devoutly together, applauded! When he shat, what a line formed to inhale (from afar) the great monstrous reek!

But one day a strange thing occurred.

Someone began to speak out against the monster. Everyone, of course, thought this was just a question of a madman declaiming, and they expected (prayed) that he would quickly be exterminated. The man who was speaking delivered an insulting speech that began more or less like this: "In that city there was a monster, too. It was a complex of suppurating arteries, tracheas pumping like furious pistons. . . ." And he went on, attacking—solitary, violent, and heroic. A few women, keeping their distance, stopped to listen. Men, always more civilized, peeked out from behind doors. But he went on shouting horrible things about the monster: "Its eyes, always bloodshot and rheumy . . ." Finally, since no one murdered him, everyone began listening to him; then, respecting him. Then they even came to admire him, and they paraphrased his tirades against the monster.

At last when his power was such that he had managed to abolish the monster and take his place, we could all see for ourselves—and he never stopped speaking against the monster—that it was all a question of a monster.

CANTO FIVE

Reading
                    (by one of those frightening turns of fate)
Cintio Vitier
                    in that hallowed little folio of his on Cuban poetry.
How sad—and irritating—it all is. This man did not include poets
because of the merits *per se* which their poems manifest, but
rather because of the poets' limitations—their pietistic mouth-
ings, their cowardliness, their resignation to things as they are,
their patience, their renunciation of life, their suffering—and the
prejudices they suffered under, accepted, assumed, or could not
overcome, and now make *us* suffer, the resigned calmness with
which they learned to tolerate or silence the slanders their time
showered on them. That is the way, then, that Cintio the Monk
sets them up and knocks them down, enthrones and deposes—
guided by a curious critical sense in which sanctimoniousness
(renunciation, penitence, abstinence, prudishness, hypocrisy, and
all sorts of other monastic priggery) forces intelligence, imagination, talent, and sensitivity to yield. . . . It is not strange, then,
that such a mentality has found its place (and such a place!) in
the current dictatorship of Cuba. Philistine Catholicism and fa-
natic, dogmatic Communism are equivalent terms for what one
might term the *special ethics of hypocrisy*. They hold life up not
to reality but to a theory of reality. They are both guided not by
experimentation, experience, but by their adoration of a dogma.
Life doesn't count. Obedience, rules, guidelines, precepts count—
and, of course, hierarchies. A devout man—that is, an obedient

man (for Christ has less and less to do with it)—must accept, must lend his support to, any humiliation imposed on his life, precisely because his religion is nothing but the chains of anti-natural limitations and impositions. The militant Communist (Marx virtually prohibited) must, *a priori*, renounce all authenticity, spontaneity, all vitality, and unconditionally obey the directives that "come down" from the Party. *Come down*—that is the expression. The Divinity (be it God or the Dictator-for-Life) is indisputably On High. Freedom (creation, love, rebelliousness, renewal—*life*) is foreign to both theories (and practices) or even worse than foreign; both theories (and practices) are irreconcilable enemies of freedom (life). Catholicism boasts of (glories in) having survived through four social systems: slavery, feudalism, capitalism, and now Communism. When it still could, it used all the blind terror which power wielded by dogma implies, to establish its hegemony. Now that the instruments of Faith (fire, persecution, and the machine gun) have passed into the hands of its enemies in the material world, it uses means more hypocritical and cunning to survive. One can expect any sort of monstrousness at all from a religion which, for the sake of survival, makes a pact with those who deny it, combat it, laugh at it, and persecute it. Communism sets in where the Church leaves off. At first, having no power, it encourages a "subtle, delicate, broad" humanistic labor. This is the period of "preconquest," when great ideas—even works of art!—are extolled, a period of "philosophical well-being" and understanding—of the weak, the poor, the miserable of the earth. Ah, how the hero, victim of the enemy, is respected then, how the debilities, defects, of future proselytes are respected!—the future slaves who, because of the very defects that inspired them to rebellion and struggle, will afterward be the most horribly conquered of men, for they will be put into the category of traitors. Once in power, Communism tends to be less tolerant than any system that has gone before it. There is no way for it to be otherwise. Ruled and sustained by an ostensible "ecumenical truth," it admits of no theory (much less practice) different from that which it propagates and which "justifies" it. Its flaws, the patches over them, its monstrosities are so great that anyone (given the slightest opportunity) could strip that misshapen body naked, that body so futilely camouflaged by all those Band-Aids, one stolen from here, another pinched from there. Communism is, without a doubt, a species of Catholicism, with the difference that whereas the latter offers a choice, heaven or hell, Communism can only promise hell—and it never forgives an enemy, even if he should recant. Its hell is all the more horrific and tedious, for since it is so strait it strips its victims of all hope as well (that far, far consolation) that they will ever be able to transcend it. Its gods, though more worldly (they so quickly grow fat), are not for that any the less inhuman. It goes without saying that they must be worshiped daily; that one must ratify and repeat their prayers, bulls, and excommunications by heart, though they increase alarmingly by the day; that one must suffer their ires and caprices, imitate their looks, gestures, voices. And do it all with great optimism, simplicity, and faith. In this respect our religion (Communism, of course) is doubtless more fetishistic and fanatical than the other. But both of them, really—and this should be kept constantly in mind (to be able to survive, or elude, them both)—deny reality, or take from it whatever they need to keep the game going. A man embracing one of these doctrines to try to come to self-realization is lost, because both of them consider man either a sheep or an enemy. Life, for both of them, is submission. Naturally, once it is in power, Communism removes its mask and, like Catholicism, its medieval character shines forth. And more brilliantly— that is, more *blackly*—and efficiently, for after all, my goodness, this technological revolution has been good for *something!* . . . Communism, apparently, is the more popular doctrine. Small-time hoodlums and the frustrated of the world are more numerous than kings, princes, marquises, landed gentry, potentates, and the like—which is not to say, forgive me, that they are any the more contemptible. . . . What most surprises me is that in this era of "great changes," poisons, and self-flagellations, bearded leftist whoremongers ensconced in Paris inventing or backing nonexistent revolutions (which are no more than unanimous prisons for forced laborers) while always retaining the copyrights for themselves—what surprises me most, I repeat, is that, still, every country is not Communist; it must be owing to some thickheadedness or negligence on the part of the ruling governments. For truly I tell thee, greedy potbellied little dictators of the world, this is the BUSINESS DEAL OF THE CENTURY: The leader whose position is "for life" becomes (once more) the lord and master of all life and property. He can modify the past, dispose the present, and arrange the future to suit his whims; moreover, as a "progressive," he is filled with glory, which confers on him the "arduous" task of handing out prizes for the hymns composed to his name, finding spaces for his statues, coining money with his image, and flooding the world with photographs of himself, not to mention, of course, accepting the Lenin Peace Prize and suffering through interviews with Barbara Walters. . . . Experience is worth a great deal. "Development" and "dialectic" are undeniable things; Communism puts into practice (and in so doing sharpens) the characteristics (which is to say those well-known barbarities) of antecedent systems. Let us take, for example, the technical term "added value," that Marxist monks' fondled flinty stone. Very well. In the new system, Communism, a worker works harder than in any other, gets less back in return, is treated worse, and what he may finally acquire is more expensive (eight or ten times its production cost and its "before" price), even though it is a product of the very poorest quality—and even though there are no longer any capitalists to rob him of the fruits of his labors. What has become, then, sir, of "added value"? (Some might say "profit," but even saying that word has become an act of subversion.) Really, and I repeat, it would be dishonest to deny that technique improves as "History marches on." Before, the state received its "tithe"; the new class (an *economic* class, basically) figured out that it is far more practical, efficient, and even "revolutionary" to abolish taxes, tariffs, and so on and to convert man into a kind of letter of exchange *ad infinitum*. No more tithes! The state is now the only usufructuary—no middlemen—and its subject, serf, slave, laborer, or comrade (call him what you will), given that he does not "belong," that he does not exist as a legal or human entity, must, naturally, obey the state. The state, a monolith, is everything to him. There can no longer be any thought of strikes and protests, since the struggle of contraries (that condition so basic to the preservation and continuation of life) has been abolished, judicially, and any insinuation to the contrary will be detected and punished with all the skill and cruelty which are the attributes of any great machine. . . . Moreover, when there are no longer any classes, but rather on the one hand the plenipotentiary and omnipresent State and on the other the monolithic block of the slave mass, who are you going to mount a protest against? A human being (if it is not absurd so to speak of him now) under the new system must put all his transcendental worries and fears behind him, for if he does not the system will annihilate him. . . . Let us strive, then, to be accorded the syndicate's permission, in a year or so, to buy a pressure cooker or a couple of chairs which, logically, the state will be paid, overpaid, for—that is to say, with what would have been our "added value," and adding on top of that what might be termed a "socialist surcharge." The black market is even in the hands of the state now. Economists, economists. . . . Everybody rise and shine, cheer, bow, entertain suspicions of the man who doesn't make those genuflections (he could well be doing it to test us); use a simple, repetitive vocabulary—if possible cheery monosyllables like Yes! Yes! Wow! Wow! Hey! Hey! Hoo-ray! . . . Out there, all is darkness, confusion, and danger—and no one will come to our rescue. Quite the contrary—they will traffick in our slavery, in our corpses. And whenever he wishes, "the God" can bestow upon us the grace of annihilation. . . . As you no doubt will have noted, both doctrines are monstrous. Therein lies their attraction, the success with which the second of them now seems to reap its harvest. Man, in his ancestral misery, in his pathetic, congenital weakness, cannot bear his own freedom. When, by some oversight of evil, he tastes it, he is filled with existential anguish, guilt, complexes, a resentment of himself and of his peers; he wishes to immolate himself, to run desperately, pitifully, in search of someone who'll put a ring through his nose and honor him with a kick in the ass. . . . Touched at once by a kind of tragic peevishness and by a memory of the herd, he ceases not to search out the object of his conquering and submission. God, Karl Marx, Mao, even some tropical subderivation—a Dictator-for-Life. . . . Choose one. I recommend, if you wish to "fit in" to the era, that you choose Communism. Its strength—doubt it not for a single second—is overwhelming. It can draw on its own property—as well as on the raped and exploited of systems opposed to it—on the weak, the frustrated, the ignorant, the angry, the repressed and impotent, the innocent (naïve) and the heavy-laden, the children sick to death of Daddy's allowance; on demagogues forging political—even artistic—careers by dealing in political opportunism; on the great publishing houses of the Western—

and Eastern—world (neither prisoners nor corpses buy books); on traffickers in words and hope; and, of course, on ex-officio villains and grand, noble ladies whom menopause or excess (read: "uterine flame") has provided with an urge for immolation. . . . That is, it can draw on almost the entire genus *Homo*. Very well, then, cheer—and cower. *You, too, can become a new man!* . . . Nonetheless, among the cracks that terror or History leaves (cracks growing narrower by the day), you will often find hiding, nourished by solitude and fire, the ever-scarce, the strange— wet blankets, Party-poopers, as it were, who have been so stubborn as not to avail themselves of any blessing. So old, so outdated, so new, so few, so inevitable and indestructible, they justify and exalt those millions upon millions of poor tame beasts— anonymous, mute, and saddled and bridled—who now (once more) bow, prostrate themselves, before the "Redeemer." Amen.

    Ah,
but have you even begun to think, sir
    (which is improbable),
what strange beast
these two entwined
doctrines
    would bequeath
    (which is probable)
to the world?
Have you even begun to consider
    (which is very difficult)
how life might be,
under the yoke of those two
confabulated
    religions
    (which is not, come now,
improbable)?
      Have you begun?
        Have you begun?
         Have you even
         begun to?

Joined.

         The sun,

you say,
and your hand seems to fondle
invisible flowers.

                                        The sun,

you say, and your hand
as it hangs diapers out to dry
seems to plunge into a garden
where there is still a tree, where
music plays.
                    (Ah, whereward, oh, whereward?)
                                        The sun,

you say,
and I see your hands
pay homage to the weather.

                                        The sun,

you say,
and your hand curves
as it caresses who can tell
what suffering, transparent beasts'
humps.
                                        The sun,

you say,
and you walk away, haloed by its glow,
your hand pointing
toward a place where
there still are jasmine flowers.
                    (Ah, whereward, whereward?)
                                        The sun,

you say,
and all the love in the world
is concentrated in that word
while your eyes
try to peer, thankfully
                    (but whereward, where).
            Today
we will not go to the ocean
for the sea is the memory
of some holy thing
which we cannot comprehend,
which strikes us.
            Today
we will not go to the ocean
for the sea is an undulating expanse,
a song to eternity,

                                    ─────────────

                                        303

which it would not be right to break into with our ephemeral
repeated cry.
                    Today
we will not go to the ocean
for the sea is yearning, a mass of desires
I will never be able to fulfill.
                    Today
we will not go to the ocean
for seeing that open water
(skyward flowing, skyward flowing)
would once more wake our ancestral urge
to cross it—
                              and that, we may not do.
                    Today
we will not go to the ocean
for the sea gives shape to avenues towers palaces
and cathedrals blazing with light
airy specters gardens and cities
which we will never see,
which, for us, have ceased to exist.
                    Today
we will not go to the ocean
for the vision of so much life, so much grandeur
flowing up to our chained feet,
is not to be borne.
                    Today
we will not go to the ocean
for its splendor offends our eyes,
which may only see fields of dirt to plow
and cities subjected to rot
and slogans.
                    Today
we will not go to the ocean
for there is always an adolescent in the sea
displaying how great it is to be alive
and that, that is no longer to be borne.
                    Today
we will not go to the ocean
for going to the sea is recognizing ourselves for what we are.
                    Let us go, then, down to the ocean.

. . .

The boys
in a futile gesture of rebellion
try to find their place in a time (another time) which now
has ceased to be theirs.
They wear tight faded jeans
they let their hair grow long and subversive
their walk speaks of vitality—the proud walk
of one of the young lords of the earth, a world-eater.
The girls
(as a consequence of the lack of communication)
turn out to be copies of American situation comedies
of the Fifties.
     Look at the boys, look at them move now.
It is almost heartbreaking, how much they want to exist.
Long sideburns, barely sprouting beards, hair
kept secretly long
     (hidden for now under their caps).
     See how they desperately try to find their place.
They have ceased to exist.
Over every splendid expression of their faces,
those elasticities, those postures,
over those bodies, those gusts of laughter,
over that desperate testament to life,
     someone is keeping watch.
     Brag as they will, *yeah, bro', m'buddy,*
what a heavy chick, oh wow, some party, as they will,
show their stuff as they will, try as they will to impress you—
Tight as they wear their tight bathing suits
     and strut, cocks of the walk, as they will,
laughing at everything,
throwing up to my eyes and to the era those world-eaters' faces,
they have ceased to exist.
     Time, the world, the epoch
have eaten them alive.

     Such dark brightness
     Such vulgar unanimity
     Such horrible sensation
     Here, there, everywhere

Horror

                                  We arrived.

We came on foot, by state-run bus packed with people,
to wash dishes and hose down the new class's cars.

                                  We arrived.

We came to understand that to play, for example,
the cello, one must first become a soldier and farmer.

                                  We arrive.

We have come late to the feast.
All the places are taken.
We are entrusted with the task of serving the table.

                We arrived

when there was no longer a place to stay in or a chance
to flee,
when no one except the Greater Cockatoo could speak anymore,
when no one except the man who imposed the slavery was free
anymore.

                You arrive,

when there are no more plays or concerts or blank pages.

                You arrive

when the only things that are constantly excellent
are the methods for inducing stupor.

                You arrive

and are presented with a machete and an infinite expanse
to chop in.

                You arrive

and they unleash a bombastic speech on you which tells you,
as they send you off to a compulsory-labor camp,
that you are building the future, building
freedom.

                                    Our generation,

poor generation,
has no expectations,
does not aspire to, or believe, or trust in anything.
Our generation,
        poor generation,
is condemned as well to wander like shades
through a hell that uses them
and scorns them.

                                                  We arrived
when the fraternal embraces
and the fireworks
were over.

                                                  We arrived
when the era offered no possibility of hope—
just an infinite terror.

                                                  We arrived
when the old privileges—the houses, diplomatic posts,
cars, foreign clothes, scholarships, trips, beaches,
special medical attention, restaurants books movies and
walks, education, jobs—of the once-privileged
had already been dealt out to the newly privileged.

                                                  We arrived
when consumers and producers had already been redesignated.

                                                  We arrived
when neither freedom nor equality was any longer
envisaged—just production goals and degrading
laws; when now that the first fanfares had faded away,
the newly enthroned jailer shows his true,
invariable face—the face of a murderer.

                                                  We arrived
when a job in the shade is a strategic post
to which only the most obedient, the dullest
need aspire.

                                                  We arrived
when thought had already been replaced
by stupefying rhetoric.

                                                  Our generation,
poor generation
(Look at them, look at them, look at me),
arrives when everything has been so swallowed into the Big Rip-
off
that you can't even point at something and say, There's the rip-
off—
and the horror is distilled when it imposes its splendid show
of cheers—and work—upon us.

                                                  Our generation,
          horrible generation,
wants to jump a bit, wear its clothes a little tighter,

let its mustache grow, dance
beside the wall.
　　　　　　　Our generation
is sick of hearing big words
and then, after the promises, being picked up in the
streets or in our very homes, dragged off to a
military school, a work camp, or a jail.
　　　　　　　Our generation is sick of them worrying so much
about us.
　　　　　　　Our generation learned to distrust
(too late, always too late) those foreign humanists
and homegrown patriots
　　　　　　　　　enjoying the very privileges of the bourgeoisie
(managed with greater excess and clumsiness)
　　　　　　　　　yet leaving to us always the fetid scum of their
　　　　　　　　　　　　　　　　　　　　　rhetoric.
　　　　　　　Our generation, poor generation,
was not born to be poets, but to drive a potato harvester
and get drunk once a year when the boss
arranges it (in his own honor).
　　　　　　　　　Our generation
arrived when there was no way out anymore—not by air
or by sea,
　　　　　　　　　not by the word,
　　　　　　　　　and not by fury.
　　　　　　　　　Our generation, accursed generation,
did not have the privilege of choosing its own hell.
We arrived when there was only one,
　　　　　　　　　and the most inescapable, most burning one, at that.
Our youth,
our only youth,
　　　　　　　　　had to subject its noblest ambitions, its
most daring desires, its most vital intuitions, its
grandest sense of self
　　　　　　　　　　　to
the hypocrisy of "I have to fake it, I have to renounce
so they won't wipe me out once and for all."
　　　　　　　Our youth
　　　　　　　　　swallowed down its torments with an ice-cream
cone from Coppelia,

limited its dreams to a pair of faded jeans,
or to the hard-won victory
of a twenty-four-hour
                    pass.

                                        For a while
                                        For a while
                                        For a while

                    How well
                I understand them
            how furiously I understand
                    them all.
Our youth,
            wonderful youth,
has ceased to be young.
                    (For a while
                    For a while.)
                    Let's go, then,
                hand in hand, to take
            a walk, make a face, and babble
                nonsense, dancing the jig
                around this emptiness
                    which we are,
                    which is us,
                        us, us
                    ourselves.

                                    (For a while.
                                    For a while.)
                    HA
            HA   HA
                    HA
Mark my words—for a while.

                    And
                everyone here
            gathered at this moment
            flowing before my eyes.
                    And
            the ocean behind
        swelling in howls of laughter.

                    ———

The ocean
        fleeing.
The ocean like some real thing within a dream,
like a reality so real that it becomes unreal.
       The ocean
             like an echo that now fades away
like a vast empty stage—waiting—
before an audience that has been waiting too,
a thousand (ten thousand) years
                For a while
                For a while

W   A   I   T   I   N   G

and, watchfully, watching
               for a while
      Mark my words—   for a while
                  I will not go.
                  I will not go.

Picasso: *Seated Woman*
Prickasso: *Seated Woman*
                  I will not go.
                  I will not go.

      Woman
I will present you with an astrolabe
a sounding line and a barometer
all sorts of instruments to measure pitch and roll and yaw
      and perform tests and corrections
        I will set before your eyes my birth certificate
and my wounded feelings
        I will open myself to you like a file full of data
painstakingly computed
        I will even turn over to you all my forgotten
memories
blood-type illnesses outbreaks suffered and to suffer
        joys
great-grandfather's eye color
      fractures
weight and I.Q.

---

color of liver at six months of age
education completed   length of eyelashes   books read   and
kicks received
            images which flooded first masturbation
sign of zodiac
love of water
            pleasure at burning a black moth
family conflict and pleasures   dark damnation
            all that and more I will turn over to you
soul   way of singing in the shower   ill-written letters
            sense of horror and of the
void
            At last
after all   the analyses   rectifications   and adjustments
tests and pondering over it all   you will see that you can come
to no conclusion
that all are possible
that you know nothing.

                                        Ah woman
            poor woman

                        in the cry unuttered
                        in the inconclusive gesture
                        in your way of placing
                        just   so
                        the knives and forks on the
                        table
                        in your open eyes
                                        Ah woman
            poor woman

                        in your peering gaze
                        in your trembling lips
                        in the way you interpret
                        my silences as wrongs
                                        Ah woman
            poor woman

                        in the ceremony of
                        the rustling cloth
                        in your light light step
                        in the way you say without
                        saying what you feel

                              Ah woman

        poor woman

                        in the gesture which doesn't
                        quite come to the point of
                        insult
                        in the image held
                        in mirrors
                        in the frightened way you peer
                        into the distance
                                    Ah woman

        poor woman

                        in the fact of living
                        conquered
                        in the sadness which
                        more than the epoch's
                        is your life's
                                    Ah woman

        poor woman

                        in the growing womb
                        in the growing womb
                        in the glowing afternoon
                        (and you at your vigil, quiet)
                        in the gathering evening
                        (and you waiting and watch-
                        ing,
                        quiet)
                    But
            what is our country
                    doing?
The horrible marmot pulls out a huge spring and shoves it
                        —ooh, that tickles!
The tentacles come now to your throat and carry out
their methodical inspection. Deep inside you they yank out
your guts and the rest of your equally necessary parts.
                    But
            what is our country
                    doing?

I will not go.
I will not go.

Boots,
gloves,
    palm-leaf
hat,
    blue workshirt
khaki
    pants—these
are the slave's dark vestments
    once more at the threshold
    once more at the threshold
    Boots
    gloves
and the weather like a brazen cackle
and the trucks braying
and farther and farther away
and farther and farther away
    that dream of evening water
flowing toward my heart
heartward flowing
    (flooding all the land)
    Pants
    hat
Horns that never stop honking
    full truck
me on top
    in the midst of an uproar
so old it is new again
    in the midst of the sway and
    shake
and the hold-tight-we're-falling
    repeating all that nonsense
me laughing by now out loud
    and farther and farther away
and farther and farther away
    that instinct for rebellion
that hymn
    (heartward flowing,
bursting within my breast).
    We arrive.

We always arrive.
(We will never leave.)
Long before dawn the booming iron clang of a gong
Shocks you awake here, where you now belong—
"You've gotta get up! Hit the ground, let's go, li'l speed,"
And join ranks and hands with this horrible breed.
Lined up and waiting, the long file of cart after cart.
We must scramble aboard, heaped like a raw mass
of hamhocks, haunches, bacon, loins, and—that too—tits and
                                                              ass.
So far away the dream of water washing my heart,
That soft cool water whose image always soothes my rest
And that laves, rocks, caresses me, calls me to its balming breast.
                                                    We go on.
The monotonous landscape cowers (light still undeliver'd).
Like a vision, a vision which unmans me
A lurking palm grove shivers
And from its fronds I hear a kind of plea
For the childhood still cradled by memory
In that swaying whose hour will once more come.
But meanwhile, thinking not of life or calm,
With blade in hand the forever-green we set upon—
Yesterday? Today? All that happens here is cause for shame.
Is it, must everything always be the same?
                                            (I will not go.)

          A man
the first thing he does
is see it, a man feels it—that one big green mass—
you know, but then again, that's because it's still early
and it's all moist—not as stiff and hard and *angry*
as it gets later, soon; so you think, at first anyway, almost
that it's a dream, like, like a (naturally) cold nightmare. A man
goes out into that big field of green with all the other men, yelling,
carrying on, making a racket, just like—and because—that's the
way everybody else does it. You've already honed down the blade,
so you go out there into the field and you just wade right in—
chop chop chop. When you go out into the field, you feel like
every step, every time you put one foot down in front of the

other, makes everything pop, crunch, crack. The ground, you know, it's like it crunches, like it was bottle glass your feet were crunching through—but what the hell, you wade on in, and you start lifting up that machete, and letting it fall, dropping it. Now the water (or the dew or sap or whatever)—you know?—the water off the leaves, runs down along the blade, or the blade flings it back at you, and it hits your face, and since a man's face isn't as cold as that water that's been standing out in the open all night, you get this feeling like hail, or sleet, is pelting you and running down your neck—but you can't stop to worry about a little thing like that, because they've already given the order to start in, *Hit it*, and you can already hear the other men going chop chop chop; so, naturally, you go along going chop chop chop too. Your feet get this, well, hot, heated-up feeling like the dead leaves in the rows were a quilt or a dry blanket—because whatever water there was on them, or in them, is gone by now—and you go along, chop chop, and since there's not any water anymore (or dew or rain or whatever) on the leaves—but I'll tell you, there's sure plenty of sun, on everything—a man thinks, naturally, logically, that it must be afternoon by now—we've been out here working at this out here for hours already. You know about that, you're pretty sure, but you'd like to be really sure, to confirm it, you know?—but then you don't have a watch, and the man closest to you there doesn't either—and yelling, specially to ask some-body what time it is, you just don't do that, it "isn't done," they say. . . . But finally somebody comes by, and you kind of get the message across, you know, you don't say a word, but you kind of tap your wrist and you look up at the sun and kind of shrug and this guy, your buddy with the watch—Wait a minute. What'd he say? Did he get me? Did I hear him right? Is that thing working?—he says it's a quarter to seven in the morning, good lord. . . . And everything—above you, under you, all around you, all over the place, everywhere, everywhere—is rustling. So a man thinks *a quarter to seven*. . . . And everything squeaks, every-thing—well, it gets, you know, sort of tough to your blade, you know, and *now*, from the sweat, the blade keeps slipping out of your hand. These Russian boots hurt your feet and you've got some ant or some itchy something, maybe a piece of dirt, in your sock. A quarter to seven. . . . The sun's up there like it, well, like it's not about to budge. Come on, buddy, let's get a move on there. . . . So you turn back to what you were doing, and you fall into the rhythm of the machete, not much breeze anymore, not thinking about lunch—which is the farthest thing from your mind—but about when the boss will say *Take ten* and a man can have a smoke, lie on his back, and then, like *that!*, at it again, *Hit it*, chop chop chop. And the sun in the very same spot. . . . You start whistling, singing, thinking about—well, I don't know, about anything at all—grabbing onto anything at all, mixing this up and that—but lord this work doesn't leave a person much for whistling, let alone thinking, because one chop can take off a man's finger, or your whole hand, like happened to this one guy. So a man has to just go on, but you look back and you see this kind of shimmer, and you look up ahead and see the same thing, green, shining, and you look up, you raise your head, you look up past your machete or hack or mulcher or whatever the hell these people are calling them now—and you don't see a thing but that heat shimmer that looks like it's melting in the air. For a second you stop chopping and breathe deep. Then, if you're by yourself just sort of standing there, you can hear, so clear, that chop chop chop of everyone else—all that chopping makes a sound, I don't know, like rain, raindrops, thundering down and echoing all across the fields. And you know, you don't see the people wielding those hacks or machetes, you just hear the way that rain, that thunder, beats down. A man *hears* them—*hard*—chopping. Shit. You hear the leaves falling chop chop. And you turn back to it again, holding your machete, and you *attack*. And you go on even when you don't think you can anymore, because not going on is worse—a person suffers more, feels worse, here, inside, not doing anything. And that dust that rises—black, you know? real grime—it sticks to a person, along with the grass and the vines that sting you—good God, and if you scratch it's worse (and who said you could scratch, anyway?) because then it spreads, and pretty soon it's on your throat and your neck (and you know it, because as it spreads, you can be sure it itches), and even worse—right up to your face—it could even get in your eyes. But bitching about it, complaining, stopping work—forget it! that's what sissies, pansies do. Good lord, and meantime, a person's own water, I mean that comes out of a person—you get sopping wet. Your fatigue shirt gets soaked, and grime and soot mixes all up with the sweat. A man looks up and he thinks, Noon, and you look at the sun, but it says, Not a minute past seven, or not even. So you come back down to earth and once more, and more furiously than ever, you set in attacking those stalks—all those stalks and all those sharp spiky leaves, all those big plants that are always ready to poke out a person's eyes—chop *chop* CHOP; and you try to latch onto—while you *ugh* and *ugh*—onto the words of some short song, anything that you can repeat, whistle, quick, trotting along, without ever stopping that machete; that's how you go along, saying or maybe sort of grunting that short something, maybe just one word, maybe not even—while a person can barely keep up that chopping, that chop chop chop—till there's so much glare that you think you'll go blind, and that noise the other men make, too, never stopping, that chop chop chop, that noise leaves you a little deaf too, so, see, now everything sounds, well, sort of far-off, funny, and a person starts feeling sort of down in a hole, deep, where it's hard to make them hear you—and where, what's more, you feel, well, drunk, high, dizzy, drowsy, dopey, really peculiar. Then, you know, things start to have a kind of beat—chop chop—and you start sort of letting yourself go with it, you might even have forgotten the words to the song, forgotten to whistle, you're more like a thing, this *thing* that raises an arm with a machete attached to it—*chop!* like that—and we go on, sort of trotting, quickstep, in time—*chop!*—and in time you forget you were thirsty, even forget the sun; a person chops—*chop!*—and the ants—shit, let 'em bite—even if, maybe, such little bastards the bastards are, the ants're all over you. We go on like that, though, *spellbound*, they told me, is the word for what it feels like, *drunk*, through the whole canefield, this big shining glary green place; we're so yoked to it, into it, that we don't even feel tired, don't even think; jog, jog, we just jog along through that glitter, trying to keep going like that, without resting, so we don't get tired. Then the whistle comes for *squeet*: that's how we say it, friend, let's go eat. You just drop onto your back, boots and all. Because if a person were to take off all that gear, what with taking it off and putting it all back on again, the time would be gone. You stretch your neck and aching back, spread-eagled—goddamned fly! There's this kind of faraway hum, somebody opening a can like, I don't know, I don't know, but you see it all through a haze of *no-can-dooth*: exhaustion, friend—far away, far off, like faded, you know?—and you hear that kind of buzzing, but you don't even have the strength to shoo it off (shoofly, teenyfly or bigasahousefly), and anyway it would just be all over you again, the stubborn son of a bitch. Everybody's gotta make a living. What it is, is, the heat makes a person drowsy and then—see?—you see, when a person is ju-u-u-ust, well, floating off—through the hullabaloo and the fly-buzz and the sweat—you hear that *clang!* and you run, shake off that sleepiness, grab your canteen, and *jump!* jump up, hook onto the truck. This time of day, people don't talk much. These people don't say a word, to tell the truth. Oh, they say things that don't really have any beginning or ending—he-e-ey, aiee, ho-o-o-o, things like that. Things that don't make any sense. A person has to push through the air, not even walk; sometimes you bump into some-body else, since it's so bright and glary a man can't even see—we must look like a bunch of drunks stumbling around. There wasn't any coffee. The trucks are like drowned in a cloud of dust and they keep running over potholes or rocks—they act like they're drunk or still asleep too. A person thinks he sees all sorts of things that just didn't happen. People keep saying all sorts of things they just got through saying, or somebody else just said. And all those wet bodies, as they, as we, I mean, go out into that green again, pulling on our gloves—they look like they're made out of smoke, it looks like they walk, or really it's like they sort of float, but walking, in sort of a dead flight, dead hop, dead step, dead weight. Because, see, there's something *dead* about a person that goes out into that canefield at this time of day. This time of day every leaf is a knife—and the field, it's like a field of tinkling, clinking glass. You put down your foot, friend, and it's as though you'd just stepped on a crazy, jumpy old hen. Some-thing—a leaf, maybe, or a piece of dried-out weed—crunches, and when it crunches like that when you step on it and it crum-bles, it sets off a chain reaction of crunching all across the field. And that's the way it goes on, like that, through the hottest part of the day. You lift your hand now, mechanically, dull, not jogging anymore. You hit that rattly tinlike thing. The ground is black. Above it, there's so much light that a person can't even see. And since you're not jogging now, you whistle, whistle, more or less the same thing, nothing, not too long, because you've got to be able to breathe and keep chopping and even once in a while pee. Don't waste your breath, I mean. You see the stream coming out of yourself and falling and disappearing, like *that!*—instantly, bubbles, you know?—that's all, like the dry leaves just swallowed it up. In the afternoon, in the middle of all that chop chop chop, if a little breeze comes up a person might even be able to think a little—think about a television set, while you whistle, if you can get enough merit points to requisition it. But the air, the air, oh, it dances, almost, it boils under your gloves. Little by little, you push yourself through all that, you keep going, not thinking now that you have to finish, that it'll be night soon and we'll finish today's day's work, not thinking about anything concrete. You raise your arm and chop, raise your arm and chop. And you see yourself there, like that, as though you were outside yourself, chop chop chop, you know? And you see (by now it must be three o'clock) all those dry leaves, one big plant after another, not like something to knock down and leave there but like something *there* that has a law that you have to obey, something there that you have to chop down so it can keep on growing, more and more every day. So a man, not jogging now anymore, sees, and he hears the other men in that rainstorm of theirs. And even though they don't say a word, or, well, whistle like a person does, something that's really nothing at all, you know that they're thinking the same thing you are, or rather feeling, experiencing, the same thing you are—that keep-on keep-on chop chop chop, maybe for the pure pleasure of it, just because. The least little excuse of a breeze comes up. And you even enjoy, a little, now, in a strange way— like a cow or a bull or a plant—this exhaustion and sweat, and this little bit of air a man has, to kick up his heels in. You don't feel the prickle of the leaves anymore, or the sting of the nettles— nothing bothers you; it cools you off, this sweat actually cools you off in that little breeze now. Chop, chop, and on that very stroke, that *chop*, it's all over. You know? You've already been here for months. . . .

Today is Sunday. There's no work until later—oh, not because it's Sunday but because of some battle somewhere that's being celebrated today. Everybody in the barracks. My buddy, my machete co-worker, is smoking on his bunk. I took a bath, and shaved; I'm lying here on my bunk smoking too. We aren't doing a thing but listening to somebody's radio, and to people, clinking spoons, bantering about chicks; somebody else playing a bench like it was a drum. Sunday. Don't have to do a thing until early tomorrow morning. Now they're hitching rides on tractors, trailers, carts passing by, to get on the road and make it to town. What a mess. My buddy even has a bottle of rotgut rum, and he offers me some. The light on Sunday is different. People brushed their teeth. I drink a little rum and we smoke a cigarette. Bunks, faces, even the flies, the ceiling, and the music from the radio, of course, is all Sunday. And if you look outside—Sunday. Do you know, the noise of the plates, the tin cups in the washbasin, it's faster today, Sunday noise. My buddy says he's going to take a walk (because it's Sunday). Everybody leaves—the planks in the barracks—Sunday. Me lying in my bunk and my buddy hurrying to get out—Sunday. My buddy motions me to follow him, there's a cart in the yard going straight to town, run. Me, no, or, to tell the truth, I groan. My buddy leaves, but he leaves the bottle behind. The empty barracks fills with Sunday. The loblolly under the washbasin—I can see it from here, lying down—is Sunday. I drink and rest—you get it?—Sunday. And my hands, that haven't done a thing for hours, so they're even more wrinkled and tough than usual—Sunday. I smell like soap, because it's Sunday. And that (Sunday) must be why I feel so, well, heavy, stupid. I walk to the latrine, I see all the things people have left lying there—pieces of mirror, pieces of soap, clothes—the products of Sunday. The soapy water is still running down the gutters. That water is Sunday water. In the barracks yard, coconut palms, zinc sheets, some other plants, some bricks—it's all Sunday. Then, in that glare, which is Sunday, I, Sunday, Sunday, pretty lazy, full of heat from it being Sunday, can afford the luxury of saying anything I want to (Boy, is it hot, I say) and not go off somewhere if I don't want to and walk down the dark sort of hallway made by the bunks all lined up like Sunday. You know— I go outside then, and something tells me that there's something beyond, besides all this, that's Sunday too, and too, all this Sunday is not good for shit, except to make me think *Sunday Sunday* and see one big Sunday while I look at the dusty road the barracks and the glare this Sunday. I go back inside. What the blazes is going on? What kind of Sunday am I seeing, what kind of Sunday fiesta, without ever having seen it? I walk, all sort of numb because since I didn't work too much I'm even number, even tireder. It's to be expected. I go outside and this Sunday fly, this Sunday

weather, attacks me, throwing that Sunday at me, you see, that
I don't see, never ever saw, you see, and will never ever see. So
I go outside, trying to run away from that other Sunday—and I
run, but there's nothing but Sunday. Empty cans that are Sunday,
garbage can which is Sunday, grass, glare, and green bottleflies
beSundayed. And, well, imagine, sir—instead of enjoying my
Sunday, the only real Sunday I've got, God only knows when I'll
get another one, I lie down in the windrow path the tamarind
trees make and hope—all Sunday—that this Sunday will get it
over with quick. So I can get on with my chopping.

                But

                      what is our country
            doing?

                    Ah,

our country
          beloved country.
Brutal, it laughs at the shrieks, the screams
Which it emits like gory streams.

            It yearns for the long pole's greasy thrusts,
Drools for it, moans for it, eyes it in lust—
But then pulls away from it and silently—bursts.

                    Ah,

our country
          beloved country
It saddles itself and draws the cinch tight
          And spurs itself bloody all day, all night.

                    Ah,

our country
          beloved country
It sucks the prick and cowers and crawls
And only whimpers when they cut off its balls—

            And that once accomplished, it thanks them and
curtsies,
Vulgar, clumsy, bungling—a klutz,
A doddering, creeping, castrated putz.

                      (For a while, for a while.)
          Ah, our country (what a laugh, what a joke)
Cheers the order imposing the yoke
And the master (what a paunch, ah, such a paunch, ah!)
       Who unleashes the slaughter.

And (what a joke, such laughter!)
He's so happy he dances a dance
       That busts his gut and throws him into a trance.
          (For a while, for a while.)
For a while—
           Terrifying smoke

Bodies passing	Thighs calves
Suntanned bodies	Navels tense buttocks
Wheeling intertwined	Backs waists
Burning, blazing bodies	Curves bulges
Reclining bodies	Where the sun crackles
Bodies rising to their feet	Smooth hands
Piercing skin	Where the sun crackles
Raised arm	Vibrant voices
Emerging head	Nothing lacking

        Terrifying smoke
   Will you go?   Won't you go?
      Living
             thinking
about a white shirt
about some memory or other
    of night and a rainstorm
    never breathed
    evoked yearned after
except sometimes, when
in a bus full of people
full of raised arms and
enormous handbags
a whirl of dirty water
there, under the bridge
         Quick, cross over—
there's music it's night
you are standing on the corner
waiting for another bus
and up there on the terrace
bright with lights there is music
    They turn, wheel
the supple figures on the balcony
lean on the railing
talk laugh there is music

by some miracle they got hold
of a record player
by some miracle today they didn't
cut off the electricity
by some miracle the police didn't
forbid them to have the party
        And they turn
you'd like to leap
up to the balcony
you'd like to run
up there and start
dancing too
you'd like to be
now in that circle of light
laugh   be that boy
coming over to the railing
talking with his hands
be *them* be forever *them*
        Be
one of those slim silhouettes
young outlined against the light
turning turning turning
        The bus comes
you get in fast she turns
she looks like she's saying something
perhaps—*ooh, this sun* she lies back
a little more on the sand she looks at me
once more she rests
stretches her legs spreads her arms
sleeps beside the child
your son looks at you I pick him up
I look at this tiny body I lift up high
        and I laugh
I look at those eyes looking at me
and just beyond that other body
        lying there
his fingers over his eyes
looking too
She I the holy family
reclining body falling light

and at last at last that beating swaying
that falling apart
that obeying
rushing footsteps
the sight and sound of pounding feet
striking my face
they crush me they fade away
jog jog
he heads for the ocean
now he comes to the water
he plunges in
he comes out dripping
he walks along the shore
he stops
                oh splendidly wholly
ineluctably lying there
yellow aircraft
rice with salt-cod
Will you go? Won't you go?
and you laugh out loud
when the waitress says
that Number 1 is the only one left
Will you still not go?
Where will we return to?
Why will we return?
What will we return for?
                      Terrifying smoke
                      Terrifying smoke
            Will you go?
            Won't you go?

PRIVILEGES OF THE SYSTEM
SHE AND I

I: Do you feel all right?
She: Wheepity, whoooopity, grmmmm! Gnnntch!
I: Thank goodness. . . . They say some soft drinks came in
       down at the corner. You want me to go?
She: What kind? Mamey? Sapodilla? Apricot? Yes? Or no?
I: Do you feel all right?

She: Yes. BeeeeEEEEEEEEE.

I: Let's cuddle up. What nice perfume. At least it isn't too cloying.

She: Yes!

I: Let's go. The buses will be less unbearable now.

She: Yes! Heeey . . . !

I: What town is this? Why are they making all that racket?

She: It's "them." . . .

I: Shall I fill up your glass?

She: Right to the bottom . . . a little more.

I: Somebody said you could get booze around here.

She: Go, if you want to.

I: Is it early or late?

She: Hush! They're looking at us! They might hear you. . . .

I: I'll fry the plantains.

She: Then is there no way out?

I: Somebody said they got a soda down at the corner.

She: It hasn't rained.

I: Interesting, I'd read that already.

She: Shall I put up the mosquito net?

I: Why worry about your belly? It doesn't make you look grotesque.

She: Seven o'clock. It's already seven o'clock!

I: One!

She: Twelve o'clock!

I: Thirteen o'clock! Ten forty-nine!

She: I'm going to take off my shoes.

I: Shall I pull the chairs out of the sun?

She: She has one son. She's a widow.

I: Did you put my hat, gloves, boots, toothbrush, and the spoon in my pack for me?

She: Fifty, sixty . . . I'm bound to make it to eighty.

I: This is the house. Let's go in.

She: Look at those people. Look at those people!

I: What did your mother say?

She: "High and alone, high and alone. . . ."

I: Yes, I know how tired you are. We should take a vacation.

She: The walls were painted, glass was enough to protect us, the laws didn't proclaim yet that it was a crime to choose, not to choose. I said to myself . . .

I: And for dessert?

She: Let's take a swim!

I: Let's sit down!

She: Let's go back!

I: They're really strange, these stones.

She: Look how I smash my head to bits now, look how I come up, look at me under the water.

I: A cigarette? I'm going to get the bottles.

She: He's gone to sleep.

I: Five o'clock.

She: Here are the glasses. A month. He's a month old!

I: It's hard always being the same person, don't you think?

She: There he comes. He's knocking. What can I say to him?

I: March, April, September.

She: Come in!

I: July, December.

She: How are you? How are you! How are you!? How are you? . . . How are you . . . ? How . . .

I: Big ones!

She: Aren't you smothering?

I: Shall I turn off the light?

She: He's on the porch with his white shorts on, he's leaving, he's walking in front of me, he lowers his head. Idiot.

I: What did you say?

She: Shall I put up the mosquito net?

I: There's a meeting! There's a meeting! There's a meeting!

She: He's getting his teeth.

I: When it gets good and dark . . .

She: That's what I said.

I: It would be in another meeting.

She: Something crashed into the porch chair.

I: Like this? *Pusschachachachachaaa. Boom. Boom. Bip!*

She: I wait for you in the rainstorm and in the now mute gibberish of the now forbidden Christmas. At the parapet, I await you. Looking out across the plain, sitting on a stool, I await you; in this frightful house listening to a Mexican ballad. I wait for you in the rectilinear city, listening to the noise of a jackhammer breaking up the pavement. What more do you want?

I: Summer, summer. Don't you feel it fermenting inside us?

How it paralyzes us, and leaves us like this, in this wavering, sweating, ambiguously gesturing state.

She: I wait for you among the chairs. I wait for you before the table set with food, to one side, face up, on top of you, off to the side, counting your wheezes, looking at this hand placed in yours. What more do you want?

I: Summer, summer, summer. I'm so tired. I feel as though there's no time anymore even to get worn out.

She: Look at me, speak to me—tell me at least that I'm the first and only object of your loathing, your scorn, that you loathe everything else through me.

I: Summer, summer. What a hellish conflagration. What tedious battering.

She: Hector? I call him. He answers, but doesn't really respond.

I: To the beach!

She: O daughters of Jerusalem. O daughters of Jerusalem.

I: You're talking about me, aren't you!

She: You hate me. Tell me you hate me, promise me you hate me. Comfort me, tell me that you hate me.

I: What a life.

She: Me! You're talking about me, aren't you!

I: Say that again!

She: He detests me so that he has never even thought of loathing me, let alone annihilating me. I'd better go back to the shore. But I depend utterly on him.

I: I'll be back after eight. See you later. Do you want to come?

She: And since his contempt is unchanging, my love, naturally, grows and grows.

I: Good evening. How has your day been?

She: Stop talking and talk to me. . . . Fine, fine, fine.

I: They're selling sodas. . . .

She: Chevrolet, Chevrolet, Chevrolet. I wonder what becomes of people three hundred miles from the ocean?

I: On this island there is no ocean anymore. In prison—

She: In prison, no gesture is sincere. Everything obeys a set of rules. Even violence, distant hope, and death. . . .

I: Floating, in the gloom, on my back, facing the wall. And behind that one, another. And beyond that one, another one. . . .

She: In prison every intention is nullified. If someone speaks it's the jailer or the would-be jailer, parodying him. He says that we're fine. He says that no one wants to leave prison. We are proud and happy. If a prisoner speaks, it isn't the prisoner talking, but the jailer through the prisoner. When someone dies it's never the jailer, it's the prisoner.

I: Tamarind, tamarind!

She: Look at them move, gesture, walk. They don't exist . . . they cannot leave. We look, look at us. . . .

I: Diaper after diaper after diaper, climbing up right to the moon.

She: We have no ocean! We have no ocean!

I: Taaaamarind-flavooooored! Boom, boom, boom, bm.

She: And what a moon, so huge, huge, huge, calling me.

I: Cigarettes? Shall we roll the chairs in?

She: An engine in the water, now not ocean but prison; signals to other guardboats. A shot.

I: Pow!

She: He's gone to sleep.

I: And what a moon, what a moon, huge, calling to me. . . .

She: Wait till sometime next year.

I: Wait till June!

She: Wait till March!

I: Wait till January!

She: Wait till August!

I: Wait till May! Wait till July! Wait till February!

She: Wait! Wait! Wait! Have you considered how cruel it is to leave us shut up alive forever, till kingdom come?

I: Till April.

She: And the moon looking at me—contemplating me, naked abandoned staggering under this load of diapers—so far from her, so far, so far that even if she spoke to me (is she calling me?) I wouldn't understand a thing. . . . So far from her . . .

I: Till the 15th of . . . October!

She and I: Have you even begun to consider? Soon the others will have arrived, will have gone, will have disappeared—will have gone to their rest—and us, here, shut up, gagged, prisoners, here in these pages, in this little corner, in this darkness, talking nonstop. Have you considered how cruel it is, granting us all eternity to spend in a dark corner where no one will ever find us, where no one will hear our cries,

where no one, though we're eternal, will know that we
exist? Have you even begun . . .

I: Watch out. Here comes a rat!

She: What are you saying? What art thou saying? Aieee!

I: I said somebody said they got sodas down at the corner.
        Aiee. Shall I bring one?

She: Hermelinda Conejeros—such a strange name, isn't it? But
        do you spell it with an *H*?

Terrifying smoke
Terrifying smoke

Bodies passing   Laziness gap and stretch
and falling light   bodies   bodies
submersion emergence   stretchings prominence
languor   somnolence
closed book   bodies   bodies
    Falling   Light

Terrifying smoke
Terrifying smoke
Will you go?
Won't you go?

And the evening
        saying you could bear no more.
The weather is saying you can bear no more.
And yet you must, and yet you mustn't.
        The afternoon shapes an aching clarity
a kind of unavoidable certainty
an almost palpable assurance of perdition.
Oh, if only, now that I am the shipwrecked sailor, desire did not
    exist.
Out of the evening a monster comes to bathe you
        a curse that swaddles you
the couching of the venom'd lily
you would melt into
and beyond all human aberration
an immense loneliness.
        The evening, beyond unforeseeable (but certain)
official offenses, shaped a crushing intemporal
light.
        The evening, revolving, transports

you to an old age, to a cry you cannot quite make out
but that you know beseeches.
                    The evening says you will not be able to go on,
or depart, or halt, or
change.
                    The evening went on breathing, an echo
that comes to you rarely but is enough
to make you lose yourself
or find yourself (it's all the same).
                    The evening, like an immense sob,
like a ridiculous yet tragic widow,
like a march of uniforms in vivid
unrest.
                    Eyes
to gaze at grazing cows with
fields sown with rocks—state plans
houses that squat one after another and disappear
in a pitiable show of zero imagination
                                    as in a dream
as in a horrible dream that goes on
when you awake
                                    Trees
conquered by a glare beating them down
and giving no quarter
seagulls catching fire
everything advancing to one unanimous stupor
secretly sapping us paralyzing us
keeping us from doing the thing
which might give us some justification.
                        Which is?   What nonsense
am I talking?
                    Leaf
that falls and pierces you
howl no one takes note of
and at this instant it sears you
and ceases not.
                    Too Late
always too late
                    that outstretched hand. Those variations
on radiant figures hounded, harassed, which shuttle back

and forth and echo each other. That splendid body
standing there firmly, gazing at you. Eyes to yearn with,
for what doesn't exist, and yet which destroys you.
                    And the sun polluted your tennis shoes.
The evening.
                              Will you go?
                              Won't you go?

    *The mother and son
are alone at a summer resort.** The mother, facing the son, is
performing some domestic operation in his honor, in honor of
her son. The son is whistling and, instinctively, wants to kill the
mother. The mother stops knitting and raises her needles, which
seem to the son to fly and stab him through the breast, the breast
of a son. The mother, needles raised, smiles at the son. The son
sees that boundless mouth, within which a storm seems to be
brewing. A gust of wind tugs at him, sucks him in. The son
pitches into the mother's cavernous maw. She stabs the needles
back into the knitting, which glows in the afternoon light. The
son, clinging to her carious molars, tries to escape the noisome
labyrinth. But the whirlpool is irresistible; he slips. The cavern
grows darker and darker, the place is so very soft. The son rolls
along through this syrup of unbearable ooze and odors. He slides,
he slides toward the huge black tunnel, toward the grotto of her
throat. He is lost, he is suffocating, and he goes on, he goes on
sliding. . . . The mother lifts her needles again and smiles, without opening her mouth. The son (feeling himself there inside),
unconsciously angered, whistling and radiant, wants to avenge
himself on the mother. What but that aim, that instinct, makes
him *son.* He looks at me—He has already chosen the instrument.
                              I won't go.
                              I won't go.
          Yesterday
was San Juan Day
and you were hiding
behind the trees
          you saw the young men naked

*Wilhelm Reich: "The Function of the Orgasm."

331

leaping into the water
                    floating on their backs
throwing themselves into the water once more.
                                        Yesterday
was San Juan Day,
the day of cleansing,
and you,
in hiding,
                    heard the noise of men
bathing in the river,
                    you saw the foam
their bodies whipped up
                    you listened to their laughter
you watched their games.
                    In awe you ran your eyes down
their shining figures.
                    You saw their leaps.
                                        Yesterday
was San Juan Day
and you ran alone across the mountain
you rolled over and over through the grass
you returned at nightfall (aunts
grandparents mothers awaited you)
you drove the yearlings to the corral
you sat down with the rest at the table.
You stayed alone in the parlor
                            under the kerosene lantern.
                        Will
                        you go?
                        Won't
                        you go?

   *The husband and wife
have entered the bedroom.* Both pummeled by the whistling. . . . To deny the body that has erected itself there, outside,
we lash out against the weather, politics, the unfailingly horrid
era, he thinks. . . . If he arrived, if that man that has never existed

*Constantin Fedin: *An Extraordinary Summer* (a novella by the leader of the
Soviet Writers' Union).

---

were to arrive now, if he were to descend on us, arrive, and all this were suddenly nothing but a dream, she thinks. . . . To deny the body that is so fixedly *there*, look instead at her—*Woman with laundered diapers of her months-old baby*, he thinks. . . . And everything were nothing but a nightmare you sometimes remember, something that can be told but that no one could bear, she thinks. . . . Woman inundated by white diapers, rising to the sky, he thinks. . . . Go to sleep, go to sleep, *run* to sleep, because perhaps (because *for sure*) you will awake in another world, yours, she thinks, pretending that she doesn't hear when he comes in, that she isn't aware of that whistling outside, that the day's brightness doesn't reach the cabin. . . . Oh, if only we could annihilate ourselves once and for all with so much love, he thinks (and now he lies down beside her). If only with a wave of our hand we could conjure away that glare and that whistling and this dark suffering-by-our-bodies-that-now-shrink-from-each-other room. If to understand each other it were only enough to show that weeping which the day's brightness transforms into sweat, into frustrated touch, or into dream. If only that gesture were credential enough, if only this falling into your closed eyes (which still observe me) could solve this. If only you knew what a horrible battle I fought, what bold knights, what fires were threatening me; but tradition decrees each man must face those things alone. . . . If only so much ocean (and so much indignation and frustration at not being able to sail across it), so much sleep and ruddy darkness, so many provocative looks, so much loud talk, confusion, mutual game-playing (mutual deception) and downright insolence, fear and complicity, insult and complicity—if only the recognition of these things could lead us to mutual recognition, mutual understanding, or at least willed ignorance of our mutual hell. . . . Oh, if only I could (what if I should) tell you that thing I have no name for and cannot say. (He draws nearer, he embraces her without touching her.) . . . I won't go, I won't go, he promises her, without opening his mouth.

Once more, without touching, they embrace.

Two hearses
Two hearses

Meanwhile
the evening opens into swelling vastnesses. No longer set in any real time at all, the water spreads, unsmirched by legends, curses,

or offerings, fully glorious, dehumanized, solitary. Darkness enters the realms of darkness. A cosmic sense of open space, of awe fully awe, descends. . . . If you stretch out your hand—that grievous certainty once more, that great fear. Night falling over deserted precincts. Shifting bodies, grudging motions, drowsing beasts and promontories, spreading fragrances, offers, rejections (you, left with nothing, calmed not in the least). Darkness receives more and more darkness until a dense unanimous void is formed. Ocean and night fuse in furious communion. Something more dreadful than night (for besides being night it is filled with most somber symbols) falls. . . . Gloom, beginning, rhythmic booming, it all confirms that merciless harmony from which man is excluded, and which he, not being night but *other*, suffers. Suffers the descending night, the night which erects her immense sensation of night and opens her loins to the stormy flood. . . . Oh, you are no longer the innocent risen from the waves, now you *know*. . . . In the cabin, glass creaks as though distressed. The lamps, the poor domestic objects—what can they do against the night? Actually, they are flashing sentinels pointing to her, enlarging her. Utter solitude, which is the night herself, grows and grows. To grow crueler yet, to be heard even better, the night takes the voice of cold. *Soon you will not be, and all my shadows will have been useless to you for giving that terror a shape that might explain them or at least make you their match.* . . . The sonorous gloom is now the shape of dread—for night and echo will always be, while you soon will not be. All restlessness and search, dissatisfaction, desire, all preferences are now foolish, foolish all second thoughts, all the paths of memory, all threats, all risks, daring, and all timidities. Night is now a plain that goes on and on, out to the high, invisible horizon. Ocean throws back his curtains to the night. Night comes onto that liquid stage, envelops undulations, surfaces, gasps, and abysses. What is that in the air? What is ringing outside the discreetly creaking bedroom? How many times do you go, come, return? . . . Nothing. And night herself descending, hurling, unmooring you. Now you have stood up. Night undermines all the objects of your security—doors, words, chairs, books, bottles. Your domain dissolves. Everything exudes a trembling secret, everything announces a secret danger. Everything is now a desperate vigil, a search in which the very—impossible—finding will multiply dissatisfactions. All desire is now frustration. Will you go? Won't you go? . . . Meanwhile the unimaginable smell of rain begins to grow. Night is now a throb fully felt. The sense of time, marked off by that throbbing, becomes more and more oppressive. Tiny tiny stones, insects with glowing shells, glowing blades of grass, or that banging of a sheet of zinc almost falling off some roof—*oppression, oppression.* The assurance of death when you are kept awake by the night incites you to even greater rebelliousness, which is an attempt to undermine (conquer) the night. Night, at her cruelest point, spreads her fundamental gloom. The drowned body, polluted with the night, rocks in the waves. Things, wiser than man, or less wounded and dying, now shadows, shrink into Night. Ordinary Being, and those most instinctive beings—woman, child, birds—close their eyes and curl up; obedient, they make their own night, an offering to the great Night. Sacrificing themselves, submitting (saving themselves), they nourish her. They pray. They know at least that they have nothing but that little arch formed by the hand or wing over the closed eyes. So they pray. The wood (the ancestral wood) emits a piercing, distant shriek. You, standing in the bedroom, do you still believe you *have* the night, do you still believe you have the ocean, do you still believe that it is they who call you, who extend to you a thick fog so you can go, skulking, to them, and at last, finding them, be *you*? Ocean and night. He and she. Extension and mystery, rhythm and coolness, fullness and abyss, confirming at last the fundamental body of your desires. Which might satisfy or conquer you. . . . But night celebrates her orgies with the ocean, and you are not invited. The ocean yields up his riches to that descending gloom. Night issues triumphant because she is the one who goes to him. The next day the ocean, peacefully for a while, begins the tale once more. They understand each other. . . . You are out of it, off to one side, under the rock. They haven't called you, they don't draw you in; they take no note of you whatever. You hold no interest for them. Miserable and timid, anonymous and out of place—growing old—you are, once more, what you do not speak.

Plan for Reform
of Article 25
of the Basic Law

establishing the death penalty
in special cases
for adults
of 16 years of age or more
has been given virtually
unanimous
approval
in all meetings
held
through-
out
the
length
and
breadth
of
the
land
National Time Radio—
Tuesday
the 25th of September, 1969.
The time is exactly one forty-
seven A.M., daylight savings
time.

I go outside.

Against the night
that moon
cold and immense
slipping through the
palm groves
Against the night
that moon
round and vulgar
spying through the
palm groves
Against the night
that moon
ages-old and glacial
enormous and leprous
sliding through the
palm groves

                    A moon
                 conventional
         and inevitable taken from
                 a painting by
                   Rousseau
                    A moon
                     with
              lowered embittered
                     face
                    A moon
                     with
                a sharp nasty
                     nose
                    A moon
                     with
                 puffy cheeks
                  and sour
                    mouth
                    A moon
                     with
              doleful laconic
                   sallow
                    face
                    A moon
                   twisted
          and accusatory with
        the face of a menopausal
            woman—the enemy
               of every vital
                  gesture

I begin walking.

                    A moon
                   frigid
               old and ashamed
        vexed besmirched spat upon
          crushed inflamed and
             whining with the face
              of a woman fated
                  to tears

                                _____

                    A moon
                 with stains
         vulgar and global who ought
         to be grabbed by her immense
                ears and kicked
                down the field
                    A moon
                   matronly
         inflamed with lust, scrappy,
            who ought to be ignored
               such an evil
                  woman
                       A moon
                    with
                 a furrowed face
            and the upset look of a
             clumsy country girl
            who after roasting the
              coffee went out
               into the night
                    dew
                       A moon
                   bovine
                and yellow
                       A moon
                   lunatic
                       A moon
                una luna
Before I get to the pine grove
I make out his figure under the trees.
In the darkness his white shirt
seems to float.

                       A moon
                 with a pimply angry
                       face

The cicadas have grown a little
quieter. They seem almost to be
the accompaniment to millions
of other insects, a background.

          ————————

      _338_

A moon
with a blood-choked
cavernous face like
a woman in difficult
menstruation

I draw closer.

A moon
with a face like a woman
who suffers bad digestion
every single
day

I come up to him—Have you
been waiting long?

A moon
with bags under her eyes
vast   and   judgmental   like
a woman who can't get a man anymore
and uses pieces of wood
long fruit something
solid and painful

He doesn't say a word. He
begins to walk away. He turns
and takes a path within the
grove.

A moon
with eyes like smoky
beads and pitiful
eyelashes

He goes on, walking ahead, sure
that I'm following him.
He makes
that sound of a body moving
through plants.

A moon
sarcastic mocking
round

We come out now onto the rocky
seashore, bathed in brightness.

A moon
like a grinning pimp
fat-cheeked and tragicomic
perfect for an
operetta
Following a narrow trail we go
deep into the mangrove swamp.
An
anachronistic
moon with the air of a
great bewildered
whore
Now in the middle of the mangrove
swamp we come to a clearing inhabited
only by dry tree trunks. Through them
you can see the ocean.

A moon
with a twisted face,
reflecting the aberrations
that evil men
undergo
We come out onto the far side of
the swamp.
A moon
matronly, double-chinned
like a retired whore
who's now chief
of security

He strides more quickly
now, though always assured-
ly. I can hear his breathing. *I'm here to be followed,*
his outline seems to say.
A huge
prophetic
meaning
moon

We come to where the cliff of rocks begins.

Although we are far from the pine grove you
can still hear the cicadas. He turns. His
face, no doubt because of his white clothes
and the night, is darker now. We gaze at
each other. Everything in him exudes a
sense of masculine firmness, of security
and pride cloaked in indifference. He begins to climb the cliff face. I stand
there, below. Not once does he turn around.
I begin to scale the cliff face as he does.
I raise my head.

A moon
shining frozen and familiar
the same moon that watched me
as a boy and that knows
who I am
now

I pause. He goes on climbing, firmly, slowly. I lower my gaze to my shoes sunk in the
moss. The ocean roars down there below, crashing into droplets. The smell of salt spray
grows stronger. I go on higher and higher.

A moon   I see the soles of his shoes, his
motherly and   legs braced agilely and then leap-
battered   ing to the end of the climb. I
     follow him. I reach the top.

A sallow
swollen yellow
full moon

He is on the other edge of the cliff. His shirt
is open, lightly billowing in the wind. The
place is a weathered boulder which forms, here
on top, a kind of wide clearing. Down below, the
ocean throws up a lash of spray from time to

time that reaches us as the merest smell of salt
spray and breath of coolness. I discover that
because of the unevenness of the terrain we
could have reached this place from the other edge,
without having to climb even a foot. I look for
a spot a little less wet and squat down, as
though waiting. I don't know how long I keep
that position. I stand up. He is there, waiting, knowing I will come.
There was no need for that climb, I say.
On the other side . . .
He then—now, in a second—turns,
simply turns. He looks at me—the presence of
his face, of his utter youthfulness planted
firmly there before me, gazing, grave, aroused at me—
and he smiles. I throw myself
onto him, clasping him, holding him. He
stops smiling. I feel him vibrating, in a way,
next to me. In a moment I strip his clothes
from him and throw off my own. I fall at his
feet, kiss his thighs, run my hands all over
his trembling body. Naked, embracing, we roll
around on the ground. I kiss his hair, his
throat, his back. I merge into his body, which
convulses silently. All my fears, all my desires
join to his. And there, while the two of us are
one, I raise my head from his back. I see his
shining neck, his glistening hair. I raise my
eyes higher and see her. Her I see, her, up there.

A moon
fixed, remote, gazing at me
—making me see—and all of it
with a hurt, shocked, and ashamed
grimace—utterly
motherly

Quickly I withdraw from his body. I leap to
the center of the clearing. I contemplate him;

for the first time he seems confused. I begin to
roar with laughter. I walk all around him, laughing. I plant myself before him and slap him.
Who did you think you were? I say to him and
slap him again. Did you think I didn't see
from the beginning what you are? Did you think
I have done all this because I felt something
for you—like others must have felt, like you're
used to having happen? And I laugh, howling, again.
I know you, I say to him. All you're interested
in is laughing at people, having yourself a
good time, having the man who wants you please
you. Ah, but the man who doesn't please you—
what integrity, what chastity! Surely you report
him to the police as a corruptor of minors,
don't you. It's fun—to them you will always
be the pure child who on top of everything
"cooperates." You can even make a good reputa-
tion for yourself, by turning in guys like me.
They're your favorite type. Ha, ha—tell me—
I scream at him again—how many times have you
turned in guys already, because they bored you,
or because suddenly you felt masculine, or because it's your job? Tell me. It's your job,
isn't it!
          I don't know what you're talking about, he says.
Yes, you do. You know perfectly well. You know
it all. And you're as pathetic as the rest of them.
          I don't know what you're talking about.
Then shut up and listen, because if you don't
know anything you're going to learn it all right
now. Listen to me, pay real close attention—
I feel sorry for you. You really don't know the
horrors waiting for you. You don't know that
you will never even be able to speak that horror?
You don't know that you will never be able to be
yourself; you'll always wear a mask, be ashamed,
be a source of derision and scandal and revenge
for other men, and of unending humiliation for

yourself? For survival alone, you will have to
betray and deny what defines you, what you precisely *are*. Listen to me, listen to me—you
will live your whole life pleading, begging par-
don of the whole world for a crime you haven't
committed, and doesn't even exist. The most you
can hope for is to be forgotten about—perhaps
to be tolerated, if you fake it. But they will
always look at you—even if you adapt, even if
you give this up—with doubt, mistrust, mis-
giving, and they'll laugh at you—and watch out,
because you show the least sign of trueness, of
sincerity, to what you are, and they will kill you!
Do you understand me? You will always be the
safety valve, in a way, for any era—for all
eras. I don't know whether you understand me,
but listen—you will be the world's shame. And
the world will use you to justify its failures
and discharge its fury. Don't dream that you'll
find a friend. You will find lots of men, it's
true, who'll blackmail you, some that will slander
you—all of them, of course, will use you. But
a true friend, friendship, a real involvement—
forget it. Your own mother when she finds out—
and she *will* find out, have no fear of that—
will live the rest of her life embarrassed,
scared, will look at you mistrustfully like the
others, will turn gray and bitter. At last she
will wish you'd never been born. . . . And it will
all be your fault. Ha, ha. . . . And I look at
him once more and slap him. And there is nothing
you will be able to do—except turn against
yourself, deny yourself, destroy yourself.
Imagine yourself old, no doubt stuck in a work
camp, filled with desires more and more difficult to satisfy. Ha, ha. And none of it is
your fault. You are so pure, so noble, so
appalling. But them—so moral!—they will
look at you with shame, and if you try to show

yourself, uncover yourself, they will annihilate you (even if they themselves have used
you) like that! with a kick in the ass. . . . The
government will let you walk down *some* streets,
will let you off with your life, if the cane
harvest was good, if there was no drought. You
will live your whole life provisionally—depending on the laws that are constantly being
passed against you. Do you think you'll be able
to go on studying? Don't think that within the
few possibilities that exist here *you* will be
able to choose one for yourself. For you there
are only jail cells and work camps where you'll
meet people like yourself, but much worse—
and you will, of course, have to become like
them. Listen to me—and I shake him again—
don't think I'm telling the whole story; this
is just part of it. Not even I can tell all of
it. . . . Oh, why did you have to pick me out,
why me when there are so many others out there
ready to fall to their knees, do whatever you
order, and leave you confident, self-assured, even
proud? . . . But listen, there's more, there's
more. There's the expression on your mother's
face when she visits you the first time in jail,
and the faces and talk of your ostensible friends
when they "find out"—Absurd! Absurd! Making
those gestures, those signs. Your friends will
be the first to "prove" your manhood and then
betray you or make some remark at a well-chosen
moment or place. Ha! And on top of everything
you are going to be alone, and are going to need
company more than anybody, need a real friend. . . .
Terrific, just terrific, with your shirt open.
Ha, ha. Look at me laugh. . . . You already know
what you are. If you hide it, you stop being;
if you show it, they destroy you. . . . I don't
know whether you've understood me, I repeat,
drawing closer and looking at him slowly,

but anyway, you *will* understand it, soon enough. . . .
It's probably better, I say, stepping away, for
a person to destroy himself, without waiting for
them to have the pleasure of doing it. I begin
to dress; I finish and once more draw near him,
who's still standing there naked. Listen, I say
to him, don't ever speak to me again or try
anything with me. Get lost, find somebody else.
Leave me alone. If you haven't understood any
of this, at least get this—I feel sorrier for
you than anything I could feel for myself. As
you will understand, there is nothing you can
do with someone you feel that way about. There
is nothing that one can do for oneself. I turn
away. Without thinking that I could leave by
the other side, I begin to climb down the same
way we had climbed up.

    And once more I crossed through the pine grove and took
the path among the mangroves
And I heard the cold litany of the cicadas
And I went on
And a car backfired in the night
And I took the avenue of the almond trees
And I came to the avenue of oleanders
And I stopped on the ocean sand
And the booming frogs sang an end to the diabolic idyll
        of the Master and Margarita
And a great sign was seen in the sky
And I pulled a few burrs off my pants
And every one of Giordano Bruno's joints and bones was crushed
        by the Inquisition
And I took the tile walk leading to the cabins
And I looked and behold a yellow horse
And the cicadas began to sound again
And the rabbit was late
And Little Red Riding Hood finally seduced the wolf
And in Andrzejewsky Forest the oriole sang

And the beast I saw was like the leopard
And Stalin abolished with a simple gesture of his mustache
      15 million human beings and granted the rest
      the honor of slavery
And an atom bomb fell
And then another
All in the name of the progress of cities
And the caravan of eroticized children disappeared
      into the abyss of sand
And I took the narrow path which went directly to my cabin
And Queen Schizabella straightened her holy tiara
And tortured, skeletal bodies swathed in green rags
      kneeling and bearing candles
      burned
And the cicadas stopped their song
And the head of a man who had come in a cart rolled
      bloody to the thunder of cheers
And the line of those waiting their turn wound out of sight
      beyond the civilized metropolis
And the rabbit was late
And Virginia Woolf finally floated down the Thames
And Hitler lifted his arm
And there was this prickly sensation at my throat
And our angry tropical skunk, with a bray, forbade
      the use of the word, the stomach, deodorant,
      paper, public transportation, sex, the ocean,
      anger, and hope
And I began to climb the cabin steps
And the Great Pharaoh, out of boredom or caprice,
      strangled his favorite eunuch, who looked at him,
      looked at him
And I came to the porch
And I saw an ocean of glass mixed with fire
And the rabbit ran, and ran, and ran, hurrier and
      hurrier, to the tea party
And now on the porch, as I raised my head I saw her,
      La Luna, blurred, floating, indifferent, simply
      mineral.
      She takes no note of me. She has never

taken any note of me.
    She doesn't even know that I exist.
And I pushed open the door
And saw three hellish demons issue from the mouth of the dragon
    and the mouth of the beast
And the boat filled with Negroes, each with his shackle,
    sank in the middle of the sea
And Louis Queen of France said, The State is MOI, so there, silly!
And our own kinglet now in an enormous tunic shrieked,
    The Revolution is ME, AIEEee! And tittered.
And the second angel spilled his glass over the ocean
And I took off my underwear
And without turning on the light, I lay down
And a guy named Jesus got all tangled up in a
    rhetoric that kept contradicting him,
    over and over again,
And the hysterical abbess at last managed to extract the
    cannonball that had lodged in her womb
And I pulled the sheet up over me
And the impassive yellow airplane lifted off into the air
And he made that gesture once more
And the whole island fled and the mountains were not found
And she began her discreet, decorous, and desperate creeping
And remembering an advertisement for some kind of pills named
    I think
    Evane (in vain) I viewed my future veiled and drifting
    stiff, stark, and rotting; I walked up and kicked him
And once more he smiled
And she put, once more, her head between my hands
And the great city was divided in three parts and
    the cities of the nations fell
And the frozen fingers of dawn perched on Katherine
    Mansfield's surprised hand
And I laughed
And I felt her tears roll slowly toward me
And I laughed
And Daphnis danced and sang for Chloe
And I laughed
And for the last time I saw him standing there naked

    and unmoving
And I laughed
And the rabbit flew
And as I saw the mosquito net faintly faintly stir
    I began to compose

FUGUE FOR A FUGITIVE POET
(Light comedy in one act)

and I slept.

CANTO SIX

"A weenie?" asks the lady.
"No. A weenie," returns the lady.
"Oh. No weenie," says the lady.
"No, a weenie," answers the lady.

And morning begins to set up all its bright lights. The air,
utterly transparent, vibrates like a symphony. The weather, fleet-
ing and therefore glorious springlike weather, is weather fully
fledged—and so it is truly impressive, even showy. Light has
taken possession of every corner. Performing virtual pirouettes
it leaps in, like a ballet dancer, at windows; like a rubbery-jointed
Bali-dancer, it writhes and stretches down hallways; in a riot of
tinklings like a belly dancer it shimmies into boarding houses
(great humanist!) and lavishes its sparkles on windows, skylights,
gratings, and the handkerchiefs and underwear hung out to dry;
scattering in leaps that no one counts—dance, dance, dance—it
runs along the avenues now: up, down, up, down, as though it
were girls skipping rope. Indefatigably it leaps trees, leaves, birds,
bald heads, and monuments to the nation. Playfully it lights up
a piece of paper blown by a whirlwind. Classically it falls over
the geraniums along the Quinta Avenida. Lickerously it bathes
teenagers' hair, the bulging roofs of buses, and tight pants. Politicized, it lashes out and strikes sparks from the gleaming tinsel
flanks of Alfa-Romeos. Oh, the houses are white; streets and
gestures, white; buses and sidewalks and everybody's fingernails

are white. The seawall and the ocean are white as well. And the roofs? What color are the roofs? . . . The sky models its own shade of white; clouds pass swift and so high, all bedecked in white. Pizza parlors are white. Benches, bites, bovine herds, and Betty the teenybopper—white. What about the roofs? . . . White sparrows scream till they're hoarse in the impeccably white air; they jump, they bloom—heavens! heavens!—over the white flamboyán trees. They sing out their tonsils, they scream, ceaselessly wheeling and fluttering over catafalques and banners, garlands and oleanders, over the weathercocks and towers of the Ministry of Communication—and all those feathers, all that hurly-burly, all those places where the kick-up-your-trills birds (which are of course white themselves) perch, are white. Jesus, and now they're perched up there on those roofs, which still don't have any color! . . . Eachurbod emerges from his cave. Though the clocks say it is five o'clock in the evening, it's ten o'clock in the morning. Tiles spread their faded cracks to soak up the warm sunshine. A natty cockroach scurries hurriedly along, umbrella in hand, dodging stomping feet and skirting the puddles of water. Them that's got get out their flashiest glad rags. Them that's not patch themselves up, dye their hair, touch up their makeup, take one stitch here, another stitch there, snicker-snack, snicker-snack. Eachurbod emerges; his eyelashes flutter so infinitely fast they seem to blur, his eyeballs revolve in their enormous pits. Hands, hair, cheeks, nose—they are all at attention; he is like living radar, scanning, alert. Oh, but those roofs that still don't have any color yet! . . . Capering, he crosses Calle 23, his hand in his pocket, his neck on ball bearings, his hanky, hairpiece, and fingers nonchalant; he is at once shivering and bathed in sweat, with the hauteur of a *grande dame* yet swishing his hips. Jesus! here in the street. A bunch of high-schoolers are jogging this way, their charming masculinities conspicuous in the shorts they wear, so very revelatory of the firmness of their physiques. Voices, looks, knock-him-dead jogging. Eachurbod, a jellyfish with sensitive tentacles floating in the waves, a dandelion seed floating through the breeze, a wind-maddened little piece of tinfoil rolling around the hillsides of Lenin Park, is alert to a place to catch on; he bounces in little hops that seem to springboard him into yet more stirring springs. Here they come! Here they come! Now he senses the place to snag; his eyes begin to follow them. Now they are crossing the park. Now as they cross it, they and she cross paths. Now they are here, their chests bursting out of their shirts, their thighs fording the dense brightness, their waists, those baby faces. Eachurbod, gazing always at the object of his desire, never caught but never abandoned, infinitely pursued, gives a discreet click of his heels; he watches them run right by him. Jog, jog, jog, how they jog—aiee, how they jog. And the earth, so fond of her sweets, lets them walk all over her. The brightness, motherly, bathes them. Aiee, who wouldn't watch them! Eachurbod, inflamed but always wise, delivers his first great thought of the day: "Teen-agers when they're all together become men, and to feel even more manly, they tease a poor queen. Well, so much for them. . . ." And he goes on, smoldering, but smiling at the same time, with a certain indifferent look, with infinite perseverance, but never losing her composure, her presence, her air of fine distinction—that, above all. He comes to the bus stop at Coppelia, where *everyone* goes for ice cream. It's still so early that besides a bunch of women with shopping bags there's not another human being in the place—if you call a woman with a shopping bag a human being. Eachurbod sniffs around, lifts his neck, sits down and springs up, with his feet and knees together, and does a kind of single-minded double-take. Searchlight, *on*; spotlight, *focused*. Serpent striped with lubricious lashes, scars dealt her by a bad man, she raises her neck and slithers on. Taking advantage of the fact that the bag-women have gotten together for their who-cares cackling, Eachurbod, on tippy-toes, performs his jeté of a swan on burning coals, not virtuoso but nonetheless pro. The bag-women lard their cackles with blasphemies. Eachurbod, slightly *fatigué*, leans against the post that also supports the *B* of the bus stop and gazes along Calle 23 as though waiting for a bus that just won't come. There, on the shining horizon, something moves, grows, draws near. Here they come. Two figures. Two simple suntanned hunks, rumpus erupting, virile gestures, and that rhythm, that rhythm. Pulling himself together, Eachurbod mentally takes inventory of his repertoire of street talk—*hey, bro'; gimme five, baby; 's happ'nin', buddy*. . . . Aiee, here they are. . . . My God, they're looking at me. Holy shit, one of them has maybe involuntarily, maybe unconsciously, maybe accidentally, raised his hand to the region where his fantastically wealthy Cyclops sleeps (and wealthy it must be, gauging by the abode it dwells in). *What is that!*

Eachurbod emits age-old exhalations. Thousands of spiders begin to emerge; on tiptoe they gush from him. The roof of his mouth produces a thunderstorm which beats down upon his tongue; his tongue, like a crater in eruption, writhes belligerently, would quake; his teeth stir, soft in his mouth; his hips, maddened, sway and emit little whimpers; his hair stands on end; his nose flares; his toes exude Chapultepecan lakes; his knees and thighs part; his hands and voice knot, remote, out of his control. Only his eyes, obeying higher orders, remain still. . . . But behold, from the other direction two brown-sugar asses approaching. And behold, the asses essentially ass and, furthermore, independent, seeing the simple hillbilly hunks, become even more Ass. Such asses! Shifting, swaying asses, creating a truly rare concussion, a (m)assive splash, whir, whir, whir, a frisky effect, a grinding effect—the sweetest thing about brown-sugar babies is their asses; or better, black asses are sweet (because if you were going to parse these arses, they'd have to be the *subject*, never the complement). Asses that come on, asses that pass by, asses that shake, asses that march. Yes, which march in procession, but these choirboys have left their tallow and their incense, their long posterior train, at home. The challenge of the ass has been thrown down. And behind the challenge, behind the asses, the great simple hunks may be descried—who (the hunks) like the asses which in front of them become more Ass, before (behind) such asses now become more Hunk. Asses! Asses! Asses! The teeth remain fixed. Fillings rush to cover the holes. The saliva surf subsides; the hand in the pocket touches a mere piece of metal, the key. Follow them! with those asses? Compare herself—her!—measure himself—him!—Eachurbod the Divine One, like Chloe and the little deer, measure his weapon—him!—who knows how to perform those perfect little pirouettes, against two black asses? Let the hunks go! Let those hunks go if they want to dress their exquisite members in mourning! For him, they've just died. He poses: a *soupçon* of premature widow; although, emphatically, he refuses to follow in such a wake. And, perhaps to comfort himself a bit, or mend his wounded pride, and because he remembered, furthermore, that heavenly gesture made, no doubt, in his honor, Eachurbod announced his second great thought of the morning: "Many men flirt with women and even exhibit themselves before them, but control themselves with queens." What profundity! . . . Ay, but

I keep forgetting the roofs! . . . The devouress sinks into long high-flying thoughts, of sex. He drifts off. He has published a book of wise sayings, *The Proverbs of Eachurbod*, Introduction and Commentary by Angel Augier: "Independent of narrative talent and . . ." My Lord—over there, on the other side of the street, who's watering the flowers at Coppelia? Supple back, blond hair falling over his shoulders, legs spread—a god, no doubt. Hose in hand, the young man in the overalls—blue overalls, couldn't you die?—waters the hideous ice-cream parlor's flower bed. The water, transformed into a kind of Technicolor rainbow, falls on the plants. The plants, wet and longing, bow down at the feet of the god. Is this not, then, a wondrous vision, still more wondrous because it is real, of Peter Pan? One of his favorite heroes? He, Peter Pan, had protected him, had accompanied, saved him, when he, Eachurbod, was a girl (tender, so tender). Just like Superman had, and Aquaman—heavens!—and Tarzan—my God!—and the Blackhawks!—they all had been his friends, had guided him, had kept him safe, oh, with such ardor, integrity, and courage, from all great danger (thunder, earthquake, monster, war and bombardment, maddened beasts, Bluto, Witch Agatha), picking him up in their arms, carrying him through branches, forests, waterfalls. And now Tarzan deposits him with a roar of passion in the soft cave. . . . He ran, he ran, cunning, poised, self-assured. He arrives. Now he's behind the delicious thing. Clever, he takes out a cigarette. Excuse me, do you have a light? The quarry turns. An old man. No less than a middle-aged old man. A common gardener, a fright; an old fart; not blond—gray; not athletic—just plain skinny. The old gardener in his tacky blue overalls looked at that suddenly disjointed figure—eager to be jointed—he had before him. His hand, a million blue veins woven through it, rummaged through every pocket in his overalls. I left 'em in the cart, he said. And he went off toward a kind of tank on two wheels. Eachurbod, utterly unreal, watched the no-less-unreal old man paw through that can full of brooms and rakes. Farther on, under the Radio City marquee, converted now by the grace of a lurid sign into the Cine Yara—who was that man in profile looking, and with such masculine aplomb, at the movie posters? What arrogance in his carriage, what sparkle! I found them! boomed a voice behind Eachurbod. Uh-huh, said he. And hurried away without a backward glance, rushing along and ranting to himself, key chain in hand, waving it, feet near flying along the silver-puddled street, dodging and balancing between the Alfas which truly were politicized, truly wanted to rip her to pieces. But none-theless didn't manage to do it. The old man, with his hand still outstretched, observed those mortal vicissitudes; finally he stuffed the matches into his overalls and picked up the hose. . . . But what does life matter, said she to herself, now launched, what does risk matter, even perishing, if your god, your redeemer, awaits you on the other shore? Pilgrim, mystic, leapin' Lena, whirling dervish, all atremble, she approached her godhead. In-deed he was an exquisite boy, that hybrid conjunction of snow and palm grove. He was that rare product that the tropics some-times are given to offer us. Mere matter, passing through all races, sects, classes, proteins, suns, vicissitudes, invasions, and ances-tral turns and twists, sometimes absorbs the best of each ingre-dient until it blossoms into music of irresistible texture and rhythm, all airy solidity and tender fuzz, throat, tresses, shoul-ders, thighs. Where did he come from? Why have I never met him? And how he stands, and how he flaunts his holy blessings, and how he moves his . . . eyes . . . like he wanted to rape it . . . over the movie poster. THE DAUGHTER OF THE PARTY, it announced in red lettering. Jesus, how he stands there, stiff and straight, just plain *being*, lost in his own thoughts, full of his own self, satu-rated with himself, overflowing with himself—foreign to this sun which hasn't yet scorched his skin or turned his hair to straw or bleached out his eyes or disfigured his body. Do you think he has his own microclimate? Do you think some high muckety-muck, a minister or maybe higher, has built an experimental heaven for the god under god knows what patriotic ex-cuse? . . . He looks like he's always been kept under glass. He could spread his legs and the world would fall to its knees. Jesus, Jesus, and outside there, Eachurbod, all throbbing and sweat, all muttering lips, was trying to approach the bastion. But what if he's an undercover agent? An expert queentrap? A common po-liceman? You should have seen how carefully he was looking at the placard DAUGHTER OF THE PARTY—aiee, and what if he's one of those perverse angels the system gives off and then instructs so they can flush unwary pigeons? Careful, careful, Mary. Just in case, she stood over at the other pillar, at a little distance, and spied from there. How impressive, how impassive, how contained! . . . It seemed that instead of being on the faded, worn, dusty sidewalk in front of Radio City—I mean, the Yara—he was standing on a hill overlooking the Aegean Sea. Oh, what to do. . . . And no one was anywhere near him. No one else was cruising him, as had happened to her so many times in similar situations. Could it not be that everyone knew him, knew who he was? Lieutenant, maybe, and she, Eachurbod, alone, unwary, innocent, silly, had not smelled the meat, I mean bait, of the Ministry of the Interior? Ah, but behold the demigod spread his legs a little more, turn, and seem to make the very air submit, kneel. He is no longer Peter Pan, he is Superman, a distilled and concentrated Tarzan, one and all, more than the Holy Trinity and the Blackhawks and Prince Valiant. Behold, he looks at no one, there; he is indifferent, lounging at his ease across time, both hands in his pockets, observing only himself, saying, *Here I am, here I am. Come and behold me, I suffer you to adore me.* . . . Another step, another teeny cautious step. Now he is beside him. Oh, now he turns his eyes to his vast, elegant dimensions. He, unabashable, remote, receiving the homage. Oh, you've got to talk fast, about anything. What difference what. But his tongue, gone stiff and numb, can hardly obey the supreme order—his lips, drooling, make a smirk, his Adam's apple squeaks up and down in his dry throat. *Luisito, Luisito!* A voice more than a voice, the warble of a triumphant hen—behold none other than Tiki (restraint freak), a.k.a. the hippie princess, purse, bracelet, cap, little Peace (and all kinds of other) buttons everywhere, charms, bangles, shocking bright pullover—*Luisito, Luisito!*— and the god opens his divine mouth, shows his heavenly teeth. So potent, he smiles captivated and marches off (oh, fate, fate) with *la* Tiki. . . . Now Eachurbod really can't take any more. After seeing *that* (and none other than Tiki, that thieving, skinny, henna-haired, watery-eyed, whining, knobby-boned . . . *thing*, to snatch it away), what is there to hold her? But it's even more horrid—the god was waiting for that awful queen, the god left with the awful queen. Ay, that awful queen already has the god in her lair; ay, that awful queen gives the god a seat; ay, now that awful queen is on her knees worshiping the god. . . . no! No, he can't go any deeper into those suspicions, he would lose the little mind that he has left—and he'll need all of it for his revenge. For now he really did have to get with it, not only for the material satisfaction (how big he had been!) but for the moral satisfaction. Now he really had to find—as though He were the object to which he would submit himself, the Source of his final redemption, the End of his constant yearning, of his perpetual need (never sated or appeased)—that Man that until now he had never, in spite of all his hard work and cruising, been able to caress. Heavens, and the midday sun discharged all its whiteness over the queen. The sparrows fled, the asphalt shimmered and sizzled. The sky grew even whiter. The trees seemed to bury their claws in each other. Ah and the body of Eachurbod, that body of his, gnawing at itself, flaying itself, rushed away. . . . My daughter, you must be a little cleverer, he thought he heard his Patron Saint and Guardian Angel Godmother say. My daughter, if you see something you like, jump right on him. And Eachurbod formed his third thought of the day: "In cruising, what's important is a good line, not good looks." Now like a flash he went down the ice-cream line reviewing the troops—old ladies, cowlike women, awful men. At that hour in the middle of the day what little chicken would deign to stand in line to buy ice cream? What pretty thing would dare even go outside this time of day? The ones he had seen today before were simply the act of a miracle. It would be work, now, for him to bump into something not equal—never!—but at least remotely similar. Not expecting much, he popped into the men's room at Coppelia. He waited there for hours. Finally one of the employees (a horrible fat creature in a uniform) came in spitting and started pushing cleaning rags around, flushing toilets and doing other nasty chores. If it's true, as they say, that they've put up a two-way mirror in this bathroom, Eachurbod says to himself, then they've just shot a superproduction. And he left. More than a million souls applauded him. The curtain rose and fell infinitely. Do that exit again! We want to see that exit one more time! they all screamed. And she, a bouquet of roses in her arms, bowed once more before that sea of adolescents. The movie had been a success. Once more he was at the Coppelia bus stop, under the scrawny seagrape plants. Octoroon Apollo had come to a screeching stop and parked himself there. There he was, standing under the steel post the bus routes were posted on. He was certainly a serious one, this brother. Nobody in the huge world of pigeons and chickens could besmirch—with any solid evidence—that dude's manliness. My sweet Mary. You should have seen him walk! Shirt, naturally, open, cock-of-the-walk, world-eater's expression on his face, such a body. And muttonchops that licked his lips. What a face. Lord, and what if he (the devouress) were the one the wolf picked out? What if she, little wounded gazelle (Giselle, they would call her) were the one chosen to scale the wall? Because this one was indeed a brick wall. Eachurbod approached. This time there was truly not a second to be lost. So many things always scheme against a poor girl in the mood for cruising. Hermes Octoroon was sort of purring; he leaned once more against the iron bar that shivered at the touch of that body. A bus comes. A number 10, full up. Racket, shoves, shrieks, bus driver mouthing off, sweaty tits, children, and other chilling things which make us realize the horror of the world. Ay, and statuesque Belvedere, black marble, impassive by the post. Eachurbod extracts from his pocket the shining chain with its keys. The bus stop mechanically fills with people again. Another number 10 likewise full up keeps the queen from making the rush openly. Octoroon Apollo, impassive. Cleverly, Eachurbod pronounces aloud, looking toward the Chocolate Macaroon, his fourth and last maxim of the day: "The bus you wait for is always the one that doesn't come." And he looks at the Dark God's marble face. Nothing, not a fiber, not a stone of the regal bulwark has been touched by the regal proverb. "Silence and cunning, then," thinks Eachurbod, as he inches closer to the wall. Picks, shovels, a rope ladder, spades, even a wood plane—useless, of course, and fairly dull; he girds his loins. There he gooooooes! Ay, another number 10. The pushing and shoving keeps Eachurbod from beginning the scaling of the wall. Gathering his accoutrements once more, he draws near, looks trembling at the great breastwork. And what does the Great Wall do? Great Wall turns toward Eachurbod, and, imposing in its distance, roundedness, and height, asserts, this time full face, his wall-like virility. . . . Ropes, lines, picks! Upward! Ay, another number 10! Completely empty this time. All the number 10 fans had already had the chance to climb on the bandwagon, so the driver of this one doesn't even bother to open his nasty thing's doors. But behold—Yummy Octoroon puts out his tree-trunklike arm, makes a faint masculine sign, and the bus driver, in a squeal of brakes worthy of a Roman charioteer, slams to a stop. And the centurion, the athlete, the imposing freedman, steps up onto the chariot. Ah, what have we here, thinks Eachurbod; he let three number 10's go by and now he takes the fourth one. It's because he was waiting for me to talk to him. You silly queer, he's tired of waiting for you to attack, you clumsy thing. The same thing, every time, you old cow, and you never realize that They're like that—They never show their desires straight out, although They're on fire inside, so They do it all sort of looking down their noses, sort of Who Cares. But move, honey, there's no time to lose. One second, one instant, one moment of dithering and your shining future goes *poof!* in a cloud of smoke (like Eduardo Eras's future went poof!). She who hesitates is lost, so Reynaldo Slambamthankyouman always affirmed when he was prom queen. And without further ado, Eachurbod rushes upon the rolling chariot and leaps (at the very instant the driver was closing the doors), taking a well-aimed blow on his backside and emitting a blood-curdling shriek, like a pinched streetwalker. The typical driver typically groans. Staggering like the dazed pythoness wounded by that other Apollo, aping Enrique Moliner, Eachurbod arrives at the spot where the Café au Lait (Olé!) Prince has come to rest. Typical-driver floorboards the bus, which does a sort of wheelie, or hop, a juncture which Eachurbod seizes to collapse beside Chocolate Divine. Bus stops come, bus stops go . . . so many bus stops, my lord! And driver doesn't halt— so typical. Sometimes comes from those standing waiting at the bus stops a typical curse. Leyland, the ponderous Pandarus, roars delightedly, and with its typical jerks helps Eachurbod get closer and closer to the Typically Delicious. Sarcastically, Leyland, the Pandarus, gives off an even more ovenly heat, a kind of typical steam and smell that makes the Blue-Eyed Chocolate Bunny unbutton his shirt all the way down. . . . Aiee, the typical bus driver whips on, charges forward, floorboards his typical machine, which shakes, shimmies, jerks, all throwing Her up against the Other, all spinning him around, all kneading him up and mashing her out, heating him. Ay, everything leads to this. . . . And what can the Angel of Wisdom do before those thighs so close, that virile hand resting, parked, motionless, fallen, placed as though to call attention precisely to what is covered—the holy region where the two typical thighs converge? Lifting his head a bit more, Eachurbod looks at that throat, that nose, those cheeks; his vision falls—Jesus!—to those hands, those big bulging hands. . . . Easy, Mary! the angel shrieks. Eachurbod, ay—*sí!*—for heaven's sake. . . . And he contains himself for a few seconds. But Pandarus begins to emit its steamy exhalations—gasoline, moist nook, heat, smell. And it doesn't open its door. It rocks back and forth, avuncularly; covered with decals and graffiti, it shines; covered with spatters, little colored lights, garlands and placards, strangely bejeweled, it helps, it helps the poor queen. Attack, attack, my friend! And it shimmies again. And once more emits that hot vapor and once more roars, unmoored. But what is the Velvet, Dear Apollo doing? Well-tended, wide hand, rustic oval nails, young—good lord, could this be the One that drove Ballagas mad?— lying there at the threshold, and he is looking, he hasn't stopped looking, out the window. Eachurbod looks out through the little window as well. Perhaps out there somewhere an unparalleled event is occurring—which may be the beginning of a beautiful conversation with this exquisite piece, a conversation whose beginning and end (Alpha and Omega, Miss Alexis the Carpenter would say), even if its subject were a mass murder, would be to careen toward that place where all a little bird's dreams tend, and end. . . . But behold—out there there are only typical houses that the typical afternoon makes even more desolate than usual. They cross the city, leave the city behind, cross the bridge. Leyland, just cruising along, gives full rein to its pandarous machinations. Now there are swallows in a stunted tree. A cow gazes at them. What's the fool waiting for? And the Other, what's he looking at? What makes him look out the window like that, as though the Seven Wonders of the World were filing past along that side of the bus? And why doesn't this driver stop anywhere? Eachurbod sagaciously surmises that it's a conspiracy, a conspiracy to seduce me—maybe to rape me. . . . And he contemplates those bulging hands, there, there, on the bulging threshold; that hand is doubtless an intimation of things to come, an order, even, that hand filled, that full hand, that hand fully hand, not yet touched by age or misery—the bulging hand, not yet marked by handling or manipulation, horrid veins, and the damage that every man's mean occupation causes—that hand that goes beyond hand, brilliant, tender, tense, and youthfully taut—that hand that clutches. Eachurbod once more lifts his imploring eyes. There is that face, the face of the delicious Blackhawk, the sweet face of sweet Prince Charming, the pure face of Peter Pan, the face of a page, of a prince, of an enraptured Superman. And once again her gaze falls to the region of her desire. And Tarzan, with a light back-and-forth motion (his face always turned to the window), moves his hand, his bulging fingers, across the great swelling, across the treasure. Jesus, behold the warrior, standing beneath the canopy. Lightly, distractedly, the Magnificent Heavensent palps his magnificent seven inches, and how great a fortune there is buried. It is so great, my heavens, and its interest so keeps growing, that his magnificent hand in a moment cannot cover the vast extent of its holdings. Eachurbod wiggles, twists, blinks. His eyes traverse its length, from one pole to the other. He turns red, yellow, he licks his dry lips with his tongue, speech fails him. And he contemplates, abject and adoring, blinded by the splendor the Divine One radiates, that One's face which, abstractedly, as though in another world, independent of what is going on down there below, watches the landscape—a sequence of stones and a firing range. . . . And Eachurbod turns once more to the place where the knight no longer sleeps—before Eachurbod's desperate, abstinent, imagining eyes the knight has begun to stir. . . . Slave, lower your eyes. Abashed, she puts forth her hand. Ebony-ivory-tower goes on studying the landscape. But has he not pulled away his knee? Penitent, Eachurbod returns, *à peine dure*, his hand to its original place. Leyland, Pandarus, roars, threatens, gives off gratuitous jerks which jostle the two bodies together, sings lusty ballads, and exudes a heavy incense of gasoline, piss, and semen. Octoroon Apollo pulls his leg back once more, raises his golden hand, and shows, now standing unhelmeted, the head of the warrior in all its vigor and fierceness. My God, this is no toy. Eachurbod bows. Oh, but the helmet is pulled once more onto the soldier's head. Pandarus charges along the asphalt. Roaring, it pushes the longing bodies together again. Virgin!, the warrior removes his cuirass yet again. This golden Grecian rotunda's rotund face, looking out the window, seems made of granite. The cheeks of the devouress grow the color of that dawn brought by the breezes; she looks toward the great wall which is looking professionally out the window—and coyly, Eachurbod the Untiring at last places her hand on his youthful gentility, which instantly responds with a haughty thrust of the lance. And how impassive is the face, looking out the window. . . . Jesus, what a battle was there joined. . . . I told thee, speaking of that great enameled uncle named Pandarus through whose veins or pipes ran the royal blood of the English nobility, that he was both heir and patron to all the avatars and adventures of the Breton cycle (lots of lances), and that he was a delicious and wise Pandarus, who on several occasions bestowed joy and fortune on one of his nymphs; he was the cradle of civilized amours on the interstate both for the Great Nymph and for the nymphettes. Even Coco Salas himself, hiding his disfigurement in the darkness, had managed with success; Pandarus on many occasions had offered his rear end for the delirious maneuvers of Tomasito the Goya-girl, and in one case of real urgency he had recognized the time to open his doors to the above-mentioned so as to facilitate her escape—she fled, in fact, accompanied by Delfín Prats and Reinaldo Arenas, alias the Horrid Skunk, who (all of them) prudently took refuge in the Writers' Union, pleading for asylum with Nicolás Guillotine who, terrified, and not wanting to compromise her silly self, put herself into the Cira García Hospital, feigning pulmonary edema. . . . Oh, how many secret touches, trials, squeezes, daring lips, mystical strokings, curlings, and twinings, how many vital exhalations has this regal uncle, intimate of *Queen Elizabeth* (or are they the same person?—only Vicente the Equerry knows!), succored, facilitated, and godparented? How many strategic movements, secret glances, rearings and pawings, and even deep-throatings does this Tunnel of Lust on wheels hold in his wired metal and Russian gasoline brain?— against which laws have been passed ("He who shall in a bus look . . . ," "He who shall in a bus touch . . ."). Well, in spite of the above-said, whether doubtless against his will or by upholding the tradition which Eachurbod brings to the case, Pandarus has now halted. Just like that, bang, when the queen was coming to the gates of paradise, Leyland, Pandarus, grinds to a halt. Will not take another step. That's it! It has become a plain, dusty, innocent, rattly old bus. Typical driver opens both doors and stands up. The passengers—virtually nonexistent—have arrived at the beaches of Marianao. The voyage is over. The old fart, just standing there wheezing, allows them to pull up his brakes and open his doors. Typical driver speaks to Statuesque-Hunk-of-Muscle, who is, of course, a co-worker. . . . Hey, buddy, your turn with 'im now, huh? And he gestures toward the ex-Pandarus, utterly ignoring Eachurbod. Unforgettable Mulatto stands, puts on his cap, tie, watch, and the other accoutrements typical of the typical driver, and all harnessed in, becomes just another typical bus driver impatiently waiting for Eachurbod to get off the bus. The queen (in flames) leaps from the chariot. She gives the chassis a good kick for revenge. Typical driver, ex–Admired Piece of Art, typically grunts, and speaks, devil only knows what about, with the other ex–typical driver. Queen is queen and walks like a queen through the paved park. The bus, its backing and turning done, focuses on Queen Eachurbod—lights spotlighting her. Ay, it passes so close that if she hadn't jumped aside there'd have been nothing left but a mess of feathers. Fag! screams, naturally, the typical driver, that is to say, Ex–Octoroon Apollo. The swallows have begun to roost in the almond trees along the beach. The sun gilds the erect sun umbrellas of La Concha. Screaming Queen walks along under the pine trees, and as she's sad, it immediately grows dark. Gloomy step, meditation with hands clasped behind, grazing the crack of her ass; ah, well, back to dark durance vile, a monastery (convent), perhaps—heroine in the jungle, she cures black lepers, this nurse, holy martyr (and virgin, great heavens!), or, better yet, becomes a brilliant elusive writer. Thousands of photographers stalk her, thousands of pilgrims want to approach her, kiss her hand, see her, take away the tiniest, tiniest hair of her head, but she goes on, remote from the banal world, writing behind a hermetic wall. Or better still, set herself on fire, immolate herself—she had kept a little bottle of gasoline, kerosene—in the middle of the Plaza de la Revolución, crying Patria! Patria! . . . Hold on, we'll have none of that, girl, get ahold of yourself. Once you've seen what *you*'ve seen, now there is truly no respite or retreat. And suddenly—my God!— behold, in the sky, the glowing arc of the Ferris wheel arises. She's come to Coney Island! And such laughter, such lights, such figures winking in the distance. "There you'll find the place you've been looking for. . . ." She remembered Rulfo. And went in. Now she's on the battlefield—she's passing review of the warriors who, lance at the ready, perform tight drills in honor of all those with eyes to see and hearts to flutter. Truly I tell thee, reverend chicken-hawks, that that young man from Arroyo Naranjo has nothing to envy the Apollo Belvedere. The "Followers of Camilo and Ché" flaunt their red armbands. Simple crude green cloth, where a mound shows where the impressive corpse reposes. Tanned bodies swathed in blue cloth. Sailors from the Fishing Fleet. Recruits, scholarship boys, Patriot Youths, and delinquents. All brimming over, rushing about, all, like medieval pages, weapons erect, trying to squeeze, take advantage of, squander, without wasting a single second, the three or four hours of official leave. Oh, how could one not follow those recruits whose rearing virilities are hinted at—and how—under their military khakis. Oh, and that one, that in spite of the armor the age has harnessed him into, gives his feelings vent and still finds the verve to jog. Ay, and this one here, with gray tights and a monumental cannon. What an army! And every soldier eager for the fray. Every one ready to deal lusty thrusts. To battle, to battle! No guts, no glory! Eachurbod, aflame, plunges into the jungle. A group of cadets passes beside her, all displaying under their prairie-colored uniforms their restless herd of beef; some gangs of scholarship students from the National Institute of Sports and Recreation (swimmers, cyclists, judo fighters, and ballplayers) go by too, with their earth-colored uniforms showing the young stalks beginning to sprout. A rustic, Eachurbod threw himself into the hurly-burly. But . . . God! Did you see those sailors bearing regal eels? One young tough after another, lazily fingering the place they have the magnificent loot stashed in. Ay, he wished he were a swimmer, a scuba diver, a fisherman, a trapeze artist, an aviator and could melt into them like that, squeeze them, feel them up like that, disintegrate into that parade of young men condemned—condemned precisely because they were young—and spirited—because they were young; embrace those paired-off, yoked, linked figures, swathed in buttons and bright metal insignia, caps, boots, medals, little capes, and monograms with which the system obliges them to cover themselves— and horny, too, not just because of the thickness of that rough cloth rubbing against their bodies, but as well because of all the moralistic, puritanical, and sanctimonious resolutions which by trying to put down every sexual urge only succeed in awaking them—and so urgently—and spurring the desire to satisfy them. For hatred of this hell is such, honey, that as soon as the system forbids something, even people who loathed doing whatever-it- was now can't do it quick enough, or often enough. . . . Ay, the jungle flows! The rushing, gleaming bodies flow; the thrusts, now, must be at hand; the warriors, sure of their charisma, their force, have no modesty in flashing their swords. And they do so publicly and secretly—brazenly and at once discreetly, eminently, unavoidably, and conspiratorially, indifferently, almost religiously, as only they know how to do it. . . . And Eachurbod, his stomach all butterflies (and all butterfly outside too), open-mouthed, contemplates the skirmishes, those masculine clashes, that legion of gestures always careening toward, culminating in, and dying on that battled-over bulge. So, then, surrounded by noble arms and magnanimous legs, how could he not lose his reason, judgment, and voice? Unbridled, he just takes it easy; not knowing what to do, who to look at, once and for all choose, and—with a delicious flutter of his eyelashes, worthy of being compared with the one that, according to Luis Rogelio Nogueras, Antón Arrufat slyly coquetted in The One-Eyed Cat—capture. His body, turning about, shrinking and swelling like a windsock, his eyes making whirlwinds, his hair and heart, now ruffled, standing on end. Disarmed, sweaty, clucking like a hen, behold her there, stuttering or mute, drooling, before such an overflow of Johns-of-all-trades gallantry, courtesy, and gentility. Heavens, I will mention, among the thousands of mentionables, the Flower Boys Boys' Choir who, shirts open, display the brilliance of a belly, the opulence of a belly button, and the dense trail of hair descending to the region where the very Nibelungen would have been amazed. . . . Here too are the superb young men of Los Pinos, the famed hustlers from Banta, the turned-on boys' gangs from Arroyo Arenas, the unparalleled Gorialdo, the untiring Malthea-tus of immeasurable lance which managed to smother, for five minutes (a real record), the rectal fire of Pepe the Gimp, the Brazen Hussy of Marazul. . . . Over there is Sergio, a.k.a. Mayito, with epileptic, lyrical, gangster tendencies and a leopard's walk, who for two years kept up the Buggers' Club of El Vedado, and there's Blue Boy, from the best neighborhoods. You will see also a Hercules and an Alexander, two Patrocluses and several Achilleses, all men of unfathomable dimensions, who ordered Salas to write a book cycle bearing the names of each divinity: The Book of Juan, The Book of Tato, The Book of Cheo, of Senel Paz, of David, of Abraham, of Pedrito. . . . Oh, and over there, the object of his childhood's dreams—of Eachurbod's, I mean, when his itches did not yet have names and it was a swoon alike to death—Prince Charming (Lazarito of Luyano), he that she (Ea-churbod) had secretly always awaited. How often had she (mis-takenly) accorded that name to some clerk in the grocery store, the druggist's delivery boy, or even the basketball player glimpsed for one second, from afar, through the wire fence of the Sports Center, and who afterward, according to firsthand reports brought in by Dario Mala himself, turned out to be a *real* knight? . . . But now, you might say, it was really he. . . . He even winked. He also saw the Blackhawks and Peter Pan, all in the same place, and then he couldn't take it anymore and, whirling to the music of the organ, even faster than the Carrousel, he was after them! . . . O cruel century, what happened? What curse was hers? What always came to pass with her, the Tragic One, the Mystical One, the Indefatigable One, dated but never sated, smiling outside but never satisfied, the flash-in-the-pan beefcake photographer, snooped after but never pooped, furious fire without a stick of kindling, desperate, and till today, lord, till just a few seconds ago, never spitted? She spoke, then, with a recruit who grunted and spat. She gazed with a vampire's skilled gaze on a huge Negro who muttered and clenched his fists. He asked a young sailor for a match; he said, "Got no matches," and sailed away. She danced before 3,000 Camilo followers who were squeezing and rubbing up against each other and whispering naughty things—but justifying it all because they were staring at the queen's dance; they marched away, playing grabass and fondling and rubbing each other, off to their barracks, the little heroes. . . . He offered a cigarette to a brother from Arroyo Naranjo, who took it without even saying thank you. Ay, and that impressive thing exhibiting his haughty physique and looking at the Ferris wheel while he palped himself so lewdly and lasciviously? Why those itchings and signs, if when the queen addressed him ("made a pass") he threatened to beat the shit out of her and she had, poor baby, to run for her life? Camping, nonetheless, in another corner of the lighted park, she wanted to share a joke, about a Congolese giant, with a Patriot Youth, but he looked at her shocked, asked her on the spot for a quarter, and ran off to get in the line for ice cream, where more than a dozen of his buddies were waiting. . . . What a laugh they had, on her, the Benefactress. Like a cloud of smoke she went sniffling, snuffling, slipping around—she went from carnival ride to carnival ride, from line to line, from fly to fly, discovering, understanding, seeing that almost all those treasures had already been staked out and the claims laid. And the prospectors! Pirates wearing foreign pullovers, ethnographers with thick briefcases full of chocolate bars, swishing nylon-wrapped officials (Peña, Saúl Martínez, Armando Suárez del Pullar, Eduardo Eras [Miss Pornopop] . . .), functionaries, serious-type leaders, high-school drag queens, ordinary queers, closet queens, each more regal than the last, teenage angels, gay boxers, gay cops, all of them already hitched up—some to more than one. And he (Eachurbod) understood that she (Eachurbod) was the only one who hadn't cornered the market in anything. Oh, everything now was, well, arranged. All the warriors had their partner ("uncle," "cousin," "friend," "brother," "co-worker," "buddy," so called). Jesus, and her without her Achilles; Jesus, and her still searching for her Prince Charming. There, under a colonnade, the Countess (that outrageous, ostentatious, and intriguing femme) walked off with seven sailors. . . . There among the granite benches and the statue of José Martí, the great Weird Sister was besieged by more than fifty gentlemen. Jesus, and right over there, before her eyes, that horrid Tomasito the Goya-girl struggled with six overwhelming hunks displaying, oh so seriously, their fiery manhoods and poking at Tomasito the Goya-girl's ass as he swished along. . . . She ran, she ran, ay, Eachurbod ran after a medieval god, an eighteen-year-old page, a Russian serf, a man without a country, an Ethiope, a Mongol, anything armed and tough. Thus, pursuing a lance, a spear, turning a corner, he bumped into Hiram, the Queen of Spiders, who was making the guest list for a party that was to be held that very night—and never to end—in a high muckety-muck's mansion situated naturally on the heights of El Nuevo Vedado. This restraint and S-M freak (once a person of singular talent) made every one of the aspirants to The Man's party, which made a long line, stand up on a dais. The young man now on the platform was tried out by the mistress of ceremonies, who was weighing, pinching and squeezing, sniffing, opening mouths and flies, examining teeth and testicles, measuring physique and phallus, earlobes and eyelashes, cupping her hand under ass cheeks and feeling the texture of hair, carefully studying chins and throats, shoulders, fingers, thickness of lips, waist, back, and length of leg, until at last, computations done, she presented an analysis of the youth, and if the verdict was favorable (not so easy), she placed the fortunate one in another line, while she praised, in a brilliant speech, which it shall be fitting to remember so long as the sky wheels, the gallantry of that gentleman, the noble undulations of his hidden reefs. . . . She could not, Eachurbod simply could not stand such humiliation! That rabbit-faced, dung-lunged, mad-eyed, snake-eyed, beggar-lipped, swishy-assed, pole-axed, frog-hopping, lobster-armed bitch, opening and closing her arms like a dying shipwrecked sailor, that flaming queen had a whole line of youths to choose from, and she, the devouress, official compileress of bibliographies of primary and secondary sources, mistress of Bulgarian and other dead tongues, intimate of Leopoldo Avila, María las Tallo, and even Guillén the Bad, oh, she with house, garden, and wages, could get nothing. . . . All anus (analhilated), she walked on. Had Fate, my God, singled her out for something grand? Would she, if not, have to immolate herself? Once more the little bottle of kerosene came to her mind. Ay, would it be, then, her destiny to throw herself, with no further ado, under one of those Krazy Kars or against the gilded breastplates of the Airplane of Love? How ironic. . . . First, though, why not speak to that freckled little prince who opened and closed the doors of the Midway. And there she goes. "If you don't have a ticket, beat it!" the fiery child screams. And in such a tone of voice that it was better not even to present arms. And once more, melancholy, she gazed at the wings of the Airplane of Love. "Come, crash in flames! Come, have a fiery crash!" the bitches screamed. But first, why not offer conversation and a cigarette to that exquisite child opening and closing the chain across the Waterboats? Ay—It's for kids fifteen and under! says the imp. And the queen dissolves in vain smirks and simpers and languid looks which nonetheless do not weasel even a single syllable more out of him, not even a promising signal. Now, to rub salt in the wound, Miguel Barniz goes by, scattering tulips, on the arm of a boxer who is brazenly pinching that opera singer's vast body—he, for his part, in throaty so-norities promising a bicycle. . . . And farther on, Erich, bald, cross-eyed, was talking with six real delinquents, while over here closer, Intheslammerthankyouman, also squinty, politicized, had hauled in a pre-recruit and three "Followers of Camilo and Ché" and now with sweet nothings was handcuffing them. . . . She couldn't, Eachurbod simply couldn't, take it anymore. Ah, but behold— over there a sign keeps her from doing something crazy. MEN, breathes the sign, for the sign, a sign of salvation, hope, and promise, existed for people like her—discarded, crazy queens who don't want to give in to defeat quite yet. So she runs off in that direction, sure of her redemption. . . . As she enters the urinals an atmosphere of smoke, sweat, and old urine hits her so hard, makes her so drunk, that for a few seconds she loses her footing, she floats, she doesn't clearly see what's going on in this historic place—a place where well-built, masculine young men, released from duty every Sunday, freeing themselves for a few moments from their ardent girlfriends, can come to have a little fun while they're pissing (or pretending to piss), in the mutual contemplation of their stiff members, no doubt perked up by all the attention paid them by those ladies who, touching up their hair and makeup, impatient, but not aware of what's going on, spend a good long time outside there, waiting for them. . . . But let us return to Eachurbod once more, who has by now reached the interior of the glaring men's room of Coney Island and sees— sees clearly—what's going on. Armor drawn open, waistbands unbuttoned, legs flexed, weapons at universal attention. And Mahoma, so cunning, officiating on her knees in the center of the sacred place. What in the world, sweet Virgin! That fat old queen, no hair, no teeth, monumental double chin, had at her left and at her right, before her and behind her, at hand (at tongue), the most exquisite examples that manhood could offer. And all stripped of their armor coverings, lances at the ready, they set upon her with their frenzied deeds of bravery. For a few moments, Eachurbod was frozen watching a youth of noble bearing unsheath his weapon and assail that blubberball pawing the ground and snorting colossally—sometimes triumphantly—as she unceasingly received homage at every cavernous opening. Ay, what a discharge of short-arms. . . . Just as at the wafting of the gentle southern winds which blow their breaths across the warm sea, the snow and ice of the winter storms melt, just so, before that heroic roaring, before that unleashed heat, before those trunks swaying, virtually humming, before those polished, experienced, and skillful weapons going back and forth, Eachurbod melted and flung aside all his fear; without more ado, he threw herself into the mêlée, ready for battle. . . . Aiee, but behold the evil Mahoma, as cunning as he was agéd, as ambitious as she was bitchy, as cruel as she was an old catamite; as she sees the figure of the devouress spring onto her field (now so well plowed), she is filled with wrath, and giving orders to the Horrid Skunk, the mistress of ceremonies, she prepares to do battle with wretched Eachurbod. "No one but I," she roars, Her Double-Chinness, "may enjoy these glorious shafts, do you hear me?" But Eachurbod only hears a kind of echoing crackle, only sees rosy protuberances, only attends to those virile legs which hoist on high their glorious flaming standards. But the valorous warriors led by Mahoma— and guided by that secret and fundamental law of cruising which states that anyone who doesn't play it cool, take it easy, go slow, act tough is a *loser* (because for a hustler there's nothing more dismaying, and even insulting, than to know that you're the floating plank to a desperate, drowning, yearning queen; that's enough to throw water on your ardor and fan the flames of your cruelty)—withdraw their weapons. Jesus! Eachurbod ran from one cuirass to the next, from a bulging helmet whose visor slammed in his face to a bow that though tense returned to its quiver. Ay, that act of erotic pleading infuriated the gay company even more. And as though that weren't enough, Mahoma, the cunning cunt, imitated in all her words and gestures by the Horrid Skunk who, as Pandarus always did, spoke as follows (her voice repeated and amplified by Miss Horrid), "But who does this fairy think he is? What gall! Does he think this is a brothel? We're all *men* here!" Ay, and when all those born hustlers, all those sexed-up young men heard the word *men*, something deep inside puffed up and grew haughty, awoke, and on the instant a cape of dignity, morality, machismo, "manliness" fell over their shoulders. Mama, daddy, baby. Oh, granny, granny. . . . And their buttons buttoned up, their zippers zzzipped, their shirts were "properly" tucked in, and their belts were belted. You ought to have seen it! . . . And as though that weren't enough, Mahoma's voice magnificently amplified by Miss Horrid, echoed once more, and said, "Kill that queer! Or aren't you *men* enough to do it?" Jesus, not men enough! What a challenge! What did she think? What was she insinuating? Of course they were all real men! And they'd kill not one but a thousand faggots, if necessary, to prove their manliness. Their lips tautened, their fists clenched, and now the exquisite ones did not draw their regal swords but rather ordinary knives, old-fashioned daggers, sharpened rods, and even a very, very well-honed table knife. What men, what men they were. You should have seen them advance. You should have seen them now (what men), Jesus, circling around Eachurbod, every one of them. Who's the queer here? Come on, where's the guy that tried to suck me off? Oh wow, now the queen does find herself in something of a hurry, since a catamite-of-a-thing is a reasoning being but a cata-*macho* is a thing that will *hurt* you. There is a glitter of metal. Mahoma, like a new Calpurnia, spreading his cloak, the end of which is dexterously taken by the Horrid Skunk, imposes the unappealable sentence of death. Oh, wretched one, on you now falls the bloody horde. Ay, all those high-schoolers and athletes make a beeline straight for you; now, at last, they are going to screw you. After all, the verb, the action, is almost the same for them: screw, pierce, penetrate; the pleasure is almost the same—for many of them, greater—some of them are ejaculating already. Thus it is that, oh, ill-fated one, you may as well give yourself up for fucked. Now they stab you, now at last you are going to be run through. Eachurbod sees the gleam of the weapons, realizes he has no way out, feels already at his throat the cold fury of the knife. He backs off, he dodges, he shuffles backward desperately, he nervously attempts to levitate himself. The mob closes in around him. They are sure as hell about to attack. Ay, poor queen. . . . But though to this day I don't know how to explain it, at the exact instant he was about to have his throat slit, he heard a great din, he felt a great shaking of the earth, sloshing water out of the latrines, he saw the ceiling part, and he heard a kind of honeyed tinkling from above. Eachurbod imploringly lifted his eyes. There above against the starry sky, wearing a pharmacist's cotton diadem and wrapped in clouds of rubbing alcohol incense, rose the disfigured Doctor Aurelio Cortés (better known as the grand-um-daughter of the Conqueror of Mexico); lifelong abstinence, strictest stinginess, planning even to the time and amount of defecation, mini-meals more than thirty days frozen, and with no salt, pious pilgrimages to the Cinémathèque to see "Battleship *Potemkin*" every time it played, dreams (vigils) on a mattressless board, impassive captivity and, well, renunciation (aided by his horrific physique, it is only fair to record) of all vital (that is, phallic) ambitions had in olden times led to his canonization—he was rechristened St. Nelly by the Holy Father himself at the behest of Miguel Barniz, Lázaro, Juan Peréz de la Riva, Jorge Calderón, Coco Salas, Pepe the Gimp, and a million ordinary fags who put down the dissidents' clamor. . . . Ay, and St. Nelly came down now from the heavenly vault where she lived with Galaciela herself. The fag down below, in the throes of death, saw clearly at last those bloodcurdling but lovable features, saw those horsy buckteeth smiling, saw those gray, sparse, wiry, tangled, greasy, matted locks, saw that nickel-plated-looking bony face, saw that neck like a sad heron's, saw those long skinny arms gesticulating like windmill blades, saw those fluttering hands, gazed upon that stinking venomous question-mark-shaped body, and those eyes like a cow's in painful birth, fixed on him, on the devour-ess. . . . Hoorah! Her-ray! It was *she!* There was no doubt about it, it was St. Nelly come to his rescue. She descended, descended a little more (she had lots of wings), and now exclaimed in that constipated little-old-lady voice, "Eachurbod, Eachurbod, take these free passes to eat at This Little Piggy! You'll see—not only will they stop attacking you, they'll actually start adoring you! . . ." And her huge teeth, now holy, threw off pious glints. The coupons for This Little Piggy Restaurant fell like rain. And it was the miracle of the valley. Before this manna falling at last from heaven, they all became brothers, they all quickly bent down and started gathering up the little pasteboard tickets, every one; bowing be-fore the regal queen (so they called Eachurbod now), they begged for more, more. And St. Nelly, moved by seeing the success of her first miracle, stopped being so stingy for a second and hurled another storm of coupons on Eachurbod, this time for the White Rabbit. And more for the Tower. What a triumph, what a triumph! You should have seen how the lances swelled within their sheaths, how the sabers gleamed, how the regal young gentilities reared and swayed, how everyone, ecumenically, wanted to measure his lance against this messenger from the Divine Nelly. Even Ma-homa, the cunning, had to lay down her arms before such skill and vigor; therefore the Horrid Skunk, truly dismayed, terrified, hid behind the voluminous figure of Mahoma. Both queers, at a little distance, contrite, repentant, and supplicant, disposed themselves, respectfully, to watch the skills in that battle that Eachurbod ruled not only as Marfisa but as Bradamante as well. She was the queen, or the princess rather, the Amazon, the cap-tive, for every man, every youth; every knight invested with a noble figure and brandishing a sword dashed forward to be the first to her rescue, to lift her astride his smooth swinging mount. . . . Oh, which horseman should she choose, on which of those swords should she ride? St. Nelly rose now smiling, leaving a wake of alcohol and pharmaceutical cotton balls. Eachurbod was seen once more among the howling of the youths and the deafening sound of belts unbuckling, flies unzipping; she was bathed in the gleams of weapons already unsheathed. They all wanted to pick her up, carry her, *take* her, they all wanted now, without further ado, right there, to rape her, kidnap her, and fly, eager, heroic, and fierce, with her, off to the nearby pine grove. . . . Oh, but no. She got to choose. Fainthearted but regal, the queen spun round and round within that sea that assailed her. What! a buggering hustler from Los Pinos? What! *her*, the Chosen of the Divinity, go off with a common sailor? A Negro, horrors! Not even this one, who's quite a nice piece, actually. No, no. She had to go on choosing. And she left (outside the clarions were sounding already), followed by the ardent retinue. Now at the door of the urinal, they all raised her aloft and carried her there on their swaying, surging projections, rocking her. Thus, lifted, the world at her feet, high, high, she saw at last what she had so long yearned for. There, in the midst of the night, her great night, were her true lovers. . . . Bestowing curtsies, followed now by a thunder of tympani, she trots along now on a little nag, the pony's shining bridle in her dainty hands. She rides along on the little horse, her body stiff, her locks and breasts blown by the wind; she jogs along lightly and at the same time martially. Behind, pages, couriers, bishops and ambassadors, soldiers, little dukes and dauphins. . . . Mary, Mary, what a scene that was. . . . Such anthems in praise of her! Such a flowering of passion in their bodies! She looked toward the Ferris wheel and saw it occupied by Wonder Woman, who embraced with her powerful arms the shoulders of Blondie, Dagwood's wife; on the lowest seat Porky gave himself up to the delightful caresses of Donald Duck. On another, the three nephews were expertly doing a jig on Popeye the Sailor's three legs. Pluto was taking Sandy doggy-style as Sandy wagged his tail and arfed with pleasure. Mickey Mouse was dancing with Tubby; what Little Orphan Annie and Little Lulu were doing—no, I'll never tell, no way Vicentina Antuña is going to hear about that. Farther on, under the shining confection of the Roller Coaster, Prince Charming awaited Eachurbod. But what was this—who were those three guys rushing forward, about to kidnap her? Weren't they the young, hung, and hunky Blackhawks? And there, up in the sky, about to take her away in a single bound, is that—yes, it is—it's Superman! And that bellowing, gleaming torso among the pines, God, and look at how he's swinging, it's got to be Tarzan! What about that new Paris emerging from the sea to flee with her—is that not Aquaman? God, God, she felt herself taken from behind. She felt herself lifted into the air, virile bodies raising her upward. . . . She was going, burning and embraced, well protected by those figures from her dreams, which so many times had visited her furtively—when she, the Desperate One, had called on them—and which now, at last, were here—real, ready to take her away from all this. She was leaving, leaving. The great queen was leaving. . . . Down below, a boiling sea of hustlers clamored, beckoned her with lascivious gestures. But she was leaving. There the exquisite adolescents from Arroyo Arenas and Arroyo Naranjo, the hunks of Guanabacoa, the willowy boys from the Fishing Fleet, the wet-behind-the-ears delinquents of Los Pinos, observed that extraordinary body, Eachurbod's own Body, and unable to stand it any longer, ejaculated into the night. Oh, those bursts, those popping salutes, those salvos—in her honor, gloriously passing close by her body on high, some of them even splashing her at times. . . . But she was leaving. The Great Queen, the Queenly Queen, surrounded by her amorous suite, was leaving. Rising still, she felt those hard heavenly bodies with crossed spears below her, making her a never-dreamed-of bark. Oh, why shouldn't she touch them? Why not, at last, caress them? Could anyone resist, before those Blackhawks who, rapt and erect, beheld her? Before the prodigious Tarzan? Before Mighty Mouse fluttering right before her? Or tender Peter Pan, smiling at her? Jesus! Could you believe it? And it was hers. She started to embrace it. She reached out a hand and felt her fingers crunch. She started to raise her eyes and something ripped; she tried to wiggle a foot to tickle one of those yearned-for marblelike maces, and only heard the dry sound of newsprint. Bewildered, she tried to touch one of the Blackhawks' glorious members, but only managed to bend it. She tried to wiggle hips, legs, waist, nonexistent tits, tried to dance, sail, leap from one of those divine trampolines to another, but she could only be fuzzily sure that it bent creaking, that it was slick, it crumpled and then sprang back to shape. Oh, she tried in a final gesture to bend before Superman's legs, spread almost parallel and completely irrefutable over her, and then she saw that he was absolutely flat, pasted over with dead letters and figures. Now, as they lifted her again, carried her off again—higher, higher—she tried to laugh, warble, but only managed to cough, choke. . . . When the hustlers, instigated by Mahoma and the Horrid Skunk, threw the body, riddled with stab wounds, of José Martínez Mattos (alias Eachurbod) into the ocean, what fell into the water was a page of comic strips that floated briefly, rolled, arched, and fell vertical to the seabed, where it was supported upright between two sea urchins, also erect. Since the clocks were striking 10 P.M., dawn broke. The ephemeral pink of that hour fell over the faded pine grove, over the Coney Island carnival rides, reduced for years now to useless wood and metal debris, over the ex-bars, ex-restaurants, ex-cafés, and ex-amusement parks now shuttered forever more. And over the roofs of the absurd city—Pink! Pink! That was, in spite of everything, the color of the roofs.

Go on?

Not go on?

That is the question.

How are we to suffer the slings and arrows of the mere fact of being alive, the certainty that soon we will cease to be? How, then, are we to bear the standing in line for croquettes, the insult of aging, the prime minister's speeches, the unanswerable interrogations (the mockeries) that time always slings at us, the compulsory hunger praised in "glorious" verbiage, the warmth of the tropics, the horror of the tropics, the irrevocable gestures of adolescents, the solitude without subterfuge or comfort, the tyrant's humiliation, the repeated betrayal by our friends, the weekly assembly, the food without salt, the dirty shirt, the full bus, the tap without water, the Bulgarian movies, the loss of almost all our hatreds and passions, the life reduced to one-dimensional stupor, the sexual persecution, the ostracism without appeal, the expropriation of our tiniest dreams, the most brutal repression of the way we dress and wear our hair, the implantation of a fixed crime, of a fixed lie over which infinite hymns must be intoned? How are we to bear plastic shoes, the "Internationale," the loss of hair and dignity, the methodical and domestic agony (morning, noon, evening, and night), the interminable sojourns in the fields, the immediate, desolating certainty of being a prisoner, the impotence in the face of that certainty, the TV, movie, and radio programs, the always-same rhetoric savored, repeated, reproduced in murals, signs, walls, headlines, loudspeakers, tape recorders? . . . Our unavoidable, clear condition of slavery, the fact of having been born into the muted crowing of an island, the terrifying helplessness of an island, the prison-prison-prison that is an island? . . . Oh, the reading of *Granma*! The official visitors, the demagoguery of the man who bends microphone stands in half, the promises of a future "not for today or even for tomorrow," revenge in place of truth, hatred and passion instead of love and intelligence; our common wincing at our great incredulity and the terrible injustice of being; the color of Sunday, the color of summer, the color of sagging bodies, the cowardice and opportunism of our champions, the villainy of our enemies, the betrayal of our friends, the end of all civilization—of all authenticity, of all individuality, of all grandeur (an end now swooping down upon the world), the death of man as such and of all sacred, inspired, noble futilities? . . . Ah, the shrieking of the president of a Committee for the Defense of the Revolution? The lack of deodorant, the folding chairs, the "progressive" movies made by capitalist producers, the conversion of cinéastes and millionaire fags to Communism, the stench of armpits, the evening and the sweaty hands, the toilet that won't flush and the ultimate declarations by Sartre—he's always making some ultimate declaration, that hussy—the letters from the mother and Algerian ballpoint pens and even, before the certainty that there is no longer any way out, mask in hand, at the dance that goes on till we bust and maybe even on beyond? . . . How, then, tolerate so much gibing and scorn, so much stupor, so much noise, so much implicit or explicit meanness, so much ass-wiggling, so much crowing, so many empty shrieking figures, so much sadness and impotence, fury and pain, when the light thrust of metal into my body, the sweet rope, or a bullet through the temple is enough? . . . Go on? Not go on? That is the question. . . . What, then, but the stimulus of that angry, divine, persistent hunger for revenge, for retaliation, for settling accounts, for not leaving without first speaking out, leaving a mark, stamping onto eternity, or anywhere, the truth of the ration of horror we have suffered and are suffering—what but that makes us resist, tolerate, feign, and not send to hell with a boot up its ass so much weariness, degradation, and madness? . . . To die—never to sleep? Never to sleep, never to dream? Die—or perhaps stay? Perhaps, before leaving, to print, definitively, that which they never let us say, but which we are—our unanimous, untransferable cry. To die— perhaps to be?

Quick!
Quick!

The ocean passes, the woods pass, time passes. The waters fall back, the stone house (abandoned) which in the distance you see now grows closer, closer, then falls back; only the glare, that horrible glare, on both sides and above, before and behind, is there, is there.

Oh, quick.

Quick,

compose your pain though it's already too late. Compose your pain before it gets any later. Say, point, cry, sing your suffering.

But

have you remembered the bobwhites,
cold in the moonlight, native to this island, gray,
fluttering frightened in the night through which you
ride your horse across the plain in search of a
cane-trailer the truck left on the main
highway?

Yes, you see I've remembered. So what?

Ah, but

have you remembered the bay tree spilling over
before the house, and, under it, a man,
rolling a hoop through the night, to all appearances playing?
Have you remembered that tree?
Do you see that man?

Yes, you see that I've remembered. So what?
Oh, quick.
Quick!

Time's running out on me, time's running out. Leave me alone. Enough bullshit.
Don't try to move me.

Don't try that bullshit on me
                              on me on me on me?

        Surprisingly—yet conventionally—
the sky darkens,
and the shower, the coming of the storm,
giving us no chance to find shelter, breaks over us.
It drags leaves over the asphalt, which exudes a smoky steam. It
beats against our bodies, the air, the towel held over us. By the
time we come to the cabin porch we are utterly soaked. Without
taking off my trunks, without drying off, I look out the blinds
and see the ocean and the pine grove and all the trees in a confused
mass, merging together in that bath of violent water, sweeping
fog, that thundering hail, almost, pelleting the zinc roofs, drum-
ming on the leaves, and spilling out, flooding the streets, lashing,
bending grass and trees.
        Rain, rain.
        The din of the shower, the inexpressible sensations of dis-
quiet, of desperation, of longing, of joy and sorrow, solitude and
loss, fury and desires, visions and dreams of distant places. The
inexpressible transfigurations brought about by the rain. Fullness
and desolation, diversities, song and transmigration, longing (really
a command) for integration and disintegration. Depart, return,
cross seas and landscapes, disperse ourselves. The ineffable wonder. *"I am the saint in prayer on the terrace, like the docile
creatures which graze around the Sea of Palestine. . . ."*

        Rain
        Rain
            The smell of rain
        the violence of the rainstorm
        the tumult of the rain

        On days like these, when one feels the weather burst not
only over the land but in ourselves as well, my lady Señora Doña
María de la Concepción del Manzano y Jústiz, Marquesa of Prado
Ameno (*Locus Amoenus*), is wont to deck me out, replacing
burlap with fine linen cambric, putting shoes and a hat on me,
a golden cord, a little collarless jacket, a velvet vest, braids, little
gold rings in the French manner, a red plume, and a diamond

pin. . . . I am adorned thus, as is the mansion as well, for the arrival of the distinguished guests and the rains. Black, shining, I stand and wait, always close beside her, for her to do with me what she will, call me, look at me, as only she looks at me, and for her to caress me or, suddenly, to deal me a slap that always makes my nose gush blood and lie even flatter against my face. I await her cries (prison or lashes) or her dulcet voice which will permit me to be at her side for the whole afternoon, listening to the gentlemen. And the rain comes, the wetness comes, and all those sweet perfumed gasps of the earth. I hear that splash, splash, and I wonder (though my lady does not call me) what has come of my time, why it is that I have no time. I look at the garden— that I planted and I care for—static in the storm. I think of my mother, who was so deprived and whose bones this water comes to refresh. I think of all the stages of my life—a great rake, mountains of husks I have piled up, the smell of a little geranium leaf that disfigured my face. Rats. Me running along behind a lantern. . . . The tears fall (she still doesn't call me) as though the sky had sat down to cry for me. Happiness falls from the sky, weeping falls from the sky, water falls, the lights and fires of the sky on the laughter of those whom soon I will have to serve. After all, I'm better off here, under a roof, waiting on them, and not out there in the mill, soaked with sweat and rain and stoking the fire. Lord and now this irresistible urge to practice the magic craft that only they (and of them only the best) may perform. But in spite of that and that there is no time even to throw oneself onto the bunk for a few hours, here is that uncontrollable sense of wanting to speak. It mocks me; it attacks, and if I do not carry it to conclusion it makes me feel even more wretched than if I were in the stocks. It rules me, this urge, this wanting to speak which You have bestowed on me yet will not permit me to use. . . . But after they finish the readings and I fill their cups, I remain behind the doors and copy down, as I can, snatches that have not fled from memory—and what has fled, I invent. And at last I cannot control myself. . . . I go on talking, I go on thinking, "It is here, now, it comes, now, with the rain, now it takes shape, now I will find what I seek; a few seconds more and I will be. . . ." But what comes at this moment is her voice, her high, irritating, hated and at the same time intimate, familiar, and beloved voice, ordering candelabra for the whole salon and calling me now, to prove herself. . . . Like a good little marionette I make a bow. They laugh. Her elegant hands become even more expressive, applauding. . . . And the magnificent candelabra wink, for it goes on raining still.

Water
Water
Water
coming in through the cracks of the barracks walls floats the dust along, turning it into a floating mud puddle that runs along under the cots, drags pieces of *Granma* magazine, handkerchiefs, work gloves, towels, packs, pennants, boots, canteens, posters, and flags; the water is already flooding the stewpots and pans and skillets; running over the thatch of palm leaves, it leaks in runnels through the holes in the roof; making a reddish loblolly it soaks mattresses, mosquito nets, sacks, suitcases, and chests, routs from their lairs cockroaches, scorpions, lizards, rats, ferrets, spiders, mice, and other little monsters no less demons for being domesticated. Inseparable companions. The water cracks on the rocky ground around the barracks, on the empty tins of Russian meat, on the canefield's erect lances and on the arched backs of the men with machetes, who have not yet received the order to come in. . . . I hurry to save the food (covering it with big sheets of tin and palm leaves), so I can win the approval of the men, who'll come in today hungrier than usual—which is saying a lot. Soaked to the skin, they won't even change clothes before they run to the kitchen to demand their rations, to ask for a little more soup, to insult me or kid around with me while they massage their crotches promisingly in front of the big pot I officiate over. The cleverest (or the biggest eaters) imply a nighttime visit when I'm alone, to help me wash dishes, so I'll fill the ladle with stew. I fill the ladle, slyly, gratuitously—I know they'll come anyway. Looking at the rain—they still haven't come in—not through big windows (which don't exist) but through the narrow cracks left by the thin blades and thick stalks of the palm leaves. You fairy, at this moment in history being a slave doesn't even mean you'll have pompous meditations behind barred windows or Byzantine stained glass—you'll just have endless rushing to contrive something so the streams of water don't fall into the stewpot or the sacks of

sugar. For that you can be shot. Looking, as I say, at the unstoppable current of dirty water, hearing, remembering (always hearing), their monotonous, always same, shrill conversations of prick and ass, ass and prick, prick to ass, gimme your ass, I got your ass, I wonder, hearing in spite of the rain the ceaseless chopping of machetes and hoes, I wonder—what do they expect, what are they living for, why do they accept, why don't they just rise up, for once, why, for once, don't they start killing each other, why, for once, don't they kill me, right now? . . . At noon—the sun crackling on the machete blade like this downpour on the canefield—at that hour of the day when everyone else is snoring lightly, threatened by the imminent whistle of "On your feet!," after I've washed all the cans and pots, I go outside. I pick up sacks, rotten hammocks, heavy pieces of thick palm leaves, rags, old newspapers, and other squishy trash; I pile all this near the access path, between the stalks of canes. We'll come there tonight. Some refuse to, of course, but then they wind up asking for it, calling me. Those are the most dangerous ones; they can even fall in love, and then they think they're the lords and masters, with the right to take everything we've got, even to murder us. . . . But they don't go that far. Often, being with them, I've suddenly suspended the simulated conversation and the sounding each other out. *Kill me, kill me,* I've begged them. You fag, you're crazy, one told me and ran away. But most of them, the rest of them, think that plea is just one more rite of lust. *Kill me, oh, kill me. . . .* And the rain clatters on the roof, and they, bowed under the downpour, make the landscape clatter. The water runs down their drenched clothing, soaking them, as I know only too well. Such a noise, such a cold, such horrible cold; such a way of raining. Tonight there'll be more of them coming to the kitchen. *Oh, kill me, kill me. . . .* And the shower splashing my face, and me not pulling away, smiling. . . . Sometimes, when I've already washed all the plates and crockery and I'm about to empty out the sink—what a flood of dirty water, my God—I plunge my hands to the very bottom looking for the plug I have to pull; then, instinctively, I sound the bottom, the dirty water, looking for, wanting to find, the ring left there for me to find. The ring that belongs to a prince who'll come later, this very night, to rescue me. He'll come, and this jewel will be the sign. And we will go away together forever and ever, the two of us. Well, couldn't that happen? This heat, this cold, this filth, these flames, these cockroaches, this slavery without change or direction, which you must say, moreover, is wonderful—does this *have* to be, must this be, *must* this be more real than the existence of that prince who will come this very night to take me away? And I lose myself in my meditations (the food is getting cold, they don't come in, it's raining). Either this is hell and hell is all there is and therefore life has no meaning, which is not possible, or life is something else, as it should be, and therefore this is the false, the dream, the passing nightmare which will be blotted out forever and ever, will vanish, as soon as I find the ring that is to transport me to reality. . . . *Kill me, oh, kill me, now.* Here in the darkness. No one has to know it was you. I can, if you want, leave a message, a note, anything, saying . . . But no one listens to me, or they misinterpret my plea. And as I plunge my hands into the dirty water I bump into the skimmer for serving rice—Ay! The new skimmer we were looking for everywhere and thought, since we couldn't find it, we had to serve rice with a penna from a palm tree. . . . *Kill me, kill me.* And the water splattering my smudged nose. *Kill me kill me,* and the water dragging along pots and pans, maddening the palm trees and the men who go on cutting cane, obligatorily. Now transporting the cane over to the processing plant will be a double martyrdom—they'll have to double the shifts (already doubled), they won't be able to sleep, we'll be living in mud along with the little creatures that all this implies— mosquitoes, gnats, flies. I leave my chink, go over to the wash- basin to prove to myself that I'm wrong, that it isn't true, that it cannot be, that this isn't just any old rain, that this whiteness, this violence from the sky portends the prince's arrival. And I plunge my hands into dirty water. *Kill me, kill me.* I take out the old ice pick which, you may be sure, has never been used *here.* I go back to the crack. I think that the rainstorm has spoiled the rags and palm fronds I had gathered near the access path. Tonight we'll have to do our wallowing in the cane leaves, which are so sharp they cut you, or on the other hand run the risk (big deal) and do it here, on the sugar sacks. Oh, well, we're making ten tons of sugar for *some* reason. . . . Yes, I'll cry *kill me, kill me* right here tonight. Who knows, maybe the change of scene will inspire them. I see them over there, enraged and mechanized, swinging their machetes—can you hear them?—in the rain.

                    .   .   .

                Rain
            blurs
                comes down
            ceases.
                The landscape changes scene as fast as an
electronic theater.
                An infinite gamut of little noises starts up.
It cleared off.
                Last day: She looks at the violet water of eve-
ning. She loves the evening. She walks through the mangroves.
She follows him. They slip across the clearing now. Idiots.
                                —Who said that?
                And I will wind up peacefully cutting my own
throat,
or maybe I'll be a judge in Campechuela,
debating between various Sunday outings—always looking
for the outhouse—and the now harmless certainty that I am
rotting
rotting in the mundane hell of a mundane town.
                                        —I did!
                Last day: He arrives and lies down naked. She arrives,
looks at him, and backpedals shocked. What a laugh. What a
laugh!
                                —Who said that?
            And beyond
                    the cold, unfathomable ocean
the new snub
the new infamy
beckoning us, excluding us.
                Who could ever get there, who could ever
get there.
                Who could get to that
frozen, remote place,
far from the shrill pushy orders,
from boastful promises,
and from the fixed sentence;
neglected but not persecuted,
hungry but not applauding it.

                                            ———————

—I did!

Quick!

Quick

before it's too

late

and you can't even formulate

secretly

those desires.

And you can't come to any kind of conclusion.

But,

what did you think?

That I was going to exalt, in glowing hendecasyllable lines,

the History that insults us with promises and

kick after kick?

But,

what did you think?

That I was going to become the martyr, or the hero,

so beloved by the little ladies (or the little gents)

in perpetual vaginal (or rectal) fury and by

poster sellers?

And you, sir, Mister Bourgeois,

who in order to maintain your reactionary principles

now militate in the Communist Party—did you think too

that it would all be worked out with a wave of your pink little

love wand?

Ah, old marmot, ah,

old Marxist (how awful!)

who for sure likes his balls played with.

You like it or not?

Let's go, old man, talk!

Tell me, do you like your balls played with or not?

Let's go, talk!

Quick!

Quick!

Oh, but

I'm out of time,

they steal my time, they take away my time,

they pluck me of my time, they crush

my time, they usurp my time, my time
slips away slips
                        awaaaaaaaaaaaaaay
and I still haven't pissed in the corner, and
I still haven't slapped that statue (look what
a big head they've stuck on it), and I still
haven't fathomed all the world's hell.

Quick	Look. Ah, look
quick	how you've become
	a political being
	beating obsessed
Quick	about the common theme
quick	the great theme
	the only possible theme
	anymore
Quick	
quick	

Chorus of characters (emerging from the page): Look how he comes up to us, purring like that, look, you think you can dismiss us, summon us, make us run or cry at a motion of your fingers (and he's a terrible typist, at that!), look how confidently, how passionately, he approaches us. He thinks: I've got them right here, in the palm of my hand; I know their secret yearnings, their weaknesses, their few moments of comfort, their terrors. I know everything about them, since I am the one who invented them and, by simply describing them, I give them life. . . . Look how he inches forward, a con-man, honey-tongued, look how he walks confidently into the cage. *I make them suffer and tremble*, he thinks. *I nourish them*, he thinks. *They are in my hands, I have them under my thumb, here, here*, he thinks. . . . Look how he touches us, places us; look at him pass judgment on our future, look at him, condemning us. . . . Poor devil. He doesn't know that it's us who call him, who pull him, inevitably, toward us. . . . Poor devil. He doesn't know (can it be possible?) that it's we who impose our passions, our misfortunes on him, that we force him to sing our misery, who lure him in and lock him up and tell him: *Speak. Speak. Say this and that and thisnthat.* Or *I didn't say what I said before.* Or *Today we don't want to talk.* Or *Take us to that place once more*. Or *Don't put those sandals on me; they're too tight*. And we force him to go back over it, one more time, till he's almost mad. Poor devil. . . . Look how he starts all over again, with what resigned fury, and again, scribbling over thousands of pages which, by the way, he doesn't steal from his grandfather anymore, but from Nicolás Guillén himself. . . . Look how hard he works, look how passionately he tries to keep us under control, look how he drags his eyes along look how he talks to the afternoon, look how he forgot that last comma back there (don't tell him, just for spite). Look at him walk back and forth, go downstairs, scream. Poor devil. He will perish and we will remain. He will go mad and we will go on. In a very short time he will have disappeared, but we will still be here. In time no one will even know what he had to do with us, who he was. . . . Ah, and what's even more ridiculously pathetic, he thinks he has us in the palm of his hand. Listen to him talk. He actually takes us seriously. He thinks we obey him. Listen to him talk in the darkness. He comes up waving his hands around, he's sat down in front of us. Shh. Now he puts his fingers on the keys. Listen—

        Just come home
from compulsory work
my balls bathed and powdered
my white underwear on
sitting in the living room chair now
a lemonade in my glass
a book on my lap
here is the climax the conclusion
the
disaster—

                                     Life is passing
           although you are not aware of it
although you don't perceive it
          that fleeing thing
that thing fading away
among voices shouting orders
that thing that will not return
        is life that's passing.

Although we cannot see it
although we can no longer even
suffer from it
    without noticing its arrival
in the racket that comes to an end
in the project that excludes us
in the mailman's last call
in the despot's infamy
older than an eclipse

                            life is passing.

       Last chance!
       Last chance!
     In the useless afternoons
devoted to the harvest
of minor fruits
we will never get the chance to eat

                            life is passing.

       Last chance!
       Last chance!
           In the sound of the bus
           full of people, in that strange
           sound unrecognized by
           the harmonious Greeks

                            life is passing.

           In the flight of
           mosquitoes around (and in)
           the ramshackle barracks
           and the call of a bell
           to the line for molasses

                            life is passing.

           Across your face before the
           mirror, laboriously, imper-
           fectly shaved with a
           nicked razor,

                            life is passing.

           Across the green esplanade
           or the grass or useless memory
           and the dust in corners
           and the glow and the heat

and the sweat starting again
and this feeling rising rising (ah, don't go on, easy,
easy) when I look at the face
and up across the caricatured
aching distant figures
deformed under the ocean—
    Ah and madness—
Have you forgotten madness?
And betrayal and fear
and pettiness and helplessness
and denunciation?—

                    life is passing.

    Across life
life
passing.
    Quick
    Quick
for a moment will come
when you will be too
degraded to be able to
distinguish terror from
ordinary tradition.

                 And life passing

    Quick
    Quick
for a moment will come
when your death
will interest no one
for everyone
will be
dead.

                 And life passing.

Soon you will be
too prisoned
too brutalized
too annihilated
to be able to understand
your annihilation.

And that thing marching
with its back turned
to us
that thing you aren't aware of
that thing that startles you sometimes
at dawn like a distant fanfare
that thing which, at a distance,
we managed to glimpse, once,
is life, which is
passing.
　　　　　Yes,
　　　　　　　　　they
will say (wash your face): Look who dares
criticize us! Look at him! He has no
right! With what ethics? With what
principles? What dignity and merits
give him the right to pass judgment
on us? (Dry your face.)
　　　　　　　　I
will say (clean your ears real good):
I am who can best pass judgment on you,
for I have seen it all, have taken part
in all (now the other ear), have suffered
all, have observed it all, and I have
found nothing in you but trickery and
destruction under the pretext of progress
and equality. (Splash some of that alcohol on your face.) I am the purest
because that word has never interested
me. I am outside all "generous," "loving,"
opportune, cowardly rationalization. I
have no way out, or any sort of
principles; therefore I can
afford to step on your corns.
　　　　　May I?
　　　　　　　　Aieeeeeee!
Gosh, my hand I mean my foot
slipped. (Talcum powder, talcum powder
for your navel, talcum powder for

your crotch, talcum for your ass
and your balls, talcum for your
dear, dear, dear body.)
            May I once more?
                        Aieeeeeee!
Gosh, my hoof I mean my foot slipped.

        Bl   ink   ing
    of the lights
that watch you.
        Smell of fresh earth
        Water flowing away.
                                    Night.
        What about here? What is there here?
        The son and the mother. The insolent
        and the aged. The poor wretch and
        the old woman.
        The idiot and the monster.
                        Open water leaving you be-
                        hind.
        And on the porch, before
        the invisible ocean, in the
        other cabin, the other, *I*,
        rendering explanation ridiculous, look-
        ing at his hands, imagining, listen-
        ing, feeling.
                        Open water taking its leave.
Sweetheart, bring out the glasses and the bottles. Sit here.
        And when you are far away
        (for thine is the kingdom
        of blackmail) will you long
        for this island, this ocean,
        the flight of a gull, the shine
        and smell of bodies in
        the afternoon?
Sweetheart, go see if there's any ice left in the refrigerator.
        And when you are far away
        (difficult, difficult) will
        you take solitary walks and
        yearn for this place where

you took solitary walks?
            When you are far away
(very difficult, very difficult)
will you loathe, too, the place
where you are and feel home-
sick for the place you are
now, and loathe?
When you are far away will you think
that some afternoons were
lovely in spite of every-
thing, or because of it, and
that there were even moments
when you could breathe?
            When you are far away
            When you are far away
(which on the other hand you'll
never manage) will you long
for the heat which suffocates
you, flays you now? Will you
long for the vulgarity, the
brutal language, the obscene
gestures, the too-obvious
looks?
            When you are far away
            When you are far away
(I already told you never! Do you hear?!)
will you think of the angry breeze
only sometimes cool? Will you
think of the afternoons when you
walked along the avenue of
oleanders? Will you think of the
time when you still felt proud, right-
eous and angry enough to curse
and scorn?
            When you are far away
(never, never)
say it for once, think of it
for once, will you be, like today,
pursuing a time which naturally
is impossible to recapture,

as it's impossible to recapture
childhood or that gesture (which
one, which one?) never shaped?
Will you long for these violet
waters or that brief vision and
the walk under the pine grove?
For it is images that remain,
not emotional states. Not even
climate, and not even insults.

       When you are far away the horror
you suffer now will have disappeared
from your memory. You will only
remember a man strolling through
the fragrance of an irrecoverable
pinegrove.

               (Never, never.)
       When you are far away, say it
for once—will you wish you could go back?
Oh, bring the cigarettes too.
       No, I won't wish for that.
               Won't I?
                    No!!
Nothing. Are there? Good. Thank you. It's not so hot now. Or
is it?
       But
what can he say? Look at him.
Has he no shame? Hypocrite!
Coward . . .
I'll light up another cigarette. Smoke keeps the mosquitoes off.
So many. . . .
       All of it! All of it! He can say it
all! He can tell everything! He will
stop at nothing! He will be unstint-
ing in truth. He will dazzle us. He
will annoy us—don't you see
that he is an unhappy man?
Gosh, they don't even have any respect for smoke. . . .
       Here
we become animals or go mad,
but I don't want to become an

animal. I don't want to go
mad, either. So what can I do?
So where can I go? Who do I
complain to, run to, plead with?
What

                        do I do?

Shit or go blind?

                                            Madre mía!
Our hoarse voices always echoing through another man's house.
Us always the ones that had no house or memories of our own
to die in.

Us, forever strangers, visitors, fifth wheels, lodgers,
and that, thanks to the implacable benevolence of the parents
in the bedroom next to the toilet, where there's a frog.

Us, suffocatwo'd within the alien walls.

Us, fifth wheels, respecting the other people's lack
of respect.

Us dying other people's death, without right or time
for our own.

Suffocatwo'd.

Me painting windows in an alien house; you shuffling around in a kitchen that will never belong to you, coughing
at another man's smoke, laughing at your nephew's joke; he's
the owner's, your sister's, son.

                  Our hoarse voices
                        on the threshold
                        on the threshold
on the threshold of hate
on the threshold of abandonment and fury
on the threshold of the man who hasn't even got his own misfortune to bemoan.

Madre mía.

Madre mía.
Our gravelly voices rumbling on the threshold.

On the threshold of misery
On the threshold of degradation
On the threshold of pettiness
On the threshold of unbearable pity.

And that hen cackling before us, that dog barking at

us, that child that infuriates us with its shrieks. None of those
animals belongs to us. We can't even shoo them away.

> On the threshold
> On the threshold

On the threshold of terror and cold, of sun and wind,
our hoarse voices booming,
our useless, offended voices pleading,
seeking asylum, on the threshold,

> on the threshold

of miseries. Our voices.

> And that tree that someone fells before our motion-

less eyes, that last piece of shade that sheltered us and that now
somebody pulls down before our motionless sight. That tree that
falls and we can't save it because it's in the other man's yard,
their yard, that one we clean up every day. That tree that falls,
that tree that falls.

> Our hoarse voices.
> Our resentful, but pleading, voices.
> Our limitless hatred hidden

on the threshold
on the threshold
On the threshold of family piety, of the pious aunt, the pious
cousin,

> our hatred accumulating.
> Us trying to be invisible, not to bother the gentleman,

the kindly owner, the generous uncle. Us trying not to occupy a
space that it might occur to somebody, to *them*, to, perhaps,
occupy.

> Us standing up against the walls of the other person's

house—we live in it without even being able to afford to loathe
it.

> Our voices.
> Our hoarse voices sounding discreetly on the thresh-

old

> > Mother most pure
> > Mother most loved
> > Mother most chaste

> I come to you not because you are mother most pure

(mother most pure)
not because you are mother most loved (mother most loved)

not because you are mother most chaste (mother most chaste)
but because
you won't talk to me
you won't say a word to me
you won't give me any advice
or scold me.

                                    Mother most pure (nonexistent)
             I am heavy-laden with all the system's calamities
And I really don't know what to do.

                    I don't know how to go back
                    or how to stay
                    or how to run away
                    or why go on
                    or how to end it.

                                         Lately I've had to listen
to so much bullshit (speeches, lectures, very serious opinions),
I've had to surrender my life to so many promises,
I've had to fake so much,
I've had to bear and accept—praise—so many monstrous absurd
things
                    that you'd instantly fall asleep
if I tried to explain even one of them to you—you'd drop like a
stone on the spot.

                                    Mother most loved
                                              (nonexistent)
                    hear my cry—
                         Really I have no way out.
And don't think I've stopped getting up real early every day
or have stopped being obedient and cowardly.

                    But I am not a man with decorations or medals, or
orders or sententious sayings, or guillotines for home use, or
stinging threats, or timely mottoes, or terrorist enthusiasms,
or manuals on political economy, or even *Granma* magazine.

                    I am a man (and only sometimes at that) with many
feelings that might be lovely but that are not yet more than
scribbled blasphemies, scribbled on a bus transfer on a bus that
didn't arrive at its destination, or muttered inside while someone
spies and I pretend to chat.

                                         At nightfall
             a drum

that someone improvises
beating on the seat
of a bench
indicates that we are now
headed back

              to the barracks
(our eternal return).

             Now the rumba
             begins.

All the sweaty bodies
wracked by thirst
abstinence and
the sun

        twist and sing.
They sing
They sing

        forgetting
(trying to forget)
that lunch was chick-pea soup
that dinner was chick-pea soup.
They sing
They sing

        forgetting
(trying to forget)
that we are sentenced here—

        the infamous tradition
of this vexed harsh land.

           Mother most loved

lying
on this chirping cot where a cricket I can't find,
comfortably installed, vociferates (a creature that knows how
to blend into its background, immortal creature), I hear
those chants, I repeat those chants, I watch that
frenetic dancing, I suffer that racket of drums. I am now
among them, dissolving. Shaking my ass too.

           Mother most chaste.
           Mother most pure.
           Mother most loved.

Let your strong countrywoman's arms shelter me

                                        (for I'm fed up to here al-
                                        ready)
Let your skeptical peasant gaze take me in
                                        (for I'm sweaty and smelly)
Let your immense solitary peasant heart cover me
                                        (for they're calling me)
You know too much to talk.

                                        (You will make my bed,
                                        take care of my clothes,
                                        sometimes ask me for money
                                        to buy groceries.)
You know too much to hate.

                                        (You will figure out how to
                                        fix the window,
                                        you will make deodorant with
                                        boric acid,
                                        you will make sure the
                                        towels don't get musty.)
You know too much to accept.

                                        (You will not ask me for my
                                        body,
                                        you will not ask me for my
                                        soul,
                                        you will love me at a
                                        distance.)
Ah
            mother most putrid
                I mean most pure
            most loved mother
                        Do you come?
                        Are you there?
                        Do you hear me?
                        Can you do it?
Sweetheart, let's go to bed.
                        (Can you do it?)
                                        But the horrible
                                        two-backed beast keeps you sus-
                                        pended and constantly oscillating;
                                        on the one hand it rocks you to
                                        sleep, while on the other it bites

you. Now up in the air she shows you the grotto of her throat, guarded by pious little gargoyles with pointed teeth; she nudges you along, she lifts you over the ocean (the ocean of impossible legends), deposits you on an esplanade without time, on a fixed path. Then she releases you, looks at you, and weeping draws away.

There your funeral will be held.

We go in.

"Sweetheart, are you there?"

It is the hour of synthesis. The moment to come to grips with tradition. The hour to take the body which desperately offers itself to us. To accept the body which obediently accepts us. The hour to carry out the noisy futilities, the old crime thanks to which we are here, committing it.

"Sweetheart, are you there?"

(I draw her toward me.)

It is the hour that protects and compromises us. The awaited hour of payment and reconciliations. Intermingled breathing, cries (discreet, please).

"Sweetheart, are you there?" Are you that soft (so soft) thing that yields? Are you that white (so white) thing that folds, stretches, squeezes, extracts? Sweetheart? Are you there?

But the woman seems afraid of the interrogations and holds me. My poor nut, my poor baby, she says. *She doesn't know that my evil consists of being too much a man.* And so I yield, I yield and penetrate.

She opens the chasm that unifies us, and hugs me, she bestows terror on me and we roll over and over.

She opens her bottomless grief, dedicated to me (what hate, what fury, what inevitable love).

Holding each other we dissolve. Remote, so remote, sobbing.

Ah, we are all gathered together here, so prudent, doing what our fathers would have approved of, we are here, at last, all of us, circumspect, singing in unison, like good children an *older person watches while they charmingly form a ring holding sad moist hands.**

Here

Here

The line
to desert the land snaked and curved far, far beyond the distant horizon. It faded away behind infinite days of thirst and waiting, behind infinite deaths. The deteriorated jets, still available, went on, loaded, lifting off into the burning haze; then they burst in the air—the quality of the fuel was dreadful, and if they arrived anywhere they rarely returned. What pilot would return if he was already safe far, far away? Only a man moved not by pity but by that dangerous, strange pleasure that consists of returning to the ruins which we flee in terror. Yes, one or two still came back, piloting the rickety ship that fell heavily onto the panorama stripped of green and shade. . . . Night had been eradicated a little while after trees had, when the reigning philosophy proclaimed in a thousand solemn roars and respectable quotations that everyone should live "forever in the light."

The huge line, on seeing the ancient machine, straightened up, began to stir. Then, through the death rattles of those who were staying behind and the shouts of those who were leaving, the craft gained altitude again, over the dust of old bones. Then the man, knowing by the place he occupied in the line that the wait would be as long as his life (or longer), threw himself onto the esplanade; he waved his little bag filled with personal effects, to produce a small breeze, and breathing, not without difficulty, he composed (or imagined that he was composing) a few small, incoherent stories about the life—that is, death—of that planet, withered and madly eroded, wasted, by its inhabitants—by those who claimed they represented its inhabitants—who now, dying, patient, were trying to flee.

The great Museum which had dedicated itself to collecting objects from Earth—who now dares to say, like the ancients, that that planet did not exist?—still conserves a few graphic "thoughts"

---

*Nathalie Sarraute: *Tropismes*.

which the poor quality of the artificial atmosphere somehow didn't dissolve—as, strictly speaking, ought to have happened.

At times some technical failure turns out to be very lucky for the perpetuation of History.

> (Behold us here, dazed, clinging to one another, yes, holding hands, listening, hearing, feeling.)

NEGROES

Negroes were not black now. They were extremely white. But, perhaps to uphold tradition, or from a resentment more powerful than reason and than victory itself, whites, who were completely black and held the power, went on calling the negroes Negroes—that is, those who were now absolutely white—and persecuting them to extinction. It was at the end, after the Fifth Hyperthermal War (the "Necessary War"), to consolidate the Great Monolithic Universal Free Republic, that the persecution of negroes intensified to such a degree that all of them perished. Truly that hunt had been most glorious. Invisible flamethrowers, sonic waves that split their bodies, disintegrators that hurled the bodies now turned into tiny glowing particles into the air, atomic mice, and, above all, that voracious pack of supersonic hounds bought from the Seventh Galaxy (our enemy) thanks to a cruel agreement which almost led us to total ruin, annihilated the persecuted in record time, exceeding the plans foreseen by the Ministry of Harassment. In the indefatigable flames, in the atmosphere conveniently befouled, in the metallic claws of the wild beasts of prey, in the deceptive (and now fortunately abolished) dawn, from every spot we had to listen to their shrieks, which now would never be repeated, ever. Of course, numerous were the Titans of those glorious battles, numerous the decorations bestowed, numerous the perished and the memorialized. The roll of anonymous heroes—those patriotic soldiers that almost no one remembers, those glorious dead, those children turned to hatred and anger—is almost as infinite as our empire is infinite.

Before bringing this report to an end, I should like to mention a curious fact, the brief history of one of the fiercest persecutors of the negroes. Alone, it is said, he eliminated the highest number of negroes from this holy domain. Without him (it is said), in spite of the wholehearted cooperation and the heroic attitude of our soldiers, women, and children, such a perfect extermination might perhaps not have been achieved. And even today some of those contemptible creatures might wander through the rubble and hide in secret. He was to spare us that shame. "Foremostest Great First and Foremost Eternal Great Empire!" he cried among the distant columns of the First and Foremostest Palace. "I have just wiped out all the negroes!"

Then the Great Sun—our Great Primemost Minister—came out onto the Foremost Portico.

"You are mistaken," said our Foremost Excellencity, lifting his excelsiorities. "One still remains."

And taking out his disintegrator, he eliminated the persecutor to perpetuity.

When he fell, curiously kicking, we could all witness the color of his skin—sickeningly white. He was, indisputably, a negro.

I remember his end, and those cries.

Here
Here

THE TABLE

Those times too were horrible. The enemy had taken control of all nearby stars and Earth was besieged with threats, bombardments, insults that polluted the atmosphere and spread and poisoned even our longest-cherished hopes.

The enemy had altered the laws of cosmic motion. Constellations revolved madly. The end might come at any moment. The enemy had invaded us with a strange plant that was now spreading over the ocean, over rocks and boulders, and it exerted great, suffocating pressure. . . . In the middle of that advancing brightness we saw the pocked face of the moon, also in the enemy's power, hurling fatal radiations at us. The enemy (we were told) caused those underground explosions, and we were about to perish amid din and devastation. The enemy kept on threatening. The enemy promised to eliminate all images. The enemy, once in a while, managed to make the sun radiate huge waves of brightness which, cleaving the air, evaporated part of the oceans. Rivers no longer existed. The enemy orchestrated our madness. The enemy modified our concept of terror, the enemy crushed all allegiance and all long-range plans. The enemy assumed our guilt.

The enemy, the enemy, the enemy.

Of course we starved to death. Only fury kept the planet alive.

But there was a table.

It was not a very long table. It was not a very well-made table—I think it even wobbled. Nobody had bothered to put a nice shine on it. Spilled food had made a great layer of filth, and a huge swarm of flies hovered over it. Yes, there was a table, and behind it a line began that faded off into the distance of the unsure horizon.

The people in line (the enemy never ceased hurling burning bolts at us) could barely control their hysteria. The table had only two chairs. The people in line (the enemy setting the roars of its threats rolling) scratched and struck each other. At times they unleashed such violence as they pulled each other to pieces that for a few seconds the enemy's bombardments were blotted out in the conquered air.

But all of them, that is to say, all of us, who had managed to maintain our lives in the midst of that furor and those explosions, remained firm at our posts, kicking, cutting the throat of the nearest person with tiny little knives (said to have been supplied by the enemy).

Thus we went on with our bags and bottles, plates and spoons—guarded, defended with our lives. Thus we went on, stuck in the huge line that opened at last onto that little empty table. The enemy of course did everything it could to disperse us; we, everything in our power to annihilate ourselves, each other.

But when the two of us that fate brought together came to the table and sat down, now with our back to the mob, we set out our food and drink (conserved thanks to months of abstinence) and we began to look at each other, howling with laughter. The happiness that we experienced at that moment was so great, the love was so great, that we forgot about the food, the drink, the threats, the beatings received or mutually given, the constant terror. And we used up our brief turn laughing at each other and looking at each other as over our heads the flies and stars buzzed and exploded.

> (Behold us here, circumspect, singing in unison, holding hands, swaying, still "civilized" and obedient.)

Here
Here

MONSTER II

They carried out so many explorations and interrogations, deliberations and resolutions, expeditions and investigations that at last they discovered—there was no choice—the existence of the monster.

The impact of that discovery was horrifying.

The dimensions of the monster were such that it was impossible to comprehend them—or even detect them.

It was known that "the beast" (as it was popularly called) did not rest by day or by night. But it was not known whether the monster had any notion of such ephemeral human concepts as "day" or "night." What was known very precisely was that the way in which it spread terror was indefatigable, that it crept with overwhelming rapidity—such that it appeared not to move— devouring through all the interstices of its huge thick skin. The creature did not have just one mouth, or a thousand, or yet a million; those figures, at least, could have been dealt with by the superhuman (infinite) patience of the scholars, both volunteer and professional—that is to say, by every inhabitant of the planet. But there were just too many zeroes ever to be added up. . . . And through every one of those openings, through every pore, the monster constantly swallowed one or thousands of those exalted and desperate investigators.

In truth, the creature was cantankerous, frantic. Sometimes it convulsed, emitted a roar, and suddenly absorbed a city. Other times, with furious flagellations, it wiped out a ship or a country.

But—and this was the most terrifying thing of all—although everyone was perishing because of him (or her), no one had yet been able to detect its whereabouts. And here learned men began to look distressed, dictators, presidents, kings, and prime ministers, to look at each other mistrustfully. The immense multitude began to grow uncontrollably hysterical.

On the edges of those assemblies, lectures, and universal congresses, the creature went on swallowing. So that, as a last resort, dictators, monarchs, presidents, prime ministers, friends, and enemies agreed on at least one point: *The monster had to be found,* since having only discovered its existence had turned out to be as useless as it was alarming. Something like when, millions of years earlier, a calamity at that time without remedy was discovered, called cancer or something like that.

At last, the Commission for Universal Salvation, in a vast hubbub, resolved to equip a ship with every kind of device known for not only replacing the parts that might wear out or the energy that might be consumed, but as well satisfying the most complex whims. There had been so many contributions to this desperate research that if the search for the monster were infinite, infinite would be, as well, the efficiency of the ship, which had been endowed with a reactor (or thousands of them?) capable of manufacturing a memory or a nut or bolt in space.

Down below, trillions of desperate arms were waved in farewell, bearing the inevitable flags and signs. In the ship, eyes, most of them old and weary, squinted and searched.

The flaming device slid along, reflecting on its superscreen the tiniest meteorite, the most gigantic, most distant galaxy, or the blaze of a star extinguished millions of years ago. But on neither one side nor the other, nor in limitless space before, did the figure of the monster appear.

The counsel of learned men was sought, discussed. They went on ahead, indefatigable and desperate. Until once one of those men stopped taking the perspective of infinity. He turned and saw, behind the advancing ship, the monster.

At the sound of the alarm, everyone halted and observed.

Performing ceaseless revolutions, the creature writhed

rhythmic and enraged through space. Its huge circular outline was all gloom on one side and glittering light on the other. Its avid, craggy skin, now juicy, now hard, flamed out or folded in, opened or closed, gulping up one or thousands of those tiny little figures who never stopped jumping around until the last second.

Wanting to be certain of what was developing before their eyes, the crew looked toward the superscreen. Everyone could see in perfect, overwhelming close-up the round reddened face of the Earth.

The monster, at last, had been found.

Once the enigma was cleared up, there remained only the question of fleeing. Gaining more altitude, and running through Eternity (the ship was a safe place), they crossed nebulas and constellations, the great deserted night, no less night for all its twinkling.

But, silently, they all came to the control room. They turned some buttons, flipped some switches, and, descending, they returned.

(The line stirred again, advancing a few yards, which kept the two ends from coming together and girdling the entire planet. The man, as he breathed in the rationed air, smiled, thinking that he had discovered the greatest "contribution" that the system had made to the world—the spherical line.)

Here
Here

Behold us here, always

> listening to that cry

his, her, their cry

our cry

my cry

> Quick
> Quick

Take one last look and let's go.
You others, look at me, look at us one more time and get lost.

Two hearses
Two hearses

(Going off in opposite directions?)

                        Perhaps
the suicides may serve
as the image of a lost
sincerity,
                        gods exiled
to the morning filled with racket and swill.
                Poets pursuing a metaphor
in a guava-paste factory.
                The only beast that out of pride
jeers at the hunter, and doesn't flee.
                Counterpoint of cowardly monologue
with which so much misery is justified and accepted.
                Suicides are the most
mysterious tree that remains on the earth—
they always flower, in any season.
                But
don't let it get you down.
Don't seize this chance to intone another ode.
Don't fool yourself.
Don't go, for God's sake, getting all puffed up (I know you!)—
Suicides kill themselves because they're suicides.
                        But
when you take the car
                do you still hear the scream?
        When
you turn the key
                did you put water in the radiator?
        When
you accelerate
                did you close the door well?
        When
you drive along pulverizing
        crabs
                what if he really did love you?
        When
you leave the pine grove
        behind
                do you still hear the screams?

When
you enter
the radiant

    avenue
    of oleanders

        is she crying? "Do you feel all right?" Do
        you ask her?

    When
you take
the enslaving

      highway

        can you still hear the wails of the kneel-
        ing mother?

DRIVE CAREFULLY AVOID ACCIDENTS

Last screw-up!
Last screw-up!

      A single brightness, a thousand disgusts
      A single glow, a thousand shrieks
      A single road, a thousand slogans

            (Isle, all that justifies you
is now unmentionable.)

          And then
      the angel appeared again.
      This time severely dressed as a
      civilian. (Under his guayabera, how
      could you miss the bulge of his
      pistol?) He didn't look like he'd
      come to strike up any sort of
      dialogue.

           He came to call me to ac-
           count. He came patrioti-
           cally. And I told him
    It's so horrible to *be* that sometimes (remotely)
      I envy you.
    One is condemned to feel, to see, to interpret—
      not to enjoy but to narrate—

one can never forget
and as though that weren't enough, one feels
obliged to tell our horror to everyone
and to suffer everyone's terror, plus
the angels'.
                              I don't detest you anymore.
Your visits are part of my job.
Your visits are the essence of my job.
            Here—and I handed him the pages—here
is the fruit you have inspired. Do your job,
                              as an angel.
But one day I am to be you
and you are to be me, and I will be more
cruel than you because before I was I
but then I will be you,
and I will have the horror of having been I
plus the remorse of having been I
being now you. . . . Have you ever
thought what will become of you when you
fall into the hands of that *I* that I am to be
but that will also be what I was?
                              And the angel was horrified

to recognize me.
He vanished.
                    Or was it I
who vanished and that
is why I don't see the angel? What
do you think? Which of us has vanished? Which
of us still exists? Which one is the angel? Who
am I? Perhaps both of us in different places?
Perhaps he and I in a single figure? Or perhaps I
alone exist? Well then, What
can I do?

                              Tell me, what is your opin-
                              ion of the case? Tell me, huh?
                              You are going to say some-
                              thing, eh?
                              Speak. Huh?
                              Did you already say some-
                              thing, eh?

You don't want to compro-
mise yourself,
eeeeeeeh?
Last chance!
Last chance!
Dead men don't brood over their furies.
They don't ooze sweat and semen.
The don't give off sparks like vast submerged thermoelectric
plants
(across bones there is no possibility of short circuits).
Dead men don't argue, or grow happy or excited, or fall sad.
They don't wear tight bathing suits or make you a conspiratorial
unignorable sign.
They don't get suntanned.
They don't stand there in the middle of the poem
with their legs spread.
They aren't frightening.
But look,
hold on,
wait a second,
listen to me, let's go to the country dressed as workers
of the revolution
(as shepherds we'd attract too much attention at this
stage of the business),
let's pretend we're them, let's pretend, as so many do, that we're
just like everybody else. . . . Later, very late at night let's
sneak out to the woods. I'll be out there waiting for you.
And every night, with our meeting, we will conquer them.
(But he doesn't answer,
he doesn't return. Moreover, he never clearly said what he wanted.)
Quick.
Quick.
Now the shining centipede enters the white fields.
Now, sly, the scorpion introduces his dark fury into the eye-
socket.
The circling spider ecstatically contemplates the tall
columns. The cricket occupies the definitive orifice.
A fly
sacrifices to empty spaces
the triumphant rubbing of his front legs.

Theirs is the kingdom of eternity.

> Oh, wait for me.

Oh, wait for me.

> I am coming to you
> I want to come to you
> To you and no one else
> I can give myself now
> > worthily
> > with dignity.
>
> > Oh, wait for me!

Quick! Quick! Now the horrible city—our own—shows us its grotesque profile. Its horrific silhouette hovers over the ocean, now whitens under the sky, now can be made out in the air, now pollutes our sight. Quick, quick, don't wait any longer. A city which seen from afar seems still to exist, a city which is a white-hot prison; a city whose houses seen from afar seem really to be houses, whose buildings, buildings, whose streets, streets; a city which is a poisoned field where the word is kept prisoner, the dream is watched, steps are followed, and the cursed hymns constantly echo. A city which seen from afar seems still to exist, a city which from within is an immense sarcophagus—sealed, well sealed. . . . A city which seen from afar seems still to possess trees, an avenue where at times it is pleasant to breathe, a city which is a roaring throat, a horrid pollution, a pure venom, a sordid, supervised corner, a huge spotlight illuminating us. . . . Do you feel all right? Do you want a cigarette? (Are you still beside me?) Does the wind let you light a match? . . . Ah, don't arrive, don't ever get here. The barbarous fanfare is already echoing, you hear it already, you yourself are already parodying it. Last snafu, last snafu: Let's make a ring with pleading, mute gestures and, as though we were singing a farandola, but with our lips shut tight, walk toward that bridge and stop there awhile. Then, come back. That's all. Quick, quick! Now you have to slow down, now you have to slow down. Now you have to observe the traffic laws. Here, the prickly cane silk and the flaming flags. Here, the glare disintegrating us. Quick, quick. Don't arrive, don't ever get here, because arriving is turning yourself over to them. Faster, faster, because arriving is giving up once and for all. Fast, fast, because going back is throwing yourself in jail, because going back is repeating, giving up, being humiliated, backing down. Because going back is dying the death of the obedient, the useless, shameful death of the coward. Don't arrive, don't ever get here, because arriving is being defeated. And the great billboard awaiting us— ALWAYS ONWARD TO VICTORY—but whose is the victory? What victory are they talking about? What does "victory" mean? The dark mouth opening. We enter the crematorium now. We go along the tunnel that communicates with the unanimous crematorium. Who will sing to those suffocated bones? Who will gather the mute fury of those blows against the nickeled wall? Who above all will I tell my terror to, my guilt, my rationalizations, my love? Who, if I managed to do it, would be able to believe me? Who, if he believed me, would be able to help me? . . . Look, look. And the final din of voices—our voices— comes to us. A little beyond, oh, happiness, and will the testimony of our death prevail? Will it be legible? But listen, but listen, have you remembered your son looking at you? Have you thought about him? I see that you almost never name him, that you rarely mention him in your blasphemies. I see his arms, in her arms, stretched toward you. I see his gaze, under her gaze, directed toward you. Have you remembered that little creature observing you? I see his big eyes gazing at you. Have you remembered that new curse which you have been responsible for passing on? Do you really think that he exists? Or are you such an egotist that you think that only you exist? Have you ever thought about anyone not you yourself, you, and the ones that help you suffer? . . . Yes, as you see, I've remembered, I'm remembering. So what? Fast! Fast! No more bullshit. No more misery or sentimentality, no more tricks. No more cowardliness. . . . In ten minutes or so, in eight minutes, in five minutes, you'll be a slave once more, and you'll be, once more, that obscure bent-over poor devil. I speed up. Fast, fast, we're getting there; in a second we will enter the house. . . . For a time, January, February, March perhaps, the sun will not be so brutal; we will be able to get out onto the balcony from time to time; we will be able sometimes, perhaps, in the afternoon, if someone will keep the baby, to go to the movies, see a movie we've already seen a thousand times. But listen, but listen: It will only be a brief respite. The unending shifts of work in the country will return, the instant you would give anything, everything, for a glass of water, the intolerable degradations, the hateful lectures that last the day long and then are repeated, and repeated—*oh, fast, fast!*—until you yourself can repeat them from memory. . . . You will grow old, and all your dreams, and all your aspirations, and all your hopes (all your *efforts*) to be something, not this thing we are, will fade away, be forgotten, be cast aside in the face of the pressure to find a pack of cigarettes or an afternoon free of a Sunday, to sleep. . . . *Faster, faster!* In time no one will honor you with provocativeness, insolence, candor, delight. You will not be able to subjugate, destroy, anyone. Soon it will all be a shame in your memory, even in imagination. *Faster, faster!* Don't arrive, don't arrive, because arriving is also being one of them. . . . We come out into the brightness. I speed up. In four minutes. In three minutes. What have they forbidden today? What have they rationed today? How are we to behave today? What new vital instinct did they condemn today? What perhaps sincere sign did you evade, fearfully, today? What longed-for sweet body did you refuse today? What dream, what potential love did you destroy today? . . . We come out into the brightness, *faster, faster.* What poem did you sacrifice today? What dance do you dance today? What great insult like the weather do you remain silent over or, better yet, applaud today? But listen, but listen. . . . We come out into the brightness of midday. *Fast, fast.* What huge impotence muzzles your vital rebelliousness? What can you do, not to be one more in the boasting, begging, and betrayal? What can you do anymore? . . . We come out into the brightness, *fast, fast*—ah, it was so difficult getting here, leaving. There we go. The shrieking dies away, the colossal shrieks of the mother fade away. I still have time to turn around and look at the back seat, the seat beside me, empty both. There I go alone— like always—in the car. To the last second equanimity and rhythm—fantasy. *Hector, Hector,* I say, rushing forward. Imprisoned, unleashed, furious, and crashing, like the ocean.

First version disappeared, Havana, 1969
Second version confiscated, Havana, 1971
The present version smuggled out of Havana, 1974,
and published in Barcelona, 1982